DEATH

IN

DIXIE

■

DEATH IN DIXIE

■

Edited by

Billie Sue Mosiman
and Martin H. Greenberg

RUTLEDGE HILL PRESS
Nashville, Tennessee

Published in Nashville, Tennessee, by Rutledge Hill Press, Inc., 211 Seventh Avenue North, Nashville, Tennessee 37219. Distributed in Canada by H. B. Fenn & Company, Ltd., 34 Nixon Road, Bolton, Ontario L7E 1W2. Distributed in Australia by Millennium Books, 33 Maddox Street, Alexandria NSW 2015. Distributed in New Zealand by Tandem Press, 2 Rugby Road, Birkenhead, Aukland 10. Distributed in the United Kingdom by Verulam Publishing, Ltd., 152a Park Street Lane, Park Street, St. Albans, Hertfordshire AL2 2AU.

Cover and book design by Harriette Bateman
Typography by E. T. Lowe, Nashville, Tennessee

Library of Congress Cataloging-in-Publication Data

Death in Dixie / edited by Billie Sue Mosiman and Martin H. Greenberg.
    p. cm.
   ISBN 1-55853-459-8 (pbk.)
   1. Detective and mystery stories, American. 2. Crime—Southern States—Fiction. I. Mosiman, Billie Sue. II. Greenberg, Martin Harry.
PS648.D4D423   1997
813'.087208—dc21   96-54612
                                           CIP

Printed in the United States of America

1 2 3 4 5 6 7 8 9 — 00 99 98 97

CONTENTS

INTRODUCTION

Storytelling in the South is a rich tradition. In this collection of stories about murder and crime in the South, we might ask ourselves, is it the heat, suffocating and relentless, that causes violence to erupt? The fierce family loyalties and feuds? Or does crime find a home in the South because it is a place where the land is soaked in the blood of war and mired in the guilt of past transgressions against outsiders and minorities? Actually, I don't believe there is a simple reason for crime occurring anywhere in the country, but in the South it seems at times to have a distinct, personal flavor to it.

Many southern storytellers grew up in families where stories were told after supper, an entertaining pastime before the advent of the television. Crimes, from the petty to the unforgivable, were one of the subjects discussed in those days. As a child in South Alabama, I remember warm summer nights on the front porch where my grandfather regaled us with tales of his hobo-ing days during the Great Depression. My grandmother might reminisce on the time when she was a girl on the way to school and my grandfather leaped from the woods to steal a kiss. (Suffering a blow from a length of knotty pine for his trouble, she would always add.) Or an older cousin might stop by, take a seat on the steps, and join in the group. While expertly pouring just the right amount of tobacco from the Prince Albert can into a cigarette paper, he might mention his latest hunting expedition, a tale that would invariably lead to speculation on what manner of beast could be making the horrible screaming noises that summer in the neighboring woods. (It was probably a large jungle cat escaped from some traveling circus.)

But with the stories of family and conquests there were also the tales of mystery and murder. The hushed recital of the abused wife who couldn't take any more and dispatched her husband with the wood ax. The drowning that was ruled accidental, but just maybe he hadn't been swimming alone that day. The old story of the lumber gang working the woods when one member, accused of sneaking off to break into the bossman's house where a wife had to flee for her life, later disappeared, never to be seen again.

Ernest Hemingway said in *Death in the Afternoon,* "Madame, all stories, if continued far enough, end in death, and he is no true-story teller who would keep that from you."

Everyone told stories, it was an oral tradition passed down through generations. It was the way family history was kept alive and I believe it might have been a way for the elders to point out moral and acceptable behavior without lecturing their young. It was as if my southern people, who did not know Plato, knew instinctively what Plato exhorted: "We ought to esteem it of the greatest importance that the fictions which children first hear should be adapted in the most perfect manner to the promotion of virtue."

These stories you hold in your hand are to be enjoyed the way families in the past enjoyed the shared tales of life around the flickering fireplace or the porch swing on a summer night. Flannery O'Connor once said that in her own stories she found violence "strangely capable of returning my characters to reality and preparing them to accept their moment of grace." You will find complex, eccentric, and peculiar southern characters in these stories. The characters illuminate not only O'Connor's moment of grace, but a southern sensitivity to family and a certain valiant code of honor that believed although people made mistakes and sometimes naively caused harm, nevertheless, if a crime was committed against another there should be swift and sure justice.

Families, even in the South, don't sit around so much anymore, telling stories for entertainment. We come to the printed word for that today. I hope that you feel a hint of a balmy southern breeze along your skin as you read this book. If you're lucky, you might detect the heavy sensual scent of the magnolia blossom full open on a sultry summer night. But most of all I hope you will hear the voices of Dixie's story-tellers, as I did as a child, whispering in your ear about love, life, revenge, escape, death, and the importance of a final justice for wrongful deeds perpetuated against the innocent.

Billie Sue Mosiman
1996

DEATH

IN

DIXIE

■

Thomas Adcock was born on January 5, 1947, and currently lives in Manhattan with his wife. Before writing mystery stories and novels, his most famous being Precinct 19, *he was a police reporter for such newspapers as the* Detroit Free Press *and the* St. Paul Pioneer Press. *His short fiction has also appeared in* Ellery Queen's Mystery Magazine. *Here he delves into the murky world of the Louisiana bayou in a story of greed and revenge.*

Thrown-Away Child

Thomas Adcock

The little room in back where Perry stayed was "nothin' but a damn slum the way that no-'count keeps it," according to his Aunt Vivian. She had a long list of complaints about her nephew, most of which were shared by most people who knew him. But she and Perry were still family and so she loved him, too, in a quiet and abiding way.

Vivian lived in the rest of the place, a wooden cottage of four narrow connected rooms built up on hurricane stilts, with a high pitched roof, batten shutters over the windows, and French louvered doors on either end. The front steps were scrubbed every morning with a ritual mixture of steaming hot water and brick dust to keep evil spirits at bay. The back steps led from Perry's squalor to a tiny fenced garden of thick grass, a chinaberry tree, and a lilac bush. In appearance and infirmity, the cottage was nearly the same as the forty or so others crowded into a rut-filled dirt lane between lower Tchoupitoulas Street and a levee almost crumbled away from years of flood and neglect.

The neighborhood was one of many that tourists in the city were not encouraged to visit, a neighborhood where pain and fears from the hard past overlapped a generally despairing present—a haunted part of New Orleans, some claimed. Which was why, among other customs, the front steps were washed down with brick dust every day.

On most afternoons, the people in the lane would go to the levee for the coolness of the river breezes or to catch themselves a dinner of Mississippi catfish. There, ancient Creole men and widow ladies—with *tignons* covering their hair, the Madras handkerchiefs favored by voodoo women with seven points carefully twisted heavenward—would talk until dusk of the old days and the old ways.

Long ago, Vivian and her husband had been terribly proud of the cottage. It was truly theirs, no thanks to any of the banks or mortgage companies—bought and paid for with the saved-up wages of a yard man and a cleaning woman whose ancestors had once been shackled to posts in the public squares above Canal Street and sold as slaves. But on a sunny day in March of 1948, Vivian and Willis Duclat took title to a little wood cottage and became the first of their families to own their own home.

It was a long way up in a perilous, hostile world and Willis and Vivian were pleased to be gracious about their ascent. Almost everyone else in the lane shared generously in their reflected joy. One who did not was a tall, sour-faced woman next door to the Duclats, a spinster known as Miss Toni. "Ain't goin' to be no comfort to you or the rest of us down here to be buyin' your own place when it's the last one that ain't owned yet by Theo Flower. Theo wants the whole lane bad and he means to get it, one way'r other. He knows the mysteries, so that's how he'll get you yet—one way'r other."

Vivian said to pay no mind to Miss Toni. "She only says those poisonous things 'cause she's lonesome and miserable."

The pride of the Duclats was brief.

Toward the end of '48, the parish tax assessor came calling. He smiled quite a bit and seemed genuine. He shook hands with Willis, same as he'd shake a white man's hand. And he addressed Vivian properly as Mrs. Duclat. The assessor was there to explain how he had some important papers for signing, papers that would bring paving and curbing and a sewer hook-up. The Duclats didn't understand quite all of the small print on the man's papers, but since he'd been so respectful Willis and Vivian trusted him and signed where it said "Freeholder." Then by Christmas of '49, when they'd fallen impossibly far behind on the special surcharges for modern conveniences levied against them by those important papers, the Duclats' home was seized by the sheriff and put up for sale in tax-forfeiture court.

At the auction there was only one bidder—the Church of the Awakened Spirit, in the person of its pastor, The Most Reverend Doctor Theophilus Flower. At last, Theo Flower and his church owned every last cottage in the lane. Pastor Flower wasted no time. He called on the Duclats the very day he put down the cash money to retire the delinquent surcharges, plus the customary plain brown envelope full of money for his friend, the smiling tax assessor.

Pastor Flower drove straightaway from the courthouse to the Duclats' place in his big white Packard motorcar, one of the first post-war models off the Detroit assembly lines. When the neighbors saw the Packard roll in from Tchoupitoulas Street, they went to their homes and shut the doors until they knew Pastor Flower had gone away.

In the parlor of the newly dispossessed Duclats, Theo Flower was courtly and sympathetic. The pastor had no need for meanness when he bought somebody's home out from under them—the law made it all so easy and polite.

"Now, I know you can understand that our church has many missions," he said in his deep, creamy preacher's cadence, "and that among thems is providing what we can in the way of housing for our poor and unfortunate brothers and sisters."

Willis sat in a caneback chair in a sort of shock, still as a stone while Pastor Flower talked. He didn't appear to hear anything. He'd hidden from his wife for days before the court sale so that he could cry, and now his eyes looked like they might rust away with grief. Vivian sat next to him and held his big calloused hands. She looked at the floor, ashamed and resigned, and listened carefully to Theo Flower.

"I surely don't want to see fine people like you having noplace to live. You see, though, how we must serve our members first? Now, I've been giving this predicament of yours a lot of my thought and some of my most powerful prayer and I do believe I have come upon a solution—"

When at last Pastor Flower was finished, he collected twenty dollars on account toward the first year's tithe to the Church of the Awakened Spirit. And the church's two newest members, Vivian and Willis Duclat, signed some important papers their new pastor happened to have with him, pressed inside the red-leather Bible he always carried. They signed where it said "Tenant."

After scratching his name to Theo Flower's lease, Willis rose from his chair and crossed the room angrily, tearing himself away from Vivian's grip on his shirt. He stood towering over the preacher and his black eyes came alive again. Duclat's huge hands, made hard and heavy from his work with shovels and stone and earth, clenched into dark fists. His voice sounded as if it were a thousand years old.

"I ain't no educated man," he said to Flower, "and I ain't well spoken like you. But I ain't simple, neither, and I can sure as hell figure you just done somethin' crooked here. I'm goin' to think on this, then

I'm goin' to figure some way to bring you down for what you done to me and my wife, and prob'ly other poor folks besides."

The Most Reverend Doctor Theophilus Flower only smiled. When he did, Vivian saw a flash of gold at the back of his dark-brown lips. Then Flower stood up, no match in physique to Willis. He folded the lease into his Bible and answered the big angry man with the clenched fists: "It won't do to talk like that, brother. I know you're a troubled man today and I'm sorry for you, truly. But you'd best not take an adversary's tone against a man who knows the mysteries like I do. You understand what I mean, don't you, brother Willis?"

Willis understood only too well. Since he was a boy, he'd heard of Theo Flower's abilities, how he could call forth the dead from beyond, how he could "fix" an enemy, how his power came from the evil fangs of river snakes. Willis felt something cold on his neck, something like a wet wind.

Then the pastor drove off in his Packard. And later, in the silent night, Willis awoke from a nightmare with a violent fever and pains that shot through his chest and neck.

Willis never worked another day, nor did he sleep well. Then three months into the new year of 1950, on the very day that Perry was born to his younger sister, Willis Duclat dropped dead.

It happened despite his precautions. Convinced that mortal danger lay waiting in the alleyway in the form of water moccasins or copperheads that would sometimes slither up from the levee, Willis had begun a new daily protective routine. He would mix a batch of quick-lime and cayenne pepper into the boiling water left over from scrubbing the front steps and pour the potion in two parallel lines along the inside of the fence that enclosed his garden. One of the old *voodooiennes* assured him he would be safe now, back as well as front.

Just before he died, Willis was sitting on a step out back, smoking a morning pipe of tobacco. Vivian was on her way to a mansion on St. Charles Avenue, where she had a job minding three children, cleaning some, and cooking for a doctor who ate far too much. Across the river, meanwhile, in the parish of Algiers, a midwife pulled an infant boy into the world from between the legs of his very young and frightened mother.

Willis's left leg dangled off the side of the pine steps and his bare foot swung back and forth, toes brushing through the dewy grass that he'd coaxed into growing from muddy soil. Then suddenly, his body convulsed with a spasm so overwhelming it threw him to the ground, where he twisted around for a few seconds in mute torture before his heart stopped. Vivian found him when she returned home in the afternoon. He was sprawled on his back in the grass, his face covered with bits of blossoms, the white and purple petals that fell from the chinaberry tree.

She ran to a confectionary shop where there was a public telephone and rang up the doctor's house. Her employer drove over right away, breaking the speed limit even though Vivian told him that Willis was dead and already cold. The doctor examined the body there in the garden and after a minute or two pointed to a blue-black welt on Willis's left ankle. "He's full of venom more than likely," he said.

"No, sir," said Vivian. "Somebody's gone and hexed my man."

The lane was never paved, nor was it ever so much as named. And through the decades, Theo Flower bought up hundreds more ragged neighborhoods in New Orleans, building up his church membership and the sort of respectability money from any source whatever buys in the entrenched power structure of a southern town.

Along about the middle 1970s, the federal government mandated sewer hook-ups for even the lowliest neighborhoods in any city that expected revenue-sharing funds. So New Orleans obliged people like Vivian Duclat, finally. For his part, Theo Flower hiked her rent since the property would become more valuable with the addition of a modern convenience.

In July of 1983, Perry Duclat was paroled out of the Louisiana State Prison at Angola after serving half of a seven-year sentence for grand theft—auto. He'd been convicted of "borrowing" a Rolls-Royce that belonged to the doctor where his Aunt Vivian worked. In his defense, Perry told the judge, "I was helpin' out my aunt one day at the big house and the man was out of town for the weekend and there was that nice big car of his just sittin' in the garage goin' nowhere. So naturally I borrowed it. How else is a man like me ever goin' to have any style in his life? I put it back right where I found it and I never hurt it one little bit, no sir." Perry had borrowed many things in the past, many of them yet to be returned, so the judge threw the book at him and lectured him on how he'd probably never amount to anything with that sort of thieving attitude. The defendant only smiled.

And even so, even though the doctor told her she could never work at his house again. Vivian took Perry in when he was released from Angola with nowhere to go. She took him in because they were family, no matter what; because he was born on that terrible day her husband died; because in the years he'd been at Angola he'd taken on such a strong resemblance to Willis.

Every day but Sunday, Vivian would get up early in the morning and go off to work someplace. Perry would get up right after that and attend to the chores, which included keeping his aunt's part of the cottage meticulously clean and scrubbing down the front steps because she believed most of the old myths even if he didn't. By ten o'clock or so, he would be back in his own room watching television.

In the three months he'd been there, Perry's room had become wall-to-wall beer cans, hundreds of them, under a film of cigarette ash. He would light cigarettes and leave them burning on the windowsill or at the edge of the dresser. Holes were burnt into the sheets of his bed, where he sat day after day watching television game shows, talk shows, soap operas, meaningless news and witless comedies and endless commercials on a portable black-and-white set with a wire coathanger for an antenna. He liked to crush the cans after draining them, then he'd toss them aside, anywhere. Mostly, he drank Dixie beer, in the white cans with red-and-yellow lettering, or Coors in the gold cans when he had a few dollars extra.

Some days he'd stroll down to the levee. But Miss Toni had whispered around that Perry was an escaped convict, so very few neighbors would have anything to do with him. The old-timers talked to him, though, especially the widows in their *tignons,* garrulous old magpies always happy to pass along the legends that meant everything to them and practically nothing to the disrespectful younger generation.

Sometimes he would tend his late uncle's garden, where Miss Toni would spy on him from a window, ducking out of sight when he turned his face in the direction of her cottage. Or he'd sit on the back steps and read a book, which Miss Toni considered most highly suspicious. Perry had two big stacks of books in his room, one on the dresser and another that filled a corner, floor to ceiling. Sometimes, too, he would write or draw in a tablet. About once a week, he would set off by foot all the way up to the library on Rampart Street.

But mostly Perry watched television, drank and smoked and drowned himself in thought. By noon, his eyes were boozy slits and his fingers stank of nicotine. He would watch the flickering idiot box until it went dark in the wee hours of the next day. He ate very little, though he did enjoy whatever his Aunt Vivian cared to cook or bake.

The two of them seldom talked. The chat was pleasant when Vivian spoke of Perry's late uncle, when she'd show him photographs of Willis or bring out a box of Willis's personal effects or tell Perry again about the day he died, what the doctor said, and how she thought that was "nothin' but medical yap." But then it would lead inevitably to the subject of Theo Flower and their chat would quickly become an argument loud enough for Miss Toni next door to hear every word of it, even without her big ears at the window.

"That nigger Flower's nothin' but an old-timey conjure man, nothin' but a slick and cussed old fraud who's got lots of little old ladies like you and Miss Toni and all scared out of your bloomers 'cause he's supposed to 'know the mysteries,' " Perry would say, eyes rolling and his voice heavy with sarcasm. "Haw! Y'all must be crazy."

To which Vivian would reply, her jowls quivering and a finger wagging up against her nephew's nose, "You best shut that sassy trap, boy! In the first damn place, we're beholden to Pastor Flower for this house we're in. And in the second damn place, well, let's just say you ain't lived near long enough to understand that precious little in this ol' world is actually what it seems to be."

She never quite told him so, but Vivian thrilled to her nephew's boisterous arrogance on the subject of Theo Flower. She supposed this might be a womanly fault of hers, enjoying the antagonisms of men at dispute where she was concerned, so she kept quiet. But when Perry would inveigh against Pastor Flower and his church, Vivian's eyes would mist over some, and through that prism of tears and remembrance she sometimes thought she was looking at her husband again. God bless poor black men for what little arrogance they dared show the world, she thought.

And Vivian didn't care a hoot whether Miss Toni heard them carrying on—which she did, and which she dutifully passed along nearly word-for-word to Pastor Flower himself, who maintained a pervasive interest in the personal lives of his home-indentured flock.

Perry's irreverence greatly disturbed Theo Flower. His unease was compounded by the unnerving physical resemblance he saw in Perry to the late Willis Duclat, who was about Perry's age when he died. Perry had taken to attending Sunday services of the Church of the Awakened Spirit and he sat right down center and never took his eyes off Pastor Flower, never registered any expression, just stood and sat down when requested. Never had a nickel for the collection plate. But there he sat anyway, unembarrassed, looking for all the world like

Willis Duclat with his hot black eyes, taut olive-brown skin, high fore-head, and straight hawklike nose. And those wide shoulders and thickly muscled arms, with big hammer hands folded in his lap.

"You better come do somethin' on that boy here," Miss Toni warned Pastor Flower on the telephone. "I tell you, I believe Perry's got some kind of trouble-makin' designs. I see him some days on those back steps, lookin' over to my place and starin' at me and wonderin' lord only knows what! Now, you know how we don't want no trouble here. We mean to keep in our houses, Pastor Flower. Please do somethin' on him!"

"Yes, yes. You're quite right," he told Miss Toni. "We will have to stop any trouble before it has a chance to begin."

Pastor Flower said yes to a drop of brandy in his coffee and asked permission to light a cheroot in Vivian Duclat's parlor besides. "Oh my, yes, go right ahead," she said. "My Willis was a smokin' man, you know. La, yes, he had to have that pipe of his from mornin' to midnight."

"Yes, I do recall that." Flower fired a sterling Tiffany lighter and touched the yellow-blue hiss of flame to the blunt end of his cigar. In the flash of light, Vivian saw again the gold crowns of sparkle in the back of his mouth.

It was a Sunday twilight and a heavy blackness moved across the sky, overtaking what was left of the day and the week. Perry's television set droned from the back of the cottage.

"Sister Vivian, I come here to talk with you tonight on a delicate matter, one that causes me grave concern as to your welfare."

"What in the world can that be?" Vivian had enjoyed several drops of brandy in several cups of coffee before the pastor's call and her voice was thick.

"Well, Sister Vivian, you know how people will talk. Many of your neighbors and friends are worried sick about your being all alone in this house with a man fresh out of prison, a man who I am told lives like some sort of wild animal in the back room of this cottage and who does nothing besides drink all day long. Now, I must worry about this for your sake—and for the sake of the church's property, after all."

Vivian touched her lips to hide a smile, which she thought Pastor Flower might well interpret as contemptuous. "I think I know maybe just one neighbor who'd gab like that and maybe she's over there listenin' now. Besides, if I had to worry 'bout ev'ry man 'round this neighborhood who'd ever been locked up, well, shoot, I'd be a mighty nervous old hag by now. So don't you worry none 'bout my nephew Perry , 'cause *I'm* sure not worryin' and you can tell Miss Toni the same if you want."

"Well, I only mean that your husband Willis was a hard-working, sober man and this Perry is a layabout. That is what I'm told." Flower coughed, then opened his red-leather Bible and spread it out on the parlor table. "You know very well from the scriptures how the devil works through wicked drinking men and other idle folks."

"Maybe I know that," Vivian said. "I do know for sure that the devil works through schemin' folks."

She poured herself another brandy and spotted it with coffee out of respect for the ministry. The minister accepted one for himself.

"Let me set your mind at ease some, Pastor Flower. You should know a little of Perry's story, then maybe you'd understand him like I do. He's not a dangerous young man, no more than any other young man. He is sloppy, though. I'd be ashamed to have you see where he stays.

"But look here, Perry's been bruised all through his life and them bruises come one right after the other. Ain't none of them healed up completelike, which is maybe why he lays 'round all the day long. Sometimes he shows some spunk, but if he's dog-tired from life most of the time, then I figure he's got the right.

"His mother—that would be Willis's sister—was nothin' but an ignorant teenage girl livin' over in Algiers in a shack all alone near a coalyard. How d'you s'pose a girl like that made out in the world? Well, you can imagine right enough. Anyway, she gets herself in the family way and then come runnin' over here with the baby, not even knowin' her brother Willis had passed on. Not that she'd care 'bout that, mind you, not any more'n she cared for that baby she just plopped down on me.

"But I minded the child for a while and loved him. I named him, too, you know. Maybe I might have gone crazy without the baby 'round me to take my mind offa how Willis died like he did—" Her shoulders shook and she cried softly. Pastor Flowers moved to comfort her with his hands, but she backed away from his touch.

"And you know all 'bout that," she said to Flower. "Anyway, Perry's mama went up to Chicago, so I heard. She wrote how fine she was doin' up North and how she wanted to send for Perry and all. But then the man who did her come by one day with a new wife and says he wants to take his baby and raise him up over to Algiers. That's what he did, took Perry away from me and wasn't nothin' I could do 'bout it.

"But Perry started comin' back here regular when he got older, just as soon as he could get by on the ferry on his own. An' I started noticin' how beat-up lookin' he was. I got it out of him what was goin' on over to his daddy's house. His daddy's lady would be all the time hittin' him, or burnin' him with cigarettes or shamin' him in front of the other little boys by comin' after him with a belt and whuppin' his head till he'd fall over bloody, then whuppin' some more until he messed his pants.

"I tol' his daddy all this when he would come for him to take him back, and that man said his boy was possessed 'cause he wouldn't never do nothin' right or what was told him. Then he finally put little Perry in a home someplace out in the country.

"Next I heard, Perry's busted out of that home, which was more like some prison than a home, which it never had any right to be called, and he headed north lookin' for his mamma. He found her, too. He come back and tol' me how she was nothin' but a whore and a dope addict, how she looked like death itself and didn't even know Perry was her kin.

"Well, he was right. Later on, we heard from some city health official up North, how she was dead from heroin and askin' us did we know her birthday. They was so shocked to learn she was only thirty-six.

"Perry figured he'd better stay over with his father, else his daddy'd make trouble for me. But the man tossed him out soon's he showed up over there to Algiers.

"And so, you see, Perry's had trouble all the time in his life. What do you expect? He was nothin' but a thrown-away child. Least that's what he think of himself anytime he's away from here."

Pastor Flower folded his hands over the Bible. Vivian ran her fingers through her hair nervously. From the back of the house where Perry watched television came the added sound of a beer can popping open, an empty being crushed, then the clatter of it when it fell to the littered floor.

"I'm sorry for you, Sister Vivian, but I cannot stand by idly in this matter."

Her voice rising high, Vivian said, "What do you mean? Don't you be takin' my Perry away! Don't you be takin' another man from this place!"

"Quiet, woman!" Flower's voice thundered. There was stillness in the house. "What I shall do here is convene the spirits and consult the wisdom of the other side. I shall call out your own husband, Willis Duclat!"

Vivian shrieked and her cup and saucer crashed to the floor.

"Yes," Flower said, "I shall call out the spirit of Willis Duclat. He—and only he—shall guide us on the matter of your nephew!"

Pastor Flower closed his Bible and the sound of it echoed in the parlor. He stood up and moved to the door, put on his hat. "I shall request that everybody in this lane come to service next Sunday. You come, too, Sister Vivian. I know you wouldn't want to miss hearing your husband's voice."

The tall dark woman at the side of the altar began chanting in a low, melodious voice. She started in a *français africaine* dialect—

"Danse Calinda, boudoum, boudoum!
Danse Calinda, boudoum, boudoum!"

Pastor Flower, in a scarlet robe covered with *gris-gris*—dolls made of feathers and hair, skins of snakes, bits of bone—rose from a pit beneath the altar in a great plume of white and grey smoke. Beaming at the congregants in front of him, he turned and knelt at the altar as the woman's chanting grew in volume and tempo. He rapped the floor and then lit the black crucifix-shaped candles. He turned again to face his flock and he picked up the chant himself, raising his arms, commanding all to join in the calling out of spirits from beyond life.

Bodies swayed in the pews of the Church of the Awakened Spirit and the chanting rolled in waves, the single line of African French pulsating stronger and stronger through the sanctuary and out the open door into the liquid air of a savagely hot, humid Sabbath morning in New Orleans. Hands kept time and feet moved from muffled accentuation to a steady, rhythmic pounding.

Vivian Duclat, tears streaming down her face, for she had slept little during her week of anticipation, slapped her hands together determinedly and pounded her feet. She would hear her man, maybe she would even see her Willis—it didn't matter if the image were no more real than the times she thought she saw him in Perry's face. But what would Willis say of Perry? Would he send him away from her? Would Willis, too, throw the child away?

The tall dark woman stepped forward from the altar, moved her arms in an arc, and then switched to the Creole *patois* and to the uninhibited, throaty *canga*—

> *Eh! Eh! Bomba, hen! hen!*
> *Canga bafio, te,*
> *Canga moune de le,*
> *Canga do ki la,*
> *Canga li!*

All joined the chant, their massed voices now storming and frenzied, so full of pathos and longing that it became impossible for anyone to remain free of the swing and the narcotic influence of the ancient words. Everywhere, people were prepared to believe it all, for the first time in many cases. The eyes of the young were no longer disrespectful, they were full of proper fright—the old-timers clung righteously to *gris-gris* charms of their own they'd brought along to the ceremony, their little "conjure balls" of black wax and bits of their own skin or bleached lizards in glass jelly jars or dried-up rooster hearts—the curious things they kept under lock and key at home, out of embarrassment and fear. Pastor Flower then began the dance of the Voudou, the leader.

He raised a bottle of brandy from the altar, dashed some of the liquid on each side of a brown bowl full of brick dust, then tossed back his head and took a long pull of the liquor. Then he started the slow hip shuffling, moved his feet backward and then forward, accelerating his movement up to the speed of the hypnotic *canga*. Without ceasing a single step of his dance, Flower poured the rest of the brandy into the bowl, then ignited it with his silver Tiffany lighter. The bowl flamed up high over the altar and still he danced the maddening *canga*, his powerful voice starting to rise up over the waning strength of all the others.

"I call out Willis Duclat! *Eh! Eh! Bomba, hen! hen!* I call out Willis Duclat! *Eh! Eh! Bomba, hen! hen!* Willis Duclat, speak through me—"

And suddenly, a tall young man covered in a brilliant red-and-black robe and hood ran crazily from somewhere in the back of the church, whirling and leaping and howling like a dervish until he reached the altar and a stunned Pastor Flower, who tripped and fell to his knees. The mysterious figure then vaulted over a railing and turned to the panicked congregation.

He tore the hood from his head, then the robe from his body, and stood before the assembly, his olive-brown body naked and oiled, his handsome face with the straight hawklike nose held high. Women screamed, but they did not avert their eyes, for the figure before them was a perfect masculine beauty. He raised his big-fisted hands and cried out over the nearly hushed church.

"I am Willis Duclat! I *am* Willis Duclat!"

And from the pew next to Vivian Duclat, a trembling Miss Toni stood up and screamed, "Jesus, Mary, and Joseph, it's him! Oh la, it's him!"

The old ladies in *tignons* began fainting away and children squealed. Men stared, gape-mouthed, unable to help the women and the young. The tall, muscular, naked man grasped the shoulders of a terrified Theo Flower and lifted him several inches off the floor, then dropped him, crumpling, to a twitching heap. He turned again to the congregation and roared, "I, Willis Duclat, have come out!" He then knelt to Pastor Flower and whispered to him. "Time for you to blow town, chump, 'cause your number's up here."

He stripped Flower's robe of his *gris-gris,* which he dropped into the bowl of flaming brandy with elaborate gesticulation, so that all in the church could see he meant to destroy Theo Flower's control over them. "Be gone, the imposter's fakery!" he shouted.

He asked for silence. Then, he raised an arm and slowly directed it toward Miss Toni. "You," he said, "were in league with the imposter cowering at my feet. *You* placed the snake below the steps where you knew it would strike at me. You murdered me! It could have been no other way!"

Vivian sobbed.

"La, gawd-a-mercy!" Miss Toni screamed.

"Yes, yes, it was you! You and the imposter, this man called Theophilus Flower, who has oppressed you and cheated you all so cruelly for so many years since my death. It was you, Miss Toni, who killed me—to keep me from telling the truth that I do today!"

"La, mercy! Mercy! Oh la, please!" Miss Toni fell to the floor, gasping and writhing and consumed with her guilt, which took the form of what the hospital would later diagnose as massive cerebral hemorrhage.

The man then tore a lock of hair from his head and held it high over him so all could see. "Today I have destroyed the power of the imposter Theophilus Flower, who was foolish enough to call me out. I tell you all now, you must shun him! This hair I hold is the most powerful *gris-gris* of all, the hair of one from beyond. I shall give it to someone who lives amongst you. I shall plant it in his head this very night as he sleeps, and there it will grow. I shall give the power to a thrown-away child, now a grown man in my image, so that you shall always know him!"

Then he disappeared into the pit below the altar.

"Thank you for receiving me here, sir. I would have understood your refusing me."

"Well, son, I look at it this way: you done the crime and you done the time. Now that's just so much water under the bridge, don't you know. B'sides, you intrigue the hell out of me."

"Yes, sir. Thank you again." He brushed lint from the top of his sharply creased charcoal-grey slacks, part of a Parisian suit he'd had made for him by a tailor at Gauchaux's on Canal Street.

The fat man offered him one of his cigars, which he declined in favor of a pipe that used to belong to his uncle. He lit the pipe and the fat man's cigar, too, with a sterling lighter that used to belong to Theo Flower.

"Tell me," the fat man said, "how's Vivian doin' for herself these days? We all loved her so much. Damn me for casting her out like I did just 'cause of what you did."

"Nice of you to inquire, Doctor. My aunt's doin' just fine now. She had a little excitement at church a while back, but she rested lots afterward and I was able to take care of her, now that I'm runnin' the church myself and all."

"She's welcome to come back to me any time, you know."

"Thanks again, Doctor. I'll send her callin', but, you know, she likes her retirement now and she's earned it, I'd say."

"Of course, of course." The doctor shook his fleshy head. "Damn me again! Perry, I'm sorta sorry now for havin' that judge crack down on you like he did."

"That don't matter much now. You might say you straightened me out by catchin' me. I had lots of time to think things through in prison. It was sorta strange, actually. All kinds of thought just sorta took over me, and I couldn't do much more'n think, day in and day out. Finally, I figured that I had to watch close for somethin' to come along that I could grab onto to make life good for me and my aunt for a change."

"Well, sounds to me like you did a fine piece of thinkin'. Just how'd you manage to take over the church, though? I mean, Theo Flower didn't strike me as a man ready to retire, like your old aunt. All of us fellows downtown were sorta surprised when he lit out for Baton Rouge like he did, without even a bye-you-well."

Perry smiled. "He had a change of spirit, you might say. Decided on greener pastures maybe. Anyway, I was around and interested in the church, you know. Spent lots of time readin' up on it and all and figurin' how I might make my contribution. So, the moment come along when I figured I might grab on, so I done that."

He smiled again. "Of course, I had to first prove to Pastor Flower that I understood all the mysteries of his divine work. He musta been satisfied, because he signed everything over to me."

Perry emptied the contents of a satchel onto a table between him and the doctor.

"It's all legal. I didn't have to steal anything—or 'borrow,' I should say." The doctor laughed and Perry went on. "See here, it's all the deeds and titles and bank accounts—everything. That's why I come to you, sir, for some guidance in handling this all."

"You can count on me, Perry."

"I'm so glad."

"Where do you want to start?"

"Well, first thing," Perry said. "I want all the cottages down there in that lane off Tchoupitoulas deeded over to the tenants, maybe for a dollar apiece, some token like that that'd be sure to make it legal, and then—"

Avram Davidson (1923–1993) like many of the authors included, wrote in several genres during his lifetime. Getting his start in speculative fiction in the 1950s, he wrote several classic stories such as "Or All the Seas with Oysters," and "The Golem." At the urging of the editor for Ellery Queen's Mystery Magazine, *he turned to writing mysteries, and won the Ellery Queen award as well as the Edgar Allen Poe award. Here he is in top form with a tale of honor lost and regained.*

The Cobblestones of Saratoga Street

Avram Davidson

COBBLESTONES TO GO said the headline. Miss Louisa lifted her eyebrows, lifted her quizzing-glass (probably the last one in actual use anywhere in the world), read the article, passed it to her sister. Miss Augusta read it without eyeglass or change of countenance, and handed it back.

"They shan't," she said.

They glanced at a faded photograph in a silver frame on the mantelpiece, then at each other. Miss Louisa placed the newspaper next to the pewter chocolate-pot, tinkled a tiny bell. After a moment a white-haired colored man entered the room.

"Carruthers," said Miss Augusta, "you may clear away breakfast."

"Well. *I* think it is outrageous," Betty Linkhorn snapped.

"My dear," her grandfather said mildly, "you can't stop progress." He sipped his tea.

"Progress my eye! This is the only decently paved street in the whole town—you know that, don't you, Papa? Just because it's cobblestone and not concrete—or macadam—or—"

"My dear," said Edward Linkhorn, "*I* remember when several of the streets were still paved with wood. I remember it quite particularly because, in defiance of my father's orders, I went barefoot one fine summer's day and got a splinter in my heel. My mother took it out with a needle and my father thrashed me . . . Besides, don't you find the cobblestones difficult to manage in high-heeled shoes?"

Betty smiled—not sweetly. "I don't find them difficult at all. Mrs. Harris does—but, then, if *she'd* been thrashed for going barefoot . . . Come on, Papa," she said, while her grandfather maintained a diplomatic silence, "admit it—if Mrs. Harris hadn't sprained her ankle, if her husband wasn't a paving contractor, if his partner wasn't C. B. Smith, the state chairman of the party that's had the city, country *and* state sewn up for twenty years—"

Mr. Linkhorn spread honey on a small piece of toast, " 'If wishes were horses, beggars would ride—' "

"Well, what's wrong with that?"

" 'and all mankind be consumed with pride.' My dear, I will see what I can do."

His Honor was interviewing the press. "Awright, what's next? New terlets in the jail, right? Awright, if them bums and smokies wouldn't of committed no crimes they wouldn't be in no jail, right? Awright, what's next? Cobblestones? *Cobblestones?* Damn it, *again* this business with the cobblestones! You'd think they were diamonds or sumpthin'. *Awright.* Well, om, look, except for Saratoga Street, the last cobblestones inna city were tore up when I was a *boy,* for Pete's sake. Allathem people there, they're living inna past, yaknowwhatimean? Allathem gas lamps in frunna the houses, huh? Hitching posts and carriage blocks, for Pete sakes! Whadda they think we're living inna horse-and-buggy age? *Awright,* they got that park with a fence around it, private property, okay. But the streets belong to the City, see? Somebody breaks a leg on wunna them cobblestones, they can *sue* the City, right? So—*cobblestones?* Up they come, anats all there is to it. Awright, what's next?"

His comments appeared in the newspaper (the publisher of which knew what side his Legal Advertisements were buttered on) in highly polished form. *I yield to no one in my respect for tradition and history, but the cobblestoned paving of Saratoga Street is simply too dangerous to be endured. The cobblestones will be replaced by a smooth, efficient surface more in keeping with the needs of the times.*

As the Mayor put it, "What's next?"

Next was a series of protests by the local, county, and state historical societies, all of which protests were buried in two-or-three-line items in the back of the newspaper. But (as the publisher put it, "After all, C.B., business is business. And, besides, it won't make any difference in the long run, anyway.") the Saratoga Street Association reprinted

them in a full-page advertisement headed PROTECT OUR HER-
ITAGE, and public interest began to pick up.

It was stimulated by the interest shown in the metropolitan
papers, all of which circulated locally, BLUEBLOODS MAN THE
BARRICADES, said one. 20TH CENTURY CATCHES UP WITH
SARATOGA STREET, said another. BELOVED COBBLESTONES
DOOMED, HISTORICAL SARATOGA STREET PREPARES TO
SAY FAREWELL, lamented a third. And so it went.

And it also went like this: *To The Editor, Sir, I wish to point out an
error in the letter which claimed that the cobblestones were laid down in 1836.
True, the houses in Saratoga Street were mostly built in that year, but like many
local streets it was not paved at all until late in the '90s. So the cobblestones are
not so old as some people think.*

And it went like this, too:

Mr. Edward Linkhorn: Would you gentlemen care for anything else
to drink?

Reporter: Very good whiskey.

Photographer: Very good.

Linkhorn: We are very gratified that a national picture magazine is
giving us so much attention.

Reporter: Well, *you* know—human interest story. Not so much
soda, Sam.

Photographer: Say, Mr. Linkhorn, can I ask you a question?

Linkhorn: Certainly.

Photographer: Well, I notice that on all the houses—in all the windows, I mean—they got these signs, *Save Saratoga Street Cobblestones.* All
but one house. How come? They *against* the stones?

Reporter: Say, that's right, Mr. Linkhorn. How come—?

Linkhorn: Well, gentlemen, that house, number 25, belongs to the
Misses de Gray.

Reporter: de Gray? de Gray?

Linkhorn: Their father was General de Gray of Civil War fame.
His statue is in de Gray Square. We also have a de Gray Avenue.

Reporter: His *daughters* are still living? What are they like?

Linkhorn: I have never had the privilege of meeting them.

Miss Adelaide Tallman's family was every bit as good as any of
those who lived on Saratoga Street; the Tallmans had simply never *cared*
to live on Saratoga Street, that was all. The Tallman estate had been
one of the sights of the city, but nothing remained of it now except the

name *Jabez Tallman* on real estate maps used in searching land titles, and the old mansion itself—much modified now, and converted into a funeral parlor. Miss Tallman herself lived in a nursing home. Excitement was rare in her life, and she had no intention of passing up any bit of attention which came her way.

"I knew the de Gray girls well," she told the lady from the news syndicate. This was a big fib; she had never laid eyes on them in her life—but who was to know? She had *heard* enough about them to talk as if she had, and if the de Gray girls didn't like it, let them come and tell her so. Snobby people, the de Grays, always were. What if her father, Mr. Tallman, *had* hired a substitute during the Rebellion? *Hmph.*

"Oh, they were the most beautiful things! Louisa was the older, she was blonde. Augusta's hair was brown. They always had plenty of beaux—not that I didn't have my share of them too, mind you," she added, looking sharply at the newspaper lady, as if daring her to deny it. "But nobody was ever good enough for *them*. There was one young man, his name was Horace White, and—oh, he was the *hand*somest thing! I danced with him myself," she said complacently, "at the Victory Ball after the Spanish War. He had gone away to be an officer in the Navy, and he was just the most handsome thing in his uniform that you ever saw. But *he* wasn't good enough for them, either. He went away after that—went out west to Chicago or some such place—and no one ever heard from him again. Jimmy Taylor courted Augusta, and William Snow and Rupert Roberts—no, Rupert was sweet on Louisa, yes, but—"

The newspaper lady asked when Miss Tallman had last seen the de Gray sisters.

Oh, said Miss Tallman vaguely, many years ago. *Many* years ago . . . (Had she really danced with anybody at the Victory Ball? Was she still wearing her hair down then? Perhaps she was thinking of the Junior Cotillion. Oh, well, who was to know?)

"About 1905," she said firmly, crossing her fingers under her blanket. "But, you see, nobody was *good* enough for them. And so, by and by, they stopped seeing *anybody*. And that's the way it was."

That was not quite the way it was. They saw Carruthers.

Carruthers left the house on Sunday mornings only—to attend at the A.M.E. Zion Church. Sunday evenings he played the harmonium while Miss Louisa and Miss Augusta sang hymns. All food was delivered and Carruthers received it either at the basement door or the rear door. The Saratoga Street Association took care of the maintenance of the outside of the house, of course; all Carruthers had to do there was sweep the walk and polish the brass.

It must not be thought that because his employers were recluses, Carruthers was one, too; or because they did not choose to communicate with the outside world, he did not choose to do so, either. If, while engaged in his chores, he saw people he knew, he would greet them. He was, in fact, the first person to greet Mrs. Henry Harris when she moved into Saratoga Street.

"Why, hel-lo, Henrietta," he said. "What in the world are *you* doing here?"

Mrs. Harris did not seem to appreciate this attention.

Carruthers read the papers, too.

"What do they want to bother them old stones for?" he asked himself. "They been here long as I can remember."

The question continued to pose itself. One morning he went so far as to tap the Cobblestones story in the newspaper with his finger and raise his eyebrows inquiringly.

Miss Augusta answered him. "They won't," she said.

Miss Louisa frowned. "Is all this conversation necessary?"

Carruthers went back downstairs. "That sure relieves my mind," he said to himself.

"The newspapers seem to be paying more attention to the de Gray sisters than to the cobblestones," Betty Linkhorn said.

"Well," her grandfather observed, "people *are* more important than cobblestones. Still," he went on, *"House of Mystery* seems to be pitching it a little stronger than is necessary. They just want to be left alone, that's all. And I rather incline to doubt that General M. M. de Gray won the Civil War all by himself, as these articles imply."

Betty, reading further, said *Hmmm.* "Papa, except for that poor old Miss Tallman, there doesn't seem to be anyone alive—outside of their butler—who has ever *seen* them, even." She giggled. "Do you suppose that maybe they could be *dead?* For years and *years?* And old Carruthers has them covered with wax and just dusts them every day with a feather mop?"

Mr. Linkhorn said he doubted it.

Comparisons with the Collier brothers were inevitable, and newsreel and television cameras were standing by in readiness for—well, no one knew just what. And the time for the repaving of Saratoga

Street grew steadily nearer. An injunction was obtained; it expired. And then there seemed nothing more that could be done.

"It is claimed that removal would greatly upset and disturb the residents of Saratoga Street, many of whom are said to be elderly," observed the judge, denying an order of further stay; "but it is significant that the two oldest inhabitants, the daughters of General M. M. de Gray, the Hero of Chickasaw Bend, have expressed no objection whatsoever."

Betty wept. "Well, why *haven't* they?" she demanded. "Don't they realize that this is the beginning of the end for Saratoga Street? First the cobblestones, then the flagstone sidewalks, then the hitching posts and carriage blocks—then they'll tear up the common for a parking lot and knock down the three houses at the end to make it a through street. Can't you *ask* them—?"

Her grandfather spread his hands. "They never had a telephone," he said. "And to the best of my knowledge—although I've written— they haven't answered a letter for more than forty years. No, my dear, I'm afraid it's hopeless."

Said His Honor: "Nope, no change in plans. T'morra morning at eight a.m. sharp, the cobblestones *go.* Awright, what's next?"

At eight that morning a light snow was falling. At eight that morning a crowd had gathered. Saratoga Street was only one block long. At its closed end it was only the width of three houses set in their little gardens; then it widened so as to embrace the small park— "common"—then narrowed again.

The newsreel and television cameras were at work, and several announcers described, into their microphones, the arrival of the Department of Public Works trucks at the corner of Saratoga and Trenton Streets, loaded with workmen and air hammers and pickaxes, at exactly eight o'clock.

At exactly one minute after eight the front door of number 25 Saratoga Street, at the northwest corner, swung open. The interviewers and cameramen were, for a moment, intent on the rather embarrassed crew foreman, and did not at first observe the opening of the door. Then someone shouted, *"Look!"* And then everyone noticed.

First came Carruthers, very erect, carrying a number of items which were at first not identifiable. The crowd parted for him as if he had been Moses, and the crowd, the Red Sea. First he unrolled an old, but still noticeably red, carpet. Next he unfolded and set up two campstools. Then he waited.

Out the door came Miss Louisa de Gray, followed by Miss Augusta. They moved into the now absolutely silent crowd without a word; and without a word they seated themselves on the campstools— Miss Louisa facing south, Miss Augusta facing north.

Carruthers proceeded to unfurl two banners and stood—at parade rest, so to speak—with one in each hand. The snowy wind blew out their folds, revealing them to be a United States flag with 36 stars and the banner of the Army of the Tennessee.

And while at least fifty million people watched raptly at their television sets, Miss Louisa drew her father's saber from its scabbard and placed it across her knees; and Miss Augusta, taking up her father's musket, proceeded to load it with powder and ball and drove the charge down with a ramrod.

After a while the workmen debated what they ought do. Failing to have specific instructions suitable to the new situation, they built a fire in an ashcan, and stood around it, warming their hands.

The first telegram came from the Ladies of the G.A.R.; the second, from the United Daughters of the Confederacy. Both, curiously enough, without mutual consultation, threatened a protest march on the City Hall. In short and rapid succession followed indignant messages from the Senior Citizens' Congress, the Sons of Union Veterans, the American Legion, the B'nai Brith, the Ancient Order of Hibernians, the D.A.R., the N.A.A.C.P., the Society of the War of 1812, the V.F.W., the Ancient and Accepted Scottish Rite, and the Blue Star Mothers. After that it became difficult to keep track.

The snow drifted down upon them, but neither lady, nor Carruthers, moved a thirty- second of an inch.

At twenty-seven minutes after nine the Mayor's personal representative arrived on the scene—his ability to speak publicly without a script had long been regarded by the Mayor himself as something akin to sorcery.

"I have here," the personal representative declared loudly, holding up a paper, "a statement from His Honor announcing his intention to summon a special meeting of the Council for the sole purpose of turning Saratoga Street into a private street, title to be vested in the Saratoga Street Association. *Then*—" The crowd cheered, and the personal representative held up his hands for silence. "*Then*, in the event of anyone sustaining injuries because of cobblestones, the City won't be responsible."

There were scattered boos and hisses. The representative smiled broadly, expressed the Municipality's respect for Tradition, and urged the Misses de Gray to get back into their house, please, before they both caught cold.

Neither moved. The Mayor's personal representative had not reached his position of eminence for nothing. He turned to the D.P.W. crew. "Okay, boys—no work for you here. Back to the garage. In fact," he added, "take the day off!"

The crew cheered, the crowd cheered, the trucks rolled away. Miss Louisa sheathed her sword, Miss Augusta unloaded her musket by the simple expedient of firing it into the air, the Mayor's representative ducked (and was immortalized in that act by twenty cameras). The Misses de Gray then stood up. Reporters crowded in and were ignored as if they had never been born.

Miss Louisa, carrying her sword like an admiral as the two sisters made their way back to the house, observed Betty and her grandfather in the throng. "Your features look familiar," she said. "Do they not, Augusta?"

"Indeed," said Miss Augusta. "I think he must be Willie Linkhorn's little boy—are you?" Mr. Linkhorn, who was seventy, nodded; for the moment he could think of nothing to say. "Then you had better come inside. The girl may come, too. Go home, good people," she said, pausing at the door and addressing the crowd, "and be sure to drink a quantity of hot rum and tea with nutmeg on it."

The door closed on ringing cheers from the populace.

"Carruthers, please mull us all some port," Miss Louisa directed. "I would have advised the same outside, but I am not sure the common people would *care* to drink port. Boy," she said, to the gray-haired Mr. Linkhorn, "would you care to know why we have broken a seclusion of sixty years and engaged in a public demonstration so foreign to our natures?"

He blinked. "Why . . . I suppose it was your attachment to the traditions of Saratoga Street, exemplified by the cobble—"

"Stuff!" said Miss Augusta. "We don't give a hoot for the traditions of Saratoga Street. And as for the cobblestones, those dreadful noisy things, I could wish them all at the bottom of the sea!"

"Then—"

The sisters waved to a faded photograph in a silver frame on the mantelpiece. It showed a young man with a curling mustache, clad in an old-fashioned uniform. "Horace White," they said, in unison.

"He courted us," the elder said. "He never would say which he preferred. I refused Rupert Roberts for him, I gave up Morey Stone. My sister sent Jimmy Taylor away, and William Snow as well. When Horace went off to the Spanish War, he gave us that picture. He said he would make his choice when he returned. We waited."

Carruthers returned with the hot wine, and withdrew.

The younger sister took up the tale. "When he returned," she said, "we asked him whom his choice had fallen on. He smiled and said he'd changed his mind. He no longer wished to wed either of us, he said. The street had been prepared for cobblestone paving, the earth was still tolerably soft. We buried him there, ten paces from the gas lamp and fifteen from the water hydrant. And there he lies to this day, underneath those dreadful noisy cobblestones. I could forgive, perhaps, on my deathbed, his insult to myself—but his insult to my dear sister, that I can *never* forgive."

Miss Louisa echoed, "His insult to *me* I could perhaps forgive, on my deathbed, but his insult to my dear sister—that I could *never* forgive."

She poured four glasses of the steaming wine.

"Then—" said Mr. Linkhorn, "you mean—"

"I do. I pinioned him by the arms and my sister Louisa shot him through his black and faithless heart with Father's musket. Father was a heavy sleeper, and never heard a thing."

Betty swallowed. "Gol-*ly.*"

"I trust no word of this will ever reach other ears. The embarrassment would be severe . . . A scoundrel, yes, was Horace White," said Miss Augusta, "but—and I confess it to you—I fear I love him still."

Miss Louisa said, "And I. And I."

They raised their glasses. "To Horace White!"

Mr. Linkhorn, much as he felt the need, barely touched his drink; but the ladies drained theirs to the stem, all three of them.

Lester Dent (1904–1959) wrote much of his pulp fiction under pseudonyms, but his most enduring creation was Doc Savage, the two-fisted action hero who appeared in more than 200 novels during the 1930s and 1940s. He also wrote detective fiction in the hard-boiled Black Mask style, complete with tarnished heroes, shady dealings, and double crossings. However, he also tried to examine human ambitions and failings, rather than just churn out violent action yarns. "Sail" with his detective Oscar Sail, is one of his best works.

Sail

Lester Dent

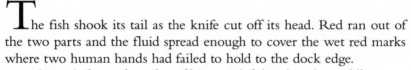

The fish shook its tail as the knife cut off its head. Red ran out of the two parts and the fluid spread enough to cover the wet red marks where two human hands had failed to hold to the dock edge.

Oscar Sail wet the palm of his own left hand in the puddle.

The small policeman kept coming out on the dock, tramping in the rear edge of glare from his flashlight.

Sail split the fish belly, shook it over the edge of the yacht dock and there were some splashes below in the water. The stuff from the fish made the red stain in the water a little larger.

When the small policeman reached Sail, he stopped and gave his cap a cock. He looked down at Sail's feet and up at Sail's head.

The cop said, "Damned if you ain't a long drink of water."

Sail said nothing.

The cop asked, "That you give that yell a minute ago?"

Sail showed plenty of teeth so that his grin would be seen in the moonlight. He picked up the fishhook and held it close to his red-wetted left palm.

"Little accident," he said.

When the cop put light on the hand, Sail tightened the thumb down and made a wrinkle in the palm. Red was squeezed out of the wrinkle and two or three drops fell on the dock. It was enough like seepage from a cut the fishhook might have torn that Sail went on breathing.

"Hook, eh?" the cop said vaguely.

He put the toe of his right shoe into the fish head's open mouthful of snake-fang teeth.

"Barracuda," he added, not sounding as if that was on his mind. "They don't eat 'em in Miami. Not when you catch the damn things in the harbor, anyhow."

Sail's laugh did not go off so well and he turned it into a throat clearing.

He said, "People get hot ideas."

The policeman did not say anything and began spearing around with his flashlight beam. He poked it over the edge of the dock at one of the fish organs floating on the stained water. He held it there for what seemed a year.

After he finally began pointing the beam at other places, the light located the bugeye. The bugeye was tied at the end of the dock with springlines. Sloping masts were shiny and black and black canvas covers were on the sails. The hull looked black, neat, new.

The cop dabbed his light up and down each of the two bugeye masts and asked, "Yours?"

Sail said, "Yep."

"What you call that kind of a boat?"

Sail began talking heartily about the boat.

He said, "Chesapeake Bay five-log bugeye. She is thirty-four feet long at the waterline and forty-five overall. Her bottom is made out of five logs drifted together with Swedish iron rods. She has twelve foot beam and only draws a little over two feet of water with the centerboard up. A bugeye has sloping masts. You tell 'em by that, and the clipper bow they always put on them. They're made—"

"Yeah," the cop said. "Uh-huh."

He splashed light on Sail.

Sail would have been all right if he had been a foot or two shorter. His face would never wear a serious look successfully. Too much mouth. Sun and salt water was on its way to ruining his hair. Some of the black had been scrubbed out of his black polo shirt and black dungarees. Bare feet had long toes. Weather had gotten to all of the man a lot.

The policeman switched off his light.

"That was a hell of a funny yell," he said. "And damned if you aren't the tallest thing I ever saw."

He stamped his feet as he walked away.

Sail shut and opened his eyes slowly and by the time he got rid of the effects of the flashlight, the officer was out of sight on shore.

Sail held both hands out about a foot from his eyes. There was enough moonlight for him to see them. A slight breeze made coolness against one side of his face. Loud music came from the Take-a-Sail-in-the-Moonlight-for-a-Dollar-a-Couple boat at the far end of the City Yacht Basin, but a barker spoiled the effect of the music. Two slot machines chugged alongside the lunch stand at Pier Six.

After he had watched his hands tremble for a while, Sail picked up hook, line, fish, knife, and got aboard the bugeye.

Sail, name of the bugeye, was in white letters on the black life preservers tied to the main stays.

Sail grasped a line, took half hitches off a cleat, and pulled a live-box made of laths partly out of the water. Some crawfish, crabs and two more live barracuda were in the live-box. He cut the line close to the live-box and let the weighted box sink.

The tiny cabin of the bugeye had headroom below for a man of ordinary height. Sail had to stoop. The usual gear was neatly, in places cleverly, stowed in the cabin.

Sail popped the fish into a kettle in the galley, hurrying.

With the point of the fishhook, he gouged a small place in his left palm, making faces over the job.

He straightened out the stuff in the tackle locker enough to get rid of signs that a hook and line had been grabbed out in haste.

After he had washed and held the mouth of a mercurochrome bottle against the gouge, he looked out of the hatch.

The young policeman was back where the fish had bled and was using his flashlight. He squatted and picked up the fish head. He squeezed it and got fresh blood out of it. After a while, he stood up and approached the dock end. When his flashlight brightened the bugeye's dark sloping masts and black sail covers, Sail was at the galley, making enough noise cutting up the fish to let the cop know where he was and what he was doing.

Sail let four or five minutes pass before he put his head out of the hatch and looked. Perspiration had made the back of his polo shirt moist by then.

The cop had gone somewhere else.

Sail was still looking and listening for the policeman when he heard a man yell and a woman curse.

The woman said, "Dam' stinker!" and more that was worse.

The man's yell was just a yell.

The sounds came out of Bayfront Park, which lay between the yacht basin and Biscayne Boulevard.

Sail got out on deck and stretched his neck around. He saw a man run among the palms in the park. The man was alone.

Then the small policeman and his flashlight appeared among the palms. During the next five minutes, the policeman and his flashlight were not motionless long enough for him to have found anything.

Sail dropped into the bugeye cabin and stripped naked, working fast. His body looked better without clothes. The hair on it was golden and long, but not thick. He put on black jersey swim trunks.

Standing in the companion and looking around, his right hand absently scratched his chest. No one was in sight.

He got over the side without being conspicuous.

The water had odor and its normal quota of floating things. The tide was high slack, almost, but still coming in a little. Sail swam under the dock.

The dock had been built strongly because of the hurricanes. There was a net of cross timbers underneath, and anything falling off the south side of the dock would be carried against them by the tide.

Sail counted pilings until he knew he was under the place on the dock where he had used the fish. He began diving and groping around underwater. He was quiet about that.

He found what he was seeking on the sixth or seventh dive. He kept in the dark places as he swam away with it.

One of the little islands in the harbor seemed to be the only place that offered privacy. He made for it.

The island—an artificial half acre put there when they dredged the City Yacht Basin—was a heap of dark silence when Sail swam tiredly to it. Pine trees on the island had been bent by the hurricanes, some uprooted. The weeds did not seem to have been affected.

Sail tried not to splash coming out of the shallows onto the sand beach. He towed the Greek under water as long as possible.

Two stubborn crabs and some seaweed hung to the Greek when Sail carried him into the pines and weeds. The knife sticking in the Greek, and what it had done, did not help. Weeds mashed under the body when Sail laid it down.

Pulpy skins in the Greek's billfold were probably greenbacks, and stiffer, smaller rectangles, business cards. Silver coins, a pocket knife, two clips for an automatic. The gun was in a clip holster under the left armpit of the corpse.

Inside the Greek's coat lining was a panel, four inches wide, five times as long, a quarter of an inch thick, hard and rigid.

The Greek's wristwatch ticked.

Sail put the business cards and the panel from the coat lining inside his swim trunks, and was down on his knees cleaning his hands with sand when the situation got the best of his stomach. By the time he finished with that, he had sweated profusely and had a headache over the eyes.

He left the Greek on the island.

The water felt cold as he swam back towards the bugeye, keeping in what dark places he could find. The water chill helped the headache.

Having reached the bugeye with the stuff still in his swim trunks, he clung to the bobstay, the chain brace which ran from the bow waterline to the end of the long bowsprit. He blew the brackish bay water off his lips quietly and listened.

There was no sign anywhere that he had been seen or heard.

He made himself sink and began feeling over the parts of the dock which would still be under water at low tide. Everything under water was inches thick with barnacles and oysters.

He found a niche that would do, took the stuff out of his trunks and wedged it there tightly enough so that there was not much danger of it working out.

Sail clung to the bugeye's bobstay until all the water ran off him that wanted to run, then scrambled aboard and ducked into the cabin.

He had started to shed the bathing suit when the woman said, "Puh-lease!"

Sail came up straight and his head thumped a ceiling carling.

She swung her legs off the forward bunk. Even then, light from the kerosene gimbal lamp did not reach more than her legs. The feet were small in dark blue sandals which showed red-enameled toenails. Her legs had not been shaved recently, and were nice.

Sail chewed an imaginary something between two eye-teeth while he squinted at the girl. He felt of his head where it had hit the ceiling. Two or three times, he seemed about to say something, but didn't and went forward into one of the pair of small staterooms. The shadow-embedded rest of her did not look bad as he passed.

He shut the stateroom door and got out of the swim trunks. He tied a three-pound fish sinker to the trunks and dropped them through a porthole into the bay, which was dredged three fathoms deep there. He put on his scrubbed dark polo and dungarees.

The girl had moved into the light when he opened the door and entered the cabin. The rest of her was interesting. Twenty something, he judged.

She smiled and said, "You don't act as if you remember me, Wesley."

Sail batted his eyes at her.

"Gosh," she said, "but you're tall!"

Sail scratched behind his right ear, changed his eyebrows around at her, gave the top of his head three hard rubs, then leaned back against the galley sink. This upset a round bottle. He caught it, looked at it, and seemed to get an idea.

He asked, "Drink?"

She had crossed her legs. Her skirt was split. "That would be nice," she smiled.

Sail, his back to her, made more noise than necessary in rattling bottles and glasses and pinking an opener into a can of condensed milk. He mixed two parts of gin, one of creme de cocoa, one of condensed milk. He put four drops from a small green bottle in one drink and gave that one to the girl, holding it out a full arm length, as if bashful.

They sipped.

"It's not bad without ice, Wesley," she murmured.

Sail said, "Thanks, lady," politely.

Her blue handbag started to slip out of the hollow of her crossed legs and she caught it quickly.

"For a husband, you're a darn polite cuss," she said.

Sail swallowed with a distinctly pigeon noise. "Eh?"

"My Gawd, don't you *remember?*"

"What?"

"If this isn't something! Two weeks ago Tuesday. Four o'clock in the morning. We were pretty tight, but we found a justice of the peace in Cocoanut Grove. You had to hock the engagement ring with the jeep for his fee and twenty dollars, and we all went out and had some drinks, and I kind of lost track of things, including you."

"I'll be——" Sail said vaguely.

The girl put her head back and laughed. The mirth did not sound just right.

"I didn't know what to do," she said. "I remembered you said you were a jewelry drummer out of Cincinnati. I sat around the hotel. Then I began to get a mad up."

An unnaturalness was growing in her voice. She pinched her eyes shut and shook her head. Her blue purse slid to the floor.

"I'm here to tell you I had a time locating you," she said. "I might have known you would be a sailor. Gawd, imagine! Anyway, Mama is right on deck now, Mister and I want something done about it. If you think you're not the man, you're going to have to prove it in a big way."

"You want me to prove my name, business and recent whereabouts? Is that it?"

"You bet."

Sail said, "That's what I figured."

She peered at him, winking both eyes. Then fright grabbed her face.

"You ain't so damn' smart!" she said through her teeth.

She started to get up, but something was wrong with her knee joints by now, and she slid off the bench and sat hard on the black battleship linoleum.

Sail moved fast and got his long fingers on the blue purse as she clawed it open. A small bright revolver fell out of the purse as they had a tug-o'-war over it.

"Blick!" the girl gasped.

Blick and a revolver came out of the oilskin locker. The gun was a small bright twin to the girl's. Blick's Panama fell off slick mahogany hair, and disarranged oilskins fell down in the locker behind him. Blick had his lips rolled in until he seemed to have no lips. He looked about old enough to have fought in the last war.

"Want it shot off?" he gritted.

Sail jerked his hand away from the girl's purse as if a bullet were already heading for it. He put his hands up as high as the cabin carlings and ceiling would allow. The upper part of his stomach jumped slightly with each beat of his heart, moving the polo shirt fabric.

The girl started to get up, couldn't. She said, "Blick!" weakly.

Blick, watching Sail, threw at her, "You hadda be a sucker and try that married-when-you-were-tight gag to find out who he is!"

The girl's lips worked with some words before they got out as sounds. ". . . was—I—know he—doped drink."

Blick gritted at Sail, "Bud, she's my sis, and if she don't come out of that, I wouldn't wanta be you!"

Sail watched the bright gun. Sweat had come out on his forehead enough to start running.

"She'll be all right," he said.

"What'd you give her?"

"Truth serum."

"You louse! Fat lot of good it'll do you."

Sail said nothing.

Blick ran his eyes up and down Sail, then said, "They sure left the faucet on too long when they poured you, didn't they, bud?"

Sail got his grin to operate. He said, "Let's see if some words will clear this any."

Blick said, "That's an idea, bud. I think I got you figured. You're some guy Andopolis rung in. It was like Andopolis to get himself some help."

"Andopolis was the one who got knifed?" Sail asked.

"You ain't that dumb."

"Was he?"

"Naw. That was Sam, my pal."

Sail rubbed the top of his head. "I'm sort of confused."

"You and us both," Blick said. "We're confused by you. We ain't seen you around before today. But me and Nola and Sam are watching Andopolis, and he starts out on this dock. You're the only boat out here, so it's a cinch he wanted to see you."

"He only made it about half way out the dock," Sail said dryly.

"Sure. Sam headed him off. Sam wanted to talk to Andopolis was all—"

"It wasn't all," Sail drawled. "What Sam really wanted was to make Andopolis tell him something. Andopolis had some information. Sam wanted it. Sam told Andopolis that if he didn't cough up on the spot he would get his entrails shot out, or words to such effect. Sam reached for his gun. But he had made the mistake of not unbuttoning his coat before he started the argument. Andopolis knew exactly where to put a knife. Sam went off the dock after he gave just one yell."

"And that brought the cop."

Sail squinted one eye. Perspiration was stinging it. He echoed, "And that brought the cop."

Blick was holding the gun steady. He said, "Andopolis ran before the cop got here. He hid in the park and Nola and I tried to get him later, but he broke away and ran."

"Then you came here."

Blick grinned thinly. "Let's get back to the time between the knifing of Sam and the arrival of the cop. You, bud, done some fast work. You were sweet, what I mean. You got a hook and line, grabbed a live fish out of your live-box, jumped on the dock and butchered the fish to hide the marks where Sam got it. You even got the insides of the fish into the water to hide any bloodstains where Sam sank. Then you fed the cop a line when he got there."

"You sure had your eyes open," Sail said.

"Did the cop go for your story?"

"I'm still wondering," Sail said thoughtfully.

Blick watched Sail. "How much do you know?"

Sail got rid of his made grin. "I'll bite. How much?"

"So you're going to start that," Blick said.

Nola was breathing noisily. Blick pointed at her, said, "Help me get her going!"

Sail grasped the girl and lifted her.

"Stay that way," Blick ordered, then searched Sail, found no weapon, and said, "Out."

Sail walked the girl up the companionway and on to the dock, then started to let go the girl and get back aboard.

"Along with us," Blick ordered. "It'd be swell if Andopolis has told you what we're trying to find out, wouldn't it?"

Sail said nothing. His breathing was as audible as the girl's. Blick got on the other side of the girl and helped hold her up. "We're tight," Blick said. "Stagger."

They staggered along the dock to the sidewalk, and along that.

Yacht sailors stood in a knot at the end of the Pier Six lunch stand, and out of the knot came the chug of the slot machines. Blick put his hand and small revolver into a coat pocket. They turned to the right, away from the lunch stand.

Sail said, "You might have the wrong idea about me."

"We'll go into that, bud," Blick said. "We'll go into that in a nice place I know about."

They scuffed over the sidewalk and Blick, walking as if he did not feel as if he weighed more than a ton, seemed to think of a possibility which pleased him.

"Hell, Nola! This guy covered up that knifing for Andopolis, so he's got to be with Andopolis all the way."

Nola did not answer. She was almost sound asleep. Blick pinched her, slapped her, and that awakened her somewhat.

A police radio car was parked at the corner of Biscayne Boulevard and the street they were traveling. Blick did not see it in time. When he did discover it, he took his breath in with a sharp noise.

"We're drunk," Blick warned. "Taking each other home."

Sail shoved a little to steer the girl to the side of the walk farthest from the prowl car. Blick shoved back to straighten them up. He also got mad.

Blick's gun was in his coat pocket, and if shooting started, it was no time for a gun to be in a pocket. Blick started to take it out, probably intending to hold it at his side where it could not be seen from the police car.

Sail watched the gun start out of the pocket. It had a high front sight and there was an even chance of it hanging on the pocket lining. It did.

Sail shoved Blick and Nola as hard as he could. Force of the effort bounced him towards the police car. He grabbed the spare tire at the back of the machine and used it to help himself around.

A policeman in the car yelled, "What the hell's this?" He wasn't excited.

Blick did not shoot. He got Nola over a shoulder and ran. A taxi-cab was on its stand at the corner. Blick made it.

Sail shouted, "Kidnappers!"

One of the cops leaned out, looked at him, said, "Huh?"

Blick leaped into the taxi with his sister. An instant later, the hack driver fell out of his own machine, holding his head. The taxi took off.

"They stole my heap!" the taxi-driver shrieked.

The police car starter began whining. It whined and whined and nothing happened. One cop wailed, "It never done this before!"

"Try turning on the switch!" Sail yelled.

The motor started.

An officer stuck his head out of the car, said, "You stick around here, wise guy!" and the machine left in pursuit of the cab.

Sail, who had the legs for it, ran away from there very fast.

Sail, when he reached the Pier Six lunch stand, planted his hip against the counter, and caught up with his breathing. A young man who looked as youths in lunch stands somehow always look came over, swiped at the counter with his towel, got a look at Sail, blinked and wanted to know, "How's the weather up there?"

"Dry," Sail said. "What you got in cans?"

Sail drank the first and second cans of beer in gulps, but did some pondering over the third. When it was down, he absent-mindedly put three dimes on the counter.

"Forty-five," the youth corrected. "Cans is fifteen."

Sail substituted a half dollar and put the nickel change in one of the slot machines, still involved with his thoughts. The one-armed bandit gave him a lemon and two bars, another bar just showing.

"Almost a jackpot," someone said.

"History," Sail said, "repeating itself."

A telephone booth was housed at the end of Pier Six. Sail dialed the 0 and asked for Police Headquarters.

The slot machines chugged at the lunch stand while he waited. A card on the phone box told how to report a fire, get the police or call an ambulance. He read part of it, and Headquarters answered.

Sail said, "I want to report an attempted robbery. This is Captain Oscar Sail of the yacht *Sail*. A few minutes ago, a man and a woman boarded my boat and marched me away at the point of a gun. I do not know why. I feel they intended to kill me. There was a police car parked at the corner of Biscayne, and I broke away. The man and woman fled in a taxi. The officers chased them. I do not know whether the officers have reported yet."

"They have."

"Did they catch the pair?"

"No."

Sail almost said that was what he had called to find out, but caught himself in time.

"It might help if you described the pair," the police voice said.

Sail described an imaginary couple that were not like Blick and Nola in any particular except that they were man and woman.

"Thanks," said the voice at Headquarters. "When you get aboard your boat, tell Patrolman Joey Cripp to give us a ring. I'm Captain Rader. You'll probably find Patrolman Cripp on your boat."

Sail was wearing a startled look as he hung up and felt for a nickel in the coin return cup of the telephone.

Three men were waiting in the cabin of *Sail* when Sail got there. Two wore police uniforms, the other had civilian clothes.

One policeman was using his tongue to lather a new cigar with saliva. The tongue was coated. His neck had some loose red skin on it. He was shaking, not very much, but shaking.

The second officer was the young small patrolman. He still had his flashlight.

The man in civilian clothes was putting bottles and test tubes in a scuffed leather bag which held more of the same stuff and a microscope off which much of the enamel had been worn. His suit was fuzzy gray, rimless spectacles were pinched tight on his nose, and he had chewed half of the cigar in his mouth without lighting it. The cigar was the same kind the policeman with the shakes was licking.

Sail said, "Captain Rader wants Patrolman Joey Cripp to call him."

"That's me," the young patrolman said, and started for the companionway.

"Wait a minute," Sail said. "You didn't happen to get a look at a man and a woman who left here with me a while ago?"

"I sure did. I was behind a bush in the park." The young officer went out.

The shaking policeman got up slowly, holding his damp cigar and looking miserable. He took a full breath and started words coming.

"Gracious but you're a tall man," he said. "I'm Captain Cripp and Joey is my son. This is Mister Waterman. You have a wonderful boat here. Some day I am going to get me a boat like this and go to the South Seas. I want to thank you for reporting your trouble to Captain Rader, which I presume you have just done. And I want to congratulate you on your narrow escape from those two. But next time, don't take such chances. Never fool with a man with a gun. We'll let you know as soon as we hear anything of your attacker and his companion. They got away from the radio car. I hope you have a good time in Miami, and no more trouble. We have a wonderful city, a wonderful climate." He shook with his chill.

Captain Cripp pulled out another cigar and a shiny cylindrical metal lighter. He took another breath.

"Smoke? Of course you do. Better light it yourself. I shake like a leaf. I've got the damned malaria, and every other day, I shake. That's an excellent cigar, if I do say so myself. One of our native products. Made right here in Miami, and as mild as an old maid's kiss. There! Didn't I tell you it was a good cigar?"

He took back his lighter. He did not touch the bright metal where Sail had held it and made fingerprints.

"Isn't admission charged to this?"

"Eh? Oh, yes, you are naturally puzzled by our presence here. Forget it. It means nothing at all. It's just an idea Captain Rader got after talking to Joey about a yell and a fish."

Patrolman Joey Cripp jumped aboard and came below.

"Captain Rader offers his apologies for sending us aboard your boat in your absence," Joey said. "And he wonders if you have anything you would like to say to us."

Sail, his scowl getting blacker and blacker, gritted, "I'm making an effort not to say it!"

Joey said, "Well, Mister Sail, if you will excuse me, we will be going."

The rabbity man, Waterman, finished putting things in his bag and picked up a camera with a photoflash attachment, pointed the camera at Sail. The outfit clicked and flashed.

"Thank you," he said, not very politely.

They left.

Sail threw the cigar overboard, then examined the cabin. Almost everything had been put back in place carefully. But in one spot, he found fingerprint powder enough to show they had printed the place.

Sail tried to sleep the rest of the night. He did get a little. The rest of the time he spent at the companion with a mirror which he had rigged on the tip joint of a fishing rod so as to look around without showing himself.

Boats at a slip do not usually have an anchor watch. But on a big Matthews at the opposite slip, somebody seemed to be standing at anchor. The watcher did not smoke, did not otherwise allow any light to get to his features. He might have been tall or short, wide or narrow. The small things he did were what any man would do during a long tiresome job.

There was one exception. The watcher frequently put a finger deep in his mouth and felt around.

Sail took a shower with the dock hose. It gave him a chance to get a better look at the Matthews. The watcher of the night was not in evidence.

The *Sail's* dinghy rode in stern davits, bugeye fashion, at enough of a tilt not to hold spray. Sail lowered it. He got a brush and the dock hose and washed down the black topsides, taking off dried salt which sea water had deposited. He dropped his brush in the water at different times. In each case, it sank, and he had to reach under for it.

The fourth time he reached under for the brush, he retrieved the stuff which he had taken off the Greek. The articles had not worked out of the niche between the dock cross braces under water, where he had jammed them.

Sail finished washing down, hauled the dink up on the davits, and during the business of coiling the dock hose around its faucet, looked around. Any of a dozen persons in sight might have been the watcher off the Matthews. The others would be tourists down for a gawk at the yachts.

He spirited the Greek's stuff below with the scrub brush.

One of the cards said Captain Santorin Gura Andopolis of the yacht *Athens Girl* chartered for Gulf Stream fishing, nobody catching more fish. The address was Pier Five.

The other twenty-six cards said Captain Sam Dokomos owned the Lignum Vitae Towing Company. An address and a telephone number for day calls only.

There was also a piece of board four by twenty inches, a quarter of an inch thick, mahogany, with screw holes in four corners. The varnish was peeled, rather than worn, as was some of the gold leaf. The gold leaf formed a letter, four figures.

K 9420

Sail burned everything in the galley Shipmate.

There was no one in the telephone booth at the end of the pier. He looked up the number of Pier Five, which was no more than two hundred feet distant, and dialed it.

"Captain Andopolis," he requested.

Through the window, he could see them go looking for Captain Andopolis. It took them almost five minutes to decide they couldn't find him.

"Maybe he went to the dentist, somebody thought," the one who had hunted suggested.

"Yeah?"

"Yeah. He's been having a toothache, somebody said."

Sail went back to the bugeye and put on a dark suit, tropical weight, a black polo shirt and black shoes. His shore cruising rig.

The cafeteria was overdone in chromium. The waiters who carried the trays were dressed in the same red that was on the walls. There were a score of customers and a boy who wandered among the tables selling newspapers and racing dope sheets. He sold more dope sheets than papers.

One man eating near the door did not put syrup on his pancakes or sugar in his coffee. When he finished, he put a finger in the back of his mouth to feel.

Sail finished his beer and doughnuts and strolled around the corner to a U-Drive-It.

The only car on which they did not want a deposit was a little six-cylinder sedan, not new. Sail drove it around, sticking his head out frequently to look for a tall building. He found it and parked in front of it.

He made a false start into the building, then came back to take another look at an upright dingus. Then he went inside.

He told the elevator operator loudly, "Five!" before they started up.

The fifth floor corridor was empty.

When the man who had felt of his tooth in the cafeteria came sneaking up the stairs, Sail was set. He had his belt strapped tight around his fist. The man got down on all fours to mew his pain. Sail hit again, then unwrapped the belt, blew on his fist, worked the fingers.

He had the senseless man in his arms when the elevator answered his signal.

"Quick! I gotta rush my friend to a place for a treatment!" he explained.

He drove five or six miles on a side road off the Tamiami Trail before he found a lonesome spot and got out. He hauled the man out.

The man began big at the top and tapered. His small hands were calloused, dirt was ground into the callouses, the nails broken. His face was darker than his hair.

A leather envelope purse held three hundred in old and new bills. There was a dollar sixty-one in change and the cashier's slip for his cafeteria breakfast in his trousers.

A knife was in a holster against the small of his back. It was flat and supported by a high belt. Sail threw it in the canal at the roadside. It was not the one with which he had knifed Sam. He had left that one in his victim.

Handfuls of water from the canal did not speed his revival much. When he finally came around, he groaned, squirmed, and started feeling of his bad tooth.

Sail stood back and showed him a fat blue revolver. "Just try to be nonchalant, Andopolis," he advised.

Andopolis immediately stood up.

"Sit down!" Sail directed sharply.

Andopolis walked towards him.

Sail shoved the gun out, gritting desperately, "This thing is loaded, you fool!"

Andopolis leaped. Sail dodged, but hardly enough. Andopolis hit him with a shoulder. The impact spun him. Since he didn't want to shoot, the gun was a handicap. It tied up his fists. Andopolis hit him on the belt buckle. Numbness grabbed the whole front of his body. Something suddenly against his back was the ground.

"Yah!" Andopolis screeched. "Yah!"

He jumped, feet together, at Sail's middle. Sail was too numb to move clear. The feet hit his chest, everything seemed to break, and red-hot pain knocked the numbness out. Sail got Andopolis' legs, jerked. Andopolis windmilled his arms, but fell.

Sail clamped on to one of the man's feet and began doing things to it and the leg. Andopolis, turning over and over, raised a dust cloud. He moaned and bellowed and made dog noises. When he judged Andopolis was dizzy enough, Sail pounced on the dust cloud. He hit, variously, an arm, the ground, a hip, and other places which he could not identify.

Andopolis, bewildered and with dirt in his eyes, failed to get his jaw out of the way.

Sail straightened, put back his head and started to take a full breath. He began coughing. Hacking, gagging, holding his chest, he sat down in the road. He began to sweat profusely. After a while, he unbuttoned his pants and pulled up his shirt. There was one purple print of the entire bottom of both of Andopolis' feet, and the chest was skinned, the loose skin mixed with the long golden hair. There was not much blood.

Andopolis got his eyes open and snarled, "Yah! I stomp you good if you don't lay off me!"

Sail coughed and got up. He kept his feet far apart, but did not teeter much.

He said thickly, "My Macedonian friend, you stood anchor watch on me all night and you were still trailing me this morning. Where do you get that lay off stuff?"

"Before that, I'm talk about," Andopolis growled.

"Eh?"

Andopolis took a breath and blew words out. "For two week now, you been follow me like dog. I go to Bimini two day, and you and that black bugeye in Bimini before long. I make the run from Bimini here yesterday. You make him too. Vat you take me for? One blind owl, huh?"

Sail asked, "Do you think you're bulletproof, too?"

Andopolis snorted. "Me, I don't theenk you shoot."

"What gave you that idea?"

"Go jump in hell," Andopolis said.

Sail coughed some, deep and low, trying to keep it from moving his ribs.

He said, "All right, now that we're being honest with each other, I'll tell you a true story about a yacht named *Lady Luck*. That's just so there won't be any misunderstanding about who knows what."

Andopolis crowded his lips into a bunch and pushed the bunch out as far as he could, but didn't say anything.

Sail began:

"The *Lady Luck,* Department of Commerce registration number K 9420, was as neat a little yacht as ever kedged off Featherbed Bank. She belonged to Bill Lord of Tulsa. Oil. Out in Tulsa, they call Bill the Osage Ogre, on account of he's got what it seems to take to find oil. Missus Bill likes jewelry, and Bill likes her, so he buys her plenty. Because Missus Bill really likes her rocks, she carries them around with her. You following me?"

Andopolis was. He still had his lips pursed.

"Bill Lord had his *Lady Luck* anchored off the vet camp on Lower Matecumbe last November," Sail continued. "Bill and the Missus were ashore, looking over the camp. Bill was in the trenches himself, back when, and is some kind of a shot in the American Legion or the democrats, so he was interested in the camp. The Missus left her pretties on the yacht. Remember that. Everybody has read about the hurricane that hit that afternoon, and maybe some noticed that Bill and his Missus were among those who hung on behind that tank car. But the *Lady Luck* wasn't so lucky, and she dragged her picks off somewhere and sank. For a while, nobody knew where."

Sail stopped to cough. He had to lay down on his back before he could stop, and he was very careful about getting erect again. Perspiration had wet most of him.

He said, "A couple of weeks ago, a guy asked the Department of Commerce lads to check and give him the name of the boat, and the name of the owner, that carried the number K 9420. That was the mistake."

"Pooey," Andopolis said, "on your story."

"The word got to me," Sail continued. "Never mind how. And it was easy to find you were the lad asking for the dope on K 9420. Inquiry brought out that you had had a fishing party down around Matecumbe and Long Key a few days before you suddenly got curious about K 9420. It was a little harder to locate the parties who had your boat hired at the time. Two Pan-American pilots. They said you anchored off Lower Matecumbe to bottom fish, and your anchor fouled something, and you had a time, and finally, when you got the anchor up, you brought aboard some bow planking off a sunken boat. From the strain as it was torn loose, it was apparent the anchor had pulled the planking off the rest of the boat, which was still down there. You checked up as a matter of course to learn what boat you had found."

Andopolis looked as if something besides his tooth hurt him.

"Tough you didn't get in touch with the insurance people instead of contacting Captain Sam Dokomas, a countryman of yours who had a towing and salvage outfit, and a bad reputation."

Andopolis growled, "Damn! You said somethin' then!"

Sail kept his voice lower to decrease the motion of his ribs in expelling air for words. "You needed help to get the *Lady Luck*. But Captain Sam Dokomas tried to make you cough up the exact location. Then you smelled a double-cross, got scared and lit for Bimini.

"I had been hanging around all this time, and not doing a good job of it, so you got wise to me. That scared you back to Miami. You had decided on a showdown, and were headed for my boat when Captain Sam collared you on the dock. You took care of part of your troubles with a knife right there. But that left Captain Sam's girl friend and her brother, Nola and Blick, or whatever their names are. They were in the know. They tried to grab you in the park after you fixed Sam up, but you outran them.

"Now, that's a very complete story, don't you think? Oh, yes. You got reckless and jumped me a minute ago because you figured I wouldn't shoot you because nobody but you knows the exact location of the *Lady Luck*. The two Pan-American boys fishing down there with you when you found the ship forgot to take bearings and didn't have a smell of an idea where they were at the time."

Andopolis was a man who did his thinking with the help of his face, and there was more disgust than anything else on his features.

"You trying to cut in?" he snarled finally.

"Not trying. Have."

Andopolis thought that over. The sun was comfortable, but mosquitoes were coming out of the swamp around the road to investigate, hungrier than land sharks.

"Yeah," Andopolis muttered finally. "I guess you have, at that."

"Let's get this straight, Andy. You and I, and nobody else."

Andopolis nodded. "Okey."

"Now just who is this Blick?"

"Nola's brother."

"Now, hell, Andy—"

"And Nola was married to that double-crosser, Sam."

Sail made a whistling mouth. "So it was Nola's husband you dirked. She'll like you for that."

"So what? She didn't go for him much."

"No?"

"Naw. That dame—"

"Skip it," Sail said suddenly. He put his shirt on, favoring his chest. "Dang, feller, you sure busted up my ribs. We've got to watch the insurance company. They paid off on Missus Bill's stuff. Over a hundred thousand. They'll have wires out."

Andopolis nodded. "What about stuff for diving?"

"There's sponger equipment aboard my bugeye," Sail said. "I tried that racket over in Tarpon Springs, but you can't compete with those Greeks over there."

"Let's go," Andopolis said.

He was feeling of his tooth when he got in the car. Sail drove slowly. The road, nothing more than a high dike built up with material scooped out to make the drainage canal, was rough. It hurt his ribs.

Sail had driven no more than half a mile when both front tires let go their air. Maybe the car would still have remained on the road. But bullets also knocked holes in the windshield. The car was in the canal before anything could be done about it.

The car broke most of its windows going down the canal bank. The canal must have been six feet deep. Its tea-colored water filled the machine at once. Sail's middle hurt, and he had lost his air, and had to breathe in, and there was nothing but water.

After the water had filled the car, it seemed to rush around inside. Sail tried the doors, but they wouldn't open. He did not touch Andopolis in his struggles. Andopolis did not seem to be in the car. Sail couldn't remember him having been thrown out.

The first window Sail found was too small. He pummeled the car roof, but hardly had strength enough to knock himself away from what he was hitting. Then he was suddenly out of the car. He didn't know just how he had managed it. He reached the top, but sank twice before he clutched a weed on shore, after which an attack of the spasms kept him at first from hearing the shots.

Yells were mixed in the shot noise. Sail squeezed water off his eyeballs with the lids, looked, and saw Andopolis on the canal bank. Andopolis was some distance away and running madly.

Blick and his sister Nola were running after Andopolis. They were shooting at Andopolis' legs, it seemed.

They all three ran out of sight, but the sounds told Sail they had winged Andopolis and grabbed him.

Sail had wrenched some of the water out of his lungs by now. He swam to a bush which hung down into the water and got under it. He managed to get his coughing stopped.

Andopolis was sobbing at the top of his voice when Blick and Nola dragged him up.

"Shoot his other leg off if he acts up, Nola," Blick said. "I'll get our tall bud."

Sail began to want to cough. He desired the cough until it was almost worth getting shot for.

"He must be a submarine," Blick said. He got a stick and poked around. "Hell, Nola, this water is eight feet deep here anyhow."

Andopolis bubbled something in Greek.

"Shut up," Blick said, "or we'll put bullets into you like we put 'em into the tires of your car."

Andopolis went on bubbling.

"His leg is bleeding bad, Blick," Nola said.

"Hell I care! He knifed your husband, didn't he?"

Air kept coming up in big bubbles from the submerged car. Sail tried to keep his mind off the cough. Blick stood for a century on the bank with his bright little pistol.

"He musta drowned," Blick said.

Andopolis moaned.

"Didn't you know we had been shaggin' you all night and mornin'?" Blick asked him. "Hell, if you hadn't been so occupied with that long lean punk, you'd have got wise, maybe."

Nola said, "We better get his leg fixed."

"If he ain't free with his information, he won't need his leg any more," Blick said. "Let's get the hell away from here."

Andopolis whimpered as they hazed him away. They apparently had a car in the bushes beside the canal some distance down the road. Its noise went away. Sail crawled out and had a good cough.

Captain Cripp looked wide-eyed and hearty and without a sign of a chill as he exclaimed, "Well, well, good morning, good morning. You know, we began to think something had happened to you."

Sail looked at him with eyes that appeared to be drained of everything but the will to carry on, then stumbled down the remaining three steps into the main cabin of *Sail*. He let himself down on the starboard seat. Pads of cotton under gauze thickened his neck and wrists. He had discovered the car windows had cut him, Iodine had run from under one of the pads and dried. He had just come from the hospital.

Young bony Patrolman Joey Cripp looked at Sail. His grin took the looseness out of the corner of his mouth.

"Tsk, tsk," he said. "Now that's terrible. You look a sight. By God, it's a wonder you're alive. I hope that didn't happen in Miami."

Sail gave them a look of bile. "This is a private boat, in case you forgot."

"Now, now, I hope we can keep things on an amiable footing," Captain Cripp murmured.

Sail said, "Drag it!" His face was more cream than any other color. He reached behind himself in the tackle locker and got a gaff hook. A four-foot shaft of varnished oak with a tempered bright steel hook of needle point. He showed them the hook and his front teeth. "I've got a six-aspirin headache, and things to go with it! You two polite public servants get out of here before I go fishing for kidneys!"

Patrolman Joey Cripp stood up. "I didn't think we'd have any trouble with you, Mister Sail. I hoped we wouldn't, on account of you acted like a gentleman last night."

"Sit the hell down, Joey," Captain Cripp put in. "Mister Sail, you're under arrest, I'm sorry to say."

Sail said, "Arrest?" He scowled. "Is this on the level?"

"It sure is."

"Pop said it," agreed young Joey.

Captain Cripp shook a finger at Sail. He said:

"Listen. Waterman found human blood in that fish mess on the dock last night. The harbor squad's diver went down this morning. He found a bathing suit with a sinker tied to it. He also found a live-box with some live barracuda in it. It was a barracuda you butchered on the dock. Your fishline you had in your hand when Joey got there was wet, but it don't take a minute to wet a line. You described a man and a woman that looked a lot different from the pair Joey saw you with. We been doing some arithmetic, and we figure you were covering up."

"Now," Sail said, "I guess I'm supposed to get scared?"

"I don't know," Captain Cripp said, "but a dead Greek was found over on the island this morning. And in your bathing suit which the diver got was some island sand, and some stickers off the pine trees like grows on the island."

"I guess," Joey said, "it does look kinda funny."

"I regret that it does," Captain Cripp agreed. "After all, evidence is evidence, and while Miami has a wonderful hospitality, we do draw lines, and when our visitors go so far as to use knives on—"

"Let's get this straight!" Sail put in. "Pine tree stickers and sand are just about alike here and in Key West, and points between."

"You may be assured—"

Sail sprang up, gripping the hook. He began to yell.

"What's the idea of this clowning? I know two lug cops when I see 'em. If you got something to say, get it off your chests."

Joey sighed. "I guess courtesy is somethin' you can't acquire. Watcha say, Pop? Hell with the chief's courtesy campaign, huh?"

"Now that you mention it, Joey, okey." Captain Cripp pulled manacles out of his hip pocket. "We're gonna fan you into the can, and we're gonna work you over until we get the straight of this."

Sail slammed the gaff into a corner.

"That's more like. If you hadn't tried to fancy pants around last night, I'd have showed you something then."

Sail shuffled into the galley and got the rearmost can of beer out of the icebox. It gurgled when he shook it, but that was because of the small sealed jar of water which fitted inside it. Stuffed around the jar were some sheets of paper. He held the documents out to the two policemen.

Joey raked his eyes over the print and penned signatures, then spelled them out, lips moving.

"Aw, this don't make no difference," he said. "Or does it?"

Captain Cripp complained, "My glasses fell off yesterday when I was having one of my infernal chills. What does it say, Joey?"

"He's a private dick commissioned to locate some stuff that sank on a yacht called the *Lady Luck*. The insurance people hired him."

Captain Cripp buttoned his coat, squared it over his hips, set his cap with a pat on the top. "Who signed the papers, Joey?"

Joey said, "They're all right, Pop. From what it says, I guess this private op is the head of something called Marine Investigations. Reckon that's an agency, huh?"

Captain Cripp sighed and ambled over to the companionway. "Beauty before age, Joey."

Joey bristled. "Shamus or no shamus, I say it don't make no difference!"

"Let the next guy have the honor, Joey."

"Look, Pop, damn it—"

"The last private op I worked over got me two years in the sticks. He said something about me chiseling in on the reward, and the skipper believed him. It was a damned lie, except—well—out, Joey."

"But Pop, this stinker—"

"Out!" Captain Cripp barked. "You're as big a fool as your maw!"

Joey licked his lips, raking Sail with malevolent eyes. Then he turned and climbed the companion steps.

Captain Cripp looked at Sail. He felt for the bottom step with one foot without looking down. As if he didn't expect it to do any good, he asked, "You wouldn't want to cooperate?"

"I wouldn't."

"Why not?"

"I've done it before."

Captain Cripp grinned slightly. "Just as you say. But if you get yourself in a sling, it'd be better if you had a reason for refusing to help the police."

"All I get out of this is ten per cent for recovering the stuff. I can't see a split. I need the dough."

"And you with a boat like this."

"Maybe I like boats and maybe it keeps me broke."

"The only reason you're not in the can right now is that any shyster could make this circumstantial evidence look funny as hell. Forget the split."

"Thanks," Sail said. "Now I'm going to sound off. It just might be that you lads think you can let me finish it out, then step in, and maybe find the location of that boat for yourselves. Then, while I was in your bastile, trying to explain things you could think to ask me, the stuff might disappear off the boat."

"That's kind of plain talk."

"I feel kind of plain right now."

Captain Cripp's ears moved up a little with the tightening of his jaw muscles. He took his foot off the companion step. He gave his cap an angry adjustment. Then he put the foot back again.

"This malaria is sure something. I feel like a lark today, only I keep thinking about the chills tomorrow."

"Try whiskey and quinine," Sail said.

"I think the whiskey part gave it to me."

The two cops went away with Joey kicking his feet down hard at the dock planks.

Sail took rye and aspirin for what ailed him, changed clothes, took a taxi uptown and entered what looked like the largest hardware store. He asked where they kept their marine charts.

The nervous old salesman in the chart department had a rip in his canvas apron. He mixed his talk in with waving gestures of a pipe off which most of the stem had been chewed.

"Mister, you must have some funny things happen to you, you being so tall," he said. "Right now, you look as if you had had an accident."

Sail steadied himself by holding to the counter edge. "Who sells government charts here, Dad?"

"Well, there's one other store besides us. Hopkins Carter. But if you're going down in the Keys, we got everything you need here. If you go inside, you'll want charts thirty-two-sixty and sixty-one. They're the strip charts. But if you take Hawk Channel, you'll need harbor chart five-eighty-three, and charts twelve-forty-nine, fifty and fifty-one. Here, I'll show—"

Sail squinted his eyes, swallowed, and said, "I don't want to buy a chart. I want you to slip out and telephone me if either of a certain two

persons comes in here and asks for chart twelve-fifty, the one which
covers Lower Matecumbe."

"Huh?"

Sail said patiently, "It's easy, Dad. You just tell the party you got to
get the chart, and go telephone me. Then stall around three or four
minutes as if you were getting the chart out of the stock room. That
will give me time to get over here and pick up their trail."

The nervous old man put his pipe in his mouth and immediately
took it out again. "What kind of shenanygin is this?"

Sail showed him a license to operate in Florida.

"One of them fellers, huh?" The old man did not seem impressed.

Sail put a five-dollar bill on the counter. "That one's got a twin.
How about it?"

The old man picked up the bill, squinted at it. "You mean this is a
counterfeit or something. What—"

"No, no, control your imagination, Dad. The five is good, and it's
yours, and another one like it, if you help me."

"You mean I keep this whether they show up or not?"

"That's the idea."

"Go ahead, Mister, and describe them people."

Sail made a word picture of Blick and Nola. Not trusting Dad's
memory, he put the salient points down on a piece of paper. He added
a telephone number. "That phone is a booth in a cigar store on the
next corner. How far is this Hopkins Carter store?"

" 'Bout two blocks, reckon."

"I'll be there for the next ten minutes. Then I'll be in the cigar
store. Ask for Chief Steward Johnson, when you call."

"That you?"

"Uh-huh."

Sail, walking off, was not as pale as he had been on the boat. He
had put on a serge suit with more black than blue and a new black
polo. When he was standing in front of the elevator, taking a pull at a
flat amber bottle which had a crown and a figure on the label, the old
man yelled, "Mister!"

Sail lowered the bottle, started coughing.

"Lemme look at this again and see if you said anything about the
way he talked," the old man said.

Sail moved back to where he could see the old fellow peering at
the paper which held the descriptions. The old man took his pipe out
of his teeth. "Mister, what does that feller talk like?"

"Well, about like the rest of these crackers. No, wait. He'll call you bud two or three times."

The old man waved his pipe. "I already sold that man a twelve-fifty."

"The hell!"

"Around half an hour ago, I reckon."

"That's swell!" Sail pumped air out of his lungs in a short laugh which had no sound except such noise as the air made going past his teeth and out of his nostrils. "There was this one chance. They would probably want a late chart for their X-marks-the-spot. And now they've got it, so they'll be off to the wars." He kissed a palm sneeringly. "That for the whole works!"

He weaved around, a lot more unsteady than he had been a minute before. He put the flat flask between his teeth and looked at the spinning ceiling fan. By the time the bottle was empty, his head and eyes were screwing around in time with the fan blades. He got his feet tracking in the general direction of the door.

The old man said, "That there chart was delivered."

Sail maneuvered a turn and halt. "Eh?"

"He ordered it over the telephone, and we delivered. I got the address somewhere." The old man thumbed his order book, stopping to point at each name with his pipe stem.

"*Whileaway*," he said finally. "A houseboat on the Miami river below the Twelfth Street Causeway."

Sail cocked the empty bottle in a wastebasket, put five dollars in front of the old man and headed for the elevator. He was a lot steadier.

The houseboat *Whileaway* was built for rivers, and not very wide ones. Sixty feet or thereabouts waterline, she had three decks that put her up like a skyscraper. She was white, or had been. A man who loved boats would have said she should never have been built.

Scattered on shore near was a gravel pile, two trucks with nobody near them, a shed, junk from the hurricane, a trailer with both tires flat and windows broken, and two rowboats in as bad shape as the trailer.

Sail was behind most of the junk at one time or another on his way to the river bank. The river ran between wooden bulkheads at this point. Between Sail and *Whileaway*, two tugs, a yawl, a cruiser and another houseboat were tied to dolphins along the bulkhead. Nobody seemed to be on any of the boats.

Sail stripped to dark blue silk underwear shorts. He hid everything else under the junk. The water had a little more smell and floating things than in the harbor. After he had eased down into it, he kept behind the moored boats, next to the bulkhead. The tide carried him. He was just coming under the bow of *Whileaway* when one of the square window ports of the houseboat opened.

Sail sank suddenly. He thought somebody was going to shoot, or use a harpoon.

Something heavy—evidently it fell out of the porthole—hit the water. It sank quickly. Touching Sail, it pushed him aside. It went on sinking. Sail got the idea that a navy anchor was at the lowermost part of the sinking object.

He swam down after it. The river had only two fathoms here. He did not have much trouble finding it. When he clung to the object, the tide stretched his legs out behind.

Whoever had tied the knots was a sailor. Sailor knots, while they hold, are made to be easily untied. Sail got them loose. He began to think he wouldn't make the top with his burden. He was out of air.

His head came out of the water with eyes open, fixed in the direction of the square port. Nobody's head was there. No weapon appeared.

Sail looked around, then threw an arm up. He missed the first springline which held the houseboat to the bulkhead. He grasped the next one. He held Nola's head out.

Water leaked from Nola's nose and mouth.

Some of the rope which had tied her to the heavy navy anchor was still wrapped around her. Sail used it to tie her to the springline, so that her head was out of the water.

Then he had to try twice before he could get up the springline to the houseboat deck. Nola began gagging and coughing. It made a racket.

Sail stumbled through the handiest door. Waves of pain jumped from his ribs to his toes, from ribs to hair. The bandages had turned red, and it was not from mercurochrome.

The houseboat furnishings must have been something fifteen years ago. Most of the varnish had alligatored. Sail got into the galley by accident. Rust, dirt, smell. He grabbed the only things in sight, a quart brass fire extinguisher and a rusted ice pick.

He found a dining salon beyond the galley. He was half across it when Andopolis came in the opposite door.

Andopolis had a rusty butcher knife in one hand. He was using the other hand to handle a chair for a crutch, riding it with the knee of the leg which Blick and Nola had put a bullet through.

Clustered around Andopolis' eyes—more on the lids than else-where—were puffy gray blisters. They were about the size burning cigarettes would make. Two fingernails were off of his hands, the one which held the butcher knife. Red ran from the mutilated fingertips down over the rusty knife.

Sail threw the fire extinguisher. He was weaker even than he had thought. The best he could do was bounce the extinguisher off the bulkhead behind Andopolis.

Andopolis said thickly, "I feex you up this time, fran!" and reversed the knife for throwing.

Sail threw his ice pick. It was a good shot. The pick stuck into Andopolis' chest over his heart. But it did not go in deep enough to trouble Andopolis. He never bothered to jerk it out. He already had enough pain elsewhere not to know it was there.

Feet banged through the boat behind Sail. They approached.

Andopolis threw. Sail dropped. His weakness seemed to help. The knife went over his head.

A uniformed cop had appeared in the door. Bad luck put him in the path of the knife. He made a bleating sound, took spraddling steps and leaned against a bulkhead, his hands trying to cover the handle of the butcher knife and his left shoulder. He made a poor job of it.

Sail got up and lurched around Andopolis. The chair crutch made Andopolis clumsy.

Once through the door behind Andopolis, Sail found himself in what had once been the main cabin, and pretended to be, still.

Blick sat on the cabin floor, his face a mess. His visage was smeared with blue ink. The ink bottle was upside down under a table on which a new marine chart was spread open. A common writing pen lay on the chart.

Andopolis came in after Sail, banging on the chair crutch. The ice pick still stuck in his chest by its point. He came at Sail, hopped on one leg, and swung his chair with the other.

Sail, coughing, hurting all over, tried to dodge. He made it, but fell down. Andopolis swung the chair. Sail rolled, and the chair went to pieces on the floor.

Nola was still screaming. Men were swearing outside. More men were running around on the houseboat, trying to find the way below. A police siren was whining.

Andopolis held a leg of his chair still. It was heavy enough to knock the brains out of an ox. He hopped for Sail.

Sail, looking about wildly, saw the fire extinguisher on the floor. It must have bounced in here. Maybe somebody had kicked it in accidentally. He rolled to it.

Andopolis lifted the chair leg.

The extinguisher made sickly noises as Sail pumped it. No tetrachloride came out. Nothing happened to indicate it ever would. Then a first squirt ran out about a foot. The second was longer. The third wet Andopolis' chest. Sail aimed and pumped. The tetrachloride got into Andopolis' eyes.

Andopolis made snarling sounds and couldn't see any more.

Sail got up and weaved to the table.

The chart on the table had two inked lines forming a V with arms that ran to landmarks on Lower Matecumbe island in the Florida Keys. Compass bearings were printed beside each arm, and the point where the lines came together was ringed.

Several times, Sail's lips moved, repeating the bearings, the landmarks.

Then Sail picked up the pen. He made a NE into a NNE and a SSE out of an E.

His letters looked enough like the others that nobody would guess the difference. And the lines of the V were wavy. They had not been laid out with a protractor from the compass roses. Therefore, they did not indicate an exact spot. Probably they varied as much as a mile, for the *Lady Luck* seemed to lie well off Matecumbe. Nobody would locate any sunken boat from that chart now.

Sail was repeating the true bearings to fix them in his memory when Andopolis came hopping in. Andopolis was still blind, still had his chair leg.

Blick, on the floor, called, "Nola—kid—what's wrong?" He didn't seem to know where he was or what was happening.

Andopolis weaved for Blick's mumbling voice.

"Blick!" Sail yelled thickly. "Jump!"

Blick said foolishly, "Was that—you—Nola?"

Sail was stumbling towards him, fully aware he would not make it in time. He didn't. He woke up nights for quite a while hearing the sound Andopolis' chair leg and Blick's head made.

Andopolis hopped around, still quite blind, and made for Sail. He had his chair leg raised. Hair, blood and brains stuck to the hickory chair leg. Sail got out of the way.

Andopolis stopped, stood perfectly still, and listened. Sail did not move. He was pale, swaying. He squatted, got his hands on the floor, sure he was going to fall if he didn't. He tried not to breathe loudly enough for Andopolis to hear.

Captain Cripp, Patrolman Joey Cripp and the old man from the hardware store came in together looking around.

The old man pointed at Sail and began, "There's the man who asked about the feller that got the chart. I told you I told him the chart was delivered here, and he probably had come right—"

Andopolis rushed the voice, holding his chair leg up.

"Look out!" Sail croaked.

Andopolis instantly veered for where he thought Sail's voice had come from. He was a little wrong. It was hard for him to maintain a direction hopping on one leg. He hopped against a wall. Hard.

Andopolis sighed, leaned over backward and hit the floor. He had a fit. A brief fit, ending by Andopolis straightening out and relaxing. Hitting the wall had driven the ice pick the rest of the way into his chest.

Sail remained on all fours on the floor. He felt, except for the pain, as if he were very drunk on bad liquor. He must have remained on his hands and knees a long time, for he was vaguely aware that Captain Cripp and Joey had walked around and around him, but without speaking. Then they went over to the table and found the chart.

They divided their looking between the chart and each other.

"It's it," Joey said.

"Yeah." Captain Cripp sounded thoughtful. "What about it, Joey?"

"You're the boss, Pop."

Captain Cripp turned the corners of his mouth down. He folded the chart, stuck it inside his clothing, under his belt. Then he straightened his uniform.

A doctor came in at last. He seemed to be a very silent doctor. He picked up Andopolis' wrist, held it a while, then put it back on the floor carefully. The wrist and arm were more flexible than that much rubber would have been. The doctor did not speak.

Sail was still on all fours. The doctor upset him gently. Sail had his tongue between his teeth. The doctor explored with his hands, when he came to Sail's chest, a small amount of sound escaped between Sail's tongue and teeth.

"My God!" the doctor said.

Four men helped with the stretcher as far as the ambulance, but only two when it came to getting the stretcher into the ambulance. Two could manage it better, using a system which they had. The ambulance motor started.

Captain Cripp got into the ambulance with Sail. He was holding his right hand to his nose.

"About Joey," he said. "I been wondering if Joey believed in something on the side, when he could get it. You know, kinda the modern idea."

He took his hand from his nose and quickly put a handkerchief in its place. The handkerchief got red at once.

Then he put the folded marine chart under Sail's head.

"Joey," he chuckled, "is as old-fashioned as angels, only he about busted my beak before I could explain."

Joan Hess first started out writing romances, but switched to mysteries on the advice of her agent, and has never looked back. Her novels, usually set in small Arkansas towns, have won the Agatha, American Mystery, and Macavity awards. Her shorter fiction has appeared in Cat Crimes *and* Crimes of Passion. *Currently she is editing an anthology of humorous crime fiction along the lines of her own books. In the following story, she visits Maggody, Arkansas, once again for another unique mystery.*

The Maggody Files: Hillbilly Cat

Joan Hess

I was reduced to whittling away the morning, and trying to convince myself that I was in some obscure way whittling away at the length of my sentence in Maggody, Arkansas (pop. 755). Outside the red-bricked PD, the early morning rain came down steadily, and, as Ruby Bee Hanks (proprietress of a bar and grill of the same name, and incidentally, my mother) would say, it was turning a mite crumpy. I figured the local criminal elements would be daunted enough to stay home, presuming they were smart enough to come in out of the rain in the first place. This isn't to say they rampaged when the sun shone. Mostly they ran the stoplight, fussed and cussed at their neighbors, stole such precious commodities as superior huntin' dawgs, and occasionally raced away from the self-service station without paying for gas. There'd been some isolated violence during my tenure, but every last person in town still based their historical perspective on before-or-after Hiram Buchanon's barn burned to the ground.

I suppose I ought to mention that my sentence was self-imposed, in that I scampered home from Manhattan to lick my wounds after a nasty divorce. In that I was the only person stupid enough to apply for the job, I was not only the Chief of Police, but also the entirety of the department. For a while I'd had a deputy, who just happened to be the mayor's cousin, but he'd gotten himself in trouble over his unrequited love for a bosomy barmaid. Now I had a beeper.

That October morning I had a block of balsa wood that was harder than granite, and a pocket knife that was duller than most of the population. I also had some bizarre dreams of converting the wood into something that remotely resembled a duck—a marshland mallard, to be precise. Those loyal souls who're schooled in the local lore know I tried this a while back, with zero success. Same wood, for the record, and thus far, same rate of success.

So I had my feet on the corner of my desk, my cane-bottomed chair propped back against the wall, and an unholy mess of wood shavings scattered all over the place when the door opened. The man who came in wore a black plastic raincoat and was wrestling with a brightly striped umbrella more suited to a swanky golf course (in Maggody, we don't approve of golf—or any other sissified sport in which grown men wear shorts). He appeared to be forty or so, with a good ol' boy belly and the short, wavy hair of a used car salesman.

Strangers come into the PD maybe three times a year, usually to ask directions or to sell me subscriptions to magazines like *Field and Stream* or *Sports Illustrated*. I guess it's never occurred to any of them that some of us backwoods cops might prefer *Cosmopolitan*.

He finally gave up on the umbrella and set it in a corner to drip. Flashing two rows of pearly white teeth at me, he said, "Hey, honey, some weather, isn't it? Is the chief in?"

"It sure is some weather," I said politely, "and the chief is definitely in." I did not add that the chief was mildly insulted, but by no means incensed or inclined to explain further.

This time I got a wink. "Could I have a word with him?"

"You're having a word with *her* at this very moment," I said as I dropped my duck in a drawer and crossed my arms, idly wondering how long it'd take him to work it out. He didn't look downright stupid like the clannish Buchanons, who're obliged to operate solely on animal instinct, but he had squinty eyes, flaccid lips, and minutes earlier had lost a battle to an umbrella.

"Sorry, honey." His shrug indicated he wasn't altogether overwhelmed with remorse. "I'm Nelson Mullein from down near Pine Bluff. The woman at the hardware store said the chief's name was Arly, and I sort of assumed I was looking for a fellow. My mistake."

"How may I help you, Mr. Mullein?" I said.

"Call me Nelson, please. My great-grandaunts live here in Maggody, out on County 102 on the other side of the low-water bridge.

Everybody's always called them the Banebury girls, although Miss Columbine is seventy-eight and Miss Larkspur's seventy-six."

"I know who they are."

"Thought you might." He sat down on the chair across from my desk and took out a cigar. When he caught my glare, he replaced it in his pocket, licked his lips, and made a production of grimacing and sighing so I'd appreciate how carefully he was choosing his words. "The thing is," he said slowly, "I'm worried about them. As I said, they're old and they live in that big, ramshakle house by themselves. It ain't in the ghetto, but it's a far cry from suburbia. Neither one of them can see worth a damn. Miss Larkspur took a fall last year while she was climbing out of the tub, and her hip healed so poorly she's still using a walker. Miss Columbine is wheezier than a leaky balloon."

"So I should arrest them for being old and frail?"

"Of course not," he said, massaging his rubbery jowls. "I was hoping you could talk some sense into them, that's all, 'cause I sure as hell can't, even though I'm their only relative. It hurts me to see them living the way they do. They're as poor as church mice. When I went out there yesterday, it was colder inside than it was outside, and the only heat was from a wood fire in a potbelly stove. Seems they couldn't pay the gas bill last month and it was shut off. I took care of that immediately and told the gas company to bill me in the future. If Miss Columbine finds out, she'll have a fit, but I didn't know what else to do."

He sounded so genuinely concerned that I forgave him for calling me "honey," and tried to recall what little I knew about the Banebury girls. They'd been reclusive even when I was a kid, although they occasionally drove through town in a glossy black Lincoln Continental, nodding regally at the peasants. One summer night twenty or so years ago, they'd caught a gang of us skinny-dipping at the far side of the field behind their house. Miss Columbine had been outraged. After she carried on for a good ten minutes, Miss Larkspur persuaded her not to report the incident to our parents and we grabbed our clothes and high-tailed it. We stayed well downstream the rest of the summer. We avoided their house at Halloween, but only because it was isolated and not worth the risk of having to listen to a lecture on hooliganism in exchange for a stale popcorn ball.

"I understand your concern," I said. "I'm afraid I don't know them well enough to have any influence."

"They told me they still drive. Miss Columbine has macular degeneration, which means her peripheral vision's fine but she can't see anything in front of her. Miss Larkspur's legally blind, but that works out just fine—she navigates. I asked them how on earth either had a driver's license, and damned if they didn't show 'em to me. The date was 1974."

I winced. "Maybe once or twice a year, they drive half a mile to church at a speed of no more than ten miles an hour. When they come down the middle of the road, everybody in town knows to pull over, all the way into a ditch if need be, and the children have been taught to do their rubberneckin' from their yards. It's actually kind of a glitzy local event that's discussed for days afterwards. I realize it's illegal, but I'm not about to go out there and tell them they can't drive anymore."

"Yeah, I know," he said, "but I'm going to lose a lot of sleep if I don't do something for them. I'm staying at a motel in Farberville. This morning I got on the phone and found out about a retirement facility for the elderly. I went out and looked at it, and it's more like a boardinghouse than one of those smelly nursing homes. Everybody has a private bedroom, and meals are provided in a nice, warm dining room. There was a domino game going on while I was there, and a couple of the women were watching a soap opera. There's a van to take them shopping or to doctor appointments. It's kind of expensive, but I think I can swing it by using their social security checks and setting up an income from the sale of the house and property. I had a real estate agent drive by it this morning, and he thought he could get eight, maybe ten, thousand dollars."

"And when you presented this, they said . . . ?"

"Miss Columbine's a hardheaded woman, and she liked to scorch my ears," he admitted ruefully. "I felt like I was ten years old and been caught with a toad in the pocket of my choir robe. Miss Larkspur was interested at first, and asked some questions, but when they found out they couldn't take Eppie, the discussion was over, and before I knew what hit me, I was out on the porch shivering like a hound dog in a blizzard."

"Eppie?"

"Their cat. In spite of the sweet-sounding name, it's an obese yellow tomcat with one eye and a tattered ear. It's mangy and mean and moth-eaten, and that's being charitable. But they won't even consider giving it away, and the residence home forbids pets because of a health department regulation. I went ahead and put down a deposit, but the director said she can't hold the rooms for more than a few days and she expects to be filled real soon. I hate to say it, but it's now or never." He spread his hands and gave me a beseeching look. "Do you think you or anybody else in town can talk them into at least taking a look at this place?"

I suspected I would have more luck with my balsa wood than with the Banebury sisters, but I promised Nelson I'd give it a shot and wrote down the telephone number of his motel room. After a display of effusively moist gratitude, he left.

I decided the matter could wait until after lunch. The Banebury sisters had been going about their business nearly four score years, after all, I told myself righteously as I darted through the drizzle to my car and headed for Ruby Bee's Bar & Grill.

"So what's this about Miss Columbine and Miss Larkspur being dragged off to an old folks' home?" Ruby Bee demanded as I walked across the tiny dance floor. It was too early for the noon crowd, and only one booth was occupied by a pair of truck drivers working on blue plate specials and a pitcher of beer.

"And who'd pay ten thousand dollars for that old shack?" Estelle Oppers added from her favorite stool at the end of the bar, convenient to the pretzels and the rest room.

I wasn't particularly amazed by the questions. Maggody has a very sturdy grapevine, and it definitely curls through the barroom on its way from one end of town to the other. That was one of the reasons I'd left the day after I graduated, and eventually took refuge in the anonymity of Manhattan, where one can caper in the nude on the street and no one so much as bothers with a second look. In Maggody, you can hear about what you did before you're finished planning to do it.

"To think they'd give up their cat!" Ruby Bee continued, her hands on her hips and her eyes flashing as if I'd suggested we drown dear Eppie in Boone Creek. Beneath her unnaturally blond hair, her face was screwed up with indignation. "It ain't much to look at, but they've had it for fourteen years and some folks just don't understand how attached they are."

I opened my mouth to offer a mild rebuttal, but Estelle leapt in with the agility of a trout going after a mayfly. "Furthermore, I think it's mighty suspicious, him coming to town all of a sudden to disrupt their lives. I always say, when there's old ladies and a cat, the nephew's up to no good. Just last week I read a story about how the nephew tried to trick his aunt so he could steal all her money."

I chose a stool at the opposite end of the bar. "From what Nelson told me, they don't have any money."

"I still say he's up to no good," Estelle said mulishly, which is pretty much the way she said everything.

Ruby Bee took a dishrag and began to wipe the pristine surface of the bar. "I reckon that much is true, but Eula said she happened to see him in the hardware store, and he had a real oily look about him, like a carnival roustabout. She said she wouldn't have been surprised if he had tattoos under his clothes. He was asking all kinds of questions, too."

"Like what?" I said, peering at the pies under glass domes and ascertaining there was a good-sized piece of cherry left.

"Well, he wanted to know where to go to have all their utility bills sent to him, on account of he didn't think they had enough money to pay 'em. He also wanted to know if he could arrange for groceries to be delivered to their house every week, but Eula stepped in and explained that the church auxiliary already sees to that."

I shook my head and made a clucking noise. "The man's clearly a scoundrel, a cad, a veritable devil in disguise. How about meatloaf, mashed potatoes and gravy, and cherry pie with ice cream?"

Ruby Bee was not in her maternal mode. "And wasn't there an old movie about a smarmy nephew trying to put his sweet old aunts in some sort of insane asylum?" she asked Estelle.

"That was because they were poisoning folks. I don't recollect anyone accusing the Banebury girls of anything like that. Miss Columbine's got a sharp tongue, but she's got her wits about her. I wish I could say the same thing about Miss Larkspur. She can be kind of silly and forgetful, but she ain't got a mean bone in her body. Now if the cat was stalking me on a dark street, I'd be looking over my shoulder and fearing for my life. He lost his eye in a fight with old Shep Hume's pit bull. When Shep tried to pull 'em apart, he liked to lose both of his eyes and a couple of fingers, and he said he cain't remember when he heard a gawdawful racket like that night."

"Meatloaf?" I said optimistically. "Mashed potatoes?"

Still wiping the bar, Ruby Bee worked her way towards Estelle. "The real estate agent says he can sell that place for ten thousand dollars?"

"He didn't sound real sure of it, and Eilene said Earl said the fellow didn't think the house was worth a dollar. It was the forty acres he thought might sell." Estelle popped a pretzel in her mouth and chewed it pensively. "I took them a basket of cookies last year just before Christmas, and the house is in such sad shape that I thought to myself, I'm gonna sit right down and cry. The plaster's crumbling off the walls, and there was more than one window taped with cardboard. It's a matter of time before the house falls down on 'em."

Aware I was about to go down for the third time, I said, "Meatloaf?"

Ruby Bee leaned across the bar, and in a melodramatic whisper that most likely was audible in the next county, said, "Do you think they're misers with a fortune buried in jars in the back yard? If this Mullein fellow knows it, then he'd want to get rid of them and have all the time he needs to dig up the yard searching for the money."

"Them?" Estelle cackled. "There was some family money when their daddy owned the feed store, but he lost so much money when that fancy co-op opened in Starley City that he lost the store and upped and died within the year. After that, Miss Larkspur had to take piano students and Miss Columbine did mending until they went on social security. Now how are they supposed to have acquired this fortune? Are you accusing them of putting on ski masks and robbing liquor stores?"

"For pity's sake, I was just thinking out loud," Ruby Bee retorted.

"The next thing, you'll be saying you saw them on that television show about unsolved crimes."

"At least some of us have better things to do than read silly mystery stories about nephews and cats," Ruby Bee said disdainfully. "I wouldn't be surprised if you didn't have a whole book filled with them."

"So what if I do?" Estelle slapped the bar hard enough to dump the pretzels.

It seemed the only thing being served was food for thought. I drove to the Dairee Dee-Lishus and ate a chilidog in my car while I fiddled with the radio in search of anything but whiny country music. I was doing so to avoid thinking about the conversation at Ruby Bee's. Nelson Mullein wasn't my type, but that didn't automatically relegate him to the slime pool. He had good reason to be worried about his great-grandaunts. Hell, now I was worried about them, too.

Then again, I thought as I drove out County 102 and eased across the low-water bridge, Estelle had a point. There was something almost eerie about the combination of old ladies, cats, and ne'er-do-well nephews (although, as far as I knew, Nelson was doing well at whatever he did; I hadn't asked). But we were missing the key element in the plot, and that was the fortune that kicked in the greed factor. Based on what Estelle had said, the Banebury girls were just as poor as Nelson had claimed.

The appearance of the house confirmed it. It was a squatty old farmhouse that had once been white, but was weathered to a lifeless gray. What shingles remained on the roof were mossy, and the chimney had collapsed. A window on the second floor was covered with cardboard; broken glass was scattered on the porch. The detached garage across the weedy yard had fared no better.

Avoiding puddles, I hurried to the front door and knocked, keenly and uncomfortably aware of the icy rain slithering under my collar. I was about to knock a second time when the door opened a few cautious inches.

"I'm Arly Hanks," I said, trying not to let my teeth chatter too loudly. "Do you mind if I come in for a little visit?"

"I reckon you can." Miss Columbine stepped back and gestured for me to enter. To my astonishment, she looked almost exactly the same as she had the night she stood on the bank of Boone Creek and bawled us out. Her hair was white and pinned up in tight braids, her nose was sharp, her cheekbones prominent above concave cheeks. Her head was tilted at an angle, and I remembered what Nelson had said about her vision.

"Thanks," I murmured as I rubbed my hands together.

"Hanks, did you say? You're Ruby Bee's gal," she said in the same steely voice. "Now that you're growed up, are you keeping your clothes on when you take a moonlight swim?"

I was reduced to an adolescent. "Yes, ma'am."

"Do we have a visitor?" Miss Larkspur came into the living room, utilizing an aluminum walker to take each awkward step. "First Nelson and now this girl. I swear, I don't know when we've had so much company, Columbine."

The twenty years had been less compassionate to Miss Larkspur. Her eyes were so clouded and her skin so translucent that she looked as if she'd been embalmed. Her body was bent, one shoulder hunched and the other undefined. The fingers that gripped the walker were swollen and misshapen.

"I'm Arly Hanks," I told her.

"Gracious, girl, I know who you are. I heard about how you came back to Maggody after all those years in the big city. I don't blame you one bit. Columbine and I went to visit kin in Memphis when we were youngsters, and I knew then and there that I'd never be able to live in a place like that. There were so many cars and carriages and streetcars that we feared for our very lives, didn't we?"

"Yes, I seem to recall that we did, Larkspur."

"Shall I put on the tea kettle?"

Miss Columbine smiled sadly. "That's all right, sister; I'll see to it. Why don't you sit down with our company while I fix a tray? Be sure and introduce her to Eppie."

The room was scantily furnished with ugly, battered furniture and a rug worn so badly that the wooden floor was visible. It smelled of decay, and no doubt for a very good reason. Plaster had fallen in several places, exposing the joists and yellowed newspaper that served as insulation. Although it was warmer than outside, it was a good twenty degrees below what I considered comfortable. Both sisters wore shawls. I hoped they had thermal underwear beneath their plain, dark dresses.

I waited until Miss Larkspur had made it across the room and was seated on a sofa. I sat across from her and said, "I met Nelson this morning. He seems concerned about you and your sister."

"So he says," she said without interest. She leaned forward and clapped her hands. "Eppie? Are you hiding? It's quite safe to come out. This girl won't hurt you. She'd like the chance to admire you."

An enormous cat stalked from behind the sofa, his single amber eye regarding me malevolently and his tail swishing as if he considered it a weapon. He was everything Nelson had described, and worse. He paused to rake his claws across the carpet, then leapt into Miss Larkspur's lap and settled down to convey to me how very deeply he resented my presence. Had I been a less rational person, I would have wondered if he knew I was there to promote Nelson's plan. Had I been, as I said.

"Isn't he a pretty kitty?" cooed Miss Larkspur. "He acts so big and tough, but him's just a snuggly teddy bear."

"Very pretty," I said, resisting an urge to lapse into baby-talk and tweak Eppie's whiskers. He would have taken my hand off in a flash. Or my arm.

Miss Columbine came into the room, carrying a tray with three cups and saucers and a ceramic teapot. There were more chips than rosebuds, but I was delighted to take a cup of hot tea and cradle it in my hands. "Did Nelson send you?" she said as she served her sister and sat down beside her. Eppie snuggled between them to continue his surly surveillance.

"He came by the PD this morning and asked me to speak to you," I admitted.

"Nelson is a ninny," she said with a tight frown. "Always has been, always will be. When he came during the summers, I had to watch him like a hawk to make sure he wasn't tormenting the cat or stealing pennies from the sugar bowl. His grandmother, our youngest sister, married poor white trash, and although she never said a word against them, we were all of a mind that she regretted it to her dying day." She paused to take a sip of tea, and the cup rattled against the saucer as she replaced it. "I suppose Nelson's riled up on account of our Sunday drives, although it seems to me reporting us to the police is extreme. Did you come out here to arrest us?"

Miss Larkspur giggled. "Whatwould Papa say if he were here to see us being arrested? Can't you imagine the look on his face, Columbine? He'd be fit to be tied, and he'd most likely throw this nice young thing right out the door."

"I didn't come out here to arrest you," I said hastily, "and I didn't come to talk about your driving. As long as you don't run anybody down, stay on this road, and never ever go on the highway, it's okay with me."

"But not with Nelson." Miss Columbine sighed as she finished her tea. "He wants us to give up our home, our car, our beloved Eppie, and go live in a stranger's house with a bunch of old folks. Who knows what other fool rules they'd have in a house where they don't allow pets?"

"But, Columbine," Miss Larkspur said, her face puckering wistfully, "Nelson says they serve nice meals and have tea with sandwiches and pound cake every afternoon. I can't recollect when I last tasted pound cake—unless it was at Mama's last birthday party. She died of influenza back in September of fifty-eight, not three weeks after Papa brought the new car all the way from Memphis, Tennessee." She took a tissue from her cuff and dabbed her eyes. "Papa died the next year, some say on account of losing the store, but I always thought he was heartsick over poor—"

"Larkspur, you're rambling like a wild turkey," Columbine said sternly but with affection. "This girl doesn't want to hear our family history. Frankly, I don't find it that interesting. I think we'd better hear what she has to say so she can be on her way." She stroked Eppie's head, and the cat obligingly growled at yours truly.

"Is Eppie the only reason you won't consider this retirement house?" I asked. I realized it was not such an easy question and plunged ahead. "You don't have to make a decision until you've visited. I'm sure Nelson would be delighted to take you there at tea time."

"Do you think he would?" Miss Larkspur clasped her hands together and her cloudy eyes sparkled briefly.

Miss Columbine shook her head. "We cannot visit under false pretenses, Larkspur, and come what may, we will not abandon Eppie after all these years. When the Good Lord sees fit to take him from us, we'll think about moving to town."

The object of discussion stretched his front legs and squirmed until he was on his back, his claws digging into their legs demandingly. When Miss Columbine rubbed his bloated belly, he purred with all the delicacy of a truck changing gears.

"Thank you for tea," I said, rising. "I'll let myself out." I was almost at the front door when I stopped and turned back to them. "You won't be driving until Easter, will you?"

"Not until Easter," Miss Columbine said firmly.

I returned to the PD, dried myself off with a handful of paper towels, and called Nelson at the motel to report my failure.

"It's the cat, isn't it?" he said. "They're willing to live in squalor because they won't give up that sorry excuse for a cat. You know, honey, I'm beginning to wonder if they haven't wandered too far out in left field to know what's good for them. I guess I'd better talk to a lawyer when I get back to Pine Bluff."

"You're going to force them to move?"

"I feel so bad, honey, but I don't know what else to do and it's for their own good."

"What's in it for you, Nelson?"

"Nothing." He banged down the receiver.

"My shoe's full of water," Ruby Bee grumbled as she did her best to avoid getting smacked in the face by a bunch of soggy leaves. It wasn't all that easy, since she had to keep her flashlight trained on the ground in case of snakes or other critters. The worst of it was that Estelle had hustled her out the door on this harebrained mission without giving her a chance to change clothes, and now her best blue dress was splattered with mud and her matching blue suede shoes might as well go straight into the garbage can. "Doncha think it's time to stop acting like overgrown Girl Scouts and just drive up to the door, knock real politely, and ask our questions in the living room?"

Estelle was in the lead, mostly because she had the better flash-light. "At least it's stopped raining, Miss Moanie Mouth. You're carry-ing on like we had to go miles and miles, but it ain't more than two hundred feet to begin with and we're within spittin' distance already."

"I'd be within spittin' distance of my bed if we'd dropped in and asked them." Ruby Bee stepped over a log and right into a puddle, this time filling her other shoe with cold water and forcing her to bite her tongue to keep from blurting out something unseemly. However, she figured she'd better pay more attention to the job at hand, which was sneaking up on the Banebury girls' garage through the woods behind it.

"I told you so," Estelle said as she flashed her light on the backside of the building. "Now turn out your light and stay real close. If that door's not locked, we'll be inside quicker than a preacher says his prayers at night."

The proverbial preacher would have had time to bless a lot of folks. The door wasn't locked, but it was warped something awful and it took a good five minutes of puffing and grunting to get it open far enough for them to slip inside.

Ruby Bee stopped to catch her breath. "I still don't see why you're so dadburned worried about them seeing us. They're both blind as bats."

"Hush!" Estelle played her light over the black sedan. "Lordy, they made 'em big in those days, didn't they? You could put one of those little Japanese cars in the trunk of this one, and have enough room left for a table and four chairs. And look at all that chrome!"

"This ain't the showroom of a car dealership," Ruby Bee said in the snippety voice that always irritated Estelle, which was exactly what she intended for it to do, what with her ruined shoes and toes nigh onto frozen. "If you want to stand there and admire it all night, that's fine, but I for one have other plans. I'll see if it says the model on the back, and you try the interior."

She was shining her light on the license plate and calculating how many years it had been since it expired when Estelle screamed. Before she could say a word, Estelle dashed out the door, the beam from the flashlight bobbling like a ping-pong ball. Mystified but not willing to linger on her own, Ruby Bee followed as fast as she dared, and only when she caught Estelle halfway through the woods did she learn what had caused the undignified retreat.

According to Estelle, there'd been a giant rat right in the front seat of the car, its lone amber eye glaring like the devil's own. Ruby Bee snorted in disbelief, but she didn't go back to have a look for herself.

The next morning, sweet inspiration slapped me up the side of the head like a two by four. It had to be the car. I lunged for the telephone so hastily that my poor duck fell to the floor, and called Plover, a state cop with whom I occasionally went to a movie or had dinner. "What do you know about antique cars?" I demanded, bypassing pleasantries.

"They're old. Some of them are real old."

"Did you forget to jump start your brain this morning? I need to find out the current value of a particular car, and I assumed you were up on something macho like this."

He let out a long-suffering sort of sigh. "I can put gas in one at the self-service pump, and I know how to drive it. That's the extent of my so-called macho knowledge."

"Jesus, Plover," I said with a sigh of my own, "you'd better get yourself a frilly pink shirt and a pair of high heel sneakers. While you're doing that, let me talk to someone in the barracks with balls who knows about cars, okay?"

He hung up on what I thought was a very witty remark. State cops were not renowned for their humor, I told myself as I flipped open the telephone directory and hunted up the number of the Lincoln dealer in Farberville. The man who answered was a helluva lot more congenial, possibly (and mistakenly) in hopes he was dealing with a potential buyer.

Alas, he was no better informed than Plover about the current market value of a '58 Lincoln Continental, but his attitude was much brighter and he promised to call me back as soon as possible.

Rather than waste the time patting myself on the back, I called Plover, apologized for my smart-mouthed remark, and explained what I surmised was going on. "It's the car he's after," I concluded. "The house and land are close to worthless, but this old Lincoln could be a collector's dream."

"Maybe," he said without conviction, "but you can't arrest him for anything. I don't know if what he tried to do constitutes fraud, but in any case, he failed. He can't get his hands on the car until they die."

"Or he has them declared incompetent," I said. "I suppose I could let him know that I'm aware of his scheme, and that I'll testify on their behalf if he tries anything further."

We chatted aimlessly for a while, agreed to a dinner date in a few days, and hung up. I was preparing to dial the number of Nelson's motel room when the phone rang.

The dealer had my information. I grabbed a pencil and wrote down a few numbers, thanked him, and replaced the receiver with a scowl of disappointment. If the car was in mint condition (aka in its original wrapper), it might bring close to ten thousand dollars. The amounts then plummeted: sixty-five hundred for very good, less than five thousand for good, and on down to four hundred fifty as a source for parts.

It wasn't the car, after all, but simply a case of letting myself listen to the suspicious minds in Ruby Bee's Bar & Grill. I picked up the balsa wood and turned my attention to its little webbed feet.

It normally doesn't get dark until five-thirty or so, but the heavy clouds had snuffed out the sunset. I decided to call it a day (not much of one, though) and find out if Ruby Bee was in a more hospitable mood. I had locked the back door and switched off the light when the telephone rang. After a short debate centering around meatloaf versus professional obligations, I reluctantly picked up the receiver.

"Arly! You got to do something! Somebody's gonna get killed if you don't do something!"

"Calm down, Estelle," I said, regretting that I hadn't heeded the plea from my stomach. "What's the problem?"

"I'm so dadburned all shook up I can barely talk!"

I'd had too much experience with her to be overcome with alarm. "Give it your best shot."

"It's the Banebury girls! They just drove by my house, moving real smartly down the middle of the road, and no headlights! I was close enough to my driveway to whip in and get out of their way, but I'm thanking my lucky stars I saw 'em before they ran me over with that bulldozer of a car."

I dropped the receiver, grabbed my car keys, and ran out to the side of the highway. I saw nothing coming from the south, but if they were driving without lights, I wouldn't be the only one not to see them coming . . . relentlessly, in a great black death machine.

"Damn!" I muttered as I got in my car, maneuvered around, and headed down the highway to the turnoff for County 102. Miss Columbine couldn't see anything in front of her, and Miss Larkspur was legally blind. A dynamite duo. I muttered a lot more things, none of them acceptable within my mother's earshot.

It was supper time, and the highway was blessedly empty. I squealed around the corner and stopped, letting my lights shine down the narrow road. The wet pavement glistened like a snakeskin. They had passed Estelle's house at least three or four minutes ago. Presuming they were not in a ditch, they would arrive at the intersection any minute. Maybe Nelson had a justifiable reason to have them declared incompetent, I thought as I gripped the steering wheel and peered into the darkness. I hadn't seen any bunnies hopping outside my window, and if there were chocolate eggs hidden in the PD, I hadn't found them.

It occurred to me that I was in more than minimal danger, parked as I was in their path. However, I couldn't let them go on their merry way. A conscientious cop would have forbidden them to drive and confiscated the keys. I'd practically given them my blessing.

My headlights caught the glint of a massive black hood bearing down on me. With a yelp, I changed the beam to high, fumbled with a switch until the blue light on the roof began to rotate, grabbed a flashlight, and jumped out of my car. I waved the light back and forth as the monster bore down on me, and I had some sharp insights into the last thoughts of potential roadkill.

All I could see was the reflection on the chrome as the car came at me, slowly yet determinedly. The blue light splashed on the windshield, as did my flashlight. "Miss Columbine!" I yelled. "Miss Larkspur! You've got to stop!" I retreated behind my car and continued yelling.

The car shuddered, then, at the last moment, stopped a good six inches from my bumper (and a six-hour session with the mayor, trying to explain the bill from the body shop).

I pried my teeth off my lower lip, switched off the flashlight, and went to the driver's window. Miss Columbine sat rigidly behind the wheel, but Miss Larkspur leaned forward and, with a little wave, said, "It's Arly, isn't it? How are you, dear?"

"Much better than I was a minute ago," I said. "I thought we agreed that you wouldn't be driving until this spring, Miss Columbine. A day later you're not only out, but at night without headlights."

"When you're blind," she said tartly, "darkness is not a factor. This is an emergency. Since we don't have a telephone, we had no choice but to drive for help."

"That's right," said Miss Larkspur. "Eppie has been catnapped. We're beside ourselves with worry. He likes to roam around the yard during the afternoon, but this evening he did not come to the back door to demand his supper. Columbine and I searched as best we could, but poor Eppie has disappeared. It's not like him, not at all."

"Larkspur is correct," Miss Columbine added. Despite her gruff voice and expressionless face, a tear trickled down her cheek. She wiped it away and tilted her head to look at me. "I am loath to go jumping to conclusions, but in this case, it's hard not to."

"I agree," I said, gazing bleakly at the darkness surrounding us. It may not have been a factor for them, but it sure as hell was for me. "Let's go back to your place and I'll try to find Eppie. Maybe he's already on the porch, waiting to be fed. I'll move my car off the road, and then, if you don't object, I think it's safer for me to drive your car back for you."

A few minutes later I was sitting in the cracked leather upholstery of the driver's seat, trying to figure out the controls on the elaborate wooden dashboard. There was ample room for three of us in the front seat, and possibly a hitchhiker or two. Once I'd found first gear, I turned around in the church parking lot, took a deep breath, and let 'er fly.

"This is a daunting machine," I said.

Giggling, Miss Larkspur put her hand on my arm and said, "Papa brought it all the way from Memphis, as I told you. He'd gone there on account of Cousin Pearl being at the hospital, and we were flabbergasted when he drove up a week later in a shiny new car. This was after he'd lost the store, you see, and we didn't even own a car. We felt real badly about him going all the way to Memphis on the bus, but he and Cousin Pearl were kissin' cousins, and she was dying in the Baptist Hospital, so—"

"The Methodist Hospital," Miss Columbine corrected her. "I swear, some days you go on and on like you ain't got a brain in your head. Papa must have told us a hundred times how he met that polite young soldier whose mother was dying in the room right next to Cousin Pearl's."

"I suppose so," Miss Larkspur conceded, "but Cousin Pearl was a Baptist."

I pulled into the rutted driveway beside their house. The garage door was open, so I eased the car inside, turned off the ignition, and leaned back to offer a small prayer. "Why don't you wait in the house? I'll have a look out back."

"I can't believe our own kin would do such a thing," Miss Columbine said as she took Miss Larkspur's arm. I took the other and we moved slowly toward the back porch.

I believed it, and I had a pretty good idea why he'd done it. Once they were inside, I went back to the car, looked at the contents of the glove compartment to confirm my suspicions, and set off across the field. I'd had enough sense to bring my flashlight, but it was still treacherously wet and rough and I wasn't in the mood to end up with my feet in the air and my fanny in the mud. I could think of a much better candidate.

I froze as my light caught a glittery orb moving toward me in an erratic pattern. It came closer, and at last I made out Eppie's silhouette as he bounded past me in the direction of the house. His yowl of rage shattered the silence for a heart-stopping moment, then he was gone and I was once again alone in the field with a twenty-year-old memory of the path that led to Boone Creek.

Long before I arrived at the bank, I heard a stream of curses and expletives way too colorful for my sensitive ears. I followed the sound and stopped at a prudent distance to shine my light on Nelson Mullein. He was not a pretty picture as he futilely attempted to slither up the muddy incline, snatching at clumps of weeds that uprooted in his hands. He was soaked to the skin. His face was distorted not only by a swath of mud across one cheek, but also by angry red scratches, some of which were oozing blood.

"Who is it?" he said, blinking into the light.

"It's traditional to take your clothes off when you skinny-dip in the creek."

"It's you, the lady cop." He snatched at a branch, but it broke and he slid back to the edge of the inky water. "Can you give me a hand, honey? It's like trying to climb an oil slick, and I'm about to freeze to death."

"Oh, my goodness," I said as I scanned the ground with the light until it rested on a shapeless brown mound nearby. "Could that be a gunny sack? Why, I do believe it is. I hope you didn't put Eppie in it in an unsuccessful attempt to drown him in the creek."

"I've never seen that before in my life. I came down here to search for the cat. The damn thing was up in that tree, meowing in a right pitiful fashion, but when I tried to coax him down, I lost my footing and fell into the water. Why don't you try to find a sturdy branch so I can get up the bank?"

I squatted next to the gunny sack. "This ol' thing's nearly ripped to shreds. I guess Eppie didn't take kindly to the idea of being sent to Cat Heaven before his time. By the way, I know about the car, Mr. Mullein."

"That jalopy?" he said uneasily. He stopped skittering in the mud and wiped his face. "I reckoned on getting six, maybe seven thousand for it from an ol' boy what lives in Pine Bluff. That, along with the proceeds from the sale of the property, ought to be more than enough to keep my great-grandaunts from living the way they do, bless their brave souls."

"It ought to be more than enough for them to have the house remodeled and pay for a full-time housekeeper," I said as I rose, the gunny sack dangling between my thumb and forefinger. "I'm taking this along as evidence. If you ever again so much as set one foot in Maggody, I'll tell those brave souls what you tried to do. You may be their only relative, but someone might suggest they leave what's going to be in the range of half a million dollars to a rest home for cats!"

"You can't abandon me like this." He gave me a view of his pearly white teeth, but it was more of a snarl than a smile. "Don't be cruel like that, honey."

"Watch me." Ignoring his sputters, I took my tattered treasure and walked back across the field to the house. Miss Columbine took me into the living room, where her sister had swaddled Eppie in a towel.

"Him was just being a naughty kitty," she said, stroking the cat's remaining ear and nuzzling his head.

I accepted a cup of tea, and once we were settled as before, said, "That polite young soldier gave your papa the car, didn't he?"

Miss Columbine nodded. "Papa didn't know what to think, but the boy was insistent about how he'd gone from rags to riches and how it made him feel good to be able to give folks presents. Papa finally agreed, saying it was only on account of how excited Mama would be."

"It was charity, of course," Miss Larkspur added, "but the boy said he wanted to do it because of Papa's kindness in the waiting room. The boy even told Papa that he was a hillbilly cat himself, and never forgot the little town in Mississippi where he was born."

Eppie growled ominously, but I avoided meeting his hostile eye and said, "He was called the Hillbilly Cat, back in the earliest stage of his career. The original paperwork's in the glove compartment, and his signature is on the bill of sale and registration form." I explained how much the car would bring and agreed to supervise the sale for them. "This means, of course, that you won't be driving anymore," I added.

"But how will we get to church on Easter morning?" Miss Larkspur asked.

Miss Columbine smiled. "I reckon we can afford a limousine, Larkspur. Let's heat up some nice warm milk for Eppie. He's still shivering from his . . . adventure outside."

"Now that we'll be together, will you promise to never run away again?" Miss Larkspur gently scolded the cat.

He looked at her, then at me on the off chance I'd try to pet him and he could express his animosity with his claws.

I waved at him from the doorway, told the ladies I'd be in touch after I talked with the Lincoln dealer, and wished them a pleasant evening. I walked down the road to my car, and I was nearly there before I realized Eppie was a nickname. Once he'd been the Hillbilly Cat, and his death had broken hearts all around the world. But in the Banebury household, Elvis Presley was alive and well—and still the King.

"Give me that shovel," Estelle hissed. "All you're doing is poking the dirt like you think this is a mine field."

Ruby Bee eased the blade into the muddy soil, mindful of the splatters on the hem of her coat and the caked mud that made her shoes feel like combat boots. "Hold your horses," she hissed back, "I heard a clink. I don't want to break the jar and ruin the money."

Estelle hurried over and knelt down to dig with her fingers. "Ain't the Banebury girls gonna be excited when we find their Papa's buried treasure! I reckon we could find as much as a thousand dollars before the night is out." She daintily blotted her forehead with her wrist. "It's a darn shame about the car, but if it ain't worth much, then it ain't. It's kinda funny how that man at the Lincoln dealership rattled off the prices like he had 'em written out in front of him and was wishing somebody'd call to inquire. Of course I wasn't expecting to hear anything different. Everybody knows just because a car's old doesn't mean it's valuable."

A lot of responses went through Ruby Bee's mind, none of them kindly. She held them back, though, and it was just as well when Estelle finally produced a chunk of brick, dropped it back in the hole, stood up, and pointed her finger like she thought she was the high and mighty leader of an expedition.

"Start digging over there, Ruby Bee," she said, "and don't worry about them seeing us from inside the house. I told you time and again, they're both blind."

Edward D. Hoch occupies two unique niches in the world of mystery fiction. First, he is one of the few, perhaps the only writer to make his living solely by writing short fiction. Second, he has also had, with very few exceptions, a story in every issue of Ellery Queen's Mystery Magazine *since the early 1970s. His series characters include Captain Leopold, a brilliant police detective whose appearance in "The Oblong Room" won his creator an Edgar in 1968. Other unusual protagonists include Simon Ark, a man claiming to be 2,000 years old. Adept at the mystery story in all periods, genres and shapes, here he is up to his usual high standards in "Brothers on the Beach," a tale of murder set during the Wright brothers' first powered aircraft flight.*

Brothers on the Beach

Edward D. Hoch

The temperature was in the mid-forties on the December day when Ben Snow stepped off the train at Elizabeth City and went about the business of renting a horse and buggy for the remainder of his journey to the shores of the Atlantic.

He often felt there was something contrary about his gradual journey east at a time when the nation had just about completed its western expansion. There were forty-five states now, stretching from coast to coast, and already there was talk that the territories of Oklahoma, New Mexico, and Arizona would soon be admitted to the Union. He'd fought Indians in the West in his younger days, and even journeyed to Mexico on occasion, but now it was the East that drew him. Cities like Buffalo and Savannah and New Orleans.

Rivers like the Mississippi and the Delaware had only been names on a rarely studied map when he was young. Now that he was past forty and the nation had entered the Twentieth Century, things were different. The West didn't need Indian fighters any more, or hired guns whose draw was as fast as Billy the Kid's.

Ben Snow had never been a man to settle down as a ranch hand. He'd considered working for Pinkerton's, putting his crime-solving abilities to some use, but the detective agency's deep involvement in strike-breaking wasn't to his liking. So he drifted, taking jobs where he found them, helping out old friends when he could.

He'd never been as far east as North Carolina before, and he quickly noted that back here men didn't wear gunbelts on the street in 1903. He left his in his suitcase while he dickered for the horse and buggy. "Kitty Hawk," he said to the man at the stable. "How far is it?"

"About thirty-five miles," the man answered. "You take the road east to Barco and then turn south along the coast. It's on a narrow cape that runs all the way down to Hatteras and beyond, but you can get a ferry to take you across. Why'd anyone want to go to Kitty Hawk in December, though? There's nothing there but a beach, and it's too damn cold for swimming. The wind beats across there like a gale most of the time."

"I have to see a man," Ben answered. "How much for the horse and buggy?"

They dickered a bit before Ben finally drove off in the buggy. He'd noticed a few automobiles—as people were starting to call them—on the streets of the city, but he hadn't felt brave enough to try one. Besides, he didn't know what sort of roads awaited him along the coastal sand spit.

It was shortly after he'd passed through Barco and headed south along the coast, getting his first view of the turbulent Atlantic, when a lone horseman overtook him. The man was young and handsome, with curly blond hair, and he sat well in the saddle. "Would you be Ben Snow?" he asked, drawing abreast of the buggy.

"That's me."

He leaned over to offer his hand. "Roderick Claymore. My brother Rudolph hired you, but he had to go to the state capital on business and he asked that I meet you."

They pulled up and Ben swung down from the buggy. "I'm a lot more comfortable on a horse," he admitted, "but with my suitcase, the buggy seemed best."

Claymore took out a cigar and offered Ben one. "How much did my brother tell you?"

"Only that he was hiring me to guard a section of beach at Kitty Hawk for the next week or so. He wanted someone from far away, and that's what he got. He hired me last week in St. Louis."

Roderick Claymore nodded, puffing on the thin cigar. "About three years ago, a pair of brothers from Dayton, the Wrights, started coming here and flying gliders off the dunes at Kitty Hawk. Seems they wrote the Weather Bureau and were told this was the best testing area for gliders because the winds off the ocean blow at a fairly constant twenty miles an hour or better."

"Does this glider-testing bother you?"

"It didn't at first. No one paid much attention to them. But now things are changing. We own some land nearby and it's important that we don't have a lot of trespassers. They're planning something for Monday that could bring the whole country to our door."

"What would that be?"

"Last summer they started shipping in parts for a powered craft they've been constructing there on the beach. They built their own lightweight gasoline engine—four cylinders, watercooled."

"I don't know much about engines," Ben admitted.

"It's to drive two eight-foot wooden propellers mounted to the rear of the wings. This craft won't be a glider. It'll take off and fly by itself, with one of the Wrights aboard. That's why we need you."

Ben Snow smiled slightly. "To shoot it down?"

"Hardly."

"Back in '96, out West, there was a fellow billed himself as The Flying Man. He strapped wings to his arms and tried to glide off hilltops. Somebody killed him one day during an exhibition, and I helped solve the murder. I'm just telling you so you'll know which side of the fence I'm on. I've killed plenty of men in my day, but never one who didn't deserve it. I'm not a hired gun, despite what you and your brother might have heard."

"Look here, Snow, we don't want any hired guns. But if those crazy Wrights bring a thousand people to that beach to see their flight on Monday, we want them kept off our property any way that's necessary."

"All right," Ben agreed. "Where am I staying?"

"There's a lady teacher has a house in Kill Devil Hills, just a few miles from Kitty Hawk. We rented a room there for you."

"That'll be just fine."

It seemed ironic to Ben that he'd had to travel east to North Carolina to find the legendary pretty schoolmarm who was supposed to inhabit every western town. Elizabeth Boyers was a dark-haired beauty, probably past thirty but with a fine girlish figure and a smile that could melt the coldest heart. She lived alone in the house across the street from the one-room school building where she taught.

"There aren't many children here," she admitted. "They're mostly from older families who've lived here all their lives. But someone has to teach them. If I left, they'd have to take the ferry to the mainland."

It was Sunday and they were strolling on the beach together, looking over the site where the Wrights would attempt their flight the following day.

"Do you think they'll make it?" he asked.

"Frankly, no. Not after what happened to Langley last Wednesday."

"Who's Langley?"

She laughed. "You don't keep up with the newspapers, Mr. Snow. Samuel Langley, the inventor, had a $50,000 grant from the War Department to develop a flying machine. He spent five years on it, and last Wednesday he tried to launch it from the roof of a houseboat in the Potomac River with boatloads of Washington reporters and government officials looking on. But a wing tip caught on its catapult and the craft broke apart in the air. Langley is secretary of the Smithsonian Institution. If he can't build a proper flying machine, these brothers from a bicycle shop in Dayton can hardly be expected to do it."

"Will there be reporters here tomorrow?"

"Not if the Wrights can help it. They're trying to keep it secret until the flight is successful. Then they'll send a telegram to their father asking that the press be notified."

"Then why is Claymore so worried?"

She hesitated before answering. "Who hired you—Roderick or Rudolph?"

"Rudolph. He's the older one, isn't he? He came to me in St. Louis and offered to pay my expenses and a week's salary if I'd come here to guard his beach. It seemed to me he could have hired someone from here in town for half the money."

"They do own some land down the beach. I've seen them digging there. I kidded them about looking for pirate treasure. These islands along the Atlantic coast have always had pirate legends connected with them."

"Why did you ask which one hired me?"

"Oh," she answered casually, "I've had a little trouble with the younger one, Roderick—the one who brought you here yesterday. I went out with him a few times last year and he asked me to marry him. I said no, but he won't accept that. Now I'm engaged to someone else and he's bothering me. I wouldn't have taken their money for the room if I didn't need it."

"What do they do for a living when they're not digging for buried treasure?"

"They have an ice business. They deliver blocks of ice to homes and businesses in all the towns around here."

"Never had anything like that out where I come from."

She smiled at him. "This is civilization. This is the Twentieth Century."

When they returned to the house after inspecting—at a distance—the Wright brothers' flying machine, Ben found Rudolph Claymore waiting for him. Rudolph was larger and tougher than his younger brother, and while Roderick sat well on a horse Ben couldn't imagine this man ever riding one. In St. Louis, where he'd hired Ben, Rudolph had seemed like a successful businessman. Here, in his home territory, there was something vaguely sinister about him.

"You saw that flying contraption of theirs?" he asked Ben.

Ben nodded. "Looks backwards to me. The tail seems to be in the front. But flying isn't my line."

"If we're in luck, they'll crash tomorrow like that fellow Langley did. But if it's successful and people start pouring in here, I'll need you to guard our beach property for the next week or so."

"Couldn't you have hired someone from one of the towns around here for that purpose?" Elizabeth said. "Why bring Mr. Snow all the way from St. Louis?"

"I want someone who'll be here today and gone tomorrow, not one of the town boys who'll have a few drinks at the bar and get to talking too much. Mr. Snow's got a good reputation out West. When I asked around for someone to hire, he was the one everyone mentioned."

Claymore took Ben aside and gave him a down payment on his fee, along with the travel expenses. "You brought your gun, didn't you?"

"I have it," Ben assured him.

"Wear it tomorrow, but keep it under your coat."

When he'd gone, Ben asked Elizabeth, "What do you think is so valuable about that strip of sand?"

"Besides the pirate treasure?" she answered with a smile. "I have no idea."

Ben slept restlessly that night, wondering what the morning would bring. What it brought was more of the same as far as the weather was concerned. A cool breeze was blowing off the ocean and he found he needed the wool jacket he'd brought with him from the Midwest. He buckled his gunbelt under it, making certain all chambers of the Colt six-shooter were loaded. He wondered vaguely if there were laws back East against carrying concealed weapons. Maybe that's why the Claymore brothers had wanted someone from far away.

"Are you up, Mr. Snow?" Elizabeth called to him through the bedroom door.

"Sure am. I'll be right down."

"Breakfast is ready. My fiancé, Mark Freen, is joining us."

Freen was an agreeable chap with brown hair and a ready smile. Like Elizabeth, he was a teacher, though his school was on the mainland. "I'm playing hooky today," he explained. "We both are. This might be an historic occasion—right here at Kitty Hawk."

Ben was surprised to see that a fair crowd of local residents had gathered along the beach. "Those are the Wright brothers," Elizabeth said, pointing out two men in caps and jackets. They seemed to be in their thirties. "Orville and Wilbur."

"Do you know them personally?"

"I've spoken with them. They've been here since September assembling the *Flyer.* That's the name of it. And last year they made over a thousand controlled glider flights here. Everyone knows them by now."

They were interrupted by the arrival of an older man with thick glasses and a beard. "Oh, Professor—I want you to meet Ben Snow!" Elizabeth Boyers performed the introductions as if they were both her oldest friends. "Ben, this is Professor Minder from the university at Raleigh."

Ben shook hands and asked, "Did you come all this distance for today's flight?"

"Not exactly," the professor replied. "I'm doing research just south of here, on Roanoke Island. You may remember it was the site of Sir Walter Raleigh's lost colony."

Ben nodded and turned up his collar against the chill wind. "I hope they get started soon. It's cold out here."

The *Flyer* had been pulled from its storage shed by the Wrights and five assistants. Ben heard someone in the crowd comment that it weighed over six hundred pounds. They positioned it on a level stretch of sand at the base of a hundred-foot-high dune named Kill Devil Hill. Then the brothers flipped a coin and Wilbur won the toss. After the

Flyer had been placed aboard a low trolley on the single sixty-foot rail of a greased launching track, he climbed aboard and lay face down in a cradlelike harness across the lower wing, working the wing and rudder controls with his body in a final check before takeoff.

The crowd tensed and Ben glanced around for some sign of the Claymores. There were figures farther down the beach, but he couldn't tell who they were. His attention returned to the *Flyer* as the gasoline engine sputtered into life. The twin propellers started to turn and the machine glided down its greased track. There was the beginning of a roar from the crowd and cameras poised to capture the moment of flight.

Then, unaccountably, the engine stalled at takeoff. The *Flyer* dropped to the sand with a soft thud.

As the crowd groaned, Orville rushed forward to pull his brother from the craft. "It's over," Elizabeth said sadly. "It'll never fly."

"Another Langley," Mark Freen said, summing it all up.

Wilbur stood up, free of the craft, and the brothers began inspecting the damage. Ben turned and noticed Professor Minder sitting on the sand. "Excitement too much for you?" he asked in fun, bending down to offer his hand.

That was when he saw the knife protruding from Minder's back and realized the man he'd just met had been murdered.

The investigation of a murder case was far different in the East than anything Ben had known out West. There a sheriff bothered little with clues or suspects. There he looked for eyewitnesses or the person with the likeliest motive, and if justice came at all it was usually swift and deadly. On that windswept beach in North Carolina, while the Wrights worked to repair their damaged aircraft, justice was slow and plodding. Justice was a pair of State Police officers with notebooks, taking down names and addresses and setting up a camera to take a photograph of the murder scene.

There was general agreement among all witnesses that the brothers Wright couldn't have had a hand in the killing, since all eyes were on them during the entire period. But that did little to narrow the field of suspects. Any one of the dozens of spectators could have been the guilty party, and in the eyes of the State Police that included Ben Snow.

"Private citizens don't wear gunbelts in North Carolina," one of them told him pointedly. "This isn't the wild West."

"Tell that to the dead man," Ben replied.

The officer's name was Rellens, and he eyed Ben as if he'd like to lock him away in a cell. "What are you doing here, anyway?"

"I was hired by the Claymore brothers to guard their strip of beach land. They feared some of the crowd might wander down that way."

"So you're guarding it from up here?"

"I can see it from here. I can see no one's on it."

"Were the Claymores here today?"

"I didn't see them."

"Pretty strange if they missed something like this," Rellens said.

Ben had been thinking the same thing as his eyes traveled over the spectators. Some had started to drift away, but the majority had stayed after giving their names, drawn by the twin spectacles of the murder investigation and the Wrights' efforts to repair their flying machine.

Then he saw Rudolph Claymore striding over the dunes in their direction. He left Rellens and went to meet his employer. "What happened here?" Rudolph demanded. "I just got word there's been a killing—"

"That's right," Ben said. "A professor named Minder."

"Minder! I know the man! He's been working on an island nearby!"

"Someone stabbed him."

"Is my brother here?"

"I haven't seen him all morning."

"He didn't come to work today and I assumed he was down here. I had to cover the entire ice route myself." Rudolph Claymore glanced along the windswept beach. "What about our property?"

"No one's gone near it," Ben assured him.

"Not Minder, before he was killed?"

"Not unless it was early this morning before I got here. You didn't say anything about guarding it day and night."

"No, no. I just thought you might have noticed him wandering down that way."

"I think it's about time you tell me what this is all about," Ben said. "I might be able to help the investigation if I knew all the facts."

"All right," Claymore agreed. "Come to my house tonight. I'll have my brother there, too, if I can find him. Here's the address. It's in the village of Kitty Hawk."

Elizabeth and Freen had been over by the damaged aircraft and were hurrying back. "Orville says the repairs will take a few days, but they hope to try again on Thursday," she said. "Will you be staying that long, Mr. Snow?"

"I expect so. The Claymores hired me for the week."

"I saw that policeman, Rellens, talking to you. Did he ask for your help?"

"Not exactly."

"Does he have any suspects?"

"Right now I may be his prime suspect. He noticed I was wearing a gunbelt."

"That's absurd! We were all standing together."

"But Professor Minder was right behind us. With all eyes on the Wrights and their machine, I suppose I could have reached around and stabbed him. Someone did."

"But why? He was a sweet old man. Why would anyone kill him?"

"What do you know about him? What was he doing here?"

"Mark knows more about him than I do. He went over to see him on Roanoke Island a few weeks ago."

"He was studying evidence of the so-called Lost Colony," Freen explained. "You know, the colony founded by Sir Walter Raleigh that vanished from that island between 1587 and 1590."

Ben's knowledge of early colonial history was vague at best, but he nodded and urged Freen to continue.

"Well, a colony of some eighty-five men and women remained on the island in 1587 while a ship returned to England for supplies. The war between England and Spain prevented the supplies from reaching Roanoke until 1590, and by that time all that could be found was a deserted, ransacked fortress. None of the settlers was ever found. The name *Croatoan* was carved into a post—apparently the name of an island to the south. They may have gone there, or they may have been killed by Indians. It's one of the mysteries of history."

"And Professor Minder thought he'd found new evidence of what happened," Elizabeth Boyers interjected. "He was over here a few times pursuing his studies."

"Interesting," Ben admitted. "But why should anyone kill him? Why would something that happened over three hundred years ago cost a man his life?"

They returned to the house without an answer. Later that afternoon, while Elizabeth and Freen were alone, Ben walked back up the beach alone. From a distance he watched the Wright brothers and their helpers working on the flying machine. He saw that Rellens was still there, too, pacing back and forth as he examined the trampled sand.

That evening Ben Snow rode over to the address Claymore had given him. It was one of a handful of houses in the tiny village of Kitty Hawk, and Rudolph came out on the porch to greet him as he parked his buggy. "Come in, Snow. My brother's already here."

Ben entered and took a chair in the sparsely furnished parlor. A woman's touch was obviously lacking and it occurred to him for the first time that the elder Claymore was probably not married. He shook hands with Roderick and said, "I didn't see you this morning."

"I had business," Roderick answered. "I hear the flying machine never got off the ground."

"They're repairing it. They plan to try again on Thursday."

Rudolph came in and sat down. "Some of the folks around here are helping them. We got more important things on our minds."

"Tell me about it," Ben suggested. "Tell me why that property of yours is so valuable. Is there really pirate treasure buried there?"

The older brother smiled slightly. "Next best thing, according to Professor Minder. You know about the Lost Colony and that business on Roanoke Island?"

"A little."

"Well, historians have always speculated that the colonists went south to another island, if they weren't killed by Indians. Minder went there and nosed around. He decided they came north instead, right here to the beach at Kitty Hawk. Look at this here map. You can see that the abandoned Fort Raleigh was at the very northern tip of Roanoke, not ten miles across the water from where we are now."

"Minder told you this?"

"Damned right!" Roderick said. "He did a little digging by our property there and came up with evidence of settlement!"

Rudolph showed Ben a bowl with a piece missing from it. "See this? It's not Indian. It's the sort the colonists brought with them from England."

"But you were keeping this a secret?" Ben asked.

"Had to! Other people own some of that beach land, especially near the village here. We started buying it up. An old settlement like that could mean a spot people would pay to see. It could make us rich."

"Who knew about this?" Ben asked.

"Only the two of us and Minder. That's why I went so far away to hire a guard. I didn't want any of the locals getting wind of what we were trying to hide."

"How much land have you bought?"

"Around twenty thousand dollars' worth so far. Minder agreed to act as a middleman so the people wouldn't know we were the buyers."

"And that's what you've been digging for?" Ben asked.

Rudolph nodded. "We uncovered some more things on our own, too—a few trinkets and a sword."

Roderick scratched at his cheek. "We'd better check on those land deeds in the morning. With Minder dead, we could be out twenty grand."

"I've already thought of that," his brother answered sourly.

Ben left them going over their records, trying to establish the extent of their possible losses.

On Tuesday afternoon, the State Police officer, Rellens, showed up at the Boyers' house to see Ben. He sat down heavily and flipped open his notebook. "This case has taken a couple of surprising turns," he said. "I need to interview witnesses again, especially those who were standing closest to the victim."

"Miss Boyers is teaching today," Ben told him.

"You'll do for a beginning. It seems one of the men in that crowd of spectators gave a false name and address. Dick Roer, of Kill Devil Hills. No such person."

"You think you let the murderer walk away?"

"Looks like it," he said glumly. "I seem to remember him vaguely. Had a Teddy Roosevelt mustache and was wearing a wool cap. Of course, the mustache could have been a fake. Do you remember anyone looking like that near you?"

"No," Ben answered honestly. "But I wasn't concentrating on the crowd."

"All right." Rellens closed his notebook, preparing to leave.

"You said the case had taken a couple of surprising turns. What else?"

"The dead man—Minder. It turns out he was a fake, too. There's no Professor Minder connected with any of the universities in Raleigh."

"Interesting," Ben admitted. "Two men with false identities on the beach yesterday—one a murderer and one a victim."

"It looks that way." Rellens nodded.

"But why was Minder using a false name? Who was he?"

"We'll find out," Rellens promised. "You'll be here for the next few days, Mr. Snow?"

"At least till after Thursday's flight."

"That's good," Rellens said and was gone.

On Wednesday Ben Snow sought out Rudolph Claymore on his ice route. He found him lugging fifty-pound blocks into a little café in Kill Devil Hills. "I wanted to ask you about your brother," he said.

"He's back at the ice house. You can find him there."

"He was in love with Elizabeth Boyers, wasn't he?"

"Still is, far as I know. But she's sappy over that teacher, Mark Freen. It hit my brother hard."

"Ever hear of someone named Dick Roer around here?"

"Can't say that I have."

"Rellens thinks that was the name the killer used on Monday."

"Never heard of him." Claymore climbed into the back of his wagon and used an ice pick to loosen another fifty-pound block.

"That looks like hard work."

Rudolph shrugged. "It's a living." He flipped the pick into the next block in line. "It pays the bills till something big like that Lost Colony comes along."

"What if the Lost Colony never happens? What if Professor Minder was a fraud?"

Rudolph Claymore blinked and stared at Ben. "What are you saying?"

"Have you and your brother checked on that property yet?"

"He's doing it today."

"I wish you luck," Ben said and started to walk away.

"Wait a minute!" Claymore said, hurrying after him. "What are you trying to tell me?"

"That Minder was a fraud. That wasn't his real name, and chances are those trinkets in the sand were put there by him so you'd find them. Out West we call it salting a mine—putting a few gold nuggets near the surface for the suckers to find."

"But the property—"

"If he was trying to swindle someone, it must have been you. He probably took your twenty thousand and faked some papers, without ever buying the land."

"That—"

Ben left him standing by his ice wagon, still swearing.

The younger Claymore was a bit more difficult to track down. He was gone from the ice house by the time Ben reached it and he had to stop at a couple of nearby bars before he spotted Roderick's horse tethered outside the village stable. He found the young man inside, seeing to the repair of one of his saddle stirrups.

"I had a talk with your brother this morning," Ben told him. "Could I have a few words with you outside?"

Roderick shrugged. "I suppose so. You going to be on guard at the beach again tomorrow?"

"I'll be there. But when you hear what I have to say, you may decide you don't need me." Ben told him quickly what he'd told his brother, about Professor Minder's false identity and the probable swindle. Roderick's reaction wasn't quite as violent as his brother's, but it was obvious he was upset.

"I always wondered about that guy. He didn't seem right for a professor."

"Have you checked on the deeds yet?"

"I was on my way there now."

"There's something else," Ben said.

"What's that?"

"The police think Minder's killer is a man named Dick Roer."

The color drained from Roderick's face.

"That's you, isn't it? Dick Roer is a simple anagram for Roderick."

"I don't know what you mean."

"You were on the beach Monday morning, wearing a wool cap and a false mustache. You killed Professor Minder."

"I didn't! That's not true!"

"Why else would you be there in disguise?"

"That's none of your business. We hired you to guard our property, not to snoop around."

"If you don't answer me, you'll have to answer to the police."

He glowered and started to walk away, then thought better of it. "All right—if you must know. I wanted to see Elizabeth!"

"See her?"

"With him. With that Freen fellow. I wanted to hear what they were talking about."

"You disguised yourself to spy on Elizabeth Boyers?"

"Yes." His voice had dropped and he wouldn't meet Ben's eyes. "I love her."

"You can't accept the fact that she might find pleasure with another man?"

"I just wanted to hear what they talked about, to see for myself if she really cared for him. That's all. I barely realized Minder was there."

"All right," Ben said, not knowing whether he believed him nor not. "Will you be there in the morning?"

"Yes," Roderick answered.

"In disguise?"

"There's no point in it now, is there?"

Thursday morning dawned clear but freezing cold. When Ben reached the beach at Kitty Hawk in the company of Mark Freen and Elizabeth, they were saying the wind off the ocean was blowing at twenty-seven miles an hour. The few spectators were bundled against the cold and some were doubting the Wright brothers would attempt the flight.

But shortly after nine A.M., Wilbur and Orville gathered up their five assistants and once more hauled the machine from its shed. It was lifted onto the trolley at the base of Kill Devil Hill.

In addition to Elizabeth and Freen, who'd taken off another day from their teaching, both Claymore brothers were in attendance. And Ben saw Rellens pacing nearby. The cast was assembled.

Rudolph came up to stand next to Ben. "What did you say to my brother yesterday? Whatever it was, he's been pretty upset by it. He didn't even want to come out here today."

"I notice he's staying clear of Elizabeth Boyers."

"Well, they used to go together. I suppose he's jealous of her friend."

It seemed to take the Wrights forever to make their adjustments to the *Flyer* and the cold wind drove a few of the less hardy souls away. Orville was busy setting up the tripod for his camera, then aiming it at the end of the launching track. If the plane became airborne, he wanted a picture for the ages.

Finally, at 10:30, they were ready.

It was young Orville's turn to be at the controls this time and he glanced around for someone to snap the shutter of his camera. He called to one of the townspeople who'd been helping out and asked him to take the picture if the plane became airborne. Then he climbed aboard the *Flyer* and strapped himself down. Wilbur pulled the cap down more snugly on his head and gripped the lower right wingtip of the biplane.

The engine started and the propellers began to turn. The *Flyer* moved on its track. Wilbur began trotting alongside, holding the wingtip steady.

"He didn't do that on Monday," Rudolph Claymore remarked.

And then Orville opened the throttle more, bringing the engine to full power. The time was 10:35.

"No, he didn't," Ben Snow agreed. "But how did you know if you weren't here?"

The *Flyer* lifted from its track, airborne. Wilbur released the wing as the camera shutter clicked. A cheer went up from the small group of spectators.

The machine wobbled and swooped down, its runner hitting the sand. The flight had lasted only twelve seconds, never more than ten feet off the ground, but it had covered 120 feet.

People were running forward. Rudolph Claymore started to move, but Ben restrained him. "You knew what happened on Monday because you were here. Because you came to murder the man who'd swindled you."

"You think I was this Dick Roer?"

"No, that was your brother, spying on Elizabeth."

"But everyone else in the crowd was accounted for!"

"You never joined the crowd, Rudolph. You hid behind a sand dune, and while all eyes were on the Wrights at the crucial moment, you sneaked up just close enough to *throw* that knife into Minder's back, just like you flipped that ice pick into the cake yesterday. You never came closer than fifteen or twenty feet, and the sand was too trampled to show footprints. No one saw you because we were all looking in the opposite direction."

"But I didn't know he was a swindler until you told me yesterday!" Rudolph argued.

"You put on a very good act, but I think you knew. When your brother met me, he said you'd gone to the state capital on business. That's Raleigh, where Minder claimed to teach. You checked on him while you were there and discovered he was a fake. You came back here and killed him the first chance you had."

Rellens had been overhearing the conversation and now he stepped forward. "Do you have anything to say, Mr. Claymore?"

The fight had gone out of Rudolph. "Only that he deserved to die for swindling us. No jury will convict me."

Ben Snow left town the following morning. The Claymores' land didn't need protection any longer and he never heard what the jury decided. For that matter, it was a few years before he heard the Wright brothers mentioned again. They made four successful flights that December 17th at Kitty Hawk, and their father spread the news, but only two newspapers in the country carried a report the following day.

No crowds came to Kitty Hawk. The Claymores hadn't needed Ben Snow after all.

California writer Clark Howard has been nominated for the Edgar award many times and won it in 1980 for "Horn Man." He has been writing since 1957, with dozens of stories published in Alfred Hitchcock's Mystery Magazine *and* Ellery Queen's Mystery Magazine. *His stories often are sympathetic towards the outcasts and drifters who are seen but passed by. He has also written several true-crime books dealing with such topics as Alcatraz and the murder of militant activist George Jackson. In "All the Heroes Are Dead," he inserts another outsider into a sleepy southern town, with unpredictable results.*

All the Heroes Are Dead

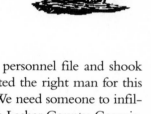

Clark Howard

The district director finished perusing the personnel file and shook his head dubiously. "Are you sure you've selected the right man for this assignment?" he asked his chief investigator. "We need someone to infiltrate a very close-knit bootlegging operation in Lasher County, Georgia. That's redneck country. This agent David Berry somehow doesn't seem the type for it. His background, I mean: political-science major at Yale, midwestern upbringing, interests in soccer and the theater—"

"His interest in the theater is precisely one of the reasons I selected Berry," the chief investigator said. "He's an amateur actor, belongs to a little-theater group in Alexandria. It's going to take someone who can put on a very good performance to fool those people in Lasher County."

"Maybe a better performance than you think," the director said. "The state authorities put an undercover man down there last year. He dropped out of sight and hasn't been heard from since. There are lots of deep woods and swamps in that part of Georgia. Good places to dispose of a body."

"I still feel Berry's the man for the job," the chief insisted.

"All right," the director said with a quiet sigh. "Have him come in."

The chief rose and summoned David Berry from an outer office. When the director saw him, his doubts were by no means assuaged. Berry's hair was styled, he wore a three-piece Brooks Brothers suit, and carried an attache case. He belonged, the director thought, in the bank examiners section, not in illegal whiskey.

"Berry, you've been with Treasury for three years now," the director said. "According to your file, all of your assignments up until now have been desk work. Do you think you can handle an undercover job?"

"Yes, sir, I do," Berry replied. "I've been eager for field work for quite some time now." His voice was precise, educated.

"You've read the Lasher County file," the director said, "so you know what the case is all about. An estimated one hundred thousand gallons of liquor is being manufactured illegally somewhere down there every year. That's not what we consider a huge operation, by any means. The government loses tax revenue on about two-and-a-half-million dollars annually based on their selling price, which is around one-third the cost of legal liquor, so we wouldn't go broke if we let them operate indefinitely. But that's not the point. The issue here is a violation of the law—manufacturing liquor without a license and distributing liquor without a tax stamp."

"Most of their sales, as you know from the file," the chief said, "are to rural residents in south Georgia and Alabama, and northern Florida. People that are commonly known as 'rednecks.' They live in and around places like the Apalachicola Forest, the Osceola Forest, and the Okefenokee Swamp. That's where we think they've got their manufacturing plant—their whiskey still: in the Okefenokee."

David Berry nodded. "Yes, sir, I noticed in the file that at one point there was nearly a six-hundred-percent increase in the sale of Mason jars in the swamp communities."

The chief smiled. "That's how we pinpointed the manufacturing site. Normally they make runs about a hundred miles away for their Mason jars, but apparently they ran out of them from their regular suppliers and had to buy locally. It was a sure tipoff—you can't bootleg hooch without Mason jars."

The director, still looking worried, sat forward and folded his hands on the desk. "Berry, I want to emphasize to you the potential peril of an assignment like this. You'll be going into a completely foreign environment, among people who are totally different from the kind you're accustomed to associating with."

"I know that, sir," Berry said. "I plan to spend a few weeks traveling around small towns in northern Georgia to learn how to act the part. I fully intend to prepare for the role."

"Your dress, your mannerisms, your speech—you'll have to change everything."

"Well, Ah don't think Ah'll have too much trouble with the speech, suh," Berry said, suddenly falling into a very good southern drawl. "Ah been listenin' to some dialect records over at that there linguistic department at the university an' Ah spect Ah'll have the talkin' down pat pretty quick like." Smiling, Berry reverted to his own speech pattern. "As for the clothes, visits to a couple of thrift shops and surplus stores will take care of that. And the mannerisms— well, just opening the beer can and drinking out of it ought to do for a start."

The chief flashed an I-told-you-so smile at the director. "We've established a complete new identity for him," he said. "His name will be Dale Barber. We chose that surname because Barber is very common in the southeastern U.S. He'll have an Alabama driver's license, army discharge, social-security card, and two membership cards to private after-hours clubs in Tuscaloosa. We picked that city because it's far enough away from where he'll be operating to make it difficult for anybody to check up on him, and it's large enough—about a hundred fifty thousand—to throw them off if they do. I think we've got all the bases covered, sir."

"It certainly seems like it." But there was still a trace of doubt in the director's voice, a gut feeling of reluctance inside him, some instinct—perhaps based on his thirty years of law-enforcement experience—that told him not to give David Berry the Lasher County assignment. It was nothing he could put his finger on and he knew if he tried to explain it to his chief investigator he would sound as if he were procrastinating. Based on the chief's recommendation and Berry's apparent ability to discharge the assignment, he was left with no choice. "All right, Berry, the job's yours," he said.

He had a feeling that he would never see the young agent again.

Three weeks later, David Berry was cruising down Highway 441, which ran parallel to the Okefenokee Swamp. He was driving a '78 Chevy pickup with a roll-bar he'd bought with agency money in Tuscaloosa. A battered suitcase and a cardboard box containing his extra clothes rode in the rear bed along with a nearly bald spare tire, a lug wrench, an empty gas can, and a six-pack of Miller's beer. In one corner of the pickup's back window was a decal of a Confederate flag.

Inside the cab was a rifle rack with a .22 pump on it. A Slim Whitman tape was playing in the dashboard deck.

When David got to DeSota, the little town that was halfway down on the edge of the swamp, he circled the tiny town square once and pulled up in front of Luther's Café.

Getting out of the truck, he stretched and twisted some of the stiffness out of his back and shoulders. He knew that several people sitting by the window in the café had already noticed him, his truck, the Alabama plates. His appearance, he knew, fit the picture—old faded Levis, an inexpensive plaid cotton shirt, a blue denim vest, and a soiled yellow visor cap with an STP patch on it. The cap was pushed to the back of his now unstyled hair. On his feet he wore low-heel Frye boots.

Going inside, David sat at the counter and looked at the hand-written menu. A waitress came over to him—redheaded, well built, a sexy wide mouth, too much mascara. She wore a white uniform that had "Tommy Sue" embroidered above her left breast.

"Hi," she said, setting a glass of water in front of him.

"Hi, Tommy Sue," he said, reading her uniform. "Ah'll have three chicken wings, some coleslaw, an' fried okra. An' iced tea."

Their eyes met just long enough for them to realize it. Then David reached down the counter and retrieved the sports section of the Tallahassee *Democrat*. He pretended to read, but he was actually thinking about Eileen, his girl friend. She was working on her master's in history at Georgetown. Eileen was tall, slim, chic, and proper—almost too proper sometimes. She had not been at all pleased about this field assignment.

"Georgia!" she had said. "Really, David. Can't you get out of it somehow? The Clarys' lawn party is coming up."

"I don't want to get out of it," he had told her. "This is my first opportunity in three years to get away from a desk."

"But *Georgia!* Couldn't you get an assignment some place close?"

"There aren't many illegal whiskey stills in Bethesda or Arlington or Alexandria," he pointed out. "We have to go where the violation is. I'm sorry about the Clarys' party."

Tommy Sue brought his food and David put the paper aside. He began to eat the chicken wings with his fingers. Out of the corner of his eye he saw the fry cook come out of the kitchen, wiping his hands on a greasy apron. "That your pickup with the 'Bama plates?" he asked.

"That's me," David said with his mouth full.

"Where'bouts in 'Bama you from?"

"Tuscaloosa. Ax'ly Ah'm from Coker, a little piece north. But ain't nobody ever heard of Coker, so Ah say Tuscaloosa."

The fry cook nodded. "Jus' passin' through?"

David shook his head. "Lookin' for work. Heard up in Waycross that y'all had a canning factory down here that might be hirin' on."

"Cannin' factory shut down last week. Soybeans done poorly this year. Nothin' to can."

David shook his head in disappointment and kept on eating. In a booth near the window sat three men he could sense listening with interest to his conversation with the fry cook.

"Know of anything else around?" he asked.

"Such as?"

David shrugged. "Ah ain't particular. Fillin' station, farm work, construction."

"Things is real slow right now. Maybe fu'ther south. Florida maybe."

David grunted. "Ah'm runnin' low on lookin' money. There a poolroom in town?"

"Right across the square. Leon's Pool Hall."

"Maybe Ah can pick up a couple dollars."

"Don't count on it," the fry cook said.

There was a motel called Harley's Motor Inn a mile out the high-way: twelve units that usually filled up only during the legal fishing season. The season was past now and the alligators were breeding in the swamp waters, so there was no one at Harley's except a notions salesman who worked the territory between Macon and Orlando. The salesman was in Unit One, so Harley put David in Unit Two when David drove out after lunch and checked in.

"How long you be staying?" Harley asked.

"Couple days maybe. Lookin' for work."

"Things is real slow around here. Be twelve-fifty a night, first night in advance. No playin' the television after midnight."

David carried his old suitcase and cardboard box into the room and unpacked. Then he pulled off his boots to stretch out on the bed for a while. It was funny about those boots. He had expected to hate them. His taste ran to Carranos: glove-leather, Italian-made. But these Frye boots, after a week of breaking in, were as comfortable as any-thing he'd ever put on his feet. It was the same with the Chevy pickup.

In Washington he drove a low-slung Datsun 280-Z and rode close to the pavement. The cab of the pickup was up high, above everything except motor homes and tractor rigs. You saw a lot more in a pickup cab than in a sportscar.

David spent the afternoon resting, then at sunset he showered, put on clean jeans and a striped shirt, and drove back uptown. He found a phonebooth next to the post office and called the chief on a blind telephone number with a memorized credit-card number. "I'm settled," he said when the chief answered. "I should be able to spot the delivery truck tonight. Unless you hear from me to the contrary, I'm ready for stage two."

"I understand," the chief said. "Good luck."

David left the booth and walked across the street to Luther's Café again. Tommy Sue was still on duty. "You work all the time?" he asked when she handed him the supper menu.

"Girl's got to make a living," she answered. While he studied the menu she said, "I saw you in the phonebooth. Calling your wife like a good little boy?"

"Don't have no wife. Let me have the fried catfish and hush puppies. Iced tea. Pecan pie for dessert."

"Calling you girl friend then?" she asked as she wrote down his order.

"Calling my mama. Your curiosity satisfied now?"

"Well, 'scuse me for livin'," she said huffily.

Throughout his meal David occasionally caught her glancing at him. Whenever he did, he threw her a smile or a wink. She turned her nose up at him. When he paid his supper check he said, "Next time Ah talk to Mama, Ah'll tell her you said hello."

"Don't bother."

"No trouble. Ah'll tell her Ah met this here little Georgia peach who's too pretty to even describe."

"You might's well save it, Alabama. You got off on the wrong foot with me with that curiosity crack. I was only makin' small talk."

Outside the window David saw a Buick drive up to Leon's Pool Hall, followed closely by a Dodge pickup. One man got out of the Buick, two out of the pickup, and they all went inside. They were the same three who had listened so intently to David's conversation with the fry cook at noon.

"Let's you and me start all over," David said, turning his attention back to Tommy Sue. "At breakfast."

"I don't work breakfast," she told him. "I come on at eleven-thirty."

"What time do you get off?"

"Nine-thirty—when we close. I work ten hours a day, four days a week. That way I get to spend three days a week with Lonnie."

"Lonnie?"

"My little boy. He's four. My mamma keeps him for me, over in Talbot."

"Oh." David glanced out the window again and his thoughts went momentarily to the Dodge pickup. It looked like the right truck, he thought. The one the department had come so close to catching several times.

Tommy Sue, taking his silence for disinterest, handed him his change, shrugged, and started to walk away.

"Hey, wait a minute. What time did you say?"

"What's it matter? You turned awful cold soon's you found out I had a kid. But don't feel bad, it's happened before."

"I didn't turn cold, I simply became distracted," David said, lapsing into his normal speech before he realized it. Tommy Sue frowned, staring curiously at him. David locked eyes with her for a moment, then forced a smile. "That was Tony Randall. Ah can do Johnny Carson too." His awkward smile faded. "Can Ah come back at nine-thirty? Take you for a beer?"

She shrugged. "I guess," she said. But there was now a trace of reluctance in her voice.

David went back to his pickup and drove out of town. Cursing himself for his momentary lapse of cover, he drove up and down the back roads for an hour, until twilight came and a grayness began to settle over the red dirt fields. Then he headed back uptown. It was fully dark when he parked in front of Leon's Pool Hall. Walking toward the door, he stopped at the Dodge, put his foot up on the back bumper, and pretended to pull a pebble out of his heel. While he was doing it, he palmed a miniature electronic transmitter with a magnet on the back of it, and attached it to the inside of the bumper. Then he went on into the pool hall.

Leon's was a prototype of every poolroom in every small town in the South. Six Brunswick tables so old their cushions could barely reject a ball. Drop pockets with net catchers. A shelf near each table holding a can of talcum for the cuestick shaft and blue chalk for its tip. A few rickety raised wooden benches for tobacco-chewing spectators.

Half a dozen spittoons. Two pinball machines that paid off in free games that could be cashed in for money. A wooden bar with an illuminated beer-logo clock over the cash register behind it. And on the bar two large jars—one of pickled eggs, one of pigs' feet. All under a cloud of gray smoke that hung at the ceiling because it had no place else to go.

David went to the bar and got a bottle of Bud. The three men who had driven up earlier were shooting nine-ball on a middle table. David stepped up on one of the benches and sat down to watch. Two of the men shooting were either twins or brothers very close in age. They wore jeans with leather belts that had their names tooled on the back of them—Merle and Earl. The latter, David noticed, also had E-A-R-L tattooed on the top joint of each finger on his right hand. The work didn't look professional. It was a jailhouse tattoo, David guessed. The third man was the oldest, probably fifty, with a pot-belly hanging over the waist of a pair of self-belted polyester trousers. He wore a shirt that had a western scene embroidered across the yoke. David sensed that he was studying him from under a pair of tinted lenses between shots.

David watched the progress of the game, waiting for an opportunity to interject a comment. To come right out with a remark would have been poor form and would have marked him at once as a total outsider, an "up-North" type. He had to be subtle about it. He waited until Earl, the one with the tattoos, missed a fairly easy straight-in corner shot, then he rolled his eyes toward the ceiling and groaned quietly. But not so quietly that Earl couldn't hear him.

"What's your problem, boy?" Earl said antagonistically. "Don't nobody ever miss a shot where you come from?"

"Not that kind," David said. Then he raised his hands, palms out. "Hey, Ah'm sorry, hear? Ah didn't have no call to remark. It just slipped out."

"You a pool player?" asked the older man, smiling across the table.

David shrugged. "Ah shoot a game ever' now and then." Which was a gross understatement. David had been president of the billiards club at college for five semesters.

The older man came around the table. He had a chaw of tobacco in one cheek, but instead of using a spittoon he kept a Dixie cup handy. "We heard you say at Luther's today that you hoped to win a little money over here. You care to shoot a game of rotation with Earl here? Say for twenty-five dollars?"

David pursed his lips. "That's mighty temptin'."

The man in the polyester trousers smiled. "What's your name, boy?"

"Dale Barber. From Tuscaloosa, Alabama."

"I didn't ask where you was from. My name's Billy Roy Latham. My friends call me Billy Roy. You can call me Mr. Latham." He peeled twenty-five dollars off a roll and stuck it in one of the corner pockets. "Anytime you're ready."

David covered the bet and beat Earl 67 to 53. He could have run the balls and blanked him, but he didn't want to look like a slicker trying to skin the locals. Neither did he want his thumbs broken. So he laid back and just won by two balls, the six and the eight. As he was fishing his winnings out of the pocket, Earl's brother Merle said, "Lemme have a crack at him, Billy Roy."

Latham nodded and put another twenty-five in the pocket. Merle was about in the same league as Earl. David beat him a little more badly, 71 to 49, winning with the two, three, seven, and ten balls.

After the game with Merle, Latham removed his tinted glasses and smiled an artificial smile at David. "Ah cain't decide if you're good or jus' lucky. How 'bout you and me shoot a game for the fifty you've won?"

David glanced around. A dozen men had idled up from the other tables and were gathered around watching. They were somber, leathery men, their eyes squinty from years in the bright sun of the fields. Maybe they worked for Latham, maybe they didn't. But David knew instinctively that even if he had wanted to there was no way he'd be allowed to walk out with the fifty he had won.

"How 'bout it, boy?" Latham pressed. "You an' me for fifty each."

"Whatever you say, Mr. Latham."

The balls were racked and Latham won the break. He made the six on the break, then ran the one, two, and three, and dropped the twelve off the three-ball. David saw at once that Latham was a much better pool shooter than Merle and Earl.

On his first shot, David ran the four, five, seven, and eight, tying it up with twenty-four points each. Latham made the nine and ten, but scratched on the ten and had to spot it back on the table. David then made it in the side pocket but missed the eleven-ball. Latham made the eleven. David made the thirteen, to go three points ahead, 47 to 44. Latham made the fourteen, to move up to forty-eight. Then he missed the fifteen and it was David's turn.

The fifteen was the game-winning ball. It was dead on the side rail, midway down from the end pocket. Its position did not present a difficult shot, merely a tricky one—the cueball had to hit the rail and the fifteen-ball at the same time in order to run the fifteen straight along the cushion into the pocket. If the cueball hit the fifteen first, the fifteen would be brought out from the rail and go nowhere, leaving the opponent a good shot. If the cueball hit the rail first, the fifteen would roll straight along the rail but wouldn't have enough momentum to go all the way to the pocket.

David chalked his cue-tip and bent low over the far end of the table. Wetting his lips, he took dead-perfect aim and let go a slow shot that hit the fifteen and the cushion at the same time. The fifteen rolled along the rail—and stopped four inches from the pocket.

There was a general murmur of approval from the onlookers: the stranger had lost. David shook his head and stepped back. Billy Ray Latham leaned casually over the side rail and eased the ball on in to win the game. He got more than a few pats on the back as he dug the fifty dollars out of the end pocket.

In the men's room, David and Latham stood side by side washing the talcum off their hands at a tin sink. "You could've made that last shot," Latham said quietly.

"Can't win 'em all," David said.

"You could've won that one. Why didn't you?"

David shrugged. "Your town, your people. No call to beat a man in his own town. 'Sides, Ah broke even."

Latham studied him for a long moment as he dried his hands. Then he made up his mind about David and nodded to himself. "There's a place called Joe's Pit out on the highway that's got good bar-becued ribs and ice-cold beer. How 'bout havin' a bite?"

"No offense," David said, "but Ah got other plans." He winked at Latham. "Tommy Sue over at the café."

Latham grinned. "You Alabama rednecks is all the same. After the sun goes down you only got one thing on your mind."

"Yep. Jus' like you Georgia rednecks." David bobbed his chin. "See you around."

He bought a cold six-pack at Luther's and drove away from the square with Tommy Sue. "Where do ya'll park around here?" he asked.

"Out by the cemetery. It's quiet there."

"Ah reckon it would be."

She showed him the way. When they were parked, David opened both doors of the pickup and two cans of the beer. They sat holding hands and sipping the beer. Someone had burned a stump during the day and there was still a smell of scorched wood in the air. It mixed with the fragrance of hackberry plants that grew wild along the side of the road. The result was an odd, almost sensual night scent. After they finished a can of beer each, David guided Tommy Sue onto the seat and put his lips on her throat. He found himself whispering things to her that he would never have dared say to Eileen. Things that made Tommy Sue draw in her breath and entwine her fingers in his hair.

It was later, when they were having their second beer, that she asked, "Who are you anyway?"

"Jus' plain ol' Dale Barber from Tuscaloosa, honey."

"You're not 'just plain ol' anybody from anywhere," she said. "And that wasn't no Tony Randall imitation you were doing earlier. That was the real you."

David looked out at the moonlight and thought it over. "Suppose it was the real me? What would you do about it?"

"Depends on who you came here to hurt. I'm not from DeSota, I'm from Talbot, but the people here been good to me. I wouldn't stick nobody in the back."

"I wouldn't ask you to. Let's get to know each other a little better first. Then we can decide what's right and what's wrong." He kissed the tips of her fingers as he talked.

"You're so gentle,"she said softly. "I can't imagine you hurting nobody." She turned her hand around. "Do that to the palm."

"Tell me about your little boy."

"I already told you. His name is Lonnie and he's four and my mama keeps him for me over in Talbot. He's just like any other little boy. Likes cowboys and trucks and beaches. I keep tellin' him we'll go down to the Florida beaches some weekend but, Lord, I never seem to find the time."

"Where's his daddy?"

"Run off with another woman. Last I heard he was on welfare out in California. He left me with Lonnie to raise. I couldn't find no work in Talbot so I come over here to DeSota. A friend of Mama's sent me to see Mr. Latham. He gave me the job at Luther's and fixed the hours so I could spend three days a week back home."

"Billy Roy Latham? He owns Luther's?"

"Sure. Luther's. Leon's Pool Hall. DeSota Market. The filling station, the canning factory, even the undertaker's parlor. He owns just about everything in Lasher County."

"When he helped you out, did he make any moves on you?"

"Not one. He's been a perfect gentleman. He's good to lots of people, and most times he don't ask nothin' in return."

A Georgia godfather, David thought. He had guessed as much from the demeanor of the men in the poolroom. But he had not imagined that Latham owned the entire county. It would be interesting to see how he reacted the following day when his illegal whiskey operation began to fall apart.

But that was tomorrow and tonight was still tonight. David slipped his hand up Tommy Sue's back under her blouse. He felt nothing except flesh.

"Where do you stay the four nights you're in DeSota?" he asked.

"Out at Harley's Motor Inn. I rent Number Twelve by the week."

"I'm in Number Two," he told her.

She put her lips on his ear. "Small world," she said.

David started the pickup.

The next day when David drove up to Luther's for breakfast, Billy Roy Latham and one of the brothers, Merle, were drinking coffee in a booth and looking worried. David nodded a greeting and sat at the counter. The fry cook was in the kitchen doorway, moving a toothpick back and forth in his mouth. "Somethin' wrong?" David asked, bobbing his chin toward the somber men in the booth.

"Revenue agents caught that fellow's brother Earl with a load of bootleg last night. Got him just after he crossed the Florida line."

David nodded. "Oh." The fry cook's wife, who worked mornings until Tommy Sue came in, handed him a menu. "Just grits and sausage," David said.

While David was eating, Merle got up and left the booth. After he was gone, Latham waved David over to join him. "Bring your plate on over," he said hospitably. David carried his coffee and the rest of his meal over.

"How'd you make out with Tommy Sue last night?" Latham asked.

"Struck out," David lied. "She's a right proper girl."

"You got that right," Latham said. "Gonna make a fine little wife for some man someday." Latham sighed wearily and took a sip of coffee.

"Fry cook tells me you got problems this morning," David said.

Latham shot an irritated look over the counter. "Fry cook's got a big mouth." Then he studied David for a moment. "But he's right. One of them boys you whipped at pool last night got caught in a revenue-agent trap." Latham narrowed his eyes. "You know anything about bootlegging?"

"A little," David admitted.

Latham tossed down his last swallow of coffee. "Come on, take a ride with me. Somethin' I want to show you."

They rode in Latham's Buick down Route 441 to a narrow county road that cut east into Okefenokee Swamp. Five miles along, Latham turned into a rutted dirt path barely wide enough for the car to negotiate. The farther they drove, the more the morning sunlight was shut out by the entangled treetops overhead and the more eerie the great swamp became. A bit of fog still clung to the ground on both sides of the car, looking wet and cold, making David think of the warmth he had left behind in Tommy Sue's bed. He shivered slightly and wished he was still there.

Before the road ended, Latham turned into a bog path and guided the car with a sure, practiced eye onto a log raft ringed with empty 55-gallon drums to keep it afloat. Sticking his head out the window, he whistled three times. Presently the raft began to float across the marsh to an island, being pulled along by unseen rope under the murky water. The trip took only three or four minutes, then Latham, who had not even shut off the engine, drove the car onto the island and into a stand of tall pines. David saw the rope and pulley that were used to bring the raft over. A black man with enormous muscles was standing next to the pulley crank. "That's Mose," said Latham. "He can crush a man's skull between his hands." David didn't doubt it for a moment.

The car drove through the shade of the pines, and up ahead David could see the whiskey still. It consisted of several large wooden tubs and a couple of cast-iron vats with kerosene burners under them. Everything was connected by wires and tubes, and with the escaping steam and the bubbling surface in two of the vats it reminded David of the mad doctors' laboratories he used to see in the movies as a kid. Latham parked and they got out. "Come on," he said, "I'll give you the ten-cent tour."

He led David to the layout of tubs, where several lean sweating white men were pouring industrial alcohol from ten-gallon cans into the first tub, then straining it through a water-and-charcoal filter into a second one. "That's how we wash the noxious chemicals out of the alky," Latham said. "Over here in this tub is where we mix water with the alky, then we run it into that iron vat and cook it some, put some caramel or butterscotch coloring in it to make it look good, then run it into the last tub there to simmer and cool." He grinned sheepishly. "I usually pour a fifth of bonded rye into the final batch to give it a little extra flavor. Like a taste?"

"Why not?" David said.

Behind the last vat were several young boys filling Mason jars with the freshly cooled liquor. Latham opened one of the jars and handed it to David. Although his taste ran to very dry martinis and good brandy, David knew he had to take a convincing drink of the bootleg stuff, as if he'd been drinking it all his life. He took a respectable swallow, prepared to forcibly hold back both cough and tears if necessary, but to his surprise the drink went down not only smoothly but with a tart good taste. He saw that Latham was smiling at him.

"Smooth, ain't it?"

"Sure is, man," David admitted. "And good too."

"Ah don't make nothin' but the best for my customers," Latham bragged. He nodded toward a picnic table and benches under a low weeping willow at the edge of the clearing. "Let's set a spell." As he spoke, Latham pulled back one side of his coat and for the first time David saw that he had a pistol stuck in his belt. Glancing around, he also now saw two men armed with rifles, one at each end of the compound. "Sure 'nuff, Mr. Latham." David said easily and followed him over to the table.

"You know," Latham said, sitting down and shaking a Camel out of a soft pack, "I sometimes wonder what the ol' world's comin' to. I read in the papers and see on the evenin' news all the stories about crime in the streets, violence in the schools, poverty in the slums, crooks in gub'ment, all that sort of thing. Makes me realize more ever' day that things is changin' too fast to keep up with—and not necessarily for the better neither. Hell, even all the heroes are dead. Harry Truman's dead. Audie Murphy's dead. John Steinbeck's dead. Ain't nobody around to admire no more. Nowadays all's a man can do is hope to keep his own little part of the world protected from outside influences that might corrupt it. You take Lasher County now. It's my own little corner of the earth and I try to look after it as best I can. I own nearly all there is to own from one end of it to the other, and ever'body except the postmaster and a couple of bankers works for me."

Latham leaned forward on the table and locked eyes with David.

"I run this county like the whole country ought to be run. We don't have no welfare recipients or food stamps down here 'cause we don't need 'em. Ever'body that *can* work *does* work. An' the ones that can't, why the others takes care of 'em. Our old people and our sick people don't want for nothin'. Nobody sleeps cold in the wintertime, nobody goes hungry at suppertime, and nobody has to be afraid *any*time. We ain't got no real crime in Lasher County—no robberies, burglaries, that sort of thing. People here *work* for what they want. They work for me—in my café, my pool hall, my grocery market, my filling station, my farms, my canning factory, and ever'thing else I own. My farms and canning factory are the economic backbone of this county. And when the economy don't stay up, when crops are bad or inflation keeps me from making enough to go around for ever'body, why then this whiskey bi'ness takes up the slack. It's this right here—" he waved an arm around "—that keeps the people of Lasher County free and independent of the rest of our dyin' and decayin' society." Now Latham's expression seemed to turn hard as stone. "And I'm here to tell you I'll do anythin' I have to do to keep it that way. Do you take my meanin'?"

David, his mouth as dry as old wood, managed to speak. "Yessir, Mr. Latham. I take your meanin'."

"Good," Latham said quietly. He sat back and seemed to relax a little, toying with the burnt-out stick match he had used to light his cigarette. "I don't know," he said matter-of-factly, "if it was just a coincidence you comin' to town one day and Earl gettin' caught with a load that same night. I don't know if you're really Dale Barber from Tuscaloosa or if you're a revenue agent from Washington. I know that Tommy Sue is crazy about you—I talked to her on the phone after Harley called to tell me you'd left the motel. Incidentally, I admire the fact that you said you struck out with her instead of braggin' the other way; that's the mark of a good man. Anyway, Tommy Sue says she thinks you're who you say you are."

She lied for me, David thought.

"But I'd like to hear it from you," Latham said. "For some funny reason I kind of like you. And I kind of trust you. Enough to give you the benefit of the doubt anyhow. I think I'll know if you lie to me. So I'll just ask you outright: who are you, boy?"

A montage of his own world saturated David's mind. Washington. Eileen. The Clarys' lawn party. Dry martinis. Sportscars. Italian shoes. Styled hair. A career in government.

Then the montage dissolved into another world. Lasher County. Frye boots and Levis. A Chevy pickup. Catfish and hush puppies. Tommy Sue's warm neck and the things he could whisper against it.

David met Billy Roy Latham's fixed stare with a calm sureness. "I'm Dale Barber, Mr. Latham. From Tuscaloosa."

The letter he wrote to the district director was brief and polite. He was sorry to resign so abruptly in the middle of a field assignment but he had been offered a job in private industry that he couldn't turn down. He wished the department luck in its pursuit of further leads in Lasher County even though based on his own investigation he didn't believe it would be possible to find an illegal whiskey still in the vast Okefenokee Swamp.

The letter to Eileen was also brief, and apologetic. He was leaving government service for private employment and he had to be honest and tell her he had become interested in another woman. He would always remember her fondly, he said, and was certain that, attractive educated woman that she was, she would find someone who deserved her much more than he did.

He mailed the letters in the box outside the DeSota post office, then pulled up in front of Luther's just as Tommy Sue was leaving for the night. She was carrying a small suitcase.

"Hop in," he said. "I'll give you a lift."

"I'm fixin' to catch the ten o'clock bus to Talbot," she told him. "My three days off starts tomorrow."

"I'll give you a lift to Talbot," he said.

"You mean it?"

"Sure I mean it. Get in."

She put her suitcase in the back and climbed into the cab.

"I start work for Mr. Latham on Monday," he told her.

Tommy Sue's eyebrows went up. "Doin' what?"

"Helping him run Lasher County, honey. He said a good ol' boy like me from Tuscaloosa would fit right in. Said that someday I might even take over and run it for him. How's that for a future?"

"Sounds like you've got the future all worked out. What about the past?"

"There isn't any past," David replied quietly. "There's just today. And tomorrow. Listen, let's pick up your little boy and drive down to Florida to the beach. Would you like that?"

"I'd like it just fine," Tommy Sue slid over close and curled up to him. "You're wrong about there bein' just today and tomorrow," she said.

"Am I? What else is there?"

"There's tonight."

The pickup drove out of town and into the Georgia night.

Lisa Lepovetsky teaches writing, literature, and communication classes for the University of Pittsburgh. She has fiction, non-fiction pieces, and poetry appearing regularly in such publications as Ellery Queen's Mystery Magazine, Cemetery Dance, *and many others. She also has work in such anthologies as* Graiis, Air Fish, Dark Destiny, Dark Destiny II, *and* 100 Wicked Little Witch Stories. *Her poetry has been collected into the chapbooks* As the Carny Goes By *and* Skeletal Remains. *In "Here Be Monsters," she reminds readers that not everybody commits crimes as a career.*

Here Be Monsters

Lisa Lepovetsky

W hen I was a little girl, I loved to be scared. Now, when crimson and gold leaves rain from the maples and birches here in North Carolina to layer the ground, I'm sometimes a bit sorry that I've become too jaded to be really frightened anymore. Then I remember the last Halloween I spent back in Willowsburg, the year I turned fourteen. And I remember why I don't like to be scared anymore.

We wore rough paper and cloth masks then, not rubber or vinyl. Nobody worried about risking their fingers in that ancient, sensuous ritual of gutting and carving great pumpkins. Homemade demons and evil spirits roamed the streets at night, hoping for nothing more than a good clean scare. We traveled in packs, imagining that would protect us from what waited for us in the dark. And we screamed in terror—and relief—when the boys jumped out at us from behind a hedgerow.

All the houses on River Road, where we lived back then, were decorated with life-size paper skeletons and whispery cornstalks and real candlelit jack-o'-lanterns. I remember those disturbing idiot smiles flickering from front-porch railings, and the smell of charred squash as flames licked at the soft carved lids. The neighbors all lurked behind their doors on Halloween to hand out fruit or home-baked goodies to those of us who braved the night. I still remember how I loved the taste of fear mixed in with the sweets.

I felt a curious combination of anticipation and regret that year, as autumn turned our small-town greens to brown. The roses had faded long ago, and the sky took on a deeper, more brittle blue behind the naked branches, a color that reminded me winter would soon be sniffing beneath the doors. I'd just started high school, and life wasn't the same anymore. I'd moved into a new world, but I'd left something behind, too.

My mother didn't get our decorations out that fall. She was working extra shifts at the tannery, since Daddy had left. The second week of October, he'd put on his frayed brown suit and Panama hat, the way he always did when he went on a sales trip. Then he'd kissed Mama and me as he went out the door, whistling.

We were used to the sales trips, but he and Mama had argued the night before when he'd flown into one of his jealous rages, and she frowned a little when he kissed her. Mama often worried about him being gone, ever since he'd had the accident. Daddy had been touring another plant several years before, when a forklift went out of control, throwing him against a cement wall. He'd been in the hospital for a week, with broken ribs and a severe concussion, and was never quite the same after that.

The doctor couldn't find anything physically wrong, but Daddy seemed secretive, suspicious all the time after that, kind of sneaking around. And he began drinking more. He and Mama fought all the time, it seemed, mostly about things he thought she was "up to." No matter how much she denied them, he found some way to convince himself she was lying. So when he kissed her and smiled the morning after their big argument, she didn't smile back. She went to the window and watched him drive away until he disappeared in the distance.

A week later, the Friday before Halloween, Mama called the shoe factory where Daddy worked. He'd rarely been gone that long; his trips never lasted longer than three days. The people at the shoe factory told her he'd been fired a month earlier for beating up a foreman. They had no idea where he'd been going every weekday since then, and certainly no idea where he was now.

I happened to walk in on the end of the conversation after school. I was surprised to see her there, because she usually left for work before I got home.

"What's up?" I asked as she cradled the receiver. Her back was still to me. As she turned around, I saw tears on her cheeks. My heart froze—I'd never seen my mother cry before, not even during one of

Daddy's tirades. In a surprisingly steady voice, she explained what the manager of the shoe factory had just told her.

"I'm sure there's some mistake," she finished. "Or he's going through some kind of psychological trauma. He'll be back any day now; he always is. Don't you worry about it."

I didn't believe her, and I didn't think she believed herself. But I nodded and agreed with her. After all, what if Daddy didn't come back? There wouldn't be any more embarrassing phone calls to the local bars, looking for him. There'd be no fights in the middle of the night, while I covered my head with a pillow, praying he wouldn't slam out the back door again.

But he was my father, and I loved him. He hadn't always been so volatile, so tense. I knew that I could make everything right again, if he'd just give me the chance.

Mama redialed the phone as I started upstairs, and I heard her ask for Sheldon Owen, her boss at the tannery. I crept partway down the stairs again. I liked Shel Owen, everybody did. He was a widower who lived on an old farm about half a mile down River Road, where it twists to the west, away from town. He raised a little vegetable garden for himself, and about a half acre of corn.

The first fall he moved into Willowsburg to take over the tannery, he hosted a neighborhood costume party/corn-roast the Saturday before Halloween. That was six years ago, but it was a huge success and became an instant tradition. Everybody on River Road prepared their costumes weeks in advance, trying to win first prize in the contest. Mr. Owen always found something interesting for the prize. That first year, Daddy won, dressed as an armchair, and he still carried the gold lighter with an evil jack-o'-lantern engraved on it. He'd been so proud of his prize, and we'd all had such fun that night. I cherished that memory.

"Shel?" Mama said quietly into the phone. "Harry's gone again— a week this time. . . . No, I don't think so. He's left before, but he always comes back after a week or so, when he gets tired of his little escapade. . . . I know, but that doesn't mean anything. Any minute now, he'll come marching through the door, wanting something to eat. I suppose we'll have to figure something out about the job, though. . . . I know you will. I just wanted you to know why I'll be a little late today. . . . I know you do. Thanks. Thanks for everything. Of course we'll be there tomorrow—wouldn't miss it. I'm bringing my carrot cake and Sammi's still working on her costume."

I'd forgotten about the picnic. I wondered whether we'd still go if
Daddy came home. We'd never missed a corn roast in the six years Mr.
Owen had hosted them. For some reason, Daddy had developed a
hatred for Shel Owen and never wanted to go now, but Mama insisted
we go anyway. He was her boss, after all, she said. How would it look?

One year, Daddy and Mama had a big fight the night before the
roast. He refused to go the next day, and forbid us to go, too. Mama just
looked him in the eye, grabbed her cake, and marched me out to the
old Ford station wagon without a word. It was the only time I ever saw
her disobey him. Daddy didn't come after us in his truck that time, but
he never missed another corn roast. I don't think he enjoyed them
anymore, but he dressed up and went along every year.

By the next morning, Daddy still hadn't come home. Mama
packed up her witch costume into a plastic bag and left early to help
Mr. Owen set up for the picnic. All his employees at the tannery
seemed to like him, but he and Mama were especially close. They were
about the same age, and never stopped talking about books and movies
they both liked, and how "one of these days" Mr. Owen was going to
help Mama plant her own vegetables. Sometimes I wondered about
their relationship, but he was her boss, after all, and she was . . . well,
she was my mother.

I got bored a couple of hours later, and decided to head over to
the farm a little early. I hadn't wanted to wear a costume because I
was afraid none of my friends would be wearing them. But Mama
had talked me into wearing the spider costume I'd made the year
before out of a leotard and four pairs of black tights. I stuffed it into a
duffel bag and left a note for Daddy, in case he came home while we
were gone.

On the way, I stopped off at my friend Alice's house, to see her
costume. We talked for a while about what boys would be there, then
had some sandwiches and a drink. I left about an hour later for Mr.
Owen's house. The afternoon was so beautiful that I decided to take
the long way, staying on the road, rather than cut through the little
woods and the cornfield.

I scuffed little waves of dirt around my sneakers as I walked,
enjoying the crisp autumn air and the musty smells of burning leaves
and dropped pine needles. I started as something scurried across my
feet, then laughed nervously as I realized it was only some dry leaves
caught in a little gust of wind. Nothing is ever what it seems to be at
Halloween. Twilit ghosts dancing in the shadows behind the garage are

no more than shirts left to dry on the line. Even the weather is infidel; in no more than the casual snap of barometric fingers, sultry warm days can leave us damp and shivering. I walked a little faster, not as happy to be alone as I had been a moment before.

I got to Mr. Owen's house just before three, still an hour before anybody else was due to show up. The garden was black, with newly filled soil, waiting for winter. I went around back first, to see whether there were any good ears of corn left in the field. I liked wandering through the dry cornstalks, listening to the papery sound they make, even on the stillest days, like little voices whispering. I noticed Mr. Owen had put up a new scarecrow in the center of the field, using scrap leather from the tannery. But, as usual, the birds were perched on its arms and the big floppy hat, not a bit scared. I always suspected Mr. Owen really didn't mind birds and animals in his cornfield that much, anyway. He even put a couple of the wormy ears out in his front yard for them every couple of days.

I headed toward the scarecrow anyway, assuming that if there were any good ears, that's where they'd be. When I got close to the center of the field, I noticed something shiny in the dirt between the stalks. I stooped to pick it up. My breath stopped and I felt goosebumps prickle on the back of my neck. *Daddy's lighter.*

I thought of Mama and Mr. Owen alone back at the house, and Daddy returning drunk from wherever he'd been. I imagined him finding my note and racing furiously through the woods and the cornfield to get there ahead of me, while I drank lemonade and chatted with Alice. I made myself stop imagining then, and ran back toward the house.

Mama and Mr. Owen came out onto the back porch just then. She had on her long black witch's dress and some makeup that I thought made her look more beautiful than frightening. Mr. Owen was carrying a paper-wrapped bundle. He took his arm from around Mama's shoulders when he saw me there, and Mama tucked a couple of strands of loose hair behind her ear with a trembling hand. Her eyes were red, and she came over and hugged me. She stepped back then and put her hands along the sides of my face. She looked into my eyes for a long time.

"Mama," I gasped, holding out the lighter. "I found this. I think Daddy's back. I was afraid that you . . . that he . . ."

Then Mr. Owen cleared his throat softly. Mama glanced at him. She smiled sadly and kissed my forehead as she took the lighter.

"Don't worry, Sammi," she said. "We're fine. See? There's nobody here but us. And look how dirty the lighter is. It must have been dropped awhile ago. Everything's fine."

She dropped the lighter into a pocket of her black dress. Before I had a chance to say more, she asked if I'd help set up the long picnic tables before everybody got there. Mr. Owen tucked the package into the pile of wood laid for the bonfire. We finished just as the first car pulled up, and I ran inside to change into my costume.

The corn roast was as fun as always, and we stuffed ourselves with buttery, salty kernels that popped in our mouths almost before we bit into them. Mr. Owen oohed and aahed over Mama's carrot cake until I was almost embarrassed for her. But she just smiled at him across the table, while everybody else nodded in agreement and dug in. The night settled onto the mountains like a cool, damp shawl, and a yellow moon began its ascent in the east.

Then came time for the bonfire. Mr. Owen let a couple of the men light it, while he brought out a tray stacked with marshmallows. The children all ran to find thin green branches for toasting them, and those of us who were too old to show that much enthusiasm found our own sticks more quietly.

When everybody was settled on a railroad tie, one of the kids called out for a ghost story. Everyone cheered. Mama turned to Mr. Owen.

"Shel, you know some good stories," she said. "Tell one." We all clapped our encouragement.

He shook his head. "Not this year," he said, looking at my mother. "I can't think of any." She looked away.

There was some good-natured booing and more clapping. Then Mr. Owen looked at me. I nodded and mouthed the word *please,* and he smiled, the same sad smile Mama had on her face earlier.

"Okay," he said, sitting back on his haunches and looking into the fire. "This one is about monsters, monsters who look like people, wear people's faces, but are deformed and evil underneath. Kind of a Halloween costume in reverse."

Mr. Owen stared into the fire for a few seconds, frowning. He looked as if he'd forgotten all about the party around him.

"These monsters find families to infiltrate," he continued. "They pick the best husbands and wives and the nicest kids because that's where they find sustenance. They're always hungry, never satisfied. They insert invisible fangs into the lives of the ones they should love the most and feed on that gentleness and love, grinding and devouring it until there isn't anything left. Those families just walk around with nothing inside, empty as the sky. Then they just blow away in the first wind."

One of the smaller children whimpered, "Mommy, that's scary." Mr. Owen glanced up as though surprised to find all of us still there. He stood and kicked a corn husk into the fire.

"You're right," he said. "That's a lousy story. I'm sorry, but I guess I'm just too tired for a good story tonight."

After that, the guests seemed rather subdued, and the party never quite got going again. It broke up early, most of the parents packing up their little ones and saying good night. A few of the older teens and single adults fiddled around with their marshmallow sticks for a while, but even they didn't stay much longer.

Mama and I were the last to leave. She went inside alone to say good night to Mr. Owen, then we headed up the road in the old station wagon. Neither of us said much; it had been a long day, and we were tired. When we got home, the note was still on the kitchen table where I'd left it. I crumpled it up and tossed it into the trash can.

I never saw Daddy again, and Mama threw out the Halloween decorations the next spring when we moved away from Willowsburg. I have my own house now, and my porch light remains off every Halloween night to discourage trick-or-treaters. I keep my door locked tightly to keep out monsters. I don't like remembering that last Halloween party at Mr. Owen's house.

Because then I remember seeing Mama silhouetted against the bonfire, after everybody had gone home. She threw something into the flames that looked a lot like a Panama hat. And I remember that tilled patch of earth behind Mr. Owen's house, and what the police found buried there after I gave them the lighter I dug back out of Mama's pocket. And I hope Mr. Owen forgives me.

John Lutz has been turning out supreme mystery fiction for the past 30 years.
His series characters are Alo Nudger, a lackluster private investigator with a
nervous stomach, and Fred Carver, an ex-cop turned P.I. Of these two
characters, Nudger is by far the most unusual, an unassuming, nonaggressive guy
who somehow manages to solve his cases. Nudger's author must be doing
something right, however, as he was awarded the Edgar Allan Poe Award for the
short story "Ride the Lightning." He has also won the Shamus award twice,
and has appeared in the pages of many mystery magazines.

The Right to Sing
the Blues

John Lutz

"There's this that you need to know about jazz," Fat Jack McGee
told Nudger with a smile. "You don't need to know a thing about it to
enjoy it, and that's all you need to know." He tossed back his huge
head, jowls quivering, and drained the final sip of brandy from his
crystal snifter. "It's feel." He used a white napkin to dab at his lips with
a very fat man's peculiar delicacy. "Jazz is pure feel."

"Does Willy Hollister have the feel?" Nudger asked. He pushed
his plate away, feeling full to the point of being bloated. The only portion of the gourmet lunch Fat Jack had bought him that remained
untouched was the grits.

"Willy Hollister," Fat Jack said, with something like reverence,
"plays ultra-fine piano."

A white-vested waiter appeared like a native from around a potted
palm, carrying chicory coffee on a silver tray, and placed cups before
Nudger and Fat Jack. "Then what's your problem with Hollister?"
Nudger asked, sipping the thick rich brew. He rated it delicious.
"Didn't you hire him to play his best piano at your club?"

"Hey, there's no problem with his music," Fat Jack said. "But first,
Nudger, I gotta know if you can hang around New Orleans till you
can clear up this matter." Fat Jack's tiny pinkish eyes glittered with
mean humor. "For a fat fee, of course."

Nudger knew the fee would be adequate. Fat Jack had a bank account as obese as his body, and he had, in fact, paid Nudger a sizable sum just to travel to New Orleans and sit in the Magnolia Blossom restaurant over lunch and listen while Fat Jack talked. The question Nudger now voiced was: "Why me?"

"Because I know a lady from your fair city." Fat Jack mentioned a name. "She says you're tops at your job; she don't say that about many.

". . . And because of your collection," Fat Jack added. An ebony dribble of coffee dangled in liquid suspension from his triple chin, glittering as he talked. "I hear you collect old jazz records."

"I used to," Nudger said a bit wistfully. "I had Willie the Lion. Duke Ellington and Mary Ann Williams from their Kansas City days."

"How come had?" Fat Jack asked.

"I sold the collection," Nudger said. "To pay the rent one dark month." He gazed beyond green palm fronds, out the window and through filigreed black wrought iron, at the tourists half a block away on Bourbon Street, at the odd combination of French and Spanish architecture and black America and white suits and broiling half-tropical sun that was New Orleans, where jazz lived as in no other place. "Damned rent," he muttered.

"Amen." Fat Jack was kidding not even himself. He hadn't worried about paying the rent in years. The drop of coffee released its grip on his chin, plummeted, and stained his white shirtfront. "So will you stay around town a while?"

Nudger nodded. His social and business calendars weren't exactly booked solid.

"Hey, it's not Hollister himself who worries me," Fat Jack said, "it's Ineida Collins. She's singing at the club now, and if she keeps practicing, someday she'll be mediocre. I'm not digging at her, Nudger; that's an honest assessment."

"Then why did you hire her?"

"Because of David Collins. He owns a lot of the French Quarter. He owns a piece of the highly successful restaurant where we now sit. In every parish in New Orleans, he has more clout than a ton of charge cards. And he's as skinny and ornery as I am fat and nice."

Nudger took another sip of coffee.

"And he asked you to hire Ineida Collins?"

"You're onto it. Ineida is his daughter. She wants to make it as a singer. And she will, if Dad has to buy her a recording studio, at double the fair price. Since David Collins also owns the building my club is in,

I thought I'd acquiesce when his daughter auditioned for a job. And Ineida isn't really so bad that she embarrasses anyone but herself. I call it diplomacy."

"I thought you were calling it trouble," Nudger said. "I thought that was why you hired me."

Fat Jack nodded, ample jowls spilling over his white collar. "So it became," he said. "Hollister, you see, is a handsome young dude, and within the first week Ineida was at the club, he put some moves on her. They became fast friends. They've now progressed beyond mere friendship."

"You figure he's attracted to Dad's money?"

"Nothing like that," Fat Jack said. "When I hired Ineida, David Collins insisted I keep her identity a secret. It was part of the deal. So she sings under the stage name Ineida Mann, which most likely is a gem from her dad's advertising department."

"I still don't see your problem," Nudger said.

"Hollister doesn't set right with me, and I don't know exactly why. I do know that if he messes up Ineida in some way, David Collins will see to it that I'm playing jazz on the Butte-Boise-Anchorage circuit."

"Nice cities," Nudger remarked, "but not jazz towns. I see your problem."

"So find out about Willy Hollister for me," Fat Jack implored. "Check him out, declare him pass or fail, but put my mind at ease either way. That's all I want, an easeful mind."

"Even we tough private eye guys want that," Nudger said.

Fat Jack removed his napkin from his lap and raised a languid plump hand. A waiter who had been born just to respond to that signal scampered over with the check. Fat Jack accepted a tiny ballpoint pen and signed with a ponderous yet elegant flourish. Nudger watched him help himself to a mint. It was like watching the grace and dexterity of an elephant picking up a peanut. Huge as Fat Jack was, he moved as if he weighed no more than ten or twelve pounds.

"I gotta get back, Nudger. Do some paperwork, count some money." He stood up, surprisingly tall in his tan slacks and white linen sport coat. Nudger thought it was a neat coat; he decided he might buy one and wear it winter and summer. "Drop around the club about eight o'clock tonight," Fat Jack said. "I'll fill you in on whatever else you need to know, and I'll show you Willy Hollister and Ineida. Maybe you'll get to hear her sing."

"While she's singing," Nudger said, "maybe we can discuss my fee."

Fat Jack grinned, his vast jowls defying gravity grandly. "Hey, you and me're gonna get along fine." He winked and moved away among the tables, tacking toward the door, dwarfing the other diners.

The waiter refilled Nudger's coffee cup. He sat sipping chicory brew and watching Fat Jack McGee walk down the sunny sidewalk toward Bourbon Street. He sure had a jaunty, bouncy kind of walk for a fat man.

Nudger wasn't as anxious about the fee as Fat Jack thought, though the subject was of more than passing interest. Actually, he had readily taken the case because years ago, at a club in St. Louis, he'd heard Fat Jack McGee play clarinet in the manner that had made him something of a jazz legend, and he'd never forgotten. Real jazz fans are hooked forever.

He needed to hear that clarinet again.

Fat Jack's club was on Dexter, half a block off Bourbon Street. Nudger paused at the entrance and looked up at its red and green neon sign. There was a red neon Fat Jack himself, a portly, herky-jerky, illuminated figure that jumped about with the same seeming lightness and jauntiness as the real Fat Jack.

Trumpet music from inside the club was wafting out almost palpably into the hot humid night. People were coming and going, among them a few obvious tourists, making the Bourbon Street rounds. But Nudger got the impression that most of Fat Jack's customers were folks who took their jazz seriously, and were there for music, not atmosphere.

The trumpet stairstepped up to an admirable high C and wild applause. Nudger went inside and looked around. Dim, smoky, lots of people at lots of tables, men in suits and in jeans and T-shirts, women in long dresses and in casual slacks. The small stage was empty now; the band was between sets. Customers were milling around, stacking up at the bar along one wall. Waitresses in "Fat Jack's" T-shirts were bustling about with trays of drinks. Near the left of the stage was a polished, dark, upright piano that gleamed like a new car even in the dimness. Fat Jack's was everything a jazz club should be, Nudger decided.

Feeling at home, he made his way to the bar and after a five-minute wait ordered a mug of draft beer. The mug was frosted, the beer ice-flecked.

The lights brightened and dimmed three times, apparently a signal the regulars at Fat Jack's understood, for they began a general movement back toward their tables. Then the lights dimmed considerably, and the stage, with its gleaming piano, was suddenly the only illuminated area in the place. A tall, graceful man in his early thirties walked onstage to the kind of scattered but enthusiastic applause that suggests respect and a common bond between performer and audience. The man smiled faintly at the applause and sat down at the piano. He had pained, haughty features, and blond hair that curled above the collar of his black Fat Jack's shirt. The muscles in his bare arms were corded; his hands appeared elegant yet very strong. He was Willy Hollister, the main gig, the one the paying customers had come to hear. The place got quiet, and he began to play.

The song was a variation of "Good Woman Gone Bad," an old number originally written for tenor sax. Hollister played it his way, and two bars into it Nudger knew he was better than good and nothing but bad luck could keep him from being great. He was backed by brass and a snare drum, but he didn't need it; he didn't need a thing in this world but that piano and you could tell it just by looking at the rapt expression on his aristocratic face.

"Didn't I tell you it was all there?" Fat Jack said softly beside Nudger. "Whatever else there is about him, the man can play piano."

Nudger nodded silently. Jazz basically is black music, but the fair, blond Hollister played it with all the soul and pain of its genesis. He finished up the number to riotous applause that quieted only when he swung into another, a blues piece. He sang that one while his hands worked the piano. His voice was as black as his music; in his tone, his inflection, there seemed to dwell centuries of suffering.

"I'm impressed," Nudger said, when the applause for the blues number had died down.

"You and everyone else." Fat Jack was sipping absinthe from a gold-rimmed glass. "Hollister won't be playing here much longer before moving up the show business ladder—not for what I'm paying him, and I'm paying him plenty."

"How did you happen to hire him?"

"He came recommended by a club owner in Chicago. Seems he started out in Cleveland playing small rooms, then moved up to better things in Kansas City, then Rush Street in Chicago. All I had to do was hear him play for five minutes to know I wanted to hire him. It's like catching a Ray Charles or a Garner on the way up."

"So what specifically is there about Hollister that bothers you?" Nudger asked. "Why shouldn't he be seeing Ineida Collins?"

Fat Jack scrunched up his padded features, seeking the word that might convey the thought. "His music is . . . uneven."

"That's hardly a crime," Nudger said, "especially if he can play so well when he's right."

"He ain't as right as I've heard him," Fat Jack said. "Believe me, Hollister can be even better then he was tonight. But it's not really his music that concerns me. Hollister acts strange at times, secretive. Sam Judman, the drummer, went by his apartment last week, found the door unlocked, and let himself in to wait for Hollister to get home. When Hollister discovered him there, he beat him up—with his fists. Can you imagine a piano player like Hollister using his hands for *that?*" Fat Jack looked as if he'd discovered a hair in his drink.

"So he's obsessively secretive. What else?" What am I doing, Nudger asked himself, trying to talk myself out of a job?

But Fat Jack went on. "Hollister has seemed troubled, jumpy and unpredictable, for the last month. He's got problems, and like I told you, if he's seeing Ineida Collins, I got problems. I figure it'd be wise to learn some more about Mr. Hollister."

"The better to know his intentions, as they used to say."

"And in some quarters still say."

The lights did their dimming routine again, the crowd quieted, and Willy Hollister was back at the piano. But this time the center of attention was the tall, dark-haired girl leaning with one hand on the piano, her other hand delicately holding a microphone. Inside her plain navy blue dress was a trim figure. She had nice ankles, a nice smile. Nice was a word that might have been coined for her. A stage name like Ineida Mann didn't fit her at all. She was prom queen and Girl Scouts and PTA and looked as if she'd blush at an off-color joke. But it crossed Nudger's mind that maybe it was simply a role; maybe she was playing for contrast.

Fat Jack knew what Nudger was thinking. "She's as straight and naïve as she looks," he said. "But she'd like to be something else, to learn all about life and love in a few easy lessons."

Someone in the backup band had announced Ineida Mann, and she began to sing, the plaintive lyrics of an old blues standard. She had control but no range. Nudger found himself listening to the backup music, which included a smooth clarinet solo. The band liked Ineida and went all out to envelop her in good sound, but the audience at Fat Jack's was too smart for that. Ineida finished to light applause, bowed prettily, and made her exit. Competent but nothing special, and look-

ing as if she'd just wandered in from suburbia. But this was what she
wanted and her rich father was getting it for her. Parental love could be
as blind as the other kind.

"So how are you going to get started on this thing?" Fat Jack
asked. "You want me to introduce you to Hollister and Ineida?"

"Usually I begin a case by discussing my fee and signing a contract," Nudger said.

Fat Jack waved an immaculately manicured, ring-adorned
hand. "Don't worry about the fee," he said. "Hey, let's make it whatever you usually charge plus twenty percent plus expenses. Trust me
on that."

That sounded fine to Nudger, all except the trusting part. He
reached into his inside coat pocket, withdrew his roll of antacid tablets,
thumbed back the aluminum foil, and popped one of the white disks
into his mouth, all in one practiced, smooth motion.

"What's that stuff for?" Fat Jack asked.

"Nervous stomach," Nudger explained.

"You oughta try this," Fat Jack said, nodding toward his absinthe.
"Eventually it eliminates the stomach altogether."

Nudger winced. "I want to talk with Ineida," he said, "but it
would be best if we had our conversation away from the club."

Fat Jack pursed his lips and nodded. "I can give you her address.
She doesn't live at home with her father; she's in a little apartment over
on Beulah Street. It's all part of the making-it-on-her-own illusion.
Anything else?"

"Maybe. Do you still play the clarinet?"

Fat Jack cocked his head and looked curiously at Nudger, one tiny
eye squinting through the tobacco smoke that hazed the air around the
bar. "Now and again, but only on special occasions."

"Why don't we make the price of this job my usual fee plus only
ten percent plus you do a set with the clarinet this Saturday night?"

Fat Jack beamed, then threw back his head and let out a roaring
laugh that turned heads and seemed to shake the bottles on the back
bar. "Agreed! You're a find, Nudger! First you trust me to pay you
without a contract, then you lower your fee and ask for a clarinet solo
instead of money. There's no place you can spend a clarinet solo! Hey,
I like you, but you're not much of a businessman."

Nudger smiled and sipped his beer. Fat Jack hadn't bothered
to find out the amount of Nudger's usual fee, so all this talk about
percentages meant nothing. If detectives weren't good businessmen,

neither were jazz musicians. He handed Fat Jack a pen and a club matchbook. "How about that address?"

Beulah Street was narrow and crooked, lined with low houses of French-Spanish architecture, an array of arches, pastel stucco, and ornamental wrought iron. The houses had long ago been divided into apartments, each with a separate entrance. Behind each apartment was a small courtyard.

Nudger found Ineida Collins' address. It belonged to a pale yellow structure with a weathered tile roof and a riot of multicolored bougainvillea blooming wild halfway up one cracked and often-patched stucco wall.

He glanced at his wristwatch. Ten o'clock. If Ineida wasn't awake by now, he decided, she should be. He stepped up onto the small red brick front porch and worked the lion's head knocker on a plank door supported by huge black iron hinges.

Ineida came to the door without delay. She didn't appear at all sleepy after her late-night stint at Fat Jack's. Her dark hair was tied back in a French braid. She was wearing slacks and a peach-colored silky blouse. Even the harsh sunlight was kind to her; she looked young, as inexperienced and naive as Fat Jack said she was.

Nudger told her he was a writer doing a piece on Fat Jack's club. "I heard you sing last night," he said. "It really was something to see. I thought it might be a good idea if we talked."

It was impossible for her to turn down what in her mind was a celebrity interview. She lit up bright enough to pale the sunlight and invited Nudger inside.

Her apartment was tastefully but inexpensively furnished. There was an imitation Oriental rug on the hardwood floor, lots of rattan furniture, a Casablanca overhead fan rotating its wide flat blades slowly and casting soothing, flickering shadows. Through sheer beige curtains the apartment's courtyard was visible, well tended and colorful.

"Can I get you a cup of coffee, Mr. Nudger?" Ineida asked.

Nudger told her thanks, watched the switch of her trim hips as she walked into the small kitchen. From where he sat he could see a Mr. Coffee brewer on the sink, its glass pot half full. Ineida poured, returned with two mugs of coffee.

"How old are you, Ineida?" he asked.

"Twenty-three."

"Then you haven't been singing for all that many years."

She sat down, placed her steaming coffee mug on a coaster. "About five, actually. I sang in school productions, then studied for a while in New York. I've been singing at Fat Jack's for about two months. I love it."

"The crowd there seems to like you," Nudger lied. He watched her smile and figured the lie was a worthy one. He pretended to take notes while he asked her a string of writer-like questions, pumping up her ego. It was an ego that would inflate only so far. Nudger decided that he liked Ineida Collins and hoped she would hurry up and realize she wasn't Ineida Mann.

"I'm told that you and Will Hollister are pretty good friends."

Her mood changed abruptly. Suspicion shone in her dark eyes, and the youthful smiling mouth became taut and suddenly ten years older.

"You're not a magazine writer," she said, in a betrayed voice.

Nudger's stomach gave a mule-like kick. "No, I'm not," he admitted.

"Then who are you?"

"Someone concerned about your wellbeing." Antacid time. He popped one of the white tablets into his mouth and chewed.

"Father sent you."

"No," Nudger said.

"Liar,"she told him. "Get out."

"I'd like to talk with you about Willy Hollister," Nudger persisted. In his business persistence paid, one way or the other. He could only hope it wouldn't be the other.

"Get out," Ineida repeated. "Or I'll call the police."

Within half a minute Nudger was outside again on Beulah Street, looking at the uncompromising barrier of Ineida's closed door. Apparently she was touchy on the subject of Willy Hollister. Nudger slipped another antacid between his lips, turned his back to the warming sun, and began walking.

He'd gone half a block when he realized that he was casting three shadows. He stopped. The middle shadow stopped also, but the larger shadows on either side kept advancing. The large bodies that cast those shadows were suddenly standing in front of Nudger, and two very big men were staring down at him. One was smiling, one wasn't. Considering the kind of smile it was, that didn't make much difference.

"We noticed you talking to Miss Mann," the one on the left said. He had wide cheekbones, dark, pockmarked skin, and gray eyes that gave no quarter. "Whatever you said seemed to upset her." His accent was a cross between a southern drawl and clipped French. Nudger recognized it as Cajun. The Cajuns were a tough, predominantly French people who had settled southern Louisiana but never themselves.

Nudger let himself hope and started to walk on. The second man, who was shorter but had a massive neck and shoulders, shuffled forward like a heavyweight boxer, to block his way. Nudger swallowed his antacid tablet.

"You nervous, friend?" the boxer asked in the same rich Cajun accent.

"Habitually."

Pockmarked said, "We have an interest in Miss Mann's welfare. What were you talking to her about?"

"The conversation was private. Do you two fellows mind introducing yourselves?"

"We mind," the boxer said. He was smiling again, nastily. Nudger noticed that the tip of his right eyebrow had turned white where it was crossed by a thin scar.

"Then I'm sorry, but we have nothing to talk about."

Pockmarked shook his head patiently in disagreement. "We have this to talk about, my friend. There are parts of this great state of Looziahna that are vast swampland. Not far from where we stand, the bayou is wild. It's the home of a surprising number of alligators. People go into the bayou, and some of them never come out. Who knows about them? After a while, who cares?" The cold gray eyes had diamond chips in them. "You understand my meaning?"

Nudger nodded. He understood. His stomach understood.

"I think we've made ourselves clear," the boxer said. "We aren't nice men, sir. It's our business not to be nice, and it's our pleasure. So a man like yourself, sir, a reasonable man in good health, should listen to us and stay away from Miss Mann."

"You mean Miss Collins."

"I mean Miss Ineida Mann." He said it with the straight face of a true professional.

"Why don't you tell Willy Hollister to stay away from her?" Nudger asked.

"Mr. Hollister is a nice young man of Miss Mann's own choosing," Pockmarked said with an odd courtliness. "You she obviously doesn't like. You upset her. That upsets us."

"And me and Frick don't like to be upset," the boxer said. He closed a powerful hand on the lapel of Nudger's sport jacket, not pushing or pulling in the slightest, merely squeezing the material. Nudger could feel the vibrant force of the man's strength as if it were electrical current. "Behave yourself," the boxer hissed through his fixed smile.

He abruptly released his grip, and both men turned and walked away.

Nudger looked down at his abused lapel. It was as crimped as if it had been wrinkled in a vise for days. He wondered if the dry cleaners could do anything about it when they pressed the coat.

Then he realized he was shaking. He loathed danger and had no taste for violence. He needed another antacid tablet and then, even though it was early, a drink.

New Orleans was turning out to be an exciting city, but not in the way the travel agencies and the chamber of commerce advertised.

"You're no jazz writer," Willy Hollister said to Nudger, in a small back room of Fat Jack's club. It wasn't exactly a dressing room, though at times it served as such. It was a sort of all-purpose place where quick costume changes were made and breaks were taken between sets. The room's pale green paint was faded and peeling, and a steam pipe jutted from floor to ceiling against one wall. Yellowed show posters featuring jazz greats were taped here and there behind the odd assortment of worn furniture. There were mingled scents of stale booze and tobacco smoke.

"But I *am* a jazz fan," Nudger said. "Enough of one to know how good you are, and that you play piano in a way that wasn't self-taught." He smiled. "I'll bet you even read music."

"You have to read music," Hollister said rather haughtily, "to graduate from Juilliard."

Even Nudger knew that Juilliard graduates weren't slouches. "So you have a classical background," he said.

"That's nothing rare; lots of jazz musicians have classical roots."

Nudger studied Hollister as the pianist spoke. Offstage, Hollister appeared older. His blond hair was thinning on top and his features were losing their boyishness, becoming craggy. His complexion was an unhealthy yellowish hue. He was a hunter, was this boy. Life's sad wisdom was in his eyes, resting on its haunches and ready to spring.

"How well do you know Ineida Mann?" Nudger asked.

"Well enough to know you've been bothering her," Hollister replied, with a bored yet wary expression. "We don't know what your angle is, but I suggest you stop. Don't bother trying to get any information out of me, either."

"I'm interested in jazz," Nudger said.

"Among other things."

"Like most people, I have more than one interest."

"Not like me, though," Hollister said. "My only interest is my music."

"What about Miss Mann?"

"That's none of your business." Hollister stood up, neatly but ineffectively snubbed out the cigarette he'd been smoking, and seemed to relish leaving it to smolder to death in the ashtray. "I've got a number coming up in a few minutes." He tucked in his Fat Jack's T-shirt and looked severe. "I don't particularly want to see you any more, Nudger. Whoever, whatever you are, it doesn't mean burned grits to me as long as you leave Ineida alone."

"Before you leave," Nudger said, "can I have your autograph?"

Incredibly, far from being insulted by this sarcasm, Hollister scrawled his signature on a nearby folded newspaper and tossed it to him. Nudger took that as a measure of the man's artistic ego, and despite himself he was impressed. All the ingredients of greatness resided in Willy Hollister, along with something else.

Nudger went back out into the club proper. He peered through the throng of jazz lovers and saw Fat Jack leaning against the bar. As Nudger was making his way across the dim room toward him, he spotted Ineida at one of the tables. She was wearing a green sequined blouse that set off her dark hair and eyes, and Nudger regretted that she couldn't sing as well as she looked. She glanced at him, recognized him, and quickly turned away to listen to a graying, bearded man who was one of her party.

"Hey, Nudger," Fat Jack said, when Nudger had reached the bar, "you sure you know what you're doing, old sleuth? You ain't exactly pussy-footing. Ineida asked me about you, said you'd bothered her at home. *Hollister* asked me who you were. The precinct captain asked me the same question."

Nudger's stomach tightened. "A New Orleans police captain?"

Fat Jack nodded. "Captain Marrivale." He smiled broad and bold, took a sip of absinthe. "You make ripples big enough to swamp boats."

"What I'd like to do now," Nudger said, "is take a short trip."

"Lots of folks would like for you to do that."

"I need to go to Cleveland, Kansas City, and Chicago," Nudger said. "A couple of days in each city. I've got to find out more about Willy Hollister. Are you willing to pick up the tab?"

"I don't suppose you could get this information with long-distance phone calls?"

"Not and get it right."

"When do you plan on leaving?"

"As soon as I can. Tonight."

Fat Jack nodded. He produced an alligator-covered checkbook, scribbled in it, tore out a check, and handed it to Nudger. Nudger couldn't make out the amount in the faint light. "If you need more, let me know," Fat Jack said. His smile was luminous in the dimness. "Hey, make it a fast trip, Nudger."

A week later Nudger was back in New Orleans, sitting across from Fat Jack McGee in the club owner's second floor office. "There's a pattern," he said, "sometimes subtle, sometimes strong, but always there, like in a forties Ellington piece."

"So tell me about it," Fat Jack said. "I'm an Ellington fan."

"I did some research," Nudger said, "read some old reviews, went to clubs and musicians' union halls and talked to people in the jazz communities where Willy Hollister played. He always started strong, but his musical career was checkered with flat spots, lapses. During those times, Hollister was just an ordinary performer."

Fat Jack appeared concerned, tucked his chin back into folds of flesh, and said, "That explains why he's falling off here."

"But the man is still making great music," Nudger said.

"Slipping from great to good," Fat Jack said. "Good jazz artists in New Orleans I can hire by the barrelful."

"There's something else about Willy Hollister," Nudger said. "Something that nobody picked up on because it spanned several years and three cities."

Fat Jack looked interested. If his ears hadn't been almost enveloped by overblown flesh, they would have perked up.

"Hollister had a steady girlfriend in each of these cities. All three women disappeared. Two were rumored to have left town on their own, but nobody knows where they went. The girlfriend in Cleveland, the first one, simply disappeared. She's still on the missing persons list."

"Whoo boy!" Fat Jack said. He began to sweat. He pulled a white handkerchief the size of a flag from the pocket of his sport jacket and mopped his brow, just like Satchmo but without the grin and trumpet.

"Sorry," Nudger said. "I didn't mean to make you uncomfortable."

"You're doing your job, is all," Fat Jack assured him. "But that's bad information to lay on me. You think Hollister had anything to do with the disappearances?"

Nudger shrugged. "Maybe the women themselves, and not Hollister, had to do with it. They were all the sort that traveled light and often. Maybe they left town of their own accord. Maybe for some reason they felt they had to get away from Hollister."

"I wish Ineida would want to get away from him," Fat Jack muttered. "But Jeez, not like that. Her old man'd boil me down for axle grease. But then she's not cut from the same mold as those other girls; she's not what she's trying to be and she's strictly local."

"The only thing she and those other women have in common is Willy Hollister."

Fat Jack leaned back, and the desk chair creaked in protest. Nudger, who had been hired to solve a problem, had so far only brought to light the seriousness of that problem. The big man didn't have to ask "What now?" It was written in capital letters on his face.

"You could fire Willy Hollister," Nudger said.

Fat Jack shook his head. "Ineida would follow him, maybe get mad at me and sic her dad on the club."

"And Hollister is still packing customers into the club every night."

"That, too," Fat Jack admitted. Even the loosest businessman could see the profit in Willy Hollister's genius. "For now," he said, "we'll let things slide while you continue to watch." He dabbed at his forehead again with the wadded handkerchief.

"Hollister doesn't know who I am," Nudger said, "but he knows who I'm not and he's worried. My presence might keep him aboveboard for a while."

"Fine, as long as a change of scenery isn't involved. I can't afford to have her wind up like those other women, Nudger."

"Speaking of winding up," Nudger said, "do you know anything about a couple of muscular robots? One has a scar across his right eyebrow and a face like an ex-pug's. His partner has a dark mustache, sniper's eyes, and is named Frick. Possibly the other is Frack. They both talk with thick Cajun accents."

Fat Jack raised his eyebrows. "Rocko Boudreau and Dwayne Frick," he said, with soft, terror-inspired awe. "They work for David Collins."

"I figured they did. They warned me to stay away from Ineida." Nudger felt his intestines twist into advanced Boy Scout knots. He got out his antacid tablets. "They suggested I might take up postmortem residence in the swamp." As he recalled his conversation with Frick and Frack, Nudger again felt a dark near-panic well up in him. Maybe it was because he was here in this small office with the huge and terrified Fat Jack McGee; maybe fear actually was contagious. He offered Fat Jack an antacid tablet.

Fat Jack accepted.

"I'm sure their job is to look after Ineida without her knowing it," Nudger said. "Incidentally, they seem to approve of her seeing Willy Hollister."

"That won't help me if anything happens to Ineida that's in any way connected to the club," Fat Jack said.

Nudger stood up. He was tired. His back still ached from sitting in an airline seat that wouldn't recline, and his stomach was still busy trying to digest itself. "I'll phone you if I hear any more good news."

Fat Jack mumbled something unintelligible and nodded, lost in his own dark apprehensions, a ponderous man grappling with ponderous problems. One of his inflated hands floated up in a parting gesture as Nudger left the stifling office. What he hadn't told Fat Jack was that immediately after each woman had disappeared, Hollister had regained his tragic, soulful touch on the piano.

When Nudger got back to his hotel, he was surprised to open the door to his room and see a man sitting in a chair by the window. It was the big blue armchair that belonged near the door.

When Nudger entered, the man turned as if resenting the interruption, as if it were his room and Nudger the interloper. He stood up and smoothed his light tan suit coat. He was a smallish man with a triangular face and very springy red hair that grew in a sharp widow's peak. His eyes were dark and intense. He resembled a fox. With a quick and graceful motion he put a paw into a pocket for a wallet-sized leather folder, flipped it open to reveal a badge.

"Police Captain Marrivale, I presume," Nudger said. He shut the door.

The redheaded man nodded and replaced his badge in his pocket. "I'm Fred Marrivale," he confirmed. "I heard you were back in town.

I think we should talk." He shoved the armchair around to face the room instead of the window and sat back down, as familiar as old shoes.

Nudger pulled out the small wooden desk chair and also sat, facing Marrivale. "Are you here on official business, Captain Marrivale?"

Marrivale smiled. He had tiny sharp teeth behind thin lips. "You know how it is, Nudger, a cop is always a cop."

"Sure. And that's the way it is when we go private," Nudger told him. "A confidential investigator is always that, no matter where he is or whom he's talking to."

"Which is kinda why I'm here," Marrivale said. "It might be better if you were someplace else."

Nudger was incredulous. His nervous stomach believed what he'd just heard, but he didn't. "You're actually telling me to get out of town?"

Marrivale gave a kind of laugh, but there was no glint of amusement in his sharp eyes. "I'm not authorized to *tell* anybody to get out of town, Nudger. I'm not the sheriff and this isn't Dodge City."

"I'm glad you realize that," Nudger told him, "because I can't leave yet. I've got business here."

"I know about your business."

"Did David Collins send you to talk to me?"

Marrivale had a good face for policework; there was only the slightest change of expression. "We can let that question go by," he said, "and I'll ask you one. Why did Fat Jack McGee hire you?"

"Have you asked him?"

"No."

"He'd rather I kept his reasons confidential," Nudger said.

"You don't have a Louisiana P.I. license," Marrivale pointed out.

Nudger smiled. "I know. Nothing to be revoked."

"There are consequences a lot more serious than having your investigator's license pulled, Nudger. Mr. Collins would prefer that you stay away from Ineida Mann."

"You mean Ineida Collins."

"I mean what I say."

"David Collins already had someone deliver that message to me."

"It's not a message from anyone but me," Marrivale said. "I'm telling you this because I'm concerned about your safety while you're within my jurisdiction. It's part of my job."

Nudger kept a straight face, got up and walked to the door, and opened it. He said, "I appreciate your concern, captain. Right now I've got things to do."

Marrivale smiled with his mean little mouth. He didn't seem rattled by Nudger's impolite invitation to leave; he'd said what needed saying. He got up out of the armchair and adjusted his suit. Nudger noticed that the suit hung on him just right and must have been tailored and expensive. No cop's-salary, J.C. Penney wardrobe for Marrivale.

As he walked past Nudger, Marrivale paused and said, "It'd behoove you to learn to discern friend from enemy, Nudger." He went out and trod lightly down the hall toward the elevators, not looking back.

Nudger shut and locked the door. Then he went over to the bed, removed his shoes, and stretched out on his back on the mattress, his fingers laced behind his head. He studied the faint water stains on the ceiling in the corner above him. They were covered by a thin film of mold. That reminded Nudger of the bayou.

He had to admit that Marrivale had left him with solid parting advice.

Though plenty of interested parties had warned Nudger to stay away from Ineida Collins, everyone seemed to have neglected to tell him to give a wide berth to Willy Hollister. And after breakfast, it was Hollister who claimed Nudger's interest.

Hollister lived on St. François, within a few blocks of Ineida Collins's apartment. Their apartments were similar. Hollister's was the end unit of a low tan stucco building that sat almost flush with the sidewalk. What yard there was had to be in the rear. Through the low branches of a huge magnolia tree, Nudger saw some of the raw cedar fencing that sectioned the back premises into private courtyards.

Hollister might be home, sleeping after his late-night gig at Fat Jack's. But whether he was home or not, Nudger decided that his next move would be to knock on Hollister's door.

He rapped on the wooden door three times, causally leaned toward it and listened. He heard no sound from inside. No one in the street seemed to be paying much attention to him, so after a few minutes Nudger idly gave the doorknob a twist.

It rotated all the way, clicked. The door opened about six inches. Nudger pushed the door open farther and stepped quietly inside.

The apartment no doubt came furnished. The furniture was old but not too worn; some of it probably had antique value. The floor was dull hardwood where it showed around the borders of a faded blue carpet. From where he stood, Nudger could see into the bedroom. The bed was unmade but empty.

The living room was dim. The wooden shutters on its windows were closed, allowing slanted light to come in through narrow slits. Most of the illumination in the room came from the bedroom and a short hall that led to a bathroom, then to a small kitchen and sliding glass doors that opened to the courtyard.

To make sure he was alone, Nudger called, "Mr. Hollister? Avon lady!"

No answer. Fine.

Nudger looked around the living room for a few minutes, examining the contents of drawers, picking up some sealed mail that turned out to be an insurance pitch and a utility bill.

He had just entered the bedroom when he heard a sound from outside the curtained window, open about six inches. It was a dull thunking sound that Nudger thought he recognized. He went to the window, parted the breeze-swayed gauzy white curtains, and bent low to peer outside.

The window looked out on the courtyard. What Nudger saw confirmed his guess about the sound. A shovel knifing into soft earth. Willy Hollister was in the courtyard garden, digging. Nudger crouched down so he could see better.

Hollister was planting rosebushes. They were young plants, but they already had red and white roses on them. Hollister had started on the left with the red roses and was alternating colors. He was planting half a dozen bushes and was working on the fifth plant, which lay with its roots wrapped in burlap beside the waiting, freshly dug hole.

Hollister was on both knees on the ground, using his hands to scoop some dirt back into the hole. He was forming a small dome over which to spread the rosebush's soon-to-be-exposed roots. He knew how to plant rosebushes, all right, and he was trying to ensure that these would live.

Nudger's stomach went into a series of spasms as Hollister stood and glanced at the apartment as if he had sensed someone's presence. He drew one of the rolled-up sleeves of his white dress shirt across his perspiring forehead. For a few seconds he seemed to debate about whether to return to the apartment. Then he turned, picked up the shovel, and began digging the sixth and final hole.

Letting out a long breath, Nudger drew back from the open window and stood up straight. He'd go out by the front door and then walk around to the courtyard and call Hollister's name, as if he'd just arrived. He wanted to get Hollister's own version of his past.

As Nudger was leaving the bedroom, he noticed a stack of pale blue envelopes on the dresser, beside a comb and brush set monogrammed with Hollister's initials. The envelopes were held together by a fat rubber band. Nudger saw Hollister's address, saw the Beulah Street return address penned neatly in black ink in a corner of the top envelope. He paused for just a few seconds, picked up the envelopes, and slipped them into his pocket. Then he left Hollister's apartment the same way he'd entered.

There was no point in talking to Hollister now. It would be foolish to place himself in the apartment at the approximate time of the disappearance of the stack of letters written by Ineida Collins.

Nudger walked up St. François for several blocks, then took a cab to his hotel. Though the morning hadn't yet heated up, the cab's air conditioner was on high and the interior was near freezing. The letters seemed to grow heavier and heavier in Nudger's jacket pocket, and to glow with a kind of warmth that gave no comfort.

Nudger had room service bring up a plain omelet and a glass of milk. He sat with his early lunch, his customary meal (it had a soothing effect on a nervous stomach), at the desk in his hotel room and ate slowly as he read Ineida Collins's letters to Hollister. He understood now why they had felt warm in his pocket. The love affair was, from Ineida's point of view at least, as soaring and serious as such an affair can get. Nudger felt cheapened by his crass invasion of Ineida's privacy. These were thoughts meant to be shared by no one but the two of them, thoughts not meant to be tramped through by a middle-aged detective not under the spell of love.

On the other hand, Nudger told himself, there was no way for him to know what the letters contained *until* he read them and determined that he shouldn't have. This was the sort of professional quandary he got himself into frequently but never got used to.

The last letter, the one with the latest postmark, was the most revealing and made the tacky side of Nudger's profession seem worthwhile. Ineida Collins was planning to run away with Willy Hollister; he had told her he loved her and that they would be married. Then, after the fact, they would return to New Orleans and inform friends and relatives of the blessed reunion. It all seemed quaint, Nudger thought, and not very believable unless you happened to be twenty-three and love-struck and had lived Ineida Collins's sheltered existence.

Ineida also referred in the last letter to something important she had to tell Hollister. Nudger could guess what that important bit of information was. That she was Ineida Collins and she was David Collins's daughter and she was rich, and that she was oh so glad that Hollister hadn't known about her until that moment. Because that meant he wanted her for her own true self alone. Ah, love! It made Nudger's business go round.

Nudger refolded the letter, replaced it in its envelope, and dropped it onto the desk. He tried to finish his omelet but couldn't. He wasn't really hungry, and his stomach had reached a tolerable level of comfort. He knew it was time to report to Fat Jack. After all, the man had hired him to uncover information, but not so Nudger would keep it to himself.

Nudger slid the rubber band back around the stack of letters, snapped it, and stood up. He considered having the letters placed in the hotel safe, but the security of any hotel safe was questionable. A paper napkin bearing the hotel logo lay next to his half-eaten omelet. He wrapped the envelopes in the napkin and dropped the bundle in the wastebasket by the desk. The maid wasn't due back in the room until tomorrow morning, and it wasn't likely that anyone would think Nudger would throw away such important letters. And the sort of person who would bother to search a wastebasket would search everywhere else and find the letters anyway.

He placed the tray with his dishes on it in the hall outside his door, hung the "Do Not Disturb" sign on the knob, and left to see Fat Jack McGee.

They told Nudger at the club that Fat Jack was out. Nobody was sure when he'd be back; he might not return until this evening when business started picking up, or he might have just strolled over to the Magnolia Blossom for a croissant and coffee and would be back any minute.

Nudger sat at the end of the bar, nursing a beer he didn't really want, and waited.

After an hour, the bartender began blatantly staring at him from time to time. Mid-afternoon or not, Nudger was occupying a bar stool and had an obligation. And maybe the man was right. Nudger was about to give in to the weighty responsibility of earning his place at the bar by ordering another drink he didn't want when Fat Jack appeared through the dimness like a light-footed, obese spirit in a white vested suit.

He saw Nudger, smiled his fat man's beaming smile, and veered toward him, diamond rings and gold jewelry flashing fire beneath pale coat sleeves. There was even a large diamond stickpin in his bib-like tie. He was a vision of sartorial immensity.

"We need to talk," Nudger told him.

"That's easy enough," Fat Jack said. "My office, hey?" He led the way, making Nudger feel somewhat like a pilot fish trailing a whale.

When they were settled in Fat Jack's office, Nudger said, "I came across some letters that Ineida wrote to Hollister. She and Hollister plan to run away together, get married."

Fat Jack raised his eyebrows so high Nudger was afraid they might become detached. "Hollister ain't the marrying kind, Nudger."

"What kind is he?"

"I don't want to answer that."

"Maybe Ineida and Hollister will elope and live happily—"

"Stop!" Fat Jack interrupted him. He leaned forward, wide forehead glistening. "When are they planning on leaving?"

"I don't know. The letter didn't say."

"You gotta find out, Nudger!"

"I could ask. But, Captain Marrivale wouldn't approve."

"Marrivale has talked with you?"

"In my hotel room. He assured me he had my best interests at heart."

Fat Jack appeared thoughtful. He swiveled in his chair and switched on the auxiliary window air conditioner. Its breeze stirred the papers on the desk, ruffled Fat Jack's graying, gingery hair.

The telephone rang. Fat Jack picked it up, identified himself. His face went as white as his suit. "Yes, sir," he said. His jowls began to quiver; loose flesh beneath his left eye started to dance. Nudger was getting nervous just looking at him. "You can't mean it," Fat Jack said. "Hey, maybe it's a joke. Okay, it ain't a joke." He listened a while longer and then said, "Yes, sir," again and hung up. He didn't say anything else for a long time. Nudger didn't say anything either.

Fat Jack spoke first. "That was David Collins. Ineida's gone. Not home, bed hasn't been slept in."

"Then she and Hollister have left as they planned."

"You mean as Hollister planned. Collins got a note in the mail."

"Note?" Nudger asked. His stomach did a flip; it was way ahead of his brain, reacting to a suspicion not yet fully formed.

"A ransom note," Fat Jack confirmed. "Unsigned, in cutout newspaper words. Collins said Marrivale is on his way over here now to talk to me about Hollister. Hollister's disappeared, too. And his clothes are missing from his closet." Fat Jack's little pink eyes were bulging in his blanched face. "I better not tell Marrivale about the letters."

"Not unless he asks," Nudger said. "And he won't." He stood up.

"Where are you going?"

"I'm leaving," Nudger said, "before Marrivale gets here. There's no sense in making this easy for him."

"Or difficult for you."

"It works out that way, for a change."

Fat Jack nodded, his eyes unfocused yet thoughtful, already rehearsing in his mind the lines he would use on Marrivale. He wasn't a man to bow easily or gracefully to trouble, and he had seen plenty of trouble in his life. He knew a multitude of moves and would use them all.

He didn't seem to notice when Nudger left.

Hollister's apartment was shuttered, and the day's mail delivery sprouted like a white bouquet from the mailbox next to his door. Nudger doubted that David Collins had officially notified the police; his first, his safest, step would be to seek the personal help of Captain Marrivale, who was probably on the Collins payroll already. So it was unlikely that Hollister's apartment was under surveillance, unless by Frick and Frack, who, like Marrivale, probably knew about Ineida's disappearance.

Nudger walked unhesitatingly up to the front door and tried the knob. The door was locked this time. He walked around the corner, toward the back of the building, and unhitched the loop of rope that held shut the high wooden gate to the courtyard.

In the privacy of the fenced courtyard, Nudger quickly forced the sliding glass doors and entered Hollister's apartment.

The place seemed almost exactly as Nudger had left it earlier that day. The matched comb and brush set was still on the dresser, though in a different position. Nudger checked the dresser drawers. They held only a few pairs of undershorts, a wadded dirty shirt, and some socks with holes in the toes. He crossed the bedroom and opened the closet door. The closet's blank back wall stared out at him. Empty. The apartment's kitchen was only lightly stocked with food; the refrigerator held a stick of butter, half a gallon of milk, various half-used condiments, and three cans of beer. It was dirty and needed defrosting. Hollister had been a lousy housekeeper.

The rest of the apartment seemed oddly quiet and in vague disorder, as if getting used to its new state of vacancy. There was definitely a deserted air about the place that suggested its occupant had shunned it and left in a hurry.

Nudger decided that there was nothing to learn here. No matchbooks with messages written inside them, no hastily scrawled, forgotten addresses or revealing ticket stubs. He never got the help that fictional detectives got—well, almost never—though it was always worth seeking.

As he was about to open the courtyard gate and step back into the street, Nudger paused. He stood still, feeling a cold stab of apprehension, of dread knowledge, in the pit of his stomach.

He was staring at the rosebushes that Hollister had planted that morning. At the end of the garden were two newly planted bushes bearing red rosebuds. Hollister hadn't planted them that way. He had alternated the bushes by color, one red one white. Their order now was white, red, white, white, red, red.

Which meant that the bushes had been dug up. Replanted.

Nudger walked to the row of rosebushes. The earth around them was loose, as it had been earlier, but now it seemed more sloppily spread about, and one of the bushes was leaning at an angle. Not the work of a methodical gardener; more the work of someone in a hurry.

As he backed away from the freshly turned soil, Nudger's legs came in contact with a small wrought iron bench. He sat down. He thought for a while, oblivious of the warm sunshine, the colorful geraniums and bougainvillea. He became aware of the frantic chirping of birds on their lifelong hunt for sustenance, of the soft yet vibrant buzzing of insects. Sounds of life, sounds of death. He stood up and got out of there fast, his stomach churning.

When he returned to his hotel room, Nudger found on the floor by the desk the napkin that had been wadded in the bottom of the wastebasket. He checked the wastebasket, but it was only a gesture to confirm what he already knew. The letters that Ineida Collins had written to Willy Hollister were gone.

Fat Jack was in his office. Marrivale had come and gone hours ago.

Nudger sat down across the desk from Fat Jack and looked appraisingly at the harried club owner. Fat Jack appeared wrung out by worry. The Marrivale visit had taken a lot out of him. Or maybe he'd had another conversation with David Collins. Whatever his problems, Nudger knew that, to paraphrase the great Al Jolson, Fat Jack hadn't seen nothin' yet.

"David Collins just phoned," Fat Jack said. He was visibly uncomfortable, a veritable Niagara of nervous perspiration. "He got a call from the kidnappers. They want half a million in cash by tomorrow night, or Ineida starts being delivered in the mail piece by piece."

Nudger wasn't surprised. He knew where the phone call had originated.

"When I was looking into Hollister's past," he said to Fat Jack, "I happened to discover something that seemed ordinary enough then, but now has gotten kind of interesting." He watched the perspiration flow down Fat Jack's wide forehead.

"So I'm interested," Fat Jack said irritably. He reached behind him and slapped at the air conditioner, as if to coax more cold air despite the frigid thermostat setting.

"There's something about being a fat man, a man as large as you. After a while he takes his size for granted, accepts it as a normal fact of his life. But other people don't. A really fat man is more memorable than he realizes, especially if he's called Fat Jack."

Fat Jack drew his head back into fleshy folds and shot a tortured, wary look at Nudger. "Hey, what are you talking toward, old sleuth?"

"You had a series of failed clubs in the cities where Willy Hollister played his music, and you were there at the times when Hollister's women disappeared."

"That ain't unusual, Nudger. Jazz is a tight little world."

"I said people remember you," Nudger told him. "And they remember you knowing Willy Hollister. But you told me you saw him for the first time when he came here to play in your club. And when I went to see Ineida for the first time, she knew my name. She bought the idea that I was a magazine writer; it fell right into place and it took her a while to get uncooperative. Then she assumed I was working for her father—as you knew she would."

Fat Jack stood halfway up, then decided he hadn't the energy for the total effort and sat back down in his groaning chair. "You missed a beat, Nudger. Are you saying I'm in on this kidnapping with Hollister? If that's true, why would I have hired you?"

"You needed someone like me to substantiate Hollister's involvement with Ineida, to find out about Hollister's missing women. It would help you to set him up. You knew him better than you pretended. You knew that he murdered those three women to add some insane, tragic dimension to his music—the sound that made him great. You knew what he had planned for Ineida."

"He didn't even know who she really was!" Fat Jack sputtered.

"But you knew from the time you hired her that she was David Collins's daughter. You schemed from the beginning to use Hollister as the fall guy in your kidnapping plan."

"Hollister is a killer—you said so yourself. I wouldn't want to get involved in any kind of scam with him."

"He didn't know you were involved," Nudger explained. "When you'd used me to make it clear that Hollister was the natural suspect, you kidnapped Ineida and demanded the ransom, figuring Hollister's past and his disappearance would divert the law's attention away from you."

Fat Jack's wide face was a study in agitation, but it was relatively calm compared to what must have been going on inside his head. His body was squirming uncontrollably, and the pain in his eyes was difficult to look into. He didn't want to ask the question, but he had to and he knew it. "If all this is true," he moaned, "where is Hollister?"

"I did a little digging in his garden," Nudger said. "He's under his roses, where he thought Ineida was going to wind up, but where you had space for him reserved all along."

Fat Jack's head dropped. His suit suddenly seemed to get two sizes too large. As his body trembled, tears joined the perspiration on his quivering cheeks. "When did you know?" he asked.

"When I got back to my hotel and found the letters from Ineida to Hollister missing. You were the only one other than myself who knew about them." Nudger leaned over the desk to look Fat Jack in the eye. "Where is Ineida?" he asked.

"She's still alive," was Fat Jack's only answer. Crushed as he was, he was still too wily to reveal his hole card. It was as if his fat were a kind of rubber, lending inexhaustible resilience to body and mind.

"It's negotiation time," Nudger told him, "and we don't have very long to reach an agreement. While we're sitting here talking, the police are digging in the dirt I replaced in Hollister's garden."

"You called them?"

"I did. But right now, they expect to find Ineida. When they find Hollister, they'll put all the pieces together the way I did and get the same puzzle-picture of you."

Fat Jack nodded sadly, seeing the truth in that prognosis. "So what's your proposition?"

"You release Ineida, and I keep quiet until tomorrow morning. That'll give you a reasonable head start on the law. The police don't know who phoned them about the body in Hollister's garden, so I can stall them for at least that long without arousing suspicion."

Fat Jack didn't deliberate for more than a few seconds. He nodded again, then stood up, supporting his ponderous weight with both hands on the desk. "What about money?" he whined. "I can't run far without money."

"I've got nothing to lend you," Nudger said. "Not even the fee I'm not going to get from you."

"All right," Fat Jack sighed.

"I'm going to phone David Collins in one hour," Nudger told him. "If Ineida isn't there, I'll put down the receiver and dial the number of the New Orleans police department."

"She'll be there," Fat Jack said. He tucked in his sweat-plastered shirt beneath his huge stomach paunch, buttoned his suit coat, and without a backward glance at Nudger glided majestically from the room. He would have his old jaunty stride back in no time.

Nudger glanced at his watch. He sipped Fat Jack's best whiskey from the club's private stock while he waited for an hour to pass. Then he phoned David Collins, and from the tone of Collins's voice he guessed the answer to his question even before he asked it.

Ineida was home.

When Nudger answered the knock on his hotel room door early the next morning, he wasn't really surprised to find Frick and Frack looming in the hall. They pushed into the room without being invited. There was a sneer on Frick's pockmarked face. Frack gave his boxer's nifty little shuffle and stood between Nudger and the door, smiling politely.

"We brought you something from Mr. Collins," Frick said, reaching into an inside pocket of his pale green sport jacket. It just about matched Nudger's complexion.

All Frick brought out, though, was an envelope. Nudger was surprised to see that his hands were steady as he opened it.

The envelope contained an airline ticket for a noon flight to St. Louis."

"You did okay, my friend," Frick said. "You did what was right for Ineida. Mr. Collins appreciates that."

"What about Fat Jack?" Nudger asked. Frack's polite smile changed subtly. It became a dreamy, unpleasant sort of smile.

"Where Fat Jack is now," Frack said, "most of his friends are alligators."

"After Fat Jack talked to you," said Frick, "he went to Mr. Collins. He couldn't make himself walk out on all that possible money; some guys just have to play all their cards. He told Mr. Collins that for a certain amount of cash he would reveal Ineida's whereabouts, but it all had to be done in a hurry." Now Frick also smiled. "He revealed her whereabouts in a hurry, all right, and for free. In fact, he kept talking till nobody was listening, till he couldn't talk any more."

Nudger swallowed dryly. He forgot about breakfast. Fat Jack had been a bad businessman to the end, dealing in desperation instead of distance. Maybe he'd had too much of the easy life; maybe he couldn't picture going on without it. That was no problem for him now.

When Nudger got home, he found a flat, padded package with a New Orleans postmark waiting for him. He placed it on his desk and cautiously opened it. The package contained two items: A check from David Collins made out to Nudger for more than twice the amount of Fat Jack's uncollectable fee. And an old jazz record in its original wrapper, a fifties rendition of *You Got the Reach but Not the Grasp.*

It featured Fat Jack McGee on clarinet.

Sharyn McCrumb lives in the Virginia Blue Ridge mountains, and uses that area as a basis for her beautifully written novels of mystery in the backwoods. Her novels have been nominated for just about every award imaginable, including the Anthony and Agatha awards and winning the Macavity for If I Ever Return Pretty Peggy O. *She has been a member of Sisters in Crime, Mystery Writers of America and the American Crime Writers League. Her most recent novel is* The Rosewood Casket.

A Wee Doch and Doris

Sharyn McCrumb

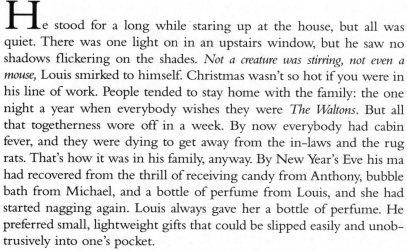

He stood for a long while staring up at the house, but all was quiet. There was one light on in an upstairs window, but he saw no shadows flickering on the shades. *Not a creature was stirring, not even a mouse,* Louis smirked to himself. Christmas wasn't so hot if you were in his line of work. People tended to stay home with the family: the one night a year when everybody wishes they were *The Waltons.* But all that togetherness wore off in a week. By now everybody had cabin fever, and they were dying to get away from the in-laws and the rug rats. That's how it was in his family, anyway. By New Year's Eve his ma had recovered from the thrill of receiving candy from Anthony, bubble bath from Michael, and a bottle of perfume from Louis, and she had started nagging again. Louis always gave her a bottle of perfume. He preferred small, lightweight gifts that could be slipped easily and unobtrusively into one's pocket.

He also preferred not to have endless discussions with his nearest and dearest over whether he was going to get a job or enroll in the auto mechanics program at the community college. Neither idea appealed to Louis. He liked his schedule: sleeping until eleven, a quick burger for brunch, and a few hours of volunteer work at the animal shelter.

Nobody at the shelter thought Louis was lazy or unmotivated. He was their star helper. He didn't mind hosing down the pens and cleaning the food dishes, but what he really enjoyed was playing with the dogs and brushing down the shaggy ones. They didn't have a lot of money at the shelter, so they couldn't afford to pay him. It took all their funds to keep the animals fed and healthy; the shelter refused to put a healthy animal to sleep. Louis heartily approved of this policy, and thus he didn't mind working for free; in fact, sometimes when the shelter's funds were low, he gave them a donation from the proceeds of his night's work. Louis thought that rich people should support local charities; he saw himself as the middleman, except that his share of the take was ninety percent. Louis also believed that charity begins at home.

Christmas was good for the shelter. Lots of people high on the Christmas spirit adopted kittens and puppies, or gave them as gifts, and the shelter saw to it that they got a donation for each adoptee. So their budget was doing okay, but Louis's personal funds were running short. Christmas is not a good time of year for a burglar. Sometimes he'd find an empty house whose occupants were spending Christmas out of town, but usually the neighborhood was packed with nosy people, eye-balling every car that went by. You'd think they were looking for Santa Claus.

If Christmas was bad for business, New Year's Eve made up for it. Lots of people went out to parties that night, and did not plan on coming home until well after midnight. Being out for just the evening made them less security conscious than the Christmas people who went out of town: New Year's party-goers were less likely to hide valuables, activate alarms, or ask the police to keep an eye on the premises. Louis had had a busy evening. He'd started around nine o'clock, when even the tardiest guests would have left for the party, and he had hit four houses, passing on one because of the Doberman Pinscher in the backyard. Louis had nothing against the breed, but he found them very unreasonable, and not inclined to give strangers the benefit of the doubt.

The other four houses had been satisfactory, though. The first one was "guarded" by a haughty white Persian whose owners had forgotten to feed it. Louis put down some canned mackerel for the cat, and charged its owners one portable television, one 35mm. camera, three pairs of earrings, a C.D. player, and a collection of compact discs. The other houses had been equally rewarding. After a day's visit to various flea markets and pawn shops, his financial standing should be greatly improved. This was much better than auto mechanics. Louis realized that larceny and auto mechanics are almost never mutually exclusive, but he felt that in free-lance burglary the hours were better.

He glanced at his watch. A little after midnight. This would be his last job of the evening. Louis wanted to be home before the drunks got out on the highway. His New Year's resolution was to campaign for gun control and for tougher drunk driving laws. He turned his attention back to the small white house with the boxwood hedge and the garden gnome next to the birdbath. No danger of Louis stealing *that*. He thought people ought to have to pay to have garden gnomes stolen. A promising sideline—he would have to consider it. But now to the business at hand.

The hedge seemed high enough to prevent the neighbors from seeing into the yard. The house across the street was vacant, with a big yellow For Sale sign stuck in the yard. The brick split-level next door was dark, but they had a chain link fence, and their front yard was floodlit like the exercise yard of a penitentiary. Louis shook his head: paranoia *and* bad taste.

There was no car in the driveway, a promising sign that no one was home. He liked the look of the rectangular kitchen window. It was partly hidden by a big azalea bush, and it looked like the kind of window that opened out at the bottom, with a catch to keep it from opening too far. It was about six feet off the ground. Louis was tempted to look under the garden gnome for a spare house key, but he decided to have a look at the window instead. Using a key was unsporting; besides, the exercise would be good for him. If you are a burglar, your physique is your fortune.

He walked a lot, too. Tonight Louis had parked his old Volkswagen a couple of streets away, not so much for the exercise as for the fact that later no one would remember seeing a strange car in the vicinity. The long walk back to the car limited Louis' take to the contents of a pillowcase or two, also from the burgled home, but he felt that most worthwhile burglary items were small and lightweight, anyway. The pillowcases he gave as baby gifts to new parents of his acquaintance, explaining that they were the perfect size to use as a cover for a bassinet mattress. Even better than a fitted crib sheet, he insisted, because after the kid grows up, you can use the pillowcases yourself. Louis was nothing if not resourceful.

He stayed close to the boxwood hedge as he edged closer to the house. With a final glance to see that no one was driving past, he darted from the azalea bush, and ended up crouched behind it, just under the rectangular window. Perfect. Fortunately it wasn't too cold tonight—temperature in the mid-thirties, about average for the Virginia Christmas season. When it got colder than that, his dexterity was impaired, making it hard to jimmy locks and tamper with windows. It was an occupational hazard. Tonight would be no problem, though, unless the window had some kind of inside lock.

It didn't. He was able to chin himself on the windowsill, and pull the window outward enough to get a hand inside and slip the catch. With that accomplished, another twenty seconds of wriggling got him through the window and onto the Formica countertop next to the sink. There had been a plant on the windowsill, but he managed to ease that onto the counter, before sliding himself all the way through. The only sound he made was a slight thump as he went from countertop to floor; no problem if the house was unoccupied.

Taking out his pen-sized flashlight, Louis checked out the kitchen. It was squeaky clean. He could even smell the lemon floor cleaner. He shone the light on the gleaming white refrigerator. Some people actually put their valuables in the freezer compartment. He always checked that last, though. In the corner next to the back door was a small washing machine and an electric dryer, with clean clothes stacked neatly on the top. Louis eased his way across the room, and inspected the laundry. Women's clothes—small sizes—towels, dish-cloths . . . ah, there they were! Pillowcases. He helped himself to the two linen cases, sniffing them appreciatively. Fabric softener. *Very* nice. Now he was all set. Time to shop around.

He slipped into the dining room and flashed the light on the round oak table and the ladderback chairs. Two places laid for breakfast. Weren't they the early birds, though? The salt and pepper shakers looked silver. They were in the shape of pheasants. Louis slid them into his pillowcase and examined the rest of the room. The glass of the china cabinet flashed his light back at him. Bunch of flowery plates. No chance that he'd be taking those. He looked around for a silver chest, but didn't see one. He'd check on it later. He wanted to examine the living room first.

Louis flashed an exploratory light at the fireplace, the chintz couch covered in throw pillows, and the glass-fronted bookcase. There were some candlesticks on the mantelpiece that looked promising. As he crept forward to inspect them, the room was flooded with light.

Squinting at the sudden brightness, Louis turned toward the stairs and saw that he wasn't alone. The overhead lights had been switched on by a sweet-faced old woman in a green velvet bathrobe. Louis braced himself for the scream, but the old lady was smiling. She kept coming daintily down the stairs. Smiling. Louis stared, trying to think up a plausible story. She couldn't have been more than five feet tall, and her blue eyes sparkled from a wrinkled but pleasant face. She patted her white permed hair into place. She looked delighted. Probably senile, Louis thought.

"Well, I'm that glad to see you!" the woman said brightly. "I was afraid it was going to be my daughter Doris."

Definitely senile, thought Louis. "No, it's just me," he said, deciding to play along. He held the pillowcase behind his back.

"Just after midnight, too, isn't it? That's grand, that is. Otherwise I'd have to ask you to go out and come in again, you know."

Louis noticed her accent now. It was sort of English, he thought. But she wasn't making any sense. "Come in again?"

"Ah, well, being an American you wouldn't know the custom, would you? Well, you're welcome all the same. Now, what can I get for you?"

Louis realized just in time that she meant food or drink, rather than jewelry and savings bonds. "Nothing for me, thanks," he said, giving her a little wave and trying to edge for the front door.

Her face fell. "Oh, no. Please! You must let me fix you something. Otherwise, you'll be taking the luck away with you. How about a piece of cake? I made it today. And a bit of strong drink? It's New Year's, after all."

She still didn't look in the least perturbed. And she wasn't trying to get to the telephone or to trip an alarm. Louis decided that he could definitely use a drink.

The old lady beamed happily up at him and motioned for him to follow her into the kitchen. "I've been baking for two days," she confided. "Now, let's see, what will you have?"

She rummaged around in a cupboard, bringing out an assortment of baked goods on glass plates, which she proceeded to spread out on the kitchen table. She handed Louis a blue-flowered plate and motioned for him to sit down. When she went in the dining room to get some cloth napkins, Louis stuffed the pillowcase under his coat, making sure that the salt and pepper shakers didn't clink together. Finally, he decided that the least suspicious thing to do would be to play along. He sat.

"Now," she announced, "we have Dundee cake with dried fruit, black bun with almonds, shortbread, petticoat tails . . ."

Louis picked up a flat yellow cookie and nibbled at it as his hostess babbled on.

"When I was a girl in Dundee—"

"Where?"

"Dundee. Scotland. My mother used to take an oat bannock—you know, a wee cake—for each one of us children. The bannocks had a hole in the middle, and they were nipped in about the edges for decorations. She flavored them with carvey—carroway seed. And we ate them on New Year's morning. They used to say that if your bannock broke while it was baking, you'd be taken ill or die in the new year. So I never baked one for my daughter Doris. Oh, but they were good!"

Louis blinked. "You're from Scotland?"

She was at the stove now, putting a large open pot on the burner and stirring it with a wooden spoon. "Yes, that's right," she said. "We've been in this country since Doris was five, though. My husband wanted to come over, and so we did. I've often thought of going home, now that he's passed on, but Doris won't hear of it."

"Doris is your daughter," said Louis. He wondered if he ought to bolt before she showed up, in case she turned out to be sane.

"Yes. She's all grown up now. She works very hard, does Doris. Can you imagine having to work on Hogmanay?"

"On what?"

"*Hogmanay.* New Year's Eve. She's out right now, poor dear, finishing up her shift. That's why I was so glad to see you tonight. We could use a bit of luck this year, starting with a promotion for Doris. Try a bit of the Dundee cake. It's awfully rich, but you can stand the calories, from the look of you."

Louis reached for another pastry, still trying to grasp a thread of sense in the conversation. He wanted to know why he was so welcome. Apparently she hadn't mistaken him for anyone else. And she didn't seem to wonder what he was doing in her house in the middle of the night. He kept trying to think of a way to frame the question without incriminating himself.

Steam was rising in white spirals from the pot on the stove. The old lady took a deep breath over the fumes and nodded briskly. "Right. That should be done now. Tell me, lad, are you old enough to take spirits?"

After a moment's hesitation, Louis realized that he was being offered a drink and not a seance. "I'm twenty-two," he mumbled.

"Right enough, then." She ladled the steaming liquid into two cups and set one in front of him.

Louis sniffed it and frowned.

"It's called a het pint," said the old lady, without waiting for him to ask. "It's an old drink given to first footers. Spirits, sugar, beer, and eggs. When I was a girl, they used to carry it round door to door in a kettle. Back in Dundee. Not that I drink much myself, of course. Doris is always on about my blood pressure. But tonight *is* Hogmanay, and I said to myself: Flora, why don't you stir up the het pint. You never know who may drop in. And, you see, I was right. Here you are!"

"Here I am," Louis agreed, taking a swig of his drink. It tasted a little like eggnog. Not bad. At least it was alcoholic. He wouldn't have more than a cup, though. He still had to drive home.

The old lady—Flora—sat down beside Louis and lifted her cup. "Well, here's to us, then. What's your name, lad?"

"Louis," he said, before he thought better of it.

"Well, Louis, here's to us! And not forgetting a promotion for Doris!" They clinked their cups together and drank to the new year.

Flora dabbed at the corners of her mouth with a linen napkin and reached for a piece of shortbread. "I must resolve to eat fewer of these during the coming year," she remarked. "Else Doris will have me out jogging."

Louis took another piece to keep her company. It tasted pretty good. Sort of like a sugar cookie with delusions of grandeur. "Did you have a nice Christmas?" he asked politely.

Flora smiled. "Perhaps not by American standards. Doris had the day off, and we went to church in the morning, and then had our roast beef for dinner. She gave me bath powder, and I gave her a new umbrella. She's always losing umbrellas. I suppose that's a rather subdued holiday by your lights, but when I was a girl, Christmas wasn't such a big festival in Scotland. The shops didn't even close for it. We considered it a religious occasion for most folk, and a lark for the children. The holiday for grown people was New Year's."

"Good idea," grunted Louis. "Over here, we get used to high expectations when we're kids, and then as adults, we get depressed every year because Christmas is just neckties and boredom."

Flora nodded. "Oh, but you should have seen Hogmanay when I was a girl! No matter what the weather, people in Dundee would gather in the City Square to wait out the old year's end. And there'd be a great time of singing all the old songs . . ."

" 'Auld Lang Syne'?" asked Louis.

"That's a Scottish song, of course," nodded Flora. "But we sang a lot of the other old tunes as well. And there was country dancing. And then just when the new year was minutes away, everyone would lapse into silence. Waiting. There you'd be in the dark square, with your breath frosting the air, and the stars shining down on the world like snowflakes on velvet. And it was so quiet you could hear the ticking of the gentlemen's pocket watches."

"Sounds like Times Square," said Louis, inspecting the bottom of his cup.

Flora took the cup and ladled another het pint for each of them. "After the carrying on to welcome in the new year, everyone would go about visiting and first footing their neighbors. My father was always in great demand for that, being tall and dark as he was. And he used to carry lumps of coal in his overcoat to be sure of his welcome."

"What," said Louis, "is *first footing*?"

"Well, it's an old superstition," said Flora thoughtfully. "Quite pagan, I expect, if the truth were told, but then, you never can be sure, can you? You don't have a lump of coal about you, by any chance?"

Louis shook his head.

"Ah, well. First footing, you asked." She took a deep breath, as if to warn him that there was a long explanation to follow. "In Scotland the tradition is that the first person to cross your threshold after midnight on Hogmanay symbolizes your luck in the year to come. The *first foot* to enter your house, you see."

Louis nodded. *It's lucky to be burgled?* he was thinking.

"The best luck of all comes if you're first footed by a tall, dark stranger carrying a lump of coal. Sometimes family friends would send round a tall, dark houseguest that our family had not met, so that we could be first footed by a stranger. The rest of the party would catch up with him a few minutes later."

"I guess I fit the bill all right," Louis remarked. He was just over six feet and looked more Italian than Tony Bennett. His uncles called him *Luigi*.

"So you do," smiled Flora. "Now the worst luck for the new year is to be first footed by a short blond woman who comes in empty-handed."

Louis remembered the first thing the old woman had said to him. "So Doris is a short blond?"

"She is that. Gets her height from me. Or the lack of it. And she can never remember to hunt up a lump of coal or bring some wee gift home with her to help the luck. Ever since Colin passed away, Doris has been first foot in this house, and where has it got us? Her with long hours and precious little time off, and me with rheumatism and a fixed income—while prices go up every year. We could use a change of luck. Maybe a sweepstakes win."

Louis leaned back in his chair, struggling between courtesy and common sense. "You really believe in all this stuff?" he asked her.

A sad smile. "Where's the harm? When you get older, it's hard to let go of the customs you knew when you were young. You'll see."

Louis couldn't think of any family customs, except eating in front of the TV set and never taking the last ice cube—so you wouldn't have to refill the tray. Other than that, he didn't think he had much in common with the people he lived with. He thought about telling Flora about his work at the animal shelter, but he decided that it would be a dangerous thing to do. She already knew his name. Any further information would enable her and the police to locate him in a matter of hours. If she ever cottoned on to the fact that she had been robbed, that is.

"Do you have any pets?" he asked.

Flora shook her head. "We used to have a wee dog, but he got old and died a few years back. I haven't wanted to get another one, and Doris is too busy with her work to help in taking care of one."

"I could get you a nice puppy, from—" He stopped himself just in time. "Well, never mind. You're right. Dogs are more work than most people think. Or they *ought* to be."

Flora beamed. "What a nice young man you are!"

He smiled back nervously.

Louis nibbled another piece of shortbread while he considered his dilemma. He had been caught breaking into a house, and the evidence from the rest of the evening's burglaries was in the trunk of his Volkswagen. The logical thing to do would be to kill the old dear, so that he wouldn't have to worry about getting caught. Logical, yes, but distasteful. Louis was not a killer. The old lady reminded him of one of the sad-eyed cocker spaniels down at the shelter. Sometimes people brought in pets because they didn't want them anymore or were moving. Or because the kid was allergic to them. Often these people asked that the animal be destroyed, which annoyed Louis no end. Did they think that if they didn't want the pet, no one else should have it?

Suppose divorce worked like that? Louis could see putting an old dog to sleep if it was feeble and suffering, but not just because the owners found it inconvenient to have it around. He supposed that his philosophy would have to apply to his hostess as well, even if she were a danger to his career. After all, Flora was old, but she was not weak or in pain. She seemed quite spry and happy, in fact, and Louis couldn't see doing away with her just for expedience. After all, people had rights, too, just like animals.

He wondered what he ought to do about her. It seemed to boil down to two choices: He could tie her up, finish robbing the house, and make his getaway, or he could finish his tea and leave, just as if he had been an ordinary—what was it?—*first footer.*

He leaned back in his chair, considering the situation, and felt a sharp jab in his side. A moment's reflection told him what it had been: the tail of the pheasant salt shaker. He had stashed the pair in the pillowcase, now concealed under his coat. He couldn't think of any way to get rid of his loot without attracting suspicion. *Then* she might realize that he was a burglar; *then* she might panic and try to call the police; *then* he would have to hit her to keep himself from being captured. It was not an appealing scenario. Louis decided that the kindest thing to do would be to tie her up, finish his job, and leave.

Flora was prattling on about Scottish cakes and homemade icing, but he hadn't been listening. He thought it would be rather rude to begin threatening his hostess while he still had a mouthful of cake, but he told himself that she had been rather rude, too. After all, she hadn't asked him anything about himself. That was thoughtless of her. A good hostess ought to express a polite interest in her guests.

Flora's interminable story seemed to have wound down at last. She looked up at the kitchen clock. It was after one. "Well," she said, beaming happily at Louis. "It's getting late. Can I get you a *wee doch and dorris?*"

Louis blinked. "A what?"

"A drink, lad. *Wee doch and dorris* is a Scottish expression for the last drink of the evening. One for the road, as you say over here. Scotch, perhaps?"

He shook his head. "I'm afraid not," he said. "I do have to be going, but I'm afraid I will have to tie you up now."

He braced himself for tears, or, even worse, a scream, but the old lady simply took another sip of her drink and waited. She wasn't smiling anymore, but she didn't look terrified, either. Louis felt his cheeks grow hot, wishing he could just get out of there. Burglars weren't sup-posed to have to interact with people; it wasn't part of the job descrip-tion. If you liked emotional scenes, you became an armed robber. Louis hated confrontations.

"I hope this won't change your luck for the New Year or any-thing," he mumbled, "but the reason I came in here tonight was to rob the house. You see, I'm a burglar."

Flora nodded, still watching him closely. Not a flicker of surprise had registered on her face.

"I really enjoyed the cakes and all, but after all, business is busi-ness."

"In Scotland, it's considered unlucky to do evil after you've accepted the hospitality of the house," the old lady said calmly.

Louis shrugged. "In America it's unlucky to miss car payments."

She made no reply to this remark, but continued to gaze up at him impassively. At least she wasn't being hysterical. He almost wished that he had given up the whole idea.

Louis cleared his throat and continued. "The reason I have to tie you up is that I have to finish getting the stuff, and I have to make sure you can't call for help until I'm long gone. But I won't beat you up or anything."

"Kind of you," she said dryly. "There is some spare clothesline in the bottom drawer of the left-hand cabinet."

He looked at her suspiciously. "Don't *try* anything, okay? I don't want to have to do anything rough." He didn't carry a gun (nobody was *supposed* to be home), but they both knew that a strong young man like Louis could do considerable damage to a frail old lady like Flora with his fists—a candlestick—almost anything could be a weapon.

Keeping his eyes on her, he edged toward the cabinet, squatting down to pull out the drawer. She watched him steadily, making no move to leave her seat. As he eased the drawer open, he saw the white rope clothesline neatly bundled above a stack of paper bags. With con-siderable relief at the ease of it all, he picked up the rope and turned back to the old lady.

"Okay," he said, a little nervously. "I'm going to tie you up. Just relax. I don't want to make it so tight it cuts off circulation, but I'm not, like, experienced, you know? Just sit in the chair with your feet flat on the floor in front of you."

She did as she was told, and he knelt and began winding the clothesline around her feet, anchoring it to the legs of the chair. He hoped it wasn't going to be too painful, but he couldn't risk her being able to escape. To cover his uneasiness at the silent reproach from his hostess, Louis began to whistle nervously as he worked. That was probably why he didn't hear anything suspicious.

His first inkling that anything was wrong was that Flora suddenly relaxed in her chair. He looked up quickly, thinking, *"Oh, God! The old girl's had a heart attack!"* But her eyes were open, and she was smiling. She seemed to be gazing at something just behind him.

Slowly Louis turned his head in the direction of the back door. There was a short blond woman of about thirty standing just inside the door. She was wearing a dark blue uniform and a positively menacing expression. But what bothered Louis the most about the intruder was the fact that her knees were bent, and she was holding a service revolver in both hands, its barrel aimed precisely at Louis's head.

Louis looked from the blond woman to Flora and back again, just beginning to make the connection. A jerk of the gun barrel made him move slowly away from the chair and put his hands up.

"This is my daughter Doris," said Flora calmly. "She's a policewoman. You see, you were lucky for us, Louis. I'm sure she'll get her promotion after this!"

Billie Sue Mosiman is the author of the Edgar-nominated novel Night Cruise. *She has published more than ninety short stories in various magazines, including* Realms of Fantasy *and in various anthologies such as* Tales From the Great Turtle *and* Tapestries: Magic the Gathering. *Her latest novel is* Stileto, *from Berkley.*

Down-Home Remedies

Billie Sue Mosiman

Toner liked jimson weed and was partial to Queen Anne's lace. He gathered armloads of the white, flat-faced lace to put into fruit jars of cool water. The flakes from the flowers covered his overalls.

"Why you gotta bring that stuff inta my house, Toner? You know I cain't abide weeds. Why don't you bring in a batch of gardenias off'n my bush? Now that's a real flower."

Toner ignored his wife's opinions. Especially when it came to which flower to harvest and which to leave dying on a stem. He liked the lace and he found nothing peculiar in wanting it in the house. Besides, Belle Anne's voice grated on his nerves and that was enough reason to cross her. She sounded like his knife blade when he sharpened it on the whetstone he carried in his pocket. She could have her cloying, yellowing gardenias.

Often in the evening, after finishing the milking and cleaning up, Toner stuck a long shaft of grass into the side of his mouth and thought about Belle Anne. Thinking was his favorite pastime, but pondering on a nagging wife wasn't much fun. She was a burden to think about.

Thoughts of her made Toner's face collapse. His features folded in on each other, the skin lapping shut in the creases. If someone spied on him, a lean figure propped against the barn door in loose twilight, they would have taken that face to mean he was in terrible physical pain, perhaps dying. Even his eyelids folded and drooped in agony. Belle Anne affected him that way. She grated. She nagged and mocked and wheezed against the sensitive grain of his spirit.

Nothing pleased her. It had always been the same from the very beginning when she had him standing ramrod straight in front of Preacher Harkins repeating marriage vows that he didn't believe in. Four years he'd been married to her now. Before that she was married for twelve years to Henry Silas, the man who had owned the land and the barn Toner leaned against. Silas died suddenly—his heart—leaving Belle Anne one of the wealthiest women in the county.

Before a year was up she picked Toner to share her wealth. Only she didn't share. If it had been left up to him, Toner might have left the place and taken a job on another farm tending to things. But Belle Anne did the choosing and proposing and she had her two muscular, hairy, mean brothers talking to Toner about marrying the poor widow. Toner married. He knew what was good for him. And getting beat to smut wasn't good for him. His wedding day was the biggest catastrophe of his miserable life. Where was peace, silence, closeness?

Before his marriage there had been no one to object to him wanting lace weeds in his tenant's shack. Or his dog, Franklin. Belle Anne made Toner take poor Franklin off the place. He was instructed to shoot "the mangy, butt-scratching animal" so they wouldn't have to worry about him wandering back to the farm. But Toner wasn't about to violate his dog. He walked two miles to the neighboring Clemmons' farm and begged them to take Franklin. It wasn't an easy thing to explain. They finally agreed when Toner said he'd be back every week and pay them five dollars for the dog's keep. After four years, Toner was still paying them the money and Franklin was fat and sleek as a water rat. Belle Anne never suspected, of course. That Toner might betray her wishes was out of the question.

Getting rid of Franklin was a sore spot between Toner and Belle Anne, but it wasn't the only ulcer that festered between them. Going to church, dressed up like some South Tennessean fool, was another. That really made Toner raw. Toner despised church services. He hated the smell of Preacher Harkins' little clapboard cave. Smelled like peaches souring and fermenting in a wood casket. And the masks people wore to church. Boy, did they try to look saintly.

Worst of all, though, was how Belle Anne changed on Sunday mornings. She became simpering, servile. She hung on Toner's arm and gave him demure, wifely glances. She always clutched a perfumed handkerchief for hiding behind when church members inquired about her health. It was pure torture.

One Sunday she said, "I've been a mite achy in the joints, but Toner is a pure-T angel. He gets the Mutt and Suet salve to rub all over my poor laigs. If it weren't for him, I don't know what'd become of me." Oh, how she could simper. Toner was shocked. His eyes grew wide and almost crossed as he stared at her lying face. She had never in four years complained about aching joints, and Toner had never in his life messed with any home remedy salve to cure her. But Belle Anne was masterful at creating sympathetic stories. She could even bring up real tears. She would be almost admirable if she weren't such a fake.

Toner heard a whippoorwill and rocked forward to the balls of his feet. He'd put off going in the house long enough. Belle Anne would come searching for him to eat his supper if he didn't get a move on.

"What's the matter now, Toner? Don't go tellin' me you don't like my chicken 'n dumplings after all this time I been fixin' 'em for you."

Toner had been unusually quiet, his food growing cold on his plate. He looked up now from where he was drawing patterns on the new Formica-topped table.

"It tastes just fine, Belle Anne. I just been thinking. You know that tractor is about worn plumb out. And with all those fields to plow, maybe we oughta buy a newer model. I seen a Massey Ferguson for sale in town. . . ."

"My God, Toner! Do you know what you're askin' for? That's like saying we gonna buy us one of them newfangled freezers when canning's just fine. Or maybe you think we oughta get us some of them milkin' machines too, so you won't havta do a lick of work around this place? You're mighty big for your breeches lately."

Toner stared straight ahead. He'd expected as much. Nothing pleased Belle Anne and nothing pleased her less than spending some of the money Henry left in the bank. She didn't have to plow the fields and get out every third row to work on the stupid engine of that old tractor. She had given him a blunt refusal. Toner knew a refusal when he heard it. Her stubbornness and stinginess thwarted him at every turn. If only she was out of the way he could. . . . But whoa, what was he thinking? He couldn't divorce Belle Anne. She wouldn't permit it. Yet if she was out of the way. . . .

The thought took hold like an oak root clenching a clod of dirt to squeeze the everlasting moisture from it. Out of the way. How to get her out of his way.

Toner's face closed in on itself forever. The problem of how to rid himself of his wife gnawed at him. Belle Anne took to calling him

Sour Puss and Persimmon Head. She laughed at the way his lips rolled in to form a mean straight line.

"You're about to suck your face right through your mouth," she said.

Toner vowed to get her for that remark. He worked on a foolproof plan. While plowing he thought up so many different ways to kill his wife that his head was a jingle of schemes. He never knew that devising a perfect murder could be so amusing. He found himself chuckling all through the long hot days while sitting on the lumbering tractor.

He considered a pitchfork. He liked the sharp tines, the tiny holes they'd make. Nasty though, real nasty. And what could he say? Belle Anne, she's clumsy, he'd say. Fell over her own big, fat feet right into the thing.

It was a tempting idea, the pitchfork, but not exactly right. Toner didn't want Belle Anne to suffer too much. He just wanted her out of the way.

He thought about dropping her twenty-two-year-old Zenith radio she played nights into her bathtub as she soaked. He could see her sizzling away. Now that was appealing too, but she'd suffer. And God, the smell she'd make. Nasty.

He thought of forcing a chicken bone down her gullet to make her choke to death at the supper table, but he might leave fingermarks by holding her down and that'd never do. Her brothers had sharp eyes and closed-trap minds. Still, it was worth a chuckle. What an appropriate end for a woman who owned one hundred and one chicken recipes! But choking to death wouldn't do. Too chancy.

At the end of the plowing week, Toner found a solution. He sat down in the cool, shadowy barn and leaned against two sacks of feed. He'd seen his solution at the edge of the woods as he plowed. Jimson weed. He would mix jimson weed fruit into Belle Anne's strong tea she drank at night. She always had a cup before bed while listening to Brother M.S. Argusy on the old radio in their bedroom. She never missed having that tea. The jimson had recently stopped blooming and the new fruit was extremely toxic. Belle Anne wouldn't suffer much. She might cramp a bit, but when was dying easy?

That night he did it. "You sit right where you are, Belle Anne. I'll pour the hot water in your teapot for you tonight. You looked tired."

Belle Anne had her head near the radio, but at Toner's offer she twisted around in her chintz chair and shot him a suspicious glance. "I can do it myself, Toner. No need to bother."

He was not to be outdone. He arrived with the hot, strong tea with its lethal potion of jimson weed juice. He gave her a crooked smile and left the room. He had never cared to listen to preachers and it wasn't a good time to start the practice now—not with what he'd have on his conscience soon. But would God despise him, he wondered? Toner was certain the Lord never had to live with a woman like Belle Anne or He'd never have gotten the world made in six days. He'd still be creating the waters.

Toner leaned against the porch post and watched fireflies spot the night. In his back pocket was a fifth of Kentucky bourbon. That was another deprivation he would soon be able to enjoy again.

In his shirt pocket he had a pack of Camels. He lit one and felt the luxurious smoke fill his lungs. Smoking was a no-no too, but not for long. He inhaled slowly and blew a plume of smoke at the fireflies who scattered to the opposite end of the porch. He'd take it easy, that's what he'd do. Relax and wait. He didn't know much about poison, but he figured it wouldn't take more than an hour to work. He wondered idly if she'd turn blue as a Tennessee summer sky. It was a pretty color and it'd suit Belle Anne.

He finished the cigarette and ground the tip between his forefinger and thumb with a certain pleasure at the pain it caused him. Only justice, he thought, and lit another. A mockingbird sung and Toner listened carefully. The world was full of sound and light and beauty. He'd hardly had time to notice before.

"Toner? You comin' to bed or you gonna stand out here all night sucking on them cancer sticks?"

Toner nearly fell off the porch edge. He twirled around.

"Whatsa matter? You look like you seen a ghost."

When Toner failed to answer, Belle Anne let the screen door shut and left him standing speechless. The radio went silent. The light blinked out. Toner made himself move. The house creaked when he tiptoed through it to the door of their bedroom. He paused on the threshold and cleared his throat, trying to speak.

"You ah . . . your ah . . . tea. . . ."

"Didn't desire it, Toner. First swallow so bitter I almost gagged. Don't you never do me no more favors, you hear? I'll make my own tea, thank you."

Toner felt faint. His mouth was cotton batting. Moonlight struck him across the eyes and made him squint horribly at the bed.

"Come to bed now, Toner. You look like some kind a idiot. I ain't gonna yell about the smoking. I been thinking about that tractor you mentioned too. Next spring maybe. But we'll talk on it. Now get over her and fan me so's I can get to sleep. It's hotter 'n Hades tonight."

Toner began to chuckle. It turned into a rumble, a throaty roar.

"What's so funny, Toner? You know a joke I don't?"

"Not lately, Belle Anne, but gimme time. I'm working on one that oughta give you a belly laugh or two."

"That right?"

"Sure, sure, I know lots of jokes. Now about that tractor. Next spring, you say?"

"Well . . . I might've been hasty. You needn't to press me. Them Masseys cost right smart come to think of it."

Toner took up the cardboard fan imprinted on the back with an advertisement from the local funeral home. He stirred the air over his wife's face. "They do cost a bunch," he agreed. His mind was plotting, racing, boiling with schemes. Maybe he'd run over her one day in the field. Be only right. Put tire tracks down the middle of her prune face.

Belle Anne drifted toward sleep beneath the cooled air. She heard Toner chuckle to himself. What a soothing sound, that chuckle. Nothing of the devil in that.

"You best not smoke," she mumbled sleepily. "Kill you one day, them nasty cigarettes."

"Right, Belle Anne. You're right. Smoking's a nasty habit."

He fanned the air furiously and smiled in the dark.

A fire in the barn, he thought. No. Lime in the stew. No. Cleaning the rifle—accidental shooting. No.

There must be a million methods—a trillion remedies for achy joints and stingy, nagging wives. And he'd figure it out. He knew he would.

The Gold-Bug

Edgar Alan Poe

> What ho! what ho! this fellow is dancing mad!
> He hath been bitten by the Tarantula.
>
> —*All in the Wrong*

Many years ago, I contracted an intimacy with a Mr. William Legrand. He was of an ancient Huguenot family, and had once been wealthy; but a series of misfortunes had reduced him to want. To avoid the mortification consequent upon his disasters, he left New Orleans, the city of his forefathers, and took up his residence at Sullivan's Island, near Charleston, South Carolina.

This island is a very singular one. It consists of little else than the sea sand, and is about three miles long. Its breadth at no point exceeds a quarter of a mile. It is separated from the mainland by a scarcely perceptible creek, oozing its way through a wilderness of reeds and slime, a favorite resort of the marsh-hen. The vegetation, as might be supposed, is scant, or at least dwarfish. No trees of any magnitude are to be seen. Near the western extremity, where Fort Moultrie stands, and where are some miserable frame buildings, tenanted, during summer, by the fugitives from Charleston dust and fever, may be found, indeed, the bristly palmetto; but the whole island, with the exception of this western point, and a line of hard, white beach on the seacoast, is covered with a dense undergrowth of the sweet myrtle so much prized by the horticulturists of England. The shrub here often attains the height of fifteen or twenty feet, and forms an almost impenetrable coppice, burdening the air with its fragrance.

In the inmost recesses of this coppice, not far from the eastern or more remote end of the island, Legrand had built himself a small hut, which he occupied when I first, by mere accident, made his acquaintance. This soon ripened into friendship—for there was much in the recluse to excite interest and esteem. I found him well educated, with unusual powers of mind, but infected with misanthropy, and subject to perverse moods of alternate enthusiasm and melancholy. He had with him many books, but rarely employed them. His chief amusements were gunning and fishing, or sauntering along the beach and through the myrtles, in quest of shells or entomological specimens—his collection of the latter might have been envied by a Swammerdamm. In these excursions he was usually accompanied by an old Negro, called Jupiter, who had been manumitted before the reverses of the family, but who could be induced, neither by threats nor by promises, to abandon what he considered his right of attendance upon the footsteps of his young "Massa Will." It is not improbable that the relatives of Legrand, conceiving him to be somewhat unsettled in intellect, had contrived to instill this obstinancy into Jupiter, with a view to the supervision and guardianship of the wanderer.

The winters in the latitude of Sullivan's Island are seldom very severe, and in the fall of the year it is a rare event indeed when a fire is considered necessary. About the middle of October 18———, there occurred, however, a day of remarkable chilliness. Just before sunset, I scrambled my way through the evergreens to the hut of my friend, whom I had not visited for several weeks—my residence being, at that time, in Charleston, a distance of nine miles from the island, while the facilities of passage and repassage were very far behind those of the present day. Upon reaching the hut I rapped, as was my custom, and getting no reply, sought for the key where I knew it was secreted, unlocked the door, and went in. A fine fire was blazing upon the hearth. It was a novelty, and by no means an ungrateful one. I threw off an overcoat, took an armchair by the crackling logs, and awaited patiently the arrival of my hosts.

Soon after dark they arrived, and gave me a most cordial welcome. Jupiter, grinning from ear to ear, bustled about to prepare some marshhens for supper. Legrand was in one of his fits—how else shall I term them?—of enthusiasm. He had found an unknown bivalve, forming a new genus, and, more than this, he had hunted down and secured, with Jupiter's assistance, a *scarabaeus* which he believed to be totally new, but in respect to which he wished to have my opinion on the morrow.

"And why not tonight?" I asked, rubbing my hands over the blaze, and wishing the whole tribe of *scarabaei* at the devil.

"Ah, if I had only known you were here!" said Legrand, "but it's so long since I saw you; and how could I foresee that you would pay me a visit this very night, of all others? As I was coming home I met Lieutenant G——, from the fort, and, very foolishly, I lent him the bug; so it will be impossible for you to see it until the morning. Stay here tonight, and I will send Jup down for it at sunrise. It is the loveliest thing in creation!"

"What?—sunrise?"

"Nonsense! No!—the bug. It is of a brilliant gold color—about the size of a large hickory-nut—with two jet-black spots near one extremity of the back, and another, somewhat longer, at the other. The antennae are—"

"Dey aint no tin in him, Massa Will, I keep a tellin on you," here interrupted Jupiter; "de bug is a goole-bug, solid, ebery bit of him, inside and all, sep him wing—neber feel half so hebby a bug in my life."

"Well, suppose it is, Jup," replied Legrand, somewhat more earnestly, it seemed to me, than the case demanded; "is that any reason for your letting the birds burn? The color—"here he turned to me—"is really almost enough to warrant Jupiter's idea. You never saw a more brilliant metallic luster than the scales emit—but of this you cannot judge till tomorrow. In the meantime I can give you some idea of the shape." Saying this, he seated himself at a small table, on which were a pen and ink, but no paper. He looked for some in a drawer, but found none.

"Never mind," he said at length, "this will answer"; and he drew from his waistcoat pocket a scrap of what I took to be very dirty foolscap, and made upon it a rough drawing with the pen. While he did this, I retained my seat by the fire, for I was still chilly. When the design was complete, he handed it to me without rising. As I received it, a loud growl was heard, succeeded by a scratching at the door. Jupiter opened it, and a large Newfoundland, belonging to Legrand, rushed in, leaped upon my shoulders, and loaded me with caresses; for I had shown him much attention during previous visits. When his gambols were over, I looked at the paper, and, to speak the truth, found myself not a little puzzled at what my friend had depicted.

"Well!" I said, after contemplating it for some minutes, "this is a strange *scarabaeus*, I must confess; new to me; never saw anything like it before—unless it was a skull, or a death's-head, which it more nearly resembles than anything else that has come under *my* observation."

"A death's-head!" echoed Legrand. "Oh—yes, well, it has something of that appearance upon paper, no doubt. The two upper black spots look like eyes, eh? And the longer ones at the bottom like a mouth—and then the shape of the whole is oval."

"Perhaps so," said I; "but, Legrand, I fear you are no artist. I must wait until I see the beetle itself, if I am to form any idea of its personal appearance."

"Well, I don't know," said he, a little nettled, "I draw tolerably—*should* do it at least—have had good masters, and flatter myself that I am not quite a blockhead."

"But, my dear fellow, you are joking, then," said I; "this is a very passable *skull*—indeed, I may say that it is a very *excellent* skull, according to the vulgar notions about such specimens of physiology—and your *scarabaeus* must be the queerest *scarabaeus* in the world if it resembles it. Why, we may get up a very thrilling bit of superstition upon this hint. I presume you will call the bug *Scarabaeus caput hominis*, or something of that kind—there are many similar titles in the natural histories. But where are the antennae you spoke of?"

"The antennae?" said Legrand, who seemed to be getting unaccountably warm upon the subject; "I am sure you must see the antennae. I made them as distinct as they are in the original insect, and I presume that is sufficient."

"Well, well," I said, "perhaps you have—still I don't see them"; and I handed him the paper without additional remark, not wishing to ruffle his temper; but I was much surprised at the turn affairs had taken; his ill humor puzzled me—and, as for the drawing of the beetle, there were positively *no* antennae visible, and the whole *did* bear a very close resemblance to the ordinary cuts of a death's-head.

He received the paper very peevishly, and was about to crumple it, apparently to throw it in the fire, when a casual glance at the design seemed suddenly to rivet his attention. In an instant his face grew violently red—in another excessively pale. For some minutes he continued to scrutinize the drawing minutely where he sat. At length he arose, took a candle from the table, and proceeded to seat himself upon a sea-chest in the furthest corner of the room. Here again he made an anxious examination of the paper; turning it in all directions. He said nothing, however, and his conduct greatly astonished me; yet I thought it prudent not to exacerbate the growing moodiness of his temper by any comment. Presently he took from his coat pocket a wallet, placed the paper carefully in it, and deposited both in a writing desk, which he locked. He now grew more composed in his demeanor; but his original air of enthusiasm had quite disappeared. Yet he seemed not so much sulky as abstracted. As the evening wore away he became more and more absorbed in reverie, from which no sallies of mine could arouse him. It had been my intention to pass the night at the hut, as I had frequently done before, but, seeing my host in this mood, I deemed it proper to take leave. He did not press me to remain, but, as I departed, he shook my hand with even more than his usual cordiality.

It was about a month after this (and during the interval I had seen nothing of Legrand) when I received a visit, at Charleston, from his man, Jupiter. I had never seen the good old Negro look so dispirited, and I feared that some serious disaster had befallen my friend.

"Well, Jup," said I, "what is the matter now?—how is your master?"

"Why, to speak de troof, massa, him not so berry well as mought be."

"Not well! I am truly sorry to hear it. What does he complain of?"

"Dar! Dat's it!—him neber plain of notin—but him berry sick for all dat."

"*Very* sick, Jupiter!—why didn't you say so at once? Is he confined to bed?"

"No, dat he aint!—he aint fin'd nowhar—dat's just whar de shoe pinch—my mind is got to be berry hebby bout poor Massa Will."

"Jupiter, I should like to understand what it is you are talking about. You say your master is sick. Hasn't he told you what ails him?"

"Why, massa, taint worf while for to git mad about de matter— Massa Will say noffin at all aint de matter wid him—but den what make him go about looking dis here way, wid he head down and he soldiers up, and as white as a gose? And den he keep a syphon all de time—"

"Keeps a what, Jupiter?"

"Keeps a syphon wid de figgurs on de slate—de queerest figgurs I ebber did see. Ise gittin to be skeered, I tell you. Hab for to keep mighty tight eye pon him noovers. Todder day he gib me slip fore de sun up and was gone de whole ob de blessed day. I had a big stick ready cut for to gib him deuced good beating when he did come—but Ise sich a fool dat I hadn't de heart arter all—he looked so berry poorly."

"Eh?—what?—ah yes!—upon the whole I think you had better not be too severe with the poor fellow—don't flog him, Jupiter— he can't very well stand it—but can you form no idea of what has occasioned this illness, or rather this change of conduct? Has anything unpleasant happened since I saw you?"

"No, massa, dey aint bin noffin onpleasant *since* den—'twas *fore* den I'm feared—'twas de berry day you was dare."

"How? what do you mean?"

"Why, massa, I mean de bug—dare now."

"The what?"

"De bug—I'm berry sartin dat Massa Will bin bit somewhere bout de head by dat goole-bug."

"And what cause have you, Jupiter, for such a supposition?"

"Claws enuff, massa, and mouff, too. I nebber did see sich a deuced bug—he kick and he bite ebery ting what cum near him. Massa Will cotch him fuss, but had for to let him go gin mighty quick, I tell you—den was de time he must ha got de bite. I didn't like de look ob de bug mouff, myself, nowhow, so I wouldn't take hold ob him wid my finger, but I cotch him wid a piece ob paper dat I found. I rap him up in de paper and stuff a piece of it in he mouff— dat was de way."

"And you think, then, that your master was really bitten by the beetle, and that the bite made him sick?"

"I don't tink noffin about it—I nose it. What make him dream bout de goole so much, if taint cause he bit by the goole-bug? Ise heerd bout dem goole-bugs fore dis."

"But how do you know he dreams about gold?"

"How I know? why, cause he talk about it in he sleep—dat's how I nose."

"Well, Jup, perhaps you are right; but to what fortunate circumstance am I to attribute the honor of a visit from you today?"

"What de matter, massa?"

"Did you bring any message from Mr. Legrand?"

"No, massa, I bring dis here pissel"; and here Jupiter handed me a note which ran thus:

My Dear———:

Why had I not seen you for so long a time? I hope you have not been so foolish as to take offense at any little brusquerie of mine; but no, that is improbable.

Since I saw you I have had great cause for anxiety. I have something to tell you, yet scarcely know how to tell it, or whether I should tell it at all.

I have not been quite well for some days past, and poor old Jup annoys me, almost beyond endurance, by his well-meant attentions. Would you believe it?—he had prepared a huge stick, the other day, with which to chastise me for giving him the slip, and spending the day, solus, among the hills on the mainland. I verily believe that my ill looks alone saved me a flogging.

I have made no addition to my cabinet since we met.

If you can, in any way, make it convenient, come over with Jupiter. Do come. I wish to see you tonight, upon business of importance. I assure you that it is of the highest importance.

Ever yours,
William Legrand

There was something in the tone of this note which gave me great uneasiness. Its whole style differed materially from that of Legrand. What could he be dreaming of? What new crotchet possessed his excitable brain? What "business of the highest importance," could *he* possibly have to transact? Jupiter's account of him boded no good. I dreaded lest the continued pressure of misfortune had, at length, fairly unsettled the reason of my friend. Without a moment's hesitation, therefore, I prepared to accompany the Negro.

Upon reaching the wharf, I noticed a scythe and three spades, all apparently new, lying in the bottom of the boat in which we were to embark.

"What is the meaning of all this, Jup?" I inquired.

"Him syfe, massa, and spade."

"Very true; but what are they doing here?"

"Him de syfe and de spade what Massa Will sis pon my buying for him in de town, and de debbil's own lot of money I had to gib for em."

"But what, in the name of all that is mysterious, is your 'Massa Will' going to do with scythes and spades?"

"Dat's more dan *I* know, and debbil take me if I don't blieve 'tis more dan he know, too. But it's all cum ob de bug."

Finding that no satisfaction was to be obtained of Jupiter, whose whole intellect seemed to be absorbed by "de bug," I now stepped into the boat, and made sail. With a fair and strong breeze we soon ran into the little cove to the northward of Fort Moultrie, and a walk of some two miles brought us to the hut. It was about three in the afternoon when we arrived. Legrand had been awaiting us in eager expectation. He grasped my hand with a nervous *empressement* which alarmed me and strengthened the suspicions already entertained. His countenance

was pale even to ghastliness, and his deep-set eyes glared with unnat-
ural luster. After some inquiries respecting his health, I asked him, not
knowing what better to say, if he had yet obtained the *scarabaeus* from
Lieutenant G——.

"Oh, yes," he replied, coloring violently, "I got it from him the
next morning. Nothing should tempt me to part with that *scarabaeus.*
Do you know that Jupiter is quite right about it?"

"In what way?" I asked, with a sad foreboding at heart.

"In supposing it to be a bug of *real gold.*" He said this with an air
of profound seriousness, and I felt inexpressibly shocked.

"This bug is to make my fortune," he continued, with a tri-
umphant smile; "to reinstate me in my family possessions. Is it any
wonder, then, that I prize it? Since fortune has thought fit to bestow it
upon me, I have only to use it properly, and I shall arrive at the gold of
which it is the index. Jupiter, bring me that *scarabaeus!*"

"What! De bug, massa? I'd rudder not go fer trubble dat bug; you
mus git him for your own self." Hereupon Legrand arose, with a grave
and stately air, and brought me the beetle from a glass case in which it
was enclosed. It was a beautiful *scarabaeus*, and, at that time, unknown
to naturalists—of course a great prize in a scientific point of view.
There were two round black spots near one extremity of the back, and
a long one near the other. The scales were exceedingly hard and glossy,
with all the appearance of burnished gold. The weight of the insect
was very remarkable, and, taking all things into consideration, I could
hardly blame Jupiter for his opinion respecting it; but what to make of
Legrand's concordance with that opinion, I could not, for the life of
me, tell.

"I sent for you," said he, in a grandiloquent tone, when I had
completed my examination of the beetle, "I sent for you that I might
have your counsel and assistance in furthering the views of fate and of
the bug—"

"My dear Legrand," I cried, interrupting him, "you are certainly
unwell, and had better use some little precautions. You shall go to bed,
and I will remain with you a few days, until you get over this. You are
feverish and—"

"Feel my pulse," said he.

I felt it, and, to say the truth, found not the slightest indication
of fever.

"But you may be ill and yet have no fever. Allow me this once to
prescribe for you. In the first place, go to bed. In the next—"

"You are mistaken," he interposed, "I am as well as I can expect to be under the excitement which I suffer. If you really wish me well, you will relieve this excitement."

"And how is this to be done?"

"Very easily. Jupiter and myself are going upon an expedition into the hills, upon the mainland, and, in this expedition, we shall need the aid of some person in whom we can confide. You are the only one we can trust. Whether we succeed or fail, the excitement which you now perceive in me will be equally allayed."

"I am anxious to oblige you in any way," I replied; "but do you mean to say that this infernal beetle has any connection with your expedition into the hills?"

"It has."

"Then, Legrand, I can become a party to no such absurd proceeding."

"I am sorry—very sorry—for we shall have to try it by ourselves."

"Try it by yourselves! The man is surely mad!—but stay!—how long do you propose to be absent?"

"Probably all night. We shall start immediately, and be back, at all events, by sunrise."

"And will you promise me, upon your honor, that when this freak of yours is over, and the bug business (good God!) settled to your satisfaction, you will then return home and follow my advice implicitly, as that of your physician?"

"Yes; I promise; and now let us be off, for we have no time to lose."

With a heavy heart I accompanied my friend. We started about four o'clock—Legrand, Jupiter, the dog, and myself. Jupiter had with him the scythe and spades—the whole of which he insisted upon carrying—more through fear, it seemed to me, of trusting either of the implements within reach of his master, than from any excess of industry or complaisance. His demeanor was dogged in the extreme, and "dat deuced bug" were the sole words which escaped his lips during the journey. For my own part, I had charge of a couple of dark lanterns, while Legrand contented himself with the *scarabaeus*, which he carried attached to the end of a bit of whip-cord; twirling it to and fro, with the air of a conjuror, as he went. When I observed this last, plain evidence of my friend's aberration of mind, I could scarcely refrain from tears. I thought it best, however, to humor his fancy, at least for the present, or until I could adopt some more energetic measures with a chance of success. In the meantime I endeavored, but all in vain, to sound him in regard to the object of the expedition. Having succeeded in inducing me to accompany him, he seemed unwilling to hold conversation upon any topic of minor importance, and to all my questions vouchsafed no other reply than "we shall see!"

We crossed the creek at the head of the island by means of a skiff, and, ascending the high grounds on the shore of the mainland, proceeded in a northwesterly direction, through a tract of country excessively wild and desolate, where no trace of a human footstep was to be seen. Legrand led the way with decision; pausing only for an instant, here and there, to consult what appeared to be certain landmarks of his own contrivance upon a former occasion.

In this manner we journeyed for about two hours, and the sun was just setting when we entered a region infinitely more dreary than any yet seen. It was a species of tableland, near the summit of an almost inaccessible hill, densely wooded from base to pinnacle, and interspersed with huge crags that appeared to lie loosely upon the soil, and in many cases were prevented from precipitating themselves into the valleys below, merely by the support of the trees against which they reclined. Deep ravines, in various directions, gave an air of still sterner solemnity to the scene.

The natural platform to which we had clambered was thickly overgrown with brambles, through which we soon discovered that it would have been impossible to force our way but for the scythe; and Jupiter, by direction of his master, proceeded to clear for us a path to the foot of an enormously tall tulip-tree, which stood, with some eight or ten oaks, upon the level, and far surpassed them all, and all other trees which I had then ever seen, in the beauty of its foliage and form, in the wide spread of its branches, and in the general majesty of its appearance. When we reached this tree, Legrand turned to Jupiter, and asked him if he thought he could climb it. The old man seemed a little staggered by the question, and for some moments made no reply. At length he approached the huge trunk, walked slowly around it and examined it with minute attention. When he had completed his scrutiny, he merely said:

"Yes, massa, Jup climb any tree he ebber see in he life."

"Then up with you as soon as possible, for it will soon be too dark to see what we are about."

"How far mus go up, massa?" inquired Jupiter.

"Get up the main trunk first, and then I will tell you which way to go—and here—stop! take this beetle with you."

"De bug, Massa Will!—de goole-bug!" cried the Negro, drawing back in dismay—"what for mus tote de bug way up de tree?—d——n if I do!"

"If you are afraid, Jup, a great big Negro like you, to take hold of a harmless little dead beetle, why you can carry it up by this string— but, if you do not take it up with you in some way, I shall be under the necessity of breaking your head with this shovel."

"What de matter now, massa?" said Jup, evidently shamed into compliance; "always want for to raise fuss wid old nigger. Was only funnin, anyhow. *Me* feered de bug! what I keer for de bug?" Here he took cautiously hold of the extreme end of the string, and, maintaining the insect as far from his person as circumstances would permit, pre- pared to ascend the tree.

In youth, the tulip-tree, or *Liriodendron tulipiferum*, the most mag- nificent of American foresters, has a trunk peculiarly smooth, and often rises to a great height without lateral branches; but, in its riper age, the bark becomes gnarled and uneven, while many short limbs make their appearance on the stem. Thus the difficulty of ascension, in the present case, lay more in semblance than in reality. Embracing the huge cylin- der, as closely as possible with his arms and knees, seizing with his hands some projections, and resting his naked toes upon others, Jupiter, after one or two narrow escapes from falling, at length wriggled him- self into the first great fork, and seemed to consider the whole business as virtually accomplished. The *risk* of the achievement was, in fact, now over, although the climber was some sixty or seventy feet from the ground.

"Which way mus go now, Massa Will?" he asked.

"Keep up the largest branch—the one on this side," said Legrand. The Negro obeyed him promptly, and apparently with but little trou- ble; ascending higher and higher, until no glimpse of his squat figure could be obtained through the dense foliage which enveloped it. Presently his voice was heard in a sort of halloo.

"How much fudder is got for go?"

"How high up are you?" asked Legrand.

"Ebber so fur," replied the Negro; "can see de sky fru de top ob de tree."

"Never mind the sky, but attend to what I say. Look down the trunk and count the limbs below you on this side. How many limbs have you passed?"

"One, two, tree, four, fibe—I done pass fibe big limb, massa, pon dis side."

"Then go one limb higher."

In a few minutes the voice was heard again, announcing that the seventh limb was attained.

"Now, Jup," cried Legrand, evidently much excited. "I want you to work your way out upon that limb as far as you can. If you see anything strange let me know."

By this time what little doubt I might have entertained of my poor friend's insanity was put finally at rest. I had no alternative but to conclude him stricken with lunacy, and I became seriously anxious about getting him home. While I was pondering upon what was best to be done, Jupiter's voice was again heard.

"Mos feered for to venture on dis limb berry far—tis dead limb putty much all de way."

"Did you say it was a *dead* limb, Jupiter?" cried Legrand in a quavering voice.

"Yes, massa, him dead as de door-nail—done up for sartin—done departed dis here life."

"What in the name of heaven shall I do?" asked Legrand, seemingly in the greatest distress.

"Do!" said I, glad of an opportunity to interpose a word, "why, come home and go to bed. Come now!—that's a fine fellow. It's getting late, and, besides, you remember your promise."

"Jupiter," cried he, without heeding me in the least, "do you hear me?"

"Yes, Massa Will, hear you ebber so plain."

"Try the wood well, then, with your knife, and see if you think it *very* rotten."

"Him rotten, massa, sure nuff," replied the Negro in a few moments, "but not so berry rotten as mought be. Mought venture out lettle way pon de limb by myself, dat's true."

"By yourself!—what do you mean?"

"Why, I mean de bug. Tis *berry* hebby bug. Spose I drop him down fuss, and den de limb won't break wid just de weight ob one nigger."

"You infernal scoundrel!" cried Legrand, apparently much relieved, "what do you mean by telling me such nonsense as that? As sure as you drop that beetle I'll break your neck. Look here, Jupiter, do you hear me?"

"Yes, massa, needn't hollo at poor nigger dat style."

"Well! Now listen!—if you will venture out on the limb as far as you think safe, and not let go the beetle, I'll make you a present of a silver dollar as soon as you get down."

"I'm gwine, Massa Will—deed I is," replied the Negro very promptly—"mos out to the eend now."

"*Out to the end!*" here fairly screamed Legrand; "do you say you are out to the end of that limb?"

"Soon be to the eend, massa—o-o-o-o-oh! Lor-gol-a-mercy! What *is* dis here pon de tree?"

"Well!" cried Legrand, highly delighted, "what is it?"

"Why, taint noffin but a skull—somebody bin lef him head up de tree, and de crows done gobble ebery bit ob de meat off."

"A skull, you say!—very well—how is it fastened to the limb?— what holds it on?"

"Sure nuff, massa; mus look. Why dis berry curious sarcum-stance, pon my word—dare's a great big nail in de skull, what fastens ob it on to de tree."

"Well now, Jupiter, do exactly as I tell you—do you hear?"

"Yes, massa."

"Pay attention then—find the left eye of the skull."

"Hum! Hoo! Dat's good! Why dey aint no lef eye at all."

"Curse your stupidity! Do you know your right hand from your left?"

"Yes, I nose dat—nose all about dat—tis my lef hand what I chops de wood wid."

"To be sure! You are left-handed; and your left eye is on the same side as your left hand. Now, I suppose, you can find the left eye of the skull, or the place where the left eye has been. Have you found it?"

Here was a long pause. At length the Negro asked:

"Is de lef eye of de skull pon de same side as de lef hand of de skull, too?—cause de skull aint got not a bit ob a hand at all—nebber mind! I got de lef eye now—here de lef eye! what mus do wid it?"

"Let the beetle drop through it, as far as the string will reach— but be careful and not let go your hold of the string."

"All dat done, Massa Will; mighty easy ting for to put de bug fru de hole—look out for him dare below!"

During this colloquy no portion of Jupiter's person could be seen; but the beetle, which he had suffered to descend, was now visible at the end of the string, and glistened, like a globe of burnished gold, in the last rays of the setting sun, some of which still faintly illumined the eminence upon which we stood. The *scarabaeus* hung quite clear of any branches, and, if allowed to fall, would have fallen at our feet. Legrand immediately took the scythe, and cleared with it a circular space, three or four yards in diameter, just beneath the insect, and, having accomplished this, ordered Jupiter to let go the string and come down from the tree.

Driving a peg, with great nicety, into the ground, at the precise spot where the beetle fell, my friend now produced from his pocket a tapemeasure. Fastening one end of this at that point of the trunk of the tree which was nearest the peg, he unrolled it till it reached the peg and thence further unrolled it, in the direction already established by the two points of the tree and the peg, for the distance of fifty feet— Jupiter clearing away the brambles with the scythe. At the spot thus attained a second peg was driven, and about this, as a center, a rude circle, about four feet in diameter, described. Taking now a spade himself, and giving one to Jupiter and one to me, Legrand begged us to set about digging as quickly as possible.

To speak the truth, I had no especial relish for such amusement at any time, and, at that particular moment, would willingly have declined it; for the night was coming on, and I felt much fatigued with the exercise already taken; but I saw no mode of escape, and was fearful of disturbing my poor friend's equanimity by a refusal. Could I have depended, indeed, upon Jupiter's aid, I would have had no hesitation in attempting to get the lunatic home by force; but I was too well assured of the old Negro's disposition to hope that he would assist me, under any circumstances, in a personal contest with his master. I made no doubt that the latter had been infected with some of the innumerable Southern superstitions about money buried, and that his fantasy had received confirmation by the finding of the *scarabaeus*, or, perhaps, by Jupiter's obstinancy in maintaining it to be "a bug of real gold." A mind disposed to lunacy would readily be led away by such suggestions—especially if chiming in with favorite preconceived ideas—and then I called to mind the poor fellow's speech about the beetle's being "the index of his fortune." Upon the whole, I was sadly vexed and puzzled, but, at length, I concluded to make a virtue of necessity—to dig with a good will, and thus the sooner to convince the visionary, by ocular demonstration, of the fallacy of the opinion he entertained.

The lanterns have been lit, we all fell to work with a zeal worthy a more rational cause; and, as the glare fell upon our persons and implements, I could not help thinking how picturesque a group we composed, and how strange and suspicious our labors must have appeared to any interloper who, by chance, might have stumbled upon our whereabouts.

We dug very steadily for two hours. Little was said; and our chief embarrassment lay in the yelping of the dog, who took exceeding interest in our proceedings. He, at length, became so obstreperous that we grew fearful of his giving the alarm to some stragglers in the vicinity—or, rather, this was the apprehension of Legrand—for myself, I should have rejoiced at any interruption which might have enabled me to get the wanderer home. The noise was, at length, very effectually silenced by Jupiter, who, getting out of the hole with a dogged air of deliberation, tied the brute's mouth up with one of his suspenders, and then returned, with a grave chuckle, to his task.

When the time mentioned had expired, we had reached a depth of five feet, and yet no signs of any treasure became manifest. A general pause ensued, and I began to hope that the farce was at an end. Legrand, however, although evidently much disconcerted, wiped his brow thoughtfully and recommenced. We had excavated the entire circle of four feet diameter, and now we slightly enlarged the limit, and went to the further depth of two feet. Still nothing appeared. The gold-seeker, whom I sincerely pitied, at length clambered from the pit, with the bitterest disappointment imprinted upon every feature, and proceeded, slowly and reluctantly, to put on his coat, which he had thrown off at the beginning of his labor. In the meantime I made no remark. Jupiter, at a signal from his master, began to gather up his tools. This done and the dog having been unmuzzled, we turned in profound silence toward home.

We had taken, perhaps, a dozen steps in this direction, when, with a loud oath, Legrand strode up to Jupiter, and seized him by the collar. The astonished Negro opened his eyes and mouth to the fullest extent, let fall the spades, and fell upon his knees.

"You scoundrel!" said Legrand, hissing out the syllables from between his clinched teeth—"you infernal black villain!—speak, I tell you!—answer me this instant, without prevarication!—which—which is your left eye?"

"Oh, my golly, Massa Will! aint dis here my lef eye for sartain?" roared the terrified Jupiter, placing his hand upon his *right* organ of vision, and holding it there with a desperate pertinacity, as if in immediate dread of his master's attempt at a gouge.

"I thought so!—I knew it! Hurrah!" vociferated Legrand, letting the Negro go and executing a series of curvets and caracols, much to the astonishment of his valet, who, arising from his knees, looked, mutely, from his master to myself, and then from myself to his master.

"Come! We must go back," said the latter, "the game's not up yet"; and he again led the way to the tulip-tree.

"Jupiter," said he, when we reached its foot, "come here! was the skull nailed to the limb with the face outward, or with the face to the limb?"

"De face was out, massa, so dat de crows could gt at de eyes good, widout any trouble."

"Well, then, was it this eye or that through which you dropped the beetle?" here Legrand touched each of Jupiter's eyes.

"'Twas dis eye, massa—de lef eye—jis as you tell me," and here it was his right eye that the negro indicated.

"That will do—we must try it again."

Here my friend, about whose madness I now saw, or fancied that I saw, certain indications of method, removed the peg which marked the spot where the beetle fell, to a spot about three inches to the westward of its former position. Taking, now, the tape measure from the nearest point of the trunk to the peg, as before, and continuing the extension in a straight line to the distance of fifty feet, a spot was indicated, removed, by several yards, from the point at which we had been digging.

Around the new position a circle, somewhat larger than in the former instance, was now described, and we again set to work with the spade. I was dreadfully weary, but, scarcely understanding what had occasioned the change in my thoughts, I felt no longer any great aversion from the labor imposed. I had become most unaccountably interested—nay, even excited. Perhaps there was something, amid all the extravagant demeanor of Legrand—some air of forethought, or of deliberation, which impressed me. I dug eagerly, and now and then caught myself actually looking, with something that very much resembled expectation, for the fancied treasure, the vision of which had demented my unfortunate companion. At a period when such vagaries of thought most fully possessed me, and when we had been at work perhaps an hour and a half, we were again interrupted by the violent howlings of the dog. His uneasiness, in the first instance, had been, evidently, but the result of playfulness or caprice, but he now assumed a bitter and serious tone. Upon Jupiter's again attempting to muzzle him, he made furious resistance, and, leaping into the hole, tore up the mould frantically with his claws. In a few seconds he had uncovered a mass of human bones, forming two complete skeletons, intermingled with several buttons of metal, and what appeared to be the dust of decayed woolen. One or two strokes of a spade upturned the blade of a large Spanish knife, and, as we dug further, three or four loose pieces of gold and silver coin came to light.

At sight of these the joy of Jupiter could scarcely be restrained, but the countenance of his master wore an air of extreme disappointment. He urged us, however, to continue our exertions, and the words were hardly uttered when I stumbled and fell forward, having caught the toe of my boot in a large ring of iron that lay half buried in the loose earth.

We now worked in earnest, and never did I pass ten minutes of more intense excitement. During this interval we had fairly unearthed an oblong chest of wood, which, from its perfect preservation and wonderful hardness, had plainly been subjected to some mineralizing process—perhaps that of the bichloride of mercury. This box was three feet and a half long, three feet broad, and two and a half feet deep. It was firmly secured by bands of wrought iron, riveted, and forming a kind of open trellis-work over the whole. On each side of the chest, near the top, were three rings of iron—six in all—by means of which a firm hold could be obtained by six persons. Our utmost united endeavors served only to disturb the coffer very slightly in its bed. We at once saw the impossibility of removing so great a weight. Luckily, the sole fastenings of the lid consisted of two sliding bolts. These we drew back—trembling and panting with anxiety. In an instant, a treasure of incalculable value lay gleaming before us. As the rays of the lanterns fell within the pit, there flashed upward a glow and a glare, from a confused heap of gold and jewels, that absolutely dazzled our eyes.

I shall not pretend to describe the feelings with which I gazed. Amazement was, of course, predominant. Legrand appeared exhausted with excitement, and spoke very few words. Jupiter's countenance wore, for some minutes, as deadly a pallor as it is possible, in the nature of things, for any Negro's visage to assume. He seemed stupefied—thunderstricken. Presently he fell upon his knees in the pit, and burying his naked arms up to the elbows in gold, let them there remain, as if enjoying the luxury of a bath. At length, with a deep sigh, he exclaimed, as if in a soliloquy:

"And dis all cum ob de goole-bug! De putty goole-bug! De poor little goole-bug, what I boosed in that sabage kind ob style! Aint you shamed ob yourself, nigger?—answer me dat!"

It became necessary, at last, that I should arouse both master and valet to the expediency of removing the treasure. It was growing late, and it behooved us to make exertion, that we might get everything housed before daylight. It was difficult to say what should be done, and much time was spent in deliberation—so confused were the ideas of all. We, finally, lightened the box by removing two-thirds of its contents, when we were enabled, with some trouble, to raise it from the hole. The articles taken out were deposited among the brambles, and the dog left to guard them, with strict orders from Jupiter neither, upon any pretense, to stir from the spot, nor to open his mouth until our return. We then hurriedly made for home with the chest; reaching the hut in safety, but after excessive toil, at one o'clock in the morning. Worn out as we were, it was not in human nature to do more immediately. We rested until two, and had supper; starting for the hills immediately afterward, armed with three stout sacks, which, by good luck, were upon the premises. A little before four we arrived at the pit, divided the remainder of the booty, as equally as might be, among us, and, leaving the holes unfilled, again set out for the hut, at which, for the second time, we deposited our golden burdens, just as the first faint streaks of the dawn gleamed over the treetops in the east.

We were now thoroughly broken down; but the intense excitement of the time denied us repose. After an unquiet slumber of some three or four hours' duration, we arose, as if by preconcert, to make examination of our treasure.

The chest had been full to the brim, and we spent the whole day, and the greater part of the next night, in a scrutiny of its contents. There had been nothing like order or arrangement. Everything had been heaped in promiscuously. Having assorted all with care, we found ourselves possessed of even vaster wealth than we had at first supposed. In coin, there was rather more than four hundred and fifty thousand dollars—estimating the value of the pieces, as accurately as we could, by the tables of the period. There was not a particle of silver. All was gold of antique date and of great variety—French, Spanish, and German money, with a few English guineas, and some counters, of which we had never seen specimens before. There were several very large and heavy coins, so worn that we could make nothing of their inscriptions. There was no American money. The value of the jewels we found more difficulty in estimating. There were diamonds—some of them exceedingly large and fine—a hundred and ten in all, and not one of them small; eighteen rubies of remarkable brilliancy; three hundred and ten emeralds, all very beautiful; and twenty-one sapphires, with an opal. These stones had all been broken from their settings and thrown loose in the chest. The settings themselves, which we picked out from among the other gold, appeared to have been beaten up with hammers, as if to prevent identification. Besides all this, there was a vast quantity of solid gold ornaments; nearly two hundred massive finger and ear rings; rich chains—thirty of these, if I remember; eighty-three very large and heavy crucifixes; five gold censers of great value; a prodigious golden punch-bowl, ornamented with richly chased vine-leaves and Bacchanalian figures; with two sword-handles exquisitely embossed, and many other smaller articles which I can not recollect. The weight of these valuables exceeded three hundred and fifty pounds avoirdupois; and in this estimate I have not included one hundred and ninety-seven superb gold watches; three of the number being worth each five hundred dollars, if one. Many of them were very old, and as timekeepers, valueless; the works having suffered, more or less, from corrosion—but all were richly jeweled and in cases of great worth. We estimated the entire contents of the chest, that night, at a million and a half of dollars; and upon the subsequent disposal of the trinkets and jewels (a few being retained for our own use), it was found that we had greatly undervalued the treasure.

When, at length, we had concluded our examination, and the intense excitement of the time had, in some measure, subsided, Legrand, who saw that I was dying with impatience for a solution of this most extraordinary riddle, entered into a full detail of all the circumstances connected with it.

"You remember," said he, "the night when I handed you the rough sketch I had made of the *scarabaeus.* You recollect, also, that I became quite vexed at you for insisting that my drawing resembled a death's-head. When you first made this assertion I thought you were jesting; but afterward I called to mind the peculiar spots on the back of the insect, and admitted to myself that your remark had some little foundation in fact. Still, the sneer at my graphic powers irritated me—for I am considered a good artist—and, therefore, when you handed me the scrap of parchment, I was about to crumple it up and throw it angrily into the fire."

"The scrap of paper, you mean," said I.

"No; it had much of the appearance of paper, and at first I supposed it to be such, but when I came to draw upon it, I discovered it at once to be a piece of very thin parchment. It was quite dirty, you remember. Well, as I was in the very act of crumpling it up, my glance fell upon the sketch at which you had been looking, and you may imagine my astonishment when I perceived, in fact, the figure of a death's-head just where, it seemed to me, I had made the drawing of the beetle. For a moment I was too much amazed to think with accuracy. I knew that my design was very different in detail from this—although there was a certain similarity in general outline. Presently I took a candle, and seating myself at the other end of the room, proceeded to scrutinize the parchment more closely. Upon turning it over, I saw my own sketch upon the reverse, just as I had made it. My first idea, now, was mere surprise at the really remarkable similarity of outline—at the singular coincidence involved in the fact that, unknown to me, there should have been a skull upon the other side of the parchment, immediately beneath my figure of the *scarabaeus*, and that this skull, not only in outline, but in size should so closely resemble my drawing. I say the singularity of this coincidence absolutely stupefied me for a time. This is the usual effect of such coincidences. The mind struggles to establish a connection—a sequence of cause and effect—and, being unable to do so, suffers a species of temporary paralysis. But, when I recovered from this stupor, there dawned upon me gradually a conviction which startled me even far more than the coincidence. I began distinctly, positively, to remember that there had been *no* drawing upon the parchment when I made my sketch of the *scarabaeus*. I became perfectly certain of this; for I recollected turning up first one side and then the other, in search of the cleanest spot. Had the skull been then there, of course, I could not have failed to notice it. Here was indeed a mystery which I felt it impossible to explain; but, even at that early moment, there seemed to glimmer, faintly, within the most remote and secret chambers of my intellect, a glowwormlike conception of that truth which last night's adventure brought to so magnificent a demonstration. I arose at once, and, putting the parchment securely away, dismissed all further reflection until I should be alone.

"When you had gone, and when Jupiter was fast asleep, I betook myself to a more methodical investigation of the affair. In the first place, I considered the manner in which the parchment had come into my possession. The spot where we discovered the *scarabaeus* was on the coast of the mainland, about a mile eastward of the island, and but a short distance over high-water mark. Upon my taking hold of it, it gave me a sharp bite, which caused me to let it drop. Jupiter, with his accustomed caution, before seizing the insect, which had flown toward him, looked about him for a leaf, or something of that nature, by which to take hold of it. It was at this moment that his eyes, and mine also, fell upon the scrap of parchment, which I then supposed to be paper. It was lying half buried in the sand, a corner sticking up. Near the spot where we found it, I observed the remnants of the hull of what appeared to have been a ship's long-boat. The wreck seemed to have been there for a very great while; for the resemblance to boat timbers could scarcely be traced.

"Well, Jupiter picked up the parchment, wrapped the beetle in it, and gave it to me. Soon afterward we turned to go home, and on the way met Lieutenant G——. I showed him the insect, and he begged me to let him take it to the fort. Upon my consenting, he thrust it forthwith into his waistcoat pocket, without the parchment in which it had been wrapped, and which I had continued to hold in my hand during his inspection. Perhaps he dreaded my changing my mind, and thought it best to make sure of the prize at once—you know how enthusiastic he is on all subjects connected with natural history. At the same time, without being conscious of it, I must have deposited the parchment in my own pocket.

"You remember that when I went to the table for the purpose of making a sketch of the beetle, I found no paper where it was usually kept. I looked in the drawer, and found none there. I searched my pockets, hoping to find an old letter, when my hand fell upon the parchment. I thus detail the precise mode in which it came into my possession; for the circumstances impressed me with peculiar force.

"No doubt you will think me fanciful—but I had already established a kind of *connection*. I had put together two links of a great chain. There was a boat lying upon a seacoast, and not far from the boat was a parchment—*not a paper*—with a skull depicted upon it. You will, of course, ask 'where is the connection?' I reply that the skull, or death's-head, is the well-known emblem of the pirate. The flag of the death's-head is hoisted in all engagements.

"I have said that the scrap was parchment, and not paper. Parchment is durable—almost imperishable. Matters of little moment are rarely consigned to parchment; since, for the mere ordinary purposes of drawing or writing, it is not nearly so well adapted as paper. This reflection suggested some meaning—some relevancy—in the death's-head. I did not fail to observe, also the *form* of the parchment. Although one of its corners had been, by some accident, destroyed, it could be seen that the original form was oblong. It was just such a slip, indeed, as might have been chosen for a memorandum—for a record of something to be long remembered and carefully preserved."

"But," I interposed, "you say that the skull was *not* upon the parchment when you made the drawing of the beetle. How then do you trace any connection between the boat and the skull—since this latter, according to your own admission, must have been designed (God only knows how or by whom) at some period subsequent to your sketching the *scarabaeus?*"

"Ah, hereupon turns the whole mystery; although the secret, at this point, I had comparatively little difficulty in solving. My steps were sure, and could afford but a single result. I reasoned, for example, thus: when I drew the *scarabaeus*, there was no skull apparent upon the parchment. When I had completed the drawing I gave it to you, and observed you narrowly until you returned it. *You*, therefore, did not design the skull, and no one else was present to do it. Then it was not done by human agency. And nevertheless it was done.

"At this stage of my reflections I endeavored to remember, and *did* remember, with entire distinctiveness, every incident which occurred about the period in question. The weather was chilly (oh, rare and happy accident!) and a fire was blazing upon the hearth. I was heated with exercise and sat near the table. You, however, had drawn a chair close to the chimney. Just as I placed the parchment in your hand, and as you were in the act of inspecting it, Wolf, the Newfoundland, entered, and leaped upon your shoulders. With your left hand you caressed him and kept him off, while your right, holding the parchment, was permitted to fall listlessly between your knees, and in close proximity to the fire. At one moment, I thought the blaze had caught it, and was about to caution you, but, before I could speak, you had withdrawn it, and were engaged in its examination. When I considered all these particulars, I doubted not for a moment that *heat* had been the agent in bringing to light, upon the parchment, the skull which I saw designed upon it. You are well aware that chemical preparations exist, and have existed time out of mind, by means of which it is possible to write upon either paper or vellum, so that the characters shall become visible only when subjected to the action of fire. Zaffre, digested in *aqua regia*, and diluted with four times its weight of water, is sometimes employed; a green tint results. The regulus of cobalt, dissolved in spirit of nitre, gives a red. These colors disappear at longer or shorter intervals after the material written upon cools, but again becomes apparent upon the reapplication of heat.

"I now scrutinized the death's-head with care. Its outer edges—the edges of the drawing nearest the edge of the vellum—were far more *distinct* than the others. It was clear that the action of the caloric had been imperfect or unequal. I immediately kindled a fire, and subjected every portion of the parchment to a glowing heat. At first, the only effect was the strengthening of the faint lines in the skull; but, upon persevering in the experiment, there became visible, at the corner of the slip, diagonally opposite to the spot in which the death's-head was delineated, the figure of what I at first supposed to be a goat. A closer scrutiny, however, satisfied me that it was intended for a kid."

"Ha! Ha!" said I, "to be sure I have no right to laugh at you—a million and a half of money is too serious a matter for mirth—but you are not about to establish a third link in your chain—you will not find any especial connection between your pirates and a goat—pirates, you know, have nothing to do with goats; they appertain to the farming interest."

"But I have just said that the figure was *not* that of a goat."

"Well, a kid, then—pretty much the same thing."

"Pretty much, but not altogether," said Legrand. "You may have heard of one *Captain* Kidd. I at once looked upon the figure of the animal as a kind of punning or hieroglyphical signature. I say signature, because its position upon the vellum suggested this idea. The death's-head at the corner diagonally opposite, had, in the same manner, the air of a stamp, or seal. But I was sorely put out by the absence of all else—of the body to my imagined instrument—of the text for my context."

"I presume you expected to find a letter between the stamp and the signature."

"Something of that kind. The fact is, I felt irresistibly impressed with a presentiment of some vast good fortune impending. I can scarcely say why. Perhaps, after all, it was rather a desire than an actual belief—but do you know that Jupiter's silly words, about the bug being of solid gold, had a remarkable effect upon my fancy? And then the series of accidents and coincidents—there were so *very* extraordinary. Do you observe how mere an accident it was that these events should have occurred upon the *sole* day of all the year in which it has been, or may be sufficiently cool for fire, and that without the fire, or without the intervention of the dog at the precise moment in which he appeared, I should never have become aware of the death's-head, and so never the possessor of the treasure?"

"But proceed—I am all impatience."

"Well; you have heard, of course, the many stories current—the thousand vague rumors afloat about money buried, somewhere upon the Atlantic coast, by Kidd and his associates. These rumors must have had some foundation in fact. And that the rumors have existed so long and so continuously, could have resulted, it appeared to me, only from the circumstance of the buried treasures still *remaining* entombed. Had Kidd concealed his plunder for a time, and afterward reclaimed it, the rumors would scarcely have reached us in their present unvarying form. You will observe that the stories told are all about money-seekers, not about money-finders. Had the pirate recovered his money, there the affair would have dropped. It seemed to me that some accident—say the loss of a memorandum indicating its locality—had deprived him of the means of recovering it, and that this accident had become known to his followers, who otherwise might never have heard that the treasure had been concealed at all, and who, busying themselves in vain, because unguided, attempts to regain it, had given first birth, and then universal currency, to the reports which are now so common. Have you ever heard of any important treasure being unearthed along the coast?"

"Never."

"But that Kidd's accumulations were immense is well known. I took it for granted, therefore, that the earth still held them; and you will scarcely be surprised when I tell you that I felt a hope, nearly amounting to certainty, that the parchment so strangely found involved a lost record of the place of deposit."

"But how did you proceed?"

"I held the vellum again to the fire, after increasing the heat, but nothing appeared. I now thought it possible that the coating of dirt might have something to do with the failure; so I carefully rinsed the parchment by pouring warm water over it, and having done this, I placed it in a tin pan, with the skull downward, and put the pan upon a furnace of lighted charcoal. In a few minutes, the pan having become thoroughly heated, I removed the slip, and, to my inexpressible joy, found it spotted, in several places, with what appeared to be figures arranged in lines. Again I placed it in the pan, and suffered it to remain another minute. Upon taking it off, the whole was just as you see it now.

Here Legrand, having reheated the parchment, submitted it to my inspection. The following characters were rudely traced, in a a red tint, between the death's-head and the goat:

53‡‡†305))6*;4826)4‡(4‡.;806*;48†8¶60)85;1‡(;:‡*8†83(88)5*
†;46(;88*96*?;8)*‡(;485);5*†2:*‡(;4956*2(5*—4)8¶8*;
4069285);)6†8)4‡‡;1(‡9;48081;8:8‡1;48†85;4)485†528806*81(
‡9;48;(88;4(‡?34;48)4‡;161;:188;‡?;

"But," said I, returning him the slip, "I am as much in the dark as
ever. Were all the jewels of Golconda awaiting me upon my solution of
this enigma, I am quite sure that I should be unable to earn them."

"And yet," said Legrand, "the solution is by no means so difficult
as you might be led to imagine from the first hasty inspection of the
characters. These characters, as anyone might readily guess, form a
cipher—that is to say, they convey a meaning; but then from what is
known of Kidd, I could not suppose him capable of constructing any
of the more abstruse cryptographs. I made up my mind, at once, that
this was of a simple species—such, however, as would appear, to the
crude intellect of the sailor, absolutely insoluble without the key."

"And you really solved it?"

"Readily; I have solved others of an abstruseness ten thousand
times greater. Circumstances, and a certain bias of mind, have led me
to take interest in such riddles, and it may well be doubted whether
human ingenuity can construct an enigma of the kind which human
ingenuity may not, by proper application, resolve. In fact, having once
established connected and legible characters, I scarcely gave a thought
to the mere difficulty of developing their import.

"In the present case—indeed, in all cases of secret writing—the
first question regards the *language* of the cipher; for the principles of
solution, so far, especially, as the more simple ciphers are concerned,
depend upon, and are varied by, the genius of the particular idiom. In
general, there is no alternative but experiment (directed by probabili-
ties) of every tongue known to him who attempts the solution, until
the true one be attained. But, with the cipher now before us all difficulty was removed by the signature. The pun upon the word 'Kidd' is
appreciable in no other language than the English. But for this consideration I should have begun my attempts with Spanish and French, as
the tongues in which a secret of this kind would most naturally have
been written by a pirate of the Spanish main. As it was, I assumed the
cryptograph to be English.

"You observe there are no divisions between the words. Had
there been divisions the task would have been comparatively easy. In
such cases I should have commenced with a collation and analysis of

the shorter words, and, had a word of a single letter occurred, as is most likely (*a* or *I*, for example), I should have considered the solution as assured. But, there being no division, my first step was to ascertain the predominant letters, as well as the least frequent. Counting all, I constructed a table thus:

Of the characters 8 there are 33.

;	"	26.
4	"	19.
‡)	"	16.
*	"	13.
5	"	12.
6	"	11.
†1	"	8.
0	"	6.
92	"	5.
:3	"	4.
?	"	3.
¶	"	2.
—.	"	1.

"Now, in English, the letter which most frequently occurs is *e.* Afterward, the succession runs thus: *a o i d h n r s t u y c f g l m w b k p q x z.* E predominates so remarkably, that an individual sentence of any length is rarely seen, in which it is not the prevailing character.

"Here, then, we have, in the very beginning, the groundwork for something more than a mere guess. The general use which may be made of the table is obvious—but, in this particular cipher, we shall only very partially require its aid. As our predominant character is 8, we will commence by assuming it as the *e* of the natural alphabet. To verify the supposition, let us observe if the 8 be seen often in cou-ples—for *e* is doubled with great frequency in English—in such words, for example, as 'meet,' 'fleet,' 'speed,' 'seen,' 'been,' 'agree,' etc. In the present instance we see it doubled no less than five times, although the cryptograph is brief.

"Let us assume 8, then, as *e.* Now, of all *words* in the language, 'the' is most usual; let us see, therefore, whether there are not repetitions of any three characters, in the same order of collocation, the last of them being 8. If we discover repetitions of such letters, so arranged, they will most probably represent the word 'the.' Upon inspection, we find no less than seven such arrangements, the characters being ;48. We may, therefore, assume that ; represents *t*, 4 represents *h*, and 8 represents *e*— the last being now well confirmed. Thus a great step has been taken.

"But, having established a single word, we are enabled to establish a vastly important point; that is to say, several commencements and terminations of other words. Let us refer, for example, to the last instance but one, in which the combination ;48 occurs—not far from the end of the cipher. We know that the ; immediately ensuing is the commencement of a word, and, of six characters succeeding this 'the,' we are cognizant of no less than five. Let us set these characters down, thus, by the letters we know them to represent, leaving a space for the unknown—

t eeth.

"Here we are enabled, at once, to discard the *th* as forming no portion of the word commencing with the first *t*; since, by experiment of the entire alphabet for a letter adapted to the vacancy, we perceive that no word can be formed of which this *th* can be a part. We are thus narrowed into

t ee,

and, going through the alphabet, if necessary, as before, we arrive at the word 'tree,' as the sole possible reading. We thus gain another letter, *r*, represented by (, with the words 'the tree' in juxtaposition.

"Looking beyond these words, for a short distance, we again see the combination ;48, and employ it by way of termination to what immediately precedes. We have thus this arrangement:

the tree ;4 (‡?34 the,

or, substituting the natural letters, where known, it reads thus:

the tree thr‡?3h the.

"Now, if, in the place of the unknown characters, we leave blank spaces, or substitute dots, we read thus:

the tree thr...h the,

when the word '*through*' makes itself evident at once. But this discovery gives us three new letters, *o, u,* and *g*, represented by ↕ , ?, and 3.

"Looking now, narrowly, through the cipher for combinations of known characters, we find, not very far from the beginning, this arrangement,

83(88, or egree,

which plainly is the conclusion of the word 'degree,' and gives us another letter, *d*, represented by ↕ .

"Four letters beyond the word 'degree,' we perceive the combination

;46(;88

"Translating the known characters, and representing the unknown by dots, as before, we read thus:

th.rtee,

an arrangement immediately suggestive of the word 'thirteen,' and again furnishing us with two new characters, *i* and *n*, represented by 6 and *.

"Referring, now, to the beginning of the cryptograph, we find the combination,

53↕↕†.

Translating as before, we obtain

.good,

which assures us that the first letter is *A*, and that the first two words are 'A good.'

"It is now time that we arrange our key, as far as discovered, in a tabular form, to avoid confusion. It will stand thus:

5	represents	a
†	"	d
8	"	e

3	"	g
4	"	h
6	"	i
*	"	n
↨	"	o
(	"	r
;	"	t
?	"	u

"We have, therefore, no less than eleven of the most important letters represented, and it will be unnecessary to proceed with the details of the solution. I have said enough to convince you that ciphers of this nature are readily soluble, and to give you some insight into the *rationale* of their development. But be assured that the specimen before us appertains to the very simplest species of cryptograph. It now only remains to give you the full translation of the characters upon the parchment as unriddled. Here it is:

A good glass in the bishop's hostel in the devil's seat forty-one degrees and thirteen minutes northeast and by north main branch seventh limb east side shoot from the left eye of the death's-head a bee-line from the tree through the shot fifty feet out.

"But," said I, "the enigma seems still in as bad a condition as ever. How is it possible to extort a meaning from all this jargon about 'devil's seats,' 'death's-head,' and 'bishop's hostels?'"

"I confess," replied Legrand, "that the matter still wears a serious aspect, when regarded with a casual glance. My first endeavor was to divide the sentence into the natural division intended by the cryptographist."

"You mean, to punctuate it?"

"Something of that kind."

"But how was it possible to effect this?"

"I reflected that it had been a *point* with the writer to run his words together without division, so as to increase the difficulty of solution. Now, a not overacute man, in pursuing such an object, would be nearly certain to overdo the matter. When, in the course of his composition, he arrived at a break in his subject which would naturally require a pause, or a point, he would be exceedingly apt to run his characters, at this place, more than usually close together. If you will observe the MS., in the present instance, you will easily detect five such cases of unusual crowding. Acting upon this hint, I made the division thus:

A good glass in the Bishop's hostel in the Devil's seat—forty-one degrees and thirteen minutes—northeast and by north—main branch seventh limb east side—shoot from the left eye of the death's-head—a bee-line from the tree through the shot fifty feet out.

"Even this division," said I, "leaves me still in the dark."

"It left me also in the dark," replied Legrand, "for a few days; during which I made diligent inquiry in the neighborhood of Sulli-van's Island, for any building which went by name of the 'Bishop's Hotel'; for, of course, I dropped the obsolete word 'hostel.' Gaining no information on the subject, I was on the point of extending my sphere of search and proceeding in a more systematic manner, when, one morning, it entered into my head, quite suddenly, that this 'Bishop's Hostel' might have some reference to an old family, of the name of Bessop, which, time out of mind, had held possession of an ancient manor-house, about four miles to the northward of the island. I accordingly went over to the plantation, and reinstituted my inquires among the older Negroes of the place. At length one of the most aged of the women said that she had heard of such a place as *Bessop's Castle,* and thought that she could guide me to it, but that it was not a castle, nor a tavern, but a high rock.

"I offered to pay her well for her trouble, and, after some demur, she consented to accompany me to the spot. We found it without much difficulty, when, dismissing her, I proceeded to examine the place. The 'castle' consisted of an irregular assemblage of cliffs and rocks—one of the latter being quite remarkable for its height as well as for its insulated and artificial appearance. I clambered to its apex, and then felt much at a loss as to what should be next done.

"While I was busied in reflection, my eyes fell upon a narrow ledge in the eastern face of the rock, perhaps a yard below the summit upon which I stood. This ledge projected about eighteen inches, and was not more than a foot wide, while a niche in the cliff just above it gave it a rude resemblance to one of the hollow-backed chairs used by our ancestors. I made no doubt that here was the 'devil's seat' alluded to in the MS., and now I seemed to grasp the full secret of the riddle.

"The 'good glass,' I knew, could have reference to nothing but a telescope; for the word 'glass' is rarely employed in any other sense by seamen. Now here, I at once saw, was a telescope to be used, and a definite point of view, *admitting no variation*, from which to use it. Nor did I hesitate to believe that the phrases, 'forty-one degrees and thirteen minutes,' and 'northeast and by north,' were intended as directions for the leveling of the glass. Greatly excited by these discoveries, I hurried home, procured a telescope, and returned to the rock.

"I let myself down to the ledge, and found that it was impossible to retain a seat upon it except in one particular position. This fact confirmed my preconceived idea. I proceeded to use the glass. Of course, the 'forty-one degrees and thirteen minutes' could allude to nothing but elevation above the visible horizon, since the horizontal direction was clearly indicated by the words, 'northeast and by north.' This latter direction I at once established by means of a pocket-compass; then, pointing the glass as nearly at an angle of forty-one degrees of elevation as I could do it by guess, I moved it cautiously up or down, until my attention was arrested by a circular rift or opening in the foliage of a large tree that overtopped its fellows in the distance. In the center of this rift I perceived a white spot, but could not, at first, distinguish what it was. Adjusting the focus of the telescope, I again looked, and now made it out to be a human skull.

"Upon this discovery I was so sanguine as to consider the enigma solved; for the phrase 'main branch, seventh limb, east side,' could refer only to the position of the skull upon the tree, while 'shoot for the left eye of the death's-head' admitted, also, of but one interpretation, in regard to a search for buried treasure. I perceived that the design was to drop a bullet from the left eye of the skull, and that a bee-line, or, in other words, a straight line, drawn from the nearest point of the trunk through the shot (or the spot where the bullet fell), and thence extended to a distance of fifty feet, would indicate a definite point— and beneath this point I thought it at least *possible* that a deposit of value lay concealed."

"All this," I said, "is exceedingly clear, and, although ingenious, still simple and explicit. When you left the Bishop's Hotel, what then?"

"Why, having carefully taken the bearings of the tree, I turned homeward. The instant that I left 'the devil's seat,' however, the circular rift vanished; nor could I get a glimpse of it afterward, turn as I would. What seems to me the chief ingenuity in this whole business, is the fact (for repeated experiment has convinced me it *is* a fact) that the circular opening in question is visible from no other attainable point of view than that afforded by the narrow ledge upon the face of the rock.

"In this expedition to the 'Bishop's Hotel' I had been attended by Jupiter, who had, no doubt, observed, for some weeks past, the abstraction of my demeanor, and took especial care not to leave me alone. But, on the next day, getting up very early, I contrived to give him the slip, and went into the hills in search of the tree. After much toil I found it. When I came home at night my valet proposed to give me a flogging. With the rest of the adventure I believe you are as well acquainted as myself."

"I suppose," said I, "you missed the spot, in the first attempt at digging, through Jupiter's stupidity in letting the bug fall through the right instead of through the left eye of the skull."

"Precisely. This mistake made a difference of about two inches and a half in the 'shot'—that is to say, in the position of the peg nearest the tree; and had the treasure been *beneath* the 'shot,' the error would have been of little moment; but 'the shot,' together with the nearest point of the tree, were merely two points for the establishment of a line of direction; of course, the error, however trivial in the beginning, increased as we proceeded with the line, and by the time we had gone fifty feet threw us quite off the scent. But for my deep-seated impressions that treasure was here somewhere actually buried, we might have had all our labor in vain."

"But your grandiloquence, and your conduct in swinging the beetle—how excessively odd! I was sure you were mad. And why did you insist upon letting fall the bug, instead of a bullet, from the skull?"

"Why, to be frank, I felt somewhat annoyed by your evident suspicions touching my sanity, and so resolved to punish you quietly, in my own way, by a little bit of sober mystification. For this reason I swung the beetle, and for this reason I let it fall from the tree. An observation of yours about its great weight suggested the latter idea."

"Yes, I perceive; and now there is only one point which puzzles me. What are we to make of the skeletons found in the hole?"

"That is a question I am no more able to answer than yourself. There seems, however, only one plausible way of accounting for them—and yet it is dreadful to believe in such atrocity as my suggestion would imply. It is clear that Kidd—if Kidd indeed secreted this treasure, which I doubt not—it is clear that he must have had assistance in the labor. But this labor concluded, he may have thought it expedient to remove all participants in his secret. Perhaps a couple of blows with a mattock were sufficient, while his coadjutors were busy in the pit; perhaps it required a dozen—who shall tell?"

Talmage Powell got his start in mystery fiction writing for the pulps, and eventually sold over 500 short stories to various markets. Although he has written a few novels, his best work is by far found in his short stories. A regular in the Alfred Hitchcock's Mystery Magazine and Ellery Queen's Mystery Magazine, his work appeared in just about every detective magazine that existed. "The Vital Element," as do so many of his stories, shows why.

The Vital Element

Talmage Powell

I would never again love the warm water of the Gulf of Mexico . . . never find beauty in its blue-green color . . . never hear music in its rustling surf . . .

The dead girl had been hurriedly buried in the Gulf. She was anchored in about thirty feet of water with a hempen rope that linked her lashed ankles to a pair of cement blocks.

I'd stirred the water, swimming down to her depth. Her body bobbed and swayed, with her bare toes about three feet off the clean, sandy bottom. It was almost as if a strange, macabre, new life had come to her. Her long blonde hair swirled about her lovely gamine face with every tremor of the water. A living ballerina might have enjoyed her grace of motion, but not her state of being. I wept silently behind my face mask.

A single stroke sent me drifting, with my shoulder stirring silt from the bottom. I touched the rope where it passed into the holes in the cement block and out again. A natural process of wear and tear had set in. The sharp, ragged edges of the blocks were cutting the rope. In a matter of time, the rope would part. Her buoyancy would drift her toward the sunlight, to the surface, to discovery.

I reeled about, careful not to look at her again, and plunged up toward the shadow of the skiff. My flippers fired me into open air with a shower of spray and a small, quick explosion in my ears.

I rolled over the side of the skiff and lay a moment with my stomach churning with reaction. Sun, blue sky, the primitive shoreline of mangrove and palmetto, everything around me was weirdly unreal. It was as if all the clocks in the world had gone *tick*, then forgot to *tock*.

"You're a too-sensitive, chicken-hearted fink," I said aloud. I forced myself to peel out of my diving gear, picked up the oars, and put my back into the job of rowing in.

I docked and tied the skiff, then walked to the cottage with my gear slung across my shoulder. Sheltered by scraggly pines, the lonely cottage creaked tiredly in the heat.

I stood on the sagging front porch. For a moment I didn't have the strength or nerve to go inside. The cottage was its usual mess, a hodgepodge of broken down furniture, dirty dishes, empty beer bottles and bean cans, none of which bothered me. But *she* was strewn all over the place, the dead girl out there in the water. She was portrayed in oil, sketched in charcoal, delicately impressed in pink and tan watercolors. She was half finished on the easel in the center of the room, like a naked skull.

Shivering and dry-throated, I slipped dingy ducks over my damp swim trunks, wriggled into a tattered T-shirt, and slid my feet into strap sandals. The greasy feeling was working again in the pit of my stomach as I half-ran from the cottage.

Palmetto City lay like a humid landscape done with dirty brushes as my eight-year-old station wagon nosed into DeSota Street. Off the beaten tourist paths, the town was an unpainted clapboard mecca for lantern-jawed farmers, fishermen, swamp muckers.

I angled the steaming wagon beside a dusty pickup at the curb and got out. On the sidewalk, I glimpsed myself in the murky window of the hardware store: six feet of bone and cartilage without enough meat; thatch of unkempt sandy hair; a lean face that wished for character; huge sockets holding eyes that looked as if they hadn't slept for a week.

Inside the store, Braley Sawyer came toward me, a flabby, sloppy man in his rumpled tropical weight suit. "Well, if it ain't Tazewell Eversham, Palmetto City's own Gauguin!" He flashed a wet, gold-toothed smile. "Hear you stopped in Willy Morrow's filling station yestiddy and gassed up for a trip to Sarasota. Going up to see them fancy art dealers, I guess."

I nodded. "Got back early this morning."

"You going to remember us country hoogers when you're famous, Gauguin?" The thought brought fat laughter from him. I let his little joke pass and in due time he waddled behind the counter and asked, "You here to buy something?"

"Chain." The word formed in my parched throat but didn't make itself heard. I cleared my throat, tried again, "I want to buy about a dozen feet of medium weight chain."

He blinked. "Chain?"

"Sure," I said. I had better control of my voice now. "I'd like to put in a garden, but I have stump problems. Thought I'd dig and cut around the roots and snake the stumps out with the station wagon."

He shrugged, his eyes hanging onto me as he moved toward the rear of the store. "I guess it would work—if that bucket of bolts holds together."

I turned and stared at a vacant point in space as the chain rattled from its reel. "Easier to carry if I put it in a gunny sack, Gauguin," Sawyer yelled at me.

"That's fine." I heard the chain clank into the sack.

Seconds later Sawyer dropped the chain at my feet. I paid him, carried the gunny sack out, and loaded it in the station wagon. Then I walked down the street to the general store and bought a few things— canned goods, coffee, flour, and two quarts of the cheapest booze available, which turned out to be a low-grade rum.

I'd stowed the stuff beside the gunny sack, closed the tailgate, and was walking around the wagon to get in when a man called to me from across the street. "Hey, Taze."

The man who barged toward me looked like the crudest breed of piney woods sheriff, which is what Jack Tully was. Big-bellied, slope-shouldered, fleshy faced with whisky veins on cheeks and nose, his protruding eyes searched with a sadistic hunger. His presence reminded me that not all Neanderthals had died out ten thousand years ago.

He thumbed back his hat, spat, guffawed. "Kinda left you high and dry, didn't she, bub?"

An arctic wind blew across my neck. "What are you talking about, Sheriff?"

He elbowed me in the ribs; I recoiled, from his touch, not the force behind it. "Bub, I ain't so dumb. I know Melody Grant's been sneaking out to your shack."

"Any law against it?"

"Not as long as the neighbors don't complain." He gave an obscene wink. "And you got no neighbors, have you, bub?"

His filthy thoughts were written in his smirking, ignorant face. No explanation could change his mind, not in a million years. Might as well try to explain a painting to him.

"Maybe she ain't told you yet, bub?"

"Told me what?"

"About young Perry Tomlin, son of the richest man in the county. She's been seeing him, too, now that he's home with his university degree. Going to marry him, I hear, honeymoon in Europe. Big come-up for a shanty cracker girl, even one as pretty as Melody. I reckon that shack'll be mighty lonesome, knowing you'll never see her again."

"Maybe it will, Sheriff, maybe it will."

"But . . ." We were suddenly conspirators. He gloated. " . . . there's one thing you can waller around in your mind."

"What's that, Sheriff?"

"Son of the county's richest man is just getting the leavings of a ragtag artist who's got hardly a bean in the pot." Laughter began to well inside of him. "Bub, I got to hand you that! Man, it would bust their blood vessels, Perry's and the old man's both, if they knew the truth."

Raucous laughter rolled out of him, to the point of strangulation. When I got in the station wagon and drove off he was standing there wiping his eyes and quaking with mirth over the huge joke.

Back at the cottage, I opened a bottle of the rum, picked up a brush, and stood before the easel. I swigged from the bottle in my left hand and made brush strokes on the unfinished canvas with my right. By the time her face was emerging from the skull-like pattern, the rum had begun its work. I knew I wasn't cut to fit a situation like this one, but the rum made up a part of the deficit.

I dropped the brush and suddenly turned from the canvas. "Why did you have to leave me? Why?"

She was, of course, still our there when the gunny sack dragged me down through thirty feet of water. Her thin cotton dress clung to her as she wavered closer. Behind and beyond her a watery forest of seaweed dipped and swayed, a green and slimy floral offering.

I felt as if my air tanks were forcing raw acid into my lungs as I spilled the chain from the gunny sack. My trembling hands made one . . . two . . . three efforts . . . and the chain was looped about her cold, slender ankles.

I passed the chain through the holes in the cement blocks, and it no longer mattered whether the hempen rope held. The job was done. No risk of floating away.

In the cottage, I picked up the rum jug and let it kick me. Then I put on a clean shirt and pants and combed my hair nice and neat.

I went to the porch and took a final look at the bloodstains on the rough planking. My eyes followed the dripping trail those blood droplets had made down to the rickety pier and the flatbottom skiff. Before my stomach started acting up again, I dropped from the porch, ran across the sandy yard, and fell into the station wagon.

I pulled myself upright behind the wheel, started the crate. Through the non-reality of the day, the wagon coughed its way over the rutted, crushed seashell road to the highway. Trucks swooshed past and passenger cars swirled about me.

On the outskirts of Palmetto City, I turned the wagon onto the private road that snaked its way across landscaped acreage. The road wound up a slight rise to a colonial mansion that overlooked half the county, the low skyline of the town, the glitter of the Gulf in the far distance. A pair of horse-sized Great Danes were chasing, tumbling, rolling like a couple of puppies on the vast manicured lawn.

A lean, trim old man had heard the car's approach and stood watching from the veranda as I got out. I walked up the short, wide steps, the shadow of the house falling over me. The man watched me narrowly. He had a crop of silver hair and his hawkish face was wrinkled. These were the only clues to his age. His gray eyes were bright, quick, hard, as cold as a snake's. His mouth was an arrogant slit. Clothed in lime slacks and riotously colored sport shirt thirty years too young for him, his poised body exuded an aura of merciless, wiry power. In my distraught and wracked imagination he was as pleasant as a fierce, deadly lizard.

"Mr. Tomlin?"

He nodded. "And you're the tramp artist who's become a local character. Didn't you see those no trespassing signs when you turned off the highway?"

"I've got some business with your son, Mr. Tomlin."

"Perry's in Washington, tending to a matter for me. He flew up yesterday and won't be back for another couple days. You call, and make a proper appointment. And get that crate out of here—unless you want me to interrupt the dogs in their play."

My stomach felt as if it were caving in, but I gave him a steady look and said in an icy voice, "If Perry's away, you must be the man I want to talk to. Sure. Perry wouldn't have killed her, but you didn't share your son's feeling for her, did you?"

"I don't believe I know what you're talking about." He knew, all right. The first glint of caution and animal cunning showed in his eyes.

"Then I'll explain, Mr. Tomlin. Yesterday I went to Sarasota to try to interest an art dealer in a one-man show. When I got back this morning I found some bloodstains. They led me to the water. I spent the morning diving, searching. I found her in about thirty feet of water."

I expected him to say something, but he didn't. He just stood there looking at me with those small, agate eyes.

"It wasn't hard to figure out," I said. "She'd come to the cottage to tell me it was all over between us. The shanty cracker girl was marrying the richest son in the county. But you didn't cotton to that idea, did you?"

"Go on," he said quietly.

"There's little more. It's all very simple. You sent Perry out of town to give you a chance to break it up between him and the cracker girl. Not much escapes your notice. You'd heard the gossip about her and the tramp artist. When you couldn't find her in town, you decided to try my place. I guess you tried to talk her off, buy her off, threaten her off. When none of it worked, you struck her in a rage. You killed her."

The old man stared blindly at the happy Great Danes.

"Realizing what you'd done," I said, "you scrounged a rope, couple of cement blocks, and planted her in thirty feet of water." I shook my head. "Not good. Not good at all. When the blocks sawed the rope in two, a nosy cop might find evidence you'd been around the place; a tire track, footprint, or maybe some fingerprints you'd left sticking around."

He studied the frolicking dogs as if planning their butchery. "You haven't named the vital element, artist; proof of guilt, proof that I did anything more than talk to her."

"Maybe so," I nodded, "but could a man in your position afford the questions, the scandal, the doubts that would arise and remain in your son's mind until the day you die? I think not. So I helped you."

His eyes flashed to me.

"I substituted a chain for the rope," I said. "The cement blocks will not cut that in two." I drew a breath. "And of course I want something in return. A thousand dollars. I'm sure you've that much handy, in a wall safe if not on your person. It's bargain day, Mr. Tomlin."

He thought it over for several long minutes. The sinking sun put a golden glitter in his eyes.

"And how about the future, artist? What if you decided you needed another thousand dollars one of these days?"

I shook my head. "I'm not that stupid. Right now I've caught you flat-footed. It's my moment. Everything is going for me. You haven't time to make a choice, think, plan. But it would be different in the future. Would I be stupid enough to try to continue blackmailing the most powerful man in the county after he's had a chance to get his forces and resources together?"

"Your question contains a most healthy logic, artist."

"One thousand bucks," I said, "and I hightail it down the driveway in the wagon. Otherwise, I'll throw the fat in the fire, all of it, including the chain about her ankles and my reason for putting it there. And we'll see which one of us has most to lose."

Without taking his eyes off my face, he reached for his wallet. He counted out a thousand dollars without turning a hair; chicken feed, pocket change to him.

I folded the sheaf of fifties and hundreds, some of them new bills, and slipped it into my pocket with care. We parted then, the old man and I, without another word being spoken.

The station wagon seemed to run with new life when I reached the highway. I felt the pressure of the money—the vital element— against my thigh.

The chain on her ankles had lured Tomlin, convinced him that he was dealing with a tramp interested only in a thousand bucks, so he had signed his confession of guilt by putting his fingerprints all over the money.

I didn't trust the gross sheriff in Palmetto City. I thought it far better to take the vital element and every detail of the nightmare directly to the state's attorney in St. Petersburg.

I was pretty sure the battered old station wagon would get me there.

"Hunter and the Widow" is one of D.L. Richardson's few short stories, a witty take on the clever detective stories of the 1930s and set in Kentucky. Reading this piece will bring to mind the snappy dialogue of the Nick and Nora films.

Hunter and the Widow

D. L. Richardson

"Say I told you so and you're fired."

Tracey, my secretary, scowled at me before continuing her ministrations. The warm water in the mixing bowl beside her thigh was a weak pink. Which is exactly how I felt. Weak pink.

"Ouch!"

I jerked my head back and reached for my cheekbone, only to have my fingers slapped away and my chin clamped in her grasp. She resumed washing the blood from the gash just under my left eye, her hazel gaze scrutinizing the damage.

"If ever anyone deserved an I-told-you-so, it's you," she said. "But since you never listen to me anyway, I won't waste my breath."

"That's not true," I said between gritted teeth. "I always listen to you." I tried to pull away but she only tightened her grip.

"Sit still!" she snapped. "And quit scrunching up your face like that. If you listened to me, neither of us would be here at three A.M. doing a bad imitation of some old movie."

She had a point. If I had listened to her, we wouldn't be watching a bowl of water turn red with my blood. She wouldn't be perched on my coffee table in jeans and an ice-blue satin pajama jacket trying to find my face amidst the cuts and scrapes and blood. I wouldn't be sitting on my couch trying to decide which hurt worse—the cheek she was cleaning or the chin she was gripping— and wondering, rather irreverently, if she was wearing anything under that blue satin.

"That cut and the one on your forehead need stitches." She surveyed her handiwork and then looked me in the eye. She scowled again. "Don't you think you've had enough trouble for one night, Adam Hunter, without asking for more?"

I had the decency to look sheepish as she gathered up the bowl and the first-aid paraphernalia and headed for the kitchen. Sometimes I had the notion that she was a witch. I mean, it wasn't natural for someone to be able to read minds the way she could read mine.

I relaxed back into the softness of the couch and closed my eyes against the dull throbbing that was steadily permeating every centimeter of my body. I could hear Tracey in the kitchen.

I hated it when Tracey was right. Probably because she was right so often.

"Here's the rough draft of your story." Tracey laid the pages in front of me. "And the phone call was your editor reminding you that he's still waiting for the last five chapters of *Murder by Yesterday*."

"He'll have to wait a little longer. I've got a job."

"Not her?" Tracey jerked her thumb in the direction of the door that, just moments before, had closed behind my new client.

"Her name is Easter Simmons, and yes, she's the one."

Tracey studied me for a moment, her lips pressed together, her eyes narrowed. With a deep breath and a single shake of her head, she left my office. I heard the rollers on her chair squeak when she sat down.

Damn! She was always doing that to me. This time I vowed not to give in. I pulled the notepad out from under the freshly typed manuscript and studied the notes I had just made. Typing sounds came from the outer office. Vicious typing sounds. Fifteen minutes later (a new endurance record for me), I was perched on the front of her desk.

"You don't think I should take the case."

"No." She pulled the page from the typewriter and scanned it.

"You don't even know what the case is."

"It's not the case that bothers me."

"What then?"

"Her."

"What about her?"

"I don't trust her."

"Why?"

She inserted a fresh piece of paper into the typewriter, the platen making clicking sounds of protest. "I never trust anyone named after a holiday." She pushed her reading glasses back up on the bridge of her nose and resumed typing without so much as a glance at me. The yellow pencil behind her ear was a sharp contrast to her short, dark hair.

Had I not known better, I would have said that Tracey's mistrust of my new client was, in actuality, a bad case of the green monsters. Easter Simmons had the looks to bring out the cat in a lot of women.

Medium height and willowy with shoulder-length, wheat-colored hair. Dazzling green eyes. Expensive clothes. The air of a woman who always got what she wanted.

Trouble was, I *did* know better, and Tracey wasn't the catty type.

"Maybe she was born on Easter and had eight or nine older brothers and sisters and her parents just ran out of favorite names," I offered.

"Maybe." She was still typing.

The subtle approach was getting me nowhere, so I reached over and flicked the switch on the electric typewriter. With a sigh, Tracey removed her glasses and swiveled her chair a quarter turn toward me. Her eyes always got to me, and the teal blouse she wore turned them a deep aquamarine that made matters worse.

"Why don't you trust her?"

"The way I understand it, she stands to lose a great deal of money if you find this long-lost stepson."

"Ah ha! You were eavesdropping."

"You left the door open."

So I had.

Tracey continued. "Her husband's been dead for over a year. Why look for the stepson now, after all this time?"

"You heard her. She *has* been looking for him. It's taken this long to get a solid lead. After all, Lexington, Kentucky, is a long way from Los Angeles." My explanation obviously didn't satisfy her suspicious mind. "What else bothers you?"

"Let's assume that she's telling the truth. That she has spent this last year looking for her stepson. That she's hired the kind of agencies only wealth can afford, agencies with lots of contacts and manpower. Why come to you now? Why not stick with the people who were able to track him down?"

"She wanted someone local who was familiar with the territory and the people."

"Then why not hire one of the larger agencies in town, like Marshall and Associates? They do security work for several of the horse farms. Why come to you, a writer, who only does this on a part-time basis?"

"If I weren't such a secure individual, I could really be hurt by that remark. Besides, you heard her. She doesn't want to make a big production out of this. She's afraid she'll scare him so far off she'll never be able to find him again."

"That simply means that she gets to keep all the money."

"Maybe, but she feels the money is his, and she can't, in good conscience, spend what isn't hers to spend."

"She said that?"

"She said that."

"And you believe her?"

"I believe her."

"I should think gullibility would be a hindrance to a private investigator."

"There's a difference between being gullible and trusting your client."

Tracey shook her head with a sigh, put her glasses on, and swiveled back to the typewriter. She flipped the switch. "Have it your way. I'm just the hired help."

I rose from the desk and headed back to my office, her voice stopping me in the doorway.

"But don't expect me to be there to put you back together again."

"Why should I need anyone to put me back together?"

"Are you forgetting that walking mountain she calls a chauffeur?"

"Lots of ladies with her kind of money have chauffeurs who double as bodyguards."

"People with bodyguards tend to draw undesirables. Otherwise they wouldn't need bodyguards."

I smiled. "It's nice to know you care."

"I just want to be sure you're around to sign my pay check at the end of the week."

I put my feet up on the coffee table, wincing at the pain in my ribs.

"You probably have two or three cracked ribs, too."

I opened my eyes to find Tracey standing in front of me, a pottery mug in her hand.

"I've already told you I'm not going to the hospital, Tracey. I'm not in the mood to make explanations."

"Suit yourself." She thrust the mug toward me. "Drink this."

I took it from her. "What is it?"

"Hemlock. It will put you out of your misery." She turned and disappeared into the kitchen.

A quick sniff confirmed it to be her special hot toddy. I took a cautious sip and welcomed the warmth that trickled down my esophagus. After two more sips, the whisky spread its own special warmth to combat the pain in my aching body.

I surveyed the mess that had been my living room. At the hospital there would be questions about my injuries, and questions meant explanations, and explanations meant lies because at this point the puzzle pieces were still scattered around the table. Hell. I wasn't too sure I even had all the pieces.

Brad Walters. Easter Simmons' stepson, Brantley Simmons, was using the name Brad Walters and had been working on a horse farm in the Lexington area for the last six months. She didn't know which one.

It wasn't much help, considering that there must be two hundred or more horse farms of varying size and prosperity within a fourteen-mile radius of Lexington. That's a lot of legwork. I decided to let my fingers do the walking and called an old friend at Marshall and Associates. They did security work for several of the local horse farms, and while finding Walters/Simmons working on one of those particular farms was a long shot, it was a place to start.

And I got lucky.

My friend had been predictably reluctant to release company information, but he owed me more than one favor, a point I was quick to make. Before long, he came up with the information I needed. Brad Walters had applied for a job at Willow Hill Farm, and a security check had netted strong recommendations from a horse breeder in Texas and a horse trainer out in L.A. As far as my friend knew, he was still there.

The next morning, after a call to the farm's manager, I left Tracey in the office and headed out Newtown Pike to Willow Hill, a small, but respected, brood mare farm a couple of miles past Ironworks Pike. It was a warm, sunny May morning, one of those days that Kentuckians dream about in February. The pastures were emerald green and lush. A few dogwoods still dotted the countryside with their white and pink lacework. A day for rolling down the car windows and inhaling the spring-scented air.

★　　★　　★

I shifted my position carefully, gritting my teeth against the pain. Another sip of Tracey's "hemlock" helped. I leaned my head back and closed my eyes.

It was hard to believe it had only been three days ago that I had bumped my way down a gravel lane to the main barn. Only three days since I had stood in the warm morning, savoring the sights and sounds of a working farm. Only three days since I had leaned against a plank fence and talked with a living, breathing Brad Walters. Too much can happen in three days.

I watched the farm manager talk to two men, point in my direction, and then disappear into the barn. I waited as the two conferred before one of them moved in my direction. With interest, I watched Brad Walters/Brantley Simmons approach.

He was about six feet tall with thick black hair, ruffled by the breeze. He wore scuffed boots, faded jeans, and a checked shirt with its long sleeves rolled up to reveal strong forearms already beginning to tan. As he got nearer, he pulled off work gloves to reveal long, blunt-ended fingers which he offered in a handshake.

"Mr. Hunter? I'm Brad Walters," he said in a clear baritone.

I returned the firm grip, studying the smooth planes of his face and the almost-black eyes. Somehow, he wasn't what I had expected.

"Mr. Trexler said you wanted to talk to me about a missing person, someone I might have met in Houston when I worked there."

"That's really only part of the truth. The person isn't actually missing. He's been found, only he doesn't know it yet. I was hired to tell him he's been found."

"I'm not sure I understand any of this, but if I can help you, I'll be glad to. Who is this guy?" he drawled.

"You."

For a brief moment he looked puzzled, and then he grinned. "Me? Who in the world would be looking for me?"

"Your stepmother."

The grin was gone, and the puzzled look was back. "My stepmother? Mr. Hunter, you must have me confused with someone else. I don't have a stepmother."

Easter's description of Brantley's departure from the Simmons household had prepared me for this reaction.

"Listen, Brad," I said, trying to maintain a friendly atmosphere by using his chosen alias, "your stepmother explained about the estrangement between you and your father that led to your leaving home. She also explained that you might be reluctant to come home."

"Wait a minute. Maybe you'd better tell me who my stepmother is."

"Easter Simmons."

I thought for an instant that something flashed in his eyes, but it was so brief that I wasn't sure.

"Easter hired you to find me?"

"Not exactly. She's been looking for you for a year, ever since—" I didn't know any better way to say it "—ever since your father died. She wasn't sure if you had even heard about his death."

"Yeah, I heard the old man got into one too many board meeting arguments and had a heart attack and died." He stuck his hands in his hip pockets. "Unless I'm badly mistaken, that makes Easter a very wealthy woman."

"It also makes you a wealthy man. Your father left a sizable portion of his estate to you. Easter hired several agencies to track you down. When they discovered that you had changed your name and were working on a horse farm in this area, she decided to come talk to you herself."

"Easter is here? In Lexington?"

I nodded. "She hired me to talk to you first. She wasn't sure you'd see her."

Brad was silent, and I gave him time to think before I continued.

"She wants you to know there are no strings attached to the inheritance. All you have to do is go back to L.A. with her to meet with the lawyers and get the paperwork taken care of."

"That's all I have to do, huh?"

Something in his voice struck a wrong chord deep in my brain, but I dismissed it. After all, I was dredging up a past he had discarded.

"That's all." I pulled a business card from my shirt pocket. "Here's my card with my office and home phones. Easter is staying at the Hyatt, and I've written her room number on the back. I won't even tell her where you work. You can call and talk to her yourself, or you can talk to her through me. It's up to you."

Brad looked at the small, buff-colored card, turning it over in his fingers and reading each side at least twice.

"When do I have to give her an answer?"

"Any time within the next two days. She said something about a clause in the will that says you have to claim your inheritance within a specific length of time or it reverts to her."

He nodded, a sardonic smile on his face. "My stepmother always did have a flair for the dramatic."

There was some bitterness in his voice. But what can you expect from someone whose stepmother is his own age?

"Don't be too hard on her. You haven't been the easiest person to find."

"Yeah. I guess not." He extended his hand again. "Thanks."

I shook his hand. "There's really nothing to thank me for."

"Oh, I don't know. You may have helped make me a wealthy man." That sardonic smile was back again. "Make sure you send my stepmother a big bill. She can afford it."

I thought about that drive back to the office. My conversation with Brad Walters had put a damper on my earlier high spirits. Something had kept nagging at me. Something I couldn't point a finger to and say, "Ah ha!"

Maybe it had been his attitude. His voice when speaking of his father's death had shown no remorse, no concern, nothing. And there had been a definite snideness in his references to his stepmother. But I didn't know the true situation. I didn't even know Brad Walters. I only knew what Easter Simmons had told me, and who was to say that was an accurate picture? No, it had to have been something else.

I had pushed it out of my mind, telling myself that I had done what I was hired for. Anything else would constitute meddling.

The sounds of Tracey moving quietly around the room broke through my thoughts. I opened one eye to see her righting a hassock. She picked up a lamp from the floor, straightened its shade, and replaced it on the table next to the chair. She disappeared down behind the chair.

"I didn't hire you to be a maid," I said.

The lamp came on.

"You didn't hire me to be a nurse either, but I seem to have done more than my share of that," she said, standing back up, hands on hips. "Besides which, this place will have to be straightened some before a maid can even get in. Most maids don't clean up after demolition derbies." She plucked a velvet pillow from the carpet.

"You could be destroying evidence, you know."

She looked me straight in the eye. "Are you planning to call the police after all?"

In the silence I regarded the score. Tyler, two; Hunter, nothing, and fading fast.

"I thought not." She returned to her self-assigned chore.

I watched her for a while. Watched her movements. Athletically graceful. No energy wasted. I found myself thinking it was a sight I could get used to and decided I must have taken a harder shot to the head than I had first thought.

I closed my eyes again only to have her image reappear in my mind. This time she was standing in front of my desk, looking too much like a knockout in red and black, a folded newspaper in her hand.

"I know you don't read the newspaper this early in the day, but I think you should make an exception today."

I looked up at her to argue but was stopped by the look in her eyes. I took the paper and began to read the story made prominent by her folding. I read the headline and lead paragraph, looked back up at her, and then finished the short item.

Brad Walters had been killed by a hit and run driver on Newtown Pike. According to coworkers, Walters, a photography buff, had walked a quarter mile up the road to photograph a dogwood. When he hadn't returned after a reasonable amount of time, one of the men had gone looking for him and found him in the ditch, dead.

"Seems hard to believe that I just talked to him yesterday morning."

"Is that all you have to say?"

"What do you want me to say? That Easter Simmons could have saved her money? Hit and run is not uncommon, Tracey. Not even here. It's just a coincidence. A rotten one, but a coincidence nonetheless."

"I don't believe in coincidences," she said in a tight voice and left, closing the door with more force than necessary.

Truth be known, neither do I. That same uneasy nagging I'd had the morning before was back. I read the article once more. Then again. And it hit me. The reason for the nagging.

According to the paper, Brad Walters was from Eagle Lake, Texas. When I had spoken with him, I had been aware that his voice hadn't sounded exactly as I'd thought it should. He had a Texas drawl, an authentic Texas drawl. The kind you don't acquire overnight. Marshall and Associates hadn't discovered that Brad Walters was Brantley Simmons either, and they were much too thorough to overlook something like that.

I grabbed my windbreaker from the antique hall tree and stepped into the outer office. Tracey was proofreading.

"I'm going to see Charlie Whisk."

"You could call him and save time."

"I need the fresh air."

I took the stairs at a half run, barely missing the guy from the pest control outfit come to check the messages on his answering machine in his tiny office across the hall from mine. When I reached the street, I turned right toward West Main Street, my back to West Vine. At the corner I turned right again. Charlie Whisk had a small work area above his cousin's camera supply store on East Main. When it came to computers, Charlie Whisk was a certified genius, and he was also a good friend. Right now I needed quick access to information from distant parts, and Charlie's computer terminal was faster than a Concorde.

I emerged an hour later and retraced my steps, having left Charlie a happy man. I had always been a little uneasy about using Charlie and had told him so once. He had laughed, rubbed his hands together, and said he could tiptoe through anybody's data banks and never leave a trace. For some reason that didn't make me feel better.

"Any calls for me?" I asked Tracey upon my return.

"No."

"None at all?"

"None."

"Are you sure?"

I recognized that look and put my hands up in surrender. "Sorry. I just expected the police to have called before now."

She followed me into my office. "Why would the police call you?"

I put my jacket back on the hall tree and sat down behind my desk. "When I talked to Brad Walters yesterday, I gave him my business card."

Tracey sat on the front of my desk. "And you think they would have checked with you even though they're calling it hit and run?"

"They should have at least been curious as to why a horse farm worker would need a private investigator."

She nodded and went off into her own thoughts.

"Do you know the number for the Hyatt?" I asked, picking up the phone.

"I'm sure it's in the book."

I ignored her sarcasm, flipped quickly through the phone directory, and penciled the number on a notepad.

"Why are you calling the Hyatt?"

I started dialing. "To see if the police have contacted Mrs. Simmons. Her room number was also on the business card."

"I'll leave the two of you alone, then," she said, slipping off my desk and out of my office, her perfume following her.

Two minutes later I was even more puzzled. The bodyguard-chauffeur had answered the phone and said that Mrs. Simmons was too upset to talk. I'd be upset, too, if I'd just inherited an extra ten million dollars. Whatever would I spend it on?

Tracey poked her head in the door. "Well?"

"The police haven't called her either."

"Curious."

"That's the word for it." I picked up the phone.

"Who are you calling now?"

"Newman."

She groaned, "I'm not here," and left.

Newman was my very limited pipeline into the Metro police department. Obnoxious and overbearing, he was not one of my favorite people, but a source is a source. Tracey didn't agree.

That uneasy feeling got worse after talking to Newman. So bad that I moved to the couch. Tracey came in and leaned against the end of my desk.

"He makes me feel the same way," she said.

"He asked for you."

"Spare me. Please."

I had to grin.

"What did you find out from Mr. Personality?"

"Zip. As far as Metro is concerned, it's straight hit and run."

"And the business card?"

I shook my head. "Nada. All he had on him was a billfold, a set of keys, and some loose change."

"Did you see where he put the card?"

"In his shirt pocket."

"Maybe it flew out when he was hit."

"Maybe."

"Or maybe he took it out before then and put it away somewhere."

"Maybe."

I looked up at her and saw that she was reading my thoughts again. I got up from the couch and grabbed my jacket.

"I'm going back out to Willow Hill. If Charlie calls, tell him I'll call him back."

I left her perched distractingly on the end of my desk.

But the trip to Willow Hill netted me nothing. Brad and two other hands shared a small house on the farm, and a search of his belongings turned up no little buff-colored card. When I got back to the office and returned Charlie's call, he confirmed my suspicions. I gave him another name to play with.

"Hunter, are you asleep?"

I opened my eyes to find Tracey leaning over me, something close to worry in her eyes, her perfume tickling my nose. Maybe the perfume was my imagination. After all, it was four A.M. Heck. Maybe the worry was my imagination.

"Just thinking." I smiled, or at least I think I did.

"I think you should go to bed and get some rest."

"You're probably right."

She frowned. "Are you all right?"

"Sure. Why?"

"Never mind. Can you manage by yourself?"

"Of course."

She stood back to give me room. She needn't have been in a rush about it. Slow was about as fast as I could manage. I finally got to my feet without too many un-macho grimaces and headed for the bedroom, grateful that Tracey was never out of reach.

"I suppose it would be chauvinistic of me to say that I don't like the idea of your driving home at this hour?"

"You should have thought of that at two A.M. when you called and asked me to come over here."

"Good point." I reached the bedroom door and stopped. "Do me a favor and be careful anyway."

"I will." There was a trace of a smile on her face.

I liked her smile. "Sweet dreams, Tyler."

The smile grew a little. "Sweet dreams, Hunter."

I entered the darkness of my bedroom, that smile following me, and made it to the bed. I managed to lower myself gently to the edge of it and shrug out of my shirt before the weariness overwhelmed me. The last thing I remember was my head hitting the pillow.

I awoke to bright sunshine and amnesia. My first movements dispelled the amnesia. I was stuck with the sunshine. A long, warm shower helped loosen the kinks in my stiff body and made the sunshine look better, too. I decided breakfast might make me feel almost human again, so I headed for the kitchen. I got sidetracked.

Tracey was asleep on my couch. I wandered over, sat on the edge of the coffee table, and watched her for a moment, curled up on her side, a blanket pulled up under her chin.

"Time to get up, Tyler."

At first there was no reaction, and then she stirred.

"Hmmmmm?"

"I said, it's time to get up."

This time her eyes flew open, and there was momentary confusion in them until her memory woke up and filled her in. She stretched her arms above her head. "What time is it?"

I grabbed her left arm and looked at her watch. "Nearly ten. I thought I told you to go home?"

She sat up on the couch, and our knees nearly touched. "Don't let it go to your head, but I was worried about leaving you alone. You didn't look too well last night." She frowned as she studied the damage. "You don't look too well this morning, either."

"Thanks."

"For spending the night or telling you that you don't look so hot?"

I returned her grin. "Both."

"You're welcome."

I was working on my second cup of coffee and she was sipping her second glass of orange juice before the case came up.

"Easter Simmons didn't take the news of your discovery too well, did she?" Tracey asked.

"What makes you say that?"

She reached out with gentle fingers and touched my face. "Two cuts needing stitches, one puffy eye, one cut lip, and assorted bruises of varying colors."

"You left out the possible cracked ribs and the headache."

"I still think you should call the police."

"And tell them what? That two men I never saw clearly used my living room as a gym and me as a punching bag? Newman would love that."

"One man has been killed, Hunter. You could have been number two."

I leaned back and stretched out my legs. They ended up next to hers. I have a small kitchen table and long legs.

"But I wasn't. Doesn't that strike you as odd?"

"How many times *did* they hit you?"

"Think about it, Tracey. Brad Walters was killed because of what he knew. I know what he knew and all I got was a slap on the wrist. Easter Simmons hired those two to deliver their late-night message. I'd bet on that. But I'd also bet she had nothing to do with Brad Walters' death."

"Simply because all you got was a beating?"

"And a warning to mind my own business."

I watched her consider.

"If she didn't kill Brad Walters, who did?"

I shrugged. "I don't know."

"Some private investigator you are."

I grinned.

"As far as I can see, Easter Simmons is the only one with a motive," Tracey pointed out.

She was right. Because Charlie Whisk's little foray had turned up some interesting facts.

Fact number one: Brantley Simmons, age forty-five, was alive and prospering in L.A. impressing the pants off his father's colleagues with his brilliance in filling his father's shoes.

Fact number two: Brad Walters was Brad Walters. Had been since he was born, thirty years ago in Eagle Lake, Texas.

Fact number three: Easter Simmons knew Brad Walters. And vice versa. On her eighteenth birthday they were married.

Fact number four: Said marriage was never legally terminated.

And that had led me to a conversation and confrontation with Easter Simmons and fact number five: Someone had been blackmailing Easter with fact number four. She thought it was Brad Walters.

So Tracey was right. Easter Simmons had an excellent motive for killing Brad. At least most people would consider ten million plus dollars a good motive for murder, and ten million plus was what Easter stood to lose if certain people were to learn she wasn't Mrs. Simmons because she was still Mrs. Walters.

It's a big step from lying to murder," I said.

"Not for some people," Tracey said. "You're going to have to tell the police what you know sooner or later."

"I know. But not until I've talked to Charlie. He's checking something out for me."

"What else is there to check out about her?"

"Not her. Edgar, her chauffeur."

"His name is Edgar?"

I grinned. "I think it fits."

"You would. Why are you checking him out?"

I thought about the way Edgar had first tried to keep me from seeing Easter and then had hovered close by, answering some questions for her, attempting to block others, until Easter had told him to get lost. She had been nervous and then outraged and then resigned. All reactions that I had expected. I hadn't expected Edgar to be so antsy. Protective, yes. Antsy, no.

"Curiosity."

"You think Edgar took the bodyguard oath a little too seriously?"

"It's possible."

"Do you think he was guarding Easter's body privately as well as publicly?"

"Your mind is in the gutter again, Tyler." I got up from the table, taking my dirty dishes to the sink. "I'll meet you at the office in an hour. Charlie should be calling about then."

"Yes, sir, boss man, sir." She got up from the table. "Excuse me for forgetting my place, sir."

Forty-five minutes later I was in the office. I rewound the tape on my answering machine and settled into my chair to listen and go through the mail. The third message made me forget the mail.

"This is Easter Simmons, Mr. Hunter. I must talk to you as soon as possible. I will be flying out of Lexington at four thirty this afternoon. Please call me here at the hotel before three o'clock. I *must* talk to you."

I listened to the message again, the effect of her sultry voice dampened by obvious agitation.

I picked up the phone and began to dial.

"You can hang that up, Hunter. Mrs. Simmons has decided she has nothing to say to you."

Edgar watched me from the doorway. With my eyes on the gun in his hand, I replaced the receiver.

"How do you know that?"

He smiled. "She told me."

He moved into the office. The doorway was again blocked by an unsmiling gentleman of the same behemoth proportions as Edgar.

"Who's your friend?"

"Just someone I brought along."

Edgar's friend had a gun exactly like Edgar's, complete with silencer. I didn't like the looks of any of them—Edgar, his friend, or the guns.

"The message from Mrs. Simmons sounded urgent. What happened, Edgar? Did she figure out that you killed Brad Walters?"

"She's a lot smarter than most people give her credit for. I must say the same thing applies to you."

"People are always thinking of me as just another pretty face."

"How did you know that I killed Walters?"

I shrugged. "Who else could it be? Easter certainly didn't. All Walters really wanted was enough money for a small horse farm, and she was more than happy to give him that. In fact, she seemed surprised that Brad would even try blackmail."

"Ah, ah, ah. Put your hands back on the desk to where I can see them."

I smiled and obeyed. "I was surprised, too. For someone who was supposedly blackmailing a wealthy woman, Brad Walters had little to show for it. According to his bank account, he had nothing to show for it. But I guess that's because Brad Walters wasn't blackmailing Easter. You were. I don't know how you found out about her first marriage, but you did. I bet your bank account would have a lot to say."

He smiled again. I was beginning to hate that smile.

"To keep suspicion off yourself, you worked out an elaborate scheme for getting the money. What did you do? Have King Kong here mail the letters from Lexington?"

"Something like that."

"Funny. He doesn't look that bright."

There was no reaction that I could see from his door-filling friend. That could mean one of two things. Either he was too dumb to know he was being insulted, or he was a very disciplined man. Either way it didn't look too good for me.

"Why did you kill Brad Walters?"

"You're the man with all the answers. You tell me."

"You knew that once he talked to Easter your little charade would be in trouble. You couldn't let that happen, so you killed him. You, or maybe Godzilla here, followed me out to Willow Hill when I went to talk to him. Lucky for you he wanted to photograph that tree. It would have been hard to get into the farm undetected."

"His little hobby made it easy."

Now I knew I hated that smile.

"That left you with two other problems. Easter and me."

"Easter's no problem. She's too scared of losing all that money. And you weren't a problem until you started snooping where you had no business. Like I said, I underestimated you."

"It was your idea to hire me and not one of the larger agencies."

"I just pointed out to her that a larger agency would be more likely to find out about her past. She picked your name out of the phone book."

The Yellow Pages really do work. "So now what?" I asked.

"So now we take a little walk." Edgar motioned with his gun. "Get up nice and easy. Tony, you make sure he's not carrying a gun."

Tony patted me down professionally, never putting himself between me and Edgar's gun.

"He's clean," he grunted.

"Oh, it talks, too."

Tony shoved me in the direction of the door. He wasn't so insensitive after all.

"We're going to take a little walk across Vine Street," Edgar said. "I want you to behave yourself, Hunter. Got that?"

I nodded.

Edgar and Tony pocketed their guns and we left the office. No one passed us in the hall, and we met no one on the stairs. Outside, they positioned themselves on either side of me and herded me toward Vine. As we waited for the light to change, it occurred to me that we must look quite normal. I didn't feel normal.

The light changed and we crossed the street. Edgar smiled pleasantly and nodded at the young woman who passed us in the middle of the crosswalk. She smiled in return. Charming fellow, that Edgar.

I began to hope the light would change again. I preferred taking my chances in Lexington traffic, and one of them might get hit by some guy impatient to be wherever. No such luck. We reached the other side without incident, and Edgar steered me toward a gutted building. Tracey had told me it was being turned into a mini-mall with offices on the three upper floors.

Funny the things you remember in times of stress. I remembered the touch of her fingers on my face and the sight of her curled up on my couch. Damn!

Edgar removed a padlock and hustled me into the gloom of the building. I tried to drag my steps, but Tony shoved me on. I suspected he took pleasure in manhandling me.

I kept my eyes open for a break, any break, but breaks are hard to come by when you find yourself wedged between a rock and a hard place. And that's where I was. Literally.

Tony must have scouted the place out beforehand because it was he who guided me through the gloom and the dirt and the work-in-progress. I wondered where the work crew was. Didn't make much difference. They weren't there.

We ended up in a cluttered corner far from where we had entered. Suddenly, the walk from the office seemed all too short.

"End of the line for you, Hunter," Edgar said. That was certainly an original remark.

There was light streaming through windows in the wall behind me. It made it easier to see the guns and the smile on Edgar's face.

"What makes you so sure Easter will keep quiet?"

It was a stall and Edgar knew it and didn't seem to mind.

"Like I said. She's too afraid of losing all that money. Brantley Simmons would just love to throw her out on her pretty little tail. And who would believe that she didn't kill Walters herself just to keep him quiet?"

"What about me? Isn't my death going to look suspicious?"

"A private investigator is bound to make enemies. And since the work here has been put on hold for two months, Easter and I will be long gone before your body is ever found. And there's nothing in particular to tie you to Walters."

"You took the business card."

"It pays to be thorough. Which is why Tony will pay a visit to your pretty secretary."

I stiffened.

"Now, now. Don't get upset. He won't kill her. Just scare her a little."

I knew Tracey didn't scare easily, but telling them would be the same as signing her death warrant.

"Put your hands over your heads, gentlemen. Now!"

Edgar and Tony whirled.

Every time I thought I had Tracey all figured out—wham!—she'd do something to blow it all away. Like the Colman party we'd gone to. She was waiting for me in the Colmans' foyer, looking terrific in a long-sleeved black dress that fell from the base of her throat to the floor, interrupted only by a red belt. Exactly what I would have expected. Fashionable, attractive, but conservative.

Until she turned and headed into the party ahead of me, and I was left to pick up my lower jaw from the floor and put my eyes back in my head. Her "conservative" dress left her back bare to the waist. Bare and beautiful.

Now here she was, surprising the hell out of me again. Feet firmly planted, .45 automatic aimed squarely and steadily at Edgar and Tony, her face, her eyes, even her body making it clear she meant business. I sidled out of the line of fire. I'm at least as smart as Tony.

"I said, hands over your heads!" she barked.

They obeyed.

"You, Edgar. Put your gun on the floor very slowly."

He obeyed.

"Take two steps back."

He did.

"You." She pointed to Tony. "Do the same thing."

He hesitated, and I saw him considering alternatives.

"Now!" Her voice echoed in the hollow building.

"You'd better do it, Tony," I said. "She's got a nasty temper."

He complied, reluctantly.

"Hunter, do you think you can get their guns without getting yourself killed?" Her eyes never left Edgar and Tony.

"I'll try." I scooped up the two guns and stood next to her.

"Now, I want you two down on the floor, spread-eagled," she said.

They didn't like the idea, but they did it anyway.

"Hunter, what did I tell you about undesirables?"

I grinned. "What brings you to this neighborhood, Tyler?"

"Charlie called me at home. He tried the office and evidently your home phone isn't working. He filled me in on Edgar. You're in the wrong profession, Hunter. According to Edgar's bank account, chauffeuring is where the money is.

"Anyway, when I got to the office, I heard voices, so I eaves-dropped until Edgar started talking about taking a walk. I went down-stairs to the pawn shop and watched until you disappeared into this building. Then I borrowed a gun from the showcase, told them to call the police, and followed you over here. Oh, by the way, you'd better point one of those guns at them. This one isn't loaded."

I chuckled and took aim. Poor Tony looked positively ill.

"You could have just called the police," I pointed out. "Coming over here was dangerous."

"I was afraid they might not get here in time."

"Why, Tyler, you really do care."

"Of course I care, Hunter. I still haven't been paid this week."

I love that smile.

Before turning to writing mystery fiction, Julie Smith was a copy editor and reporter fo rthe San Francisco Chronicle, a job that honed her observational skills and eye for detail. This would serve her well in her writing career, which now spans six novels and numerous short stories. Whether writing about the tourism industry of San Francisco or the organized chaos of Mardi Gras, her plots and characters are true to life and believable, often dealing in issues like sexual harassment, outsiders in society, and the struggle to leave the past behind. Her short stories are lighter in tone, such as this one, where a small-town sheriff solves cases that leave big city police mystified.

Crime Wave in Pinhole

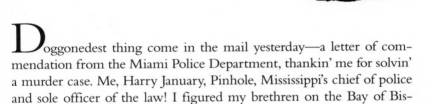

Julie Smith

Doggonedest thing come in the mail yesterday—a letter of commendation from the Miami Police Department, thankin' me for solvin' a murder case. Me, Harry January, Pinhole, Mississippi's chief of police and sole officer of the law! I figured my brethren on the Bay of Biscayne had taken leave of their senses.

But I got to studyin' on the thing a while and I looked up the date I was supposed to've perpetrated this triumph and the whole thing come back to me. Blamed if I *didn't* solve a murder for them peckerwoods—it just wasn't no big thing at the time.

It happened the day Mrs. Flossie Chestnut come in, cryin'· and takin' on cause her boy Johnny'd been kidnapped. Least that was her suspicion, but I knew that young'un pretty well and in my opinion there wasn't no kidnapper in Mississippi brave enough for such a undertakin'. Bein' as it was my duty, however, I took down a report of the incident, since he *could've* got hit by a car or fell down somebody's well or somethin'.

Mrs. Flossie said she hadn't seen a sign of him since three o'clock the day before when she caught him ridin' his pony standin' up. Naturally she told him he oughtn't to do it 'cause he could break his neck and it probably wasn't too easy on the pony neither. Then she emphasized her point by the administration of a sound hidin' and left him repentin' in the barn.

She wasn't hardly worried when he didn't show up for supper, on account of that was one of his favorite tricks when he was sulkin'. Seems his practice was to sneak in after ever'body else'd gone to sleep, raid the icebox, and go to bed without takin' a bath. Then he'd come down to breakfast just like nothin' ever happened. Only he didn't that mornin' and Mrs. Flossie had ascertained his bed hadn't been slept in.

I told Mrs. Flossie he would likely be home in time for lunch and sent her on back to her ranch-style home with heated swimmin' pool and green-house full of orchids. Come to think about it, her and her old man were 'bout the only folks in town had enough cash to warrant holdin' their offspring for ransom, but I still couldn't believe it. Some say Pinhole got its name cause it ain't no bigger'n one, and the fact is we just don't have much crime here in the country. I spend most of my mornin's playin' gin rummy with Joshua Clow, who is retired from the drygoods business, and Mrs. Flossie had already played merry heck with my schedule.

But there wasn't no sense grumblin' about it. I broadcast a missin' juvenile report on the police radio and commenced to contemplatin' what to do next. Seemed like the best thing was to wait till after lunch, see if the little varmint turned up, and, if he didn't, get up a search party. It was goin' to ruin my day pretty thorough, but I didn't see no help for it.

'Long about that time, the blessed phone rang. It was young Judy Scarborough, down at the motel, claimin' she had gone and caught a live criminal without my assistance and feelin' mighty pleased with herself. Seems she had noticed that a Mr. Leroy Livingston, who had just checked in at her establishment, had a different handwritin' when he registered than was on the credit card he used to pay in advance. Young Judy called the credit company soon as her guest went off to his room and learned the Mr. Livingston who owned the card was in his sixties, whereas her Mr. Livingston wasn't a day over twenty-five.

It sounded like she had a genuine thief on her hands, so I went on over and took him into custody. Sure enough, his driver's license and other papers plainly indicated he was James Williamson of Little Rock, Arkansas. Among his possessions he had an employee identification card for Mr. Leroy Livingston of the same town from a department store where Mr. Livingston apparently carried out janitorial chores.

So I locked up Mr. Williamson and got on the telephone to tell Mr. Livingston we had found his missin' credit card. His boss said he was on vacation and give me the number of his sister, with whom he made his home. I called Miss Livingston to give her the glad tidin's, and she said her lovin' brother was in Surfside, Florida. Said he was visitin' with a friend of his youth, a Catholic priest whose name she couldn't quite recollect, 'cept she knew he was of Italian descent.

By this time I was runnin' up quite a little phone bill for the tax-payers of Pinhole, but I can't never stand not to finish what I start. So I called my brother police in Surfside, Florida, meanwhile motionin' for Mrs. Annie Johnson to please set down, as she was just come into the station. Surfside's finest tells me there is a Father Fugazi at Holy Name Church, and I jot down the number for future reference.

"What can I do for you, Annie?" I says then, and Mrs. Annie gets so agitated I thought I was goin' to have to round up some smellin' salts. Well, sir, soon's I got her calmed down, it was like a instant replay of that mornin's colloquy with Mrs. Flossie Chestnut. Seems her boy Jimmy has disappeared under much the same circumstances as young Johnny Chestnut. She punished him the day before for somethin' he was doin' and hadn't laid eyes on him since. Just to make conversation and get her mind off what might'a happened I says, casual like, "Mind if I ax you what kind 'a misbehavior you caught him at?" And she turns every color in a Mississippi sunset.

But she sees it's her duty to cooperate with the law and she does. "I caught him makin' up his face," she says.

"Beg pardon?"

"He was experimentin' with my cosmetics," she says this time, very tight-lipped and dignified, and I begin to see why she is upset. But I figure it's my duty to be reassurin'.

"Well, now," says I, "I reckon it was just a childish prank—not that it didn't bear a lickin' for wastin' perfectly good face paint—but I don't 'spect it's nothin' to be embarrassed about. Now you run along home and see if he don't come home to lunch."

Sweat has begun to pour off me by this time as I realize I got two honest-to-Pete missin' juveniles and a live credit-card thief on my hands. Spite of myself, my mind starts wanderin' to the kind of trouble these young'uns could've got theirselves into, and it ain't pretty.

I broadcast another missin' juvenile report and start thinkin' again. Bein' as it was a Saturday I knew it wouldn't do no good callin' up the school to see if they was in attendance. But what I could do, I could call up Liza Smith, who's been principal for two generations and knows ever'thing about every kid in Pinhole.

She tells me Jimmy and Johnny is best friends and gives me two examples of where they like to play. Lord knows how she knew 'em. One is a old abandoned culvert 'bout two miles out of town and the other is a giant oak tree on ol' man Fisher's land, big enough to climb in but no good for buildin' a treehouse, on account of the boys have to trespass just to play there. Which is enough in itself to make Fisher get out his shotgun.

It was time to go home for lunch and my wife Helen is the best cook in Mississippi. But I didn't have no appetite. I called her and told her so. Then I took me a ride out to the culvert and afterwards to ol' man Fisher's place. No Jimmy and no Johnny in neither location.

So's I wouldn't have to think too much about the problem I got, I called up Father Fugazi in Surfside. He says, yes indeed, he had lunch with his ol' friend Leroy Livingston three days ago and made a date with him to go on a auto trip to DeLand the very next day. But Livingston never showed up. Father Fugazi never suspected nothin', he just got his feelin's hurt. But in the frame of mind I was in, I commenced to suspect foul play.

Now I got somethin' else to worry about, and I don't need Frannie Mendenhall, the town busybody and resident old maid, bustlin' her ample frame through my door, which she does about then. Doggone if Frannie ain't been hearin' noises again in the vacant house next door. Since this happens reg'lar every six months, I'm inclined to pay it no mind, but Frannie says the noises was different this time—kinda like voices, only more shrill. I tell Frannie I'll investigate later, but nothin' will do but what I have to do it right then.

Me and Frannie go over to that vacant house and I climb in the window I always do, but this time it's different from before. Because right away I find somethin' hadn't oughta be there—a blue windbreaker 'bout the right size for a eight-year-old, which is what Jimmy and Johnny both are. I ask Frannie if those noises coulda been kids' voices and she says didn't sound like it but it could be. I ask her if she heard any grown-ups' voices as well. She says she ain't sure. So I deduce that either Jimmy or Johnny or both has spent the night in the vacant house, either in the company of a kidnapper or not.

I go back to the station and call the Chestnuts and the Johnsons. Ain't neither Jimmy nor Johnny been home to lunch, but ain't no ransom notes arrived either. Oh, yeah, and Johnny's favorite jacket's a blue windbreaker. And sure enough, it ain't in his closet.

No sooner have I hung up the phone than my office is a reg'lar beehive of activity again. Three ladies from the Baptist church have arrived, in as big a huff as I have noticed anybody in all month. Turns out half the goods they was about to offer at a church bake sale that very afternoon have mysteriously disappeared and they are demandin' instant justice. There ain't no question crime has come to the country. I say I will launch an immediate investigation and I hustle those pillars of the community out of my office.

Course I had my suspicions 'bout who the thieves were—and I bet you can guess which young rascals I had in mind—but that still didn't get me no forrader with findin' 'em.

I made up my mind to take a walk around the block in search of inspiration, but first I called the Dade County, Florida, sheriff's office—which is in charge of Surfside, which is a suburb of Miami. I asked if they had any unidentified bodies turn up in the last few days and they acted like they thought I was touched, but said they'd check.

I walked the half block up to the square, said hello to the reg'lars sittin' on the benches there, and passed a telephone pole with some sorta advertisement illegally posted on it. I was halfway around the square without a idea in my head when all of a sudden it come to me—the meanin' of that poster on the telephone pole. It said the circus was comin' to town.

I doubled back and gave it a closer squint. It said there was gone to be a big time under the big top on October 19, which was that very Saturday. But the date had been pasted over, like on menus when they hike up the prices and paste the new ones over the old ones. I peeled the pasted-over date off and saw that the original one was October 18, which was the day before. Course I don't know when that date's been changed, but it gives me a idea. I figure long as them circus folks ain't changed their minds again, they oughta be pitchin' tents on the fairgrounds right about then.

It ain't but five minutes before I'm out there makin' inquiries, which prove fruitful in the extreme. Come to find out, two young gentlemen 'bout eight years of age have come 'round seekin' careers amid the sawdust and the greasepaint not half an hour before. They have been politely turned down and sent to pat the ponies, which is what I find 'em doin'.

In case you're wonderin', as were the Chestnuts and the Johnsons, it wasn't nothin' at all to study out once I seen that poster. I thought back to one young'un ridin' his pony standin' up and another one tryin' on his mama's pancake and I couldn't help concludin' that Johnny and Jimmy had aspirations to gainful employment, as a trick rider and a clown respectively.

Then I see that the date of the engagement has been changed and I figure the boys didn't catch onto that development till they had done run away from home and found nothin' at the fairgrounds 'cept a sign advisin' 'em accordingly. Course they could hardly go home, bein' as their pride had been sorely injured by the lickin's they had recently undergone, so they just hid out overnight in the vacant house, stole baked goods from the Baptist ladies to keep theirselves alive, and hared off to join the circus soon's it showed up.

That's all there was to it.

All's well that ends well, I says to the Chestnuts and the Johnsons, 'cept for one little detail—them kids, says I, is going to have to make restitution for them cakes and cookies they helped theirselves to. And I'm proud to say that come the next bake sale them two eight-year-olds got out in the kitchen and rattled them pots and pans till they had produced some merchandise them Baptist ladies was mighty tickled to offer for purchase.

Meanwhile, I went back to the station and found the phone ringin' dang near off the hook. It was none other than the Miami Police Department sayin' they had gotten a mighty interestin' call from the sheriff's office. Seems the body of a man in his sixties had floated up on the eighteenth hole of a golf course on the shore of Biscayne Bay three days previous and they was handlin' the case. So far's they knew, they said, it was a John Doe with a crushed skull, and could I shed any further light?

I told 'em I reckoned Father Fugazi in Surfside most likely could tell 'em their John Doe was Leroy Livingston of Little Rock, Arkansas, and that I had a pretty good idea who robbed and murdered him.

Then I hung up and had me a heart-to-heart with Mr. James Williamson, credit-card thief and guest of the people of Pinhole. He crumbled like cold bacon in no time a-tall, and waxed pure eloquent on the subject of his own cold-blooded attack on a helpless senior citizen.

I called them Miami police back and said to send for him quick, 'cause Pinhole didn't have no use in the world for him. So I guess there ain't no doubt I solved a murder in Miami. I just didn't hardly notice it.

John F. Suter has written dozens of mystery stories for Alfred Hitchcock's
Mystery Magazine *and* Ellery Queen's Mystery Magazine. *His work reveals
the sly workings of the human mind and how a crime can grow ou;of the most
ordinary happenings.* "Come Down from the Hills" *is one of his finest examples.*

Come Down
from the Hills

John F. Suter

Arlan Boley eased his backhoe down the ramp from the flatbed, cut
the motor, and climbed off. It was early in the morning in the dry
season of late August, but the dew was just starting to rise. Boley knew
that the oppressiveness of the air would pass, but he hated it all the same.

"You want me to do the first one along about here?" he asked. He
brushed at his crinkly blond hair where a strand of cobweb from an
overhanging branch had caught.

Sewell McCutcheon, who was hiring Boley's services for the
morning, walked to the edge of the creek and took a look. He picked
up a dead sycamore branch and laid it perpendicular to the stream.
"One end about here." He walked downstream about fifteen feet and
repeated the act with another branch. "Other end here."

Boley glanced across the small creek and, without looking at
McCutcheon, asked, "How far out?"

The older man grinned, the ends of his heavy brown moustache
lifting. "We do have to be careful about that." He reached into a pocket
of his blue-and-white coveralls and took out a twenty-five-foot reel of
surveyor's tape. He laid it on the ground, stooped over to remove heavy
shoes and socks, and rolled the coveralls to his knees.

He unreeled about a foot of tape and handed the end to Boley.
"Stand right at the edge and hold that," he said, picking up a pointed
stake about five feet long.

While Boley held the tape's end, McCutcheon stepped down the
low bank and entered the creek. The dark brown hair on his sinewy

legs was plastered against the dead-white skin from the knees down. When he reached the other side, he turned around. "She look square to you?"

"A carpenter couldn't do better."

McCutcheon looked down. "Fourteen and a quarter feet. Midway's seven feet, one and a half inches. I don't know about you, Boley, but I hate fractions."

He started back, reeling up tape as he came. "Seven feet, three inches from her side. I'll just give her a little more than half, then she can't complain. Not that she won't."

He plunged the stake in upright at the spot. Then he waded ashore, went to the other boundary, and repeated the performance.

"That's the first one. When you finish," he told Boley, "come down just opposite the house and we'll mark off the second one."

"How deep?" Boley asked.

"Take about two feet off the bottom," McCutcheon said. "Water's low now. When she comes back up, it'll make a good pool there. Trout ought to be happy with it."

"I'll be gettin' to 'er, then," Boley said, going back to his machine. He was already eyeing the spot where he would begin to take the first bite with the scoop. He began to work within minutes. He had moved enough dirt with his backhoe in the past to know what he was doing, even with the added presence of the water that soaked the muck. There was also an abundance of gravel in the piles he was depositing along the bank.

When he judged that he had finished the hole, he lifted the scoop until it was roughly level with the seat. Then he swung the machine around and ran it down the creek toward his next worksite.

The pebble-bottomed stream, one typical of West Virginia, was known as Squirrel Creek. It divided two farms of nearly flat land at an altitude between one and two thousand feet. On the eastern side was McCutcheon's well-kept eighty acres. McCutcheon, a recent widower, planned well and worked hard, aided by his son and daughter-in-law. Both sides of the stream were lined with trees whose root systems kept the banks from crumbling and silting the creek bed. This was deliberate on McCutcheon's part, happenstance on his neighbor's.

When Boley came down opposite McCutcheon's white frame two-story, he cut the motor and walked over to where the farmer was sitting on the steps of his porch. The house was on a small rise, with a high foundation that would protect it in the event of an unusually heavy flash flood. Because of this, Boley had to look up a few inches to talk to McCutcheon.

"See anything of her?" he asked.

"Not yet," the farmer answered.

"Maybe this isn't gonna bother her."

McCutcheon rubbed his moustache. "*Everything* about this stream bothers that woman, Arly. One of the biggest trout I ever hooked in there was givin' me one helluva fight one day. I was tryin' to play him over to this side, but I hadn't yet managed it. Then, all of a sudden, outa nowhere came the old woman, screechin' her head off. 'What d'you mean ketchin' *my* fish?' she squawks. And with that she wades right out into the water, grabs the line with both hands, and flops that trout out on the ground at her side of the creek. Whips out a knife I'da never guessed she had and cuts the line. Then off to the house with my catch."

"Well," said Boley, "it was on her half of the creek, wasn't it? Property line down the middle? That why you've been measurin'?"

"Oh, sure," the farmer replied. "I recognize that. But that's not the way she looks at it. Had the fish been over here, she'd still have done it."

"I'd better get at it while it's quiet," Boley said, mentally thankful for his own Geneva's reasonableness.

As he walked to his machine, he heard McCutcheon say, "She must be away somewhere."

Later, Boley finished piling the last of the scooped silt and rocks on the bank of the stream. McCutcheon would later sort out the rocks and use the silt in his garden.

Paid for his work, Boley put the backhoe on the flatbed and fastened it securely. He turned around to head out, when he glanced over the creek toward the brown-painted cottage on the other side. A battered red half-ton pickup was just pulling up to the front of the house, barely visible through the tangle of bushes between stream and house.

A rangy older woman with dyed jet-black hair jumped from the truck and began to force her way toward the creek.

"Arlan Boley!" she screamed. A crow's voice contained more music. "What're you doin' over there?"

Boley put the truck in gear and pushed down the accelerator. He had no wish to talk to Alice Roberts. Leave that to McCutcheon.

Six days later, Boley and his family went into town. While Geneva and the two children were making some minor purchases for the opening of school, Boley went to the courthouse to the sheriff's office.

He had just finished paying his first-half taxes and was pocketing the receipt when he was tapped on the shoulder.

"Guess I'll have to wait 'til spring now before I can get you for non-payment," a voice said.

Boley recognized the voice of his old friend, the sheriff. "Hi, McKee," he said, turning. "You want that place of mine so bad, make me an offer. I might surprise you."

"No, thanks," McKee replied. "More'n I could handle." He nodded toward the clerk's window. "You payin' with what you got from Sewell McCutcheon?"

"Some. It took a little extra." He looked at McKee with curiosity. "What's the big deal? All I did was scoop him two holes in the creek for trout to loll around in from now on."

"You did more than that, Boley. You might have provided him with a fortune. Or part of one."

Boley nudged McKee's shoulder with his fist, feeling the hardness still existing in McKee's spare frame. "Don't tell me he panned that muck and found gold."

"You're not far off the mark."

Boley's eyes widened. He noticed a tiny lift at the ends of McKee's lips and a small deepening of the lines in the sheriff's tanned face. "Well, get to it and tell me," he said.

"Maybe you heard and maybe you didn't," McKee said, "but a state geologist's been usin' a vacant office here in the courthouse for the last ten days. Been workin' in the lower end of the county tryin' to see if there's a coal seam worth explorin' by that company that owns some of the land. Anyway, today McCutcheon walked in lookin' for him. Said he needed an opinion on an object in his pocket."

"And he got his interview?"

McKee nodded. "It seems he pulled out a fair-sized rock. First glance, could have been quartz or calcite. Kinda dull—but somehow different. This state fellow thought at first it was another pebble, then he took a good look and found it wasn't."

"So what *did* he find it was?"

"A diamond."

Boley had been half anticipating the answer, but he had tried to reject it. His jaw dropped. "No kidding!"

"No kidding."

"McCutcheon's probably turning over every rock out of that stream."

The sheriff dipped his chin. "I'll bet. Geologist said it's what they call an alluvial diamond, and the probability of findin' more is very small. Said it was formed millions of years ago when these mountains were as high as the Himalayas or higher. Somewhere in all that time, water eroded away whatever surrounded this one, and it might have even washed down here from someplace else. Come down from the hills, you might say."

An odd feeling crossed Boley's mind. Several times in the past, fragments of an old ersatz folk song had made themselves recognizable at the fringe of an unpleasant situation. "Just come down from the hills" was in one of the verses.

"What's the matter?" McKee asked.

"Nothing. How big is this rock? What's it worth?"

"A little bigger than the last joint on my thumb, not as big as the whole thumb. Worth? The man told McCutcheon there's no way of knowin' until it's cut. And it might be flawed."

Boley stared into the distance. "I'd better get on home and start seein' what's in the bottom of that run that goes through my property. Everybody in the country'll be doin' the same thing wherever there's water." He paused. "Or does anybody else know?"

"Only McCutcheon, that geologist, and the two of us," McKee said. "There's sort of an agreement to keep our mouths shut. You never know who would get drawn in here, if the word got out. Don't you even tell Geneva."

"What's McCutcheon done with the thing?"

"I suggested that he should put it in a safety-deposit box."

"It's what I'd do. I hope he has," Boley said.

The quirk around McKee's mouth had gone. "You know Alice Roberts?"

"Miner's widow across the creek from McCutcheon?"

"That's the one."

"No. I've seen her. She evidently knows who I am. I don't think I want to know her."

"Not good company," McKee said. "I wonder if she's heard about this. Do me a favor, would you? Drop by McCutcheon's place before long. You have a good excuse—checkin' up on the job you did. See what you can find out, but don't let on what you know."

Boley gave him a thoughtful look. "Seems to me you know a lot already."

The following evening, Boley left home on the pretext that he wanted to look at some land where he might be asked to make a ditch for a farmer who wanted to lay plastic pipe from his well pump to a new hog house. Instead, Boley went to McCutcheon's.

He found the farmer sitting alone on his porch. The sun had not quite set. His son and daughter-in-law had gone into town.

"Hello, Sewell," Boley said, walking to the foot of the steps. "Water cleared yet where I dug 'er out?"

"If it ain't by now, it never will," McCutcheon said. "Come up."

Boley went up and sat in a cane-bottomed rocker like the farmer's. "Ever since I dug it out, I've been wonderin' why you did that," he said. "After all, you have a pretty good farm pond at the back. Fed by three springs, stocked with bass and blue gills, isn't it?"

McCutcheon smiled. "That's right. Bass and blue gills. But no trout. Running water's for trout. I like variety."

"You put all that gunk on your garden yet?"

"Oh, yeah. We just took a bunch of rakes and dragged all the rocks and pebbles out, let the muck dry some, then shoveled 'er into a small wagon, towed 'er to the garden, and that was it."

Boley looked at the gravel drive leading from the house to the main road. "I guess you can bust up the rocks and fill in some potholes when you get more."

McCutcheon seemed uninterested. "I suppose. I have a small rock pile out here. Don't know what I'll do with 'em."

Boley decided that the other man was keeping his secret. He wondered if the son and daughter-in-law knew. And if they could keep quiet. To change the subject, he said, "Anybody ever want to buy your land, Sewell?"

The farmer nodded. "Every now and then some developer comes by. Thing is, this isn't close to the lake and the recreation area, and they don't want to offer much."

"It's a good bit for the three of you to handle."

"Maybe it will be later," McCutcheon agreed. "That's when I'll think again."

Boley jerked his head toward the Roberts' property. "I'd think they'd get that over there for the price they want."

"Funny old gal," McCutcheon said. "Her husband was a miner, died of black lung. No children. He never had time to work the property. Thirty-nine acres, came down from his old man. Alice like to wore herself out years ago, tryin' to make somethin' of it, then gave up. Except she thinks the place is worth like the middle of New York City—*and* that the creek belongs to her, clear to where it touches my land. You understand any better?"

"I see the picture," Boley answered, "but I don't understand the last part."

"Neither do I," McCutcheon admitted. "How about a cold beer?"

"Fine," Boley said.

McCutcheon went into the house to get it. He had been gone for several minutes when Boley heard footsteps coming around the house from the rear. He turned and saw Alice Roberts at the foot of the steps. She began to talk in a loud voice. "So. Both of you'll be here together—the two of you who took that diamond out've my crick. And how many more we haven't heard about yet."

Boley stood up. "What diamond? I don't know what you're talkin' about, Mrs. Roberts."

She continued up the steps. Boley guessed her to be in her early sixties, but her vigor was of her forties.

"Don't you lie to me, mister!" she growled, sitting in the chair he had just vacated. "You know all about it. I saw you here the day it came out of the water. What cut is he giving you?"

Boley leaned against a porch post. "I'm not gettin' any cut of any kind, lady. I've been paid for diggin' some dirt and rocks out of the water for McCutcheon. I don't see where any diamond comes into it."

McCutcheon reappeared at the door, carrying two cans of cold beer. He gave one to Boley. "Alice," he said, "I didn't know you were here. Could I get you some cola?"

"The only thing you can get me is the diamond you stole from my crick."

McCutcheon glanced quickly at Boley, who continued to look puzzled. "There's some mistake, Alice. I never took anything of yours. Did you lose a diamond in the water?"

"No, I did not lose *anything* in the water," she snapped. "You found out a big diamond was in my crick and your crony fished it out. I want it."

"I made two fishin' holes in my side of the water," McCutcheon said. "I got some rich dirt for my garden and a heap of rocks. You can have every rock in that pile, if you like."

She got to her feet. "I'll take you up on that. There might be more diamonds in there that you missed. I'll go get the pickup." She went down the steps at a speed that awed Boley.

He turned to McCutcheon. "What was that all about?"

The farmer began to talk in a low tone. "Water's down more and she can get across on steppin' stones, so she'll be back in a hurry." He proceeded to tell Boley the same story McKee had. Boley did not admit to its familiarity. Instead, he said, "How did she find out?"

"Beats me," McCutcheon answered. "But if you don't want a bad case of heartburn, you'd better leave right now. I'm used to it. It won't bother me."

"The diamond—"

"Is in the bank."

Boley was unable to tell McKee about this for several days. He had necessary work at home, getting in apples from his small orchard. He was also getting in field corn for a very sick neighbor.

After a little more than a week, he went to the courthouse. On the walk outside he was stopped by a friend, Harry Comstock, a quiet, balding man with thick glasses, who drew maps for Border States, Inc. Border States harvested timber and was as efficient as the businesses that got everything from slaughtered pigs except the squeal. At times the company leased land for its operations; at others, it drew on its own land. Some of their holdings abutted the land owned by McCutcheon and Alice Roberts.

"Boley!" Comstock said. "Got a minute?"

"One or two."

"Won't keep you." Comstock squinted in the sun. "Didn't you do some work on Squirrel Creek for Sewell McCutcheon right recently.?"

"Yeah. Scooped out a couple of fishin' holes for him," Boley said, hoping no more information was asked for.

"Well, you must have started something. Or maybe it's just coincidence. You know what happened yesterday? He came to the office and made a deal to buy fifty more acres from us to add to his land. All rights."

"Whereabouts?"

"Beginning at the creek and going east five acres, then back upstream."

"I'll bet it costs him," Boley said.

Comstock shook his head. "Not too much. Stuff in there's mostly scrub. Company's been wishing this sort of thing might happen."

Boley began to speak, but Comstock went on. "What makes it *real* interesting is that that wild old Alice Roberts came barging in about an hour later and bought twenty acres on the opposite side of the creek. Only hers is two acres west, the west upstream. Again, all rights. What's goin' on?"

Boley looked blank. "Beats me. Did Alice Roberts pay for hers now?"

"In cash."

Boley studied the pavement. "That's the funny part, Harry. I can't give you any answers, most of all about that."

He went into the courthouse and sought McKee. The sheriff was in.

After McKee had closed his office door, Boley ran through all that had happened, including the recent land purchases.

"I figure what they're doin' is buyin' more land along that stream so they can hunt for more diamonds without Border States gettin' into it," he finished.

McKee's head was cocked to one side. "What it really sounds like is that Alice intended to go up there and buy up land on both sides of the water and cut Sewell off. He beat her to enough of it that she didn't want to push, or she would have stirred up Border States."

"Oh, well," said Boley. "It's none of our business."

"I hope you're right," said McKee, his voice dry and astringent. "I wish you'd keep your eyes and ears open, anyway. When there's somethin' in dispute that might be valuable, I always feel I might be on the hot seat. Somebody'll be in this jail out of this, is my guess."

The following morning, Boley had left home in his four-wheel-drive jeep to help an acquaintance assess the feasibility of gathering bittersweet from a difficult location in the man's woods. With autumn coming, the colorful plant was easily saleable for decorations to tourists passing through town.

He had completed the trip and was starting home after returning the man to his house. Looking down the long corridor of trees before him he couldn't see the highway. The lane swung to the right for a few hundred feet before meeting the paved road. He slowed and made the curve, then stopped abruptly. The lane was blocked by a familiar battered red pickup. Standing beside it was Alice Roberts.

He climbed from the jeep. "Mrs. Roberts. What do you want?"

The woman was expressionless. "Mornin', Boley. I want you to get back in your jeep and follow me."

Boley considered several replies. He answered evenly, "I'm afraid I can't do that. If you have work for me, there are some people ahead of you."

"I never said anything about that," she rasped. "How do you think I found where you were?"

"I suppose you called, and my wife told you."

"I didn't call, but she told me." She moved aside and opened the truck door.

Boley stared. Inside, very pale and very straight, sat Geneva.

There was a movement beside him and Boley's eyes dropped. Alice Roberts was holding a double-barrel shotgun in her hands.

"Woman," he said, "shotgun or no shotgun, if you've hurt Geneva, I'll stomp you to bits."

"Don't get excited, Boley," she replied. "Nobody's hurt—yet. Now, you get behind that wheel and follow me."

Forcing himself to be calm, Boley did as he was told. He watched Alice Roberts climb into the truck and prop the gun between the door and her left side. Then she started, turned, and drove out.

Boley followed, driving mechanically. He paid little attention to direction or time. Rage threatened to take control, but he refused to let it. He might need all of his wits.

He wasn't entirely surprised when he saw that they had reached McCutcheon's farm and were pulling into the drive leading to the front.

The truck stopped directly before the steps to the front porch. With her surprising agility, Alice Roberts came down from the driver's seat carrying the shotgun, darted around the front of the pickup, and opened the other door to urge Geneva out.

Boley pulled up behind the truck and got out. He walked over to his wife and put his arm around her quivering shoulders.

"Arly. What's this all about?" she whispered.

"I'm not sure I know," he murmured.

"Quit talkin'!" snapped the woman. "Just behave yourselves and nobody'll get hurt. Now get up there."

She followed them up to the porch and banged on the screen door. "McCutcheon! You in there? Come out!"

There was no answer. She repeated her demands.

Finally a voice came faintly through the house. "Come on around to the west side."

Boley took Geneva's arms and urged her down from the porch, Alice Roberts' footsteps impatient behind them. They went around the house to the right. Waiting for them, leaning against a beech tree, was Sewell McCutcheon.

The farmer's eyes rounded with surprise. "This is more than I expected," he said. "Why the gun, Alice?"

"To convince you I mean business. If I pointed it at *you*, you might think I was foolin'. I hear these folks got two kids, so you'll think a bit more about it. There's shells in both these chambers."

"What do you want, Alice?"

"I want to see that diamond. I want to look at it. I want to hold it."

"We'd have to go to the bank. It's in a safety-deposit box."

Alice lifted the gun. "You're a liar, Sewell McCutcheon. How do I know? I went to the bank yesterday and asked to rent a box the same size as yours. And what did the girl say? 'We don't have a box rented to Mr. McCutcheon.' Now you get that diamond out here."

McCutcheon looked from one to another of the three. "All right. You go sit on the porch. I have to go in the house. You can't ask me to give my hidin' place away to you."

"I could, but I won't," Alice answered. "And don't you try to call anybody or throw down on me with your own gun."

McCutcheon's only answer was a nod. He went rapidly up to the side door and into the house. Boley led Geneva up to a swing that hung near the front end of the porch and sat down on it with her.

Alice followed. "If you're thinkin' about those other two who live here, fergit it. They went off down to Montgomery earlier." She leaned against a stack of firewood McCutcheon had put up to season.

After what seemed to Boley to be an interminable time, the farmer reappeared. He carried a cylindrical plastic medicine container about two inches long and an inch in diameter.

"We'd best go down into the sun," he said. "You can get a better idea."

He led the way down into the yard toward the stream, out of the shade of the trees surrounding the house. He stopped, opened the container, and shook something into his right palm. He offered it to Alice.

"Here it is."

She plucked it from his hand and peered at it.

"Why, it looks just like a dirty quartz pebble or some of them other rocks," she muttered. "This is a diamond? An uncut one?"

"It is. It's real," McCutcheon answered. "I can prove it, too."

She stared at it, letting the sun shine on it. "Well, some ways you look at it—A real, honest-to-God diamond, pulled outa my crick! McCutcheon, all my life I've wanted one nice thing to call my own."

The farmer pulled at his moustache. "Well, Alice, I'm sorry for you, but it came off my property. It came outa my side."

She raised her eyes to his. "How about you get it cut? Cut in two parts. Let me have half."

McCutcheon reached over and removed the stone from her hand. "Alice, you've been too much trouble to me over the years. Threatenin' these people with a shotgun is just too much."

"Shotgun!" she yelled. "I'll give you shotgun!"

She raised the gun swiftly, reversing it, and grasping the barrels with both hands, she clubbed McCutcheon across the back of the head. He fell to the ground, bleeding.

Stooping, she pried his fingers open and took the stone from them. "I'm not gonna let you take it!" she cried, running to the creek. When she reached the bank, she drew back her arm and threw the diamond as hard as she could into the woods upstream from her house. "Now," she yelled, "it's where it belongs! I might be forever findin' it, but you ain't gonna get it!"

Boley retrieved the gun where she had dropped it. "Go inside and call the sheriff," he told Geneva. "Say we need paramedics for Sewell."

When the sheriff's car and the ambulance came, McCutcheon was unconscious. Alice Roberts sat by the creek, ignoring everything until they took her to the car in handcuffs.

Boley explained the morning's events to McKee, who had come with a deputy. The sheriff heard him out. "Sounds like we've got her for kidnapping and assault, at least."

Alice Roberts, in the police car, heard them. "Kidnapping?" she said. "They's only old empty shells in that gun."

McKee leaned in the window. "But they didn't know that, Alice." To Boley, he said, "And don't you back off on the charge."

"I won't," Boley promised. "I'm just glad it's over."

McKee gave him an odd look. "If you think that, you've got another think comin'. Let's do today's paperwork, then come see me late tomorrow afternoon."

When Boley arrived at his office late the next day, the sheriff closed the door and waved him to a seat. "Things are pretty much as I figured," he said.

"How's McCutcheon?" Boley asked. "And what about Alice?"

"Sewell's not too bad." McKee sat down. "He's gettin' a good goin' over for concussion, but that's about it. Alice is still locked up, which is where I want her." He leaned across the desk. "How's it feel to be a cat's-paw?"

Boley was startled. "There's some kind of set-up in this?"

McKee sat back. "I'll run it past you. Some of this I can't prove and we'll just have to wait and see what happens. Anyway, you know same as I do that one of this county's big hopes is to attract people with money to buy up some of this land. Build themselves a place where they can come weekends or for the summer. The trouble is, we have only one good-sized lake and one nice recreation area. There are lots of other good places, but developers want to pick 'em up for peanuts.

"Alice Roberts, poor soul, has a place that looks like the devil's back yard. But it wouldn't take a lot to make it presentable, and it lays well. Sewell's place looks good. Given the right price, he'd quit and retire."

"I'm beginning to get an idea," Boley said. "McCutcheon decided to start a diamond rush, is that it? Where'd he get the stone?"

"You dug it out for him," McKee replied. "Until then, everything was just what it seemed. You dug two fishin' holes. Then he did find the diamond, and all that hush-hush commenced.

"I'd say he called Alice over and had a talk. Showed her how they could put on an act, building things up to her sluggin' him, so his discovery would really hit the papers."

Boley said, "So they bought that land from Border States hoping to resell and clean up. But where did Alice get the money?"

"Maybe she had some put back. But I'd bet Sewell made her a loan."

"The diamond. Is it real?"

McKee grinned. "It's real. The state man wouldn't lie about that."

"You want me to press the kidnap charge."

"I do. And I've had the hospital keep McCutcheon sedated, partly to keep him from droppin' the assault charge. You hang on until I suggest you drop it."

Boley was still puzzled. "What about the diamond? She threw it into the woods. I saw her."

"You saw her throw something into the woods. Remember I said you might mistake it for dirty quartz or calcite? That's probably what Sewell let her throw away." McKee's amusement grew. "Another reason for keepin' her locked up—I want McCutcheon to have time to go over there and 'find' that stone again." He added a postscript. "Or maybe they'll leave it as an inducement for whoever buys Alice's place."